PRAI

Imagine having an account of the events in the life of Mary from before Jesus' conception to the sending of the Spirit at Pentecost all told from her perspective. Imagine it being true to Scripture, complete with all the Hebrew names for people and places, along with additional events and episodes that perfectly fit the culture and customs of the day. Imagine the story being wonderfully narrated with pathos but never melodrama, charting Mary's hopes and fears, expectations and disappointments. Well, imagine no longer. Jennifer Layte has written the account. Once you start it, you won't want to put it down.

— CRAIG L. BLOMBERG, DISTINGUISHED PROFESSOR OF NEW TESTAMENT, DENVER SEMINARY

"...and a sword will pierce your own soul, too." More than just an imaginative retelling of the life of Jesus from his mother's point of view, *Favored One* gives profound and compelling insight into the agony and the ecstasy of what it must mean to be the mother–or a disciple–of Yeshua.

— F. JAMES GROSSER, PASTOR

As one who has tried to "sit in" the skin and heart of Mary through Contemplation, I was moved and newly awakened to what it was like to be Mary through Jennifer Layte's words. Both my imagination and theological understanding were expanded by this story and the author's research. It is so important for Christ followers to understand and accept our "highly favored" status from God along with Mary. She uniquely helps us embrace our position and experience as beloved of God.

— LAUREL GRIFFITH COOLBAUGH, SPIRITUAL DIRECTOR AND PASTOR, THE SANCTUARY AT WOODVILLE

Favored One delivers a provocative and incisive look at the life of Jesus (Yeshua) from the point of view of the person who knew him best: his mother. It's an inspired narrative hook, and in the deft literary hands of Jennifer Layte it becomes a forceful celebration of the pivotal role of woman in the male-dominated history of Christianity.

— JOHN WEEKS, ARCHETYPAL LITERARY CRITIC

Over the years I have found myself unable to relate to the astounding life events of Jesus' mother Mary and how she responded to them. But Jennifer Layte's captivating portrayal in *Favored One* has helped me to emotionally connect with Mary. I find her joining with us in the human struggles of understanding God and how He chooses to work in our world. I can now relate to her as a real person and as one of the disciples of Jesus. As you read this story, allow Mary to share how she found herself in accepting God's salvation and favor while treasuring the way He brought it all about.

— JODI ROOT, THE PILGRIMAGE

Yes! Amazing! This book does for the imagination what I've always craved! These are "characters" we have known, loved and learned from. We've modeled our lives after these people. But what was it like to be them? What might it have been like to be the mother of the Savior of the world? This book expresses these possibilities in vivid color. Jennifer Layte fleshes out these beloved characters, their thoughts, their fears, their lives in such a realistic way that I would often forget that it's fiction. Amazing piece of writing!

— KIMBERLY SHAW, THE PILGRIMAGE

FAVORED ONE

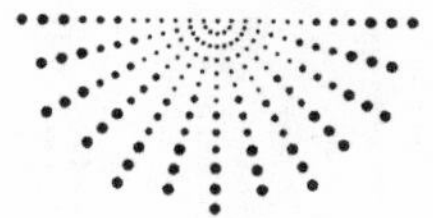

JENNIFER A. G. LAYTE

PREFACE

While preparing *Favored One* for publication, I encountered a bit of a conundrum. This book doesn't fit a genre. Depending on your point of view, it might not even fit into categories as broad as fiction or non-fiction. What on earth does one do with that? And who is meant to be the audience?

Favored One is a first person narrative of Miryam the mother of Yeshua (commonly known in the English-speaking world as Mary the mother of Jesus). I have done a little bit of direct research on the culture and the time period and the region of the world in which the events recorded in the Bible, and imaginatively fleshed out in these pages, occurred. But mostly this book has been crafted over a period of nearly two decades, through a process of *lectio divina* during personal Bible reading, and through information absorption via assorted seminary classes and discussions with Bible scholars and theologians.

Lectio divina ("divine reading") is an ancient Christian approach to reading Scripture which I have been practicing on and off for most of my adult life. My preferred engagement of the practice is to put myself "into the experience" of one of the biblical persons and imagine the recorded scene unfolding from that person's point of view. Soon after learning to do this as a young adult, I began retelling biblical narrative in short story form. After a time, I began to feel like I wanted to try "to lectio" the Gospels as Mary, the mother of Jesus. I didn't just want to pick an anecdote she was in. I wanted to read the *whole story,* from her point of view.

Since then, I've been exploring the idea of Mary as "God-bearer," and then thinking about how all Christians are supposed, in some mystical way, to be God-bearers. I have been meditating for years, particularly when the specifics of my call morph and change again—and again—over what it means to be a God-bearer–and more particularly a God-bearer who is a woman. I started the process of reading and writing the Gospels as Mary just before I turned 30. By this time I had been given a copy of the *Complete Jewish Bible,* with its Hebrew-to-English transliterations of the names, and so I began writing as Miryam.

The upshot is a story that just doesn't quite fit anywhere. It's not strictly biographical fiction, because I make no real effort in the narrative to discern or reveal who the *real* Miryam was, nor to imagine how she herself would have acted and reacted in the Biblical events. Instead, through the vehicle of *lectio divina,* this book is an attempt to imagine how *I* would have acted and reacted, had I been Miryam, and had all those events in the New Testament happened the way the Gospel writers say they did.

In the end, *Favored One* is an effort to tell a true story—about Jesus/Yeshua, and about what it means to bear Him to the world—through one person's own spiritual practice. The story of Yeshua is universal, and His call is personal, and I hope that the unusually personal process that went into crafting this book will be an aid to the reader's own experience of this Person and the Gospel stories—that it will help reader read those stories with new eyes and put themselves into those narratives, too.

As for who the reader is? Well, if you've made it through this preface, then that reader is you, of course. All you need to do next is turn the page.

Jennifer A. G. Layte
Bet Ya'ar, 2019

for my mother

Published 2019, *Notes on Pilgrimage,* an imprint of the Sanctuary at Woodville.

ISBN 9-780578-478425 (softbound)

ISBN 9-780578-478456 (e-book)

1

THERE IS A CLIFF

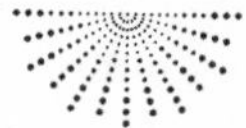

There is a cliff at the back edge of Natzeret. It is quiet there—a drop of rugged rock and tousled bushes and trees. All the mothers tell their children never to play there, for it is dangerous. A child could fall to her death there, they say, and they are right, too. But my mother died without falling off of it, when I was still quite young, so perhaps I hadn't heard the warning enough.

The original arrangements were made when my mother was still living, but a true betrothal had only been accomplished some months ago, and the wedding time was approaching. Nearly every Shabbat now found me curled sitting on an outcropping of the cliff, thinking. Praying even, I suppose. I was not a child—not since the winter, anyhow. I would not dash myself to my death sitting there, and no work was permitted on Shabbat in any case, so after some time in the synagogue in the morning I was not generally missed. Under one of the trees, out of the glare of the hot afternoon sun and just at the edge of the cliff, I hugged my knees to my chest, resting my heels on a rock and pointing my toes so that it looked as if they were suspended in midair, with the closest solid ground far enough away that small birds might fly between me and it. Shlomit knew where I was.

Sitting and thinking and praying—if praying it was—was mostly about Yosef those days. Yosef, my betrothed, was son of one of our distant Beit-Lachmi cousins. He lived in Beit-Lechem himself. In the South. In the town where our great King David had been born. I could never have been betrothed to a Southerner, and a descendent of the great David at that, were I not similarly descended.

Yosef had sisters, whom I had only seen on journeys South when I was much, much younger. Even then they made me nervous. Beit-Lechem was not such a grand place, but although their family were only craftspeople, they seemed grand enough. I was a dark little thing in comparison to their tall paleness. Sometimes, on the outcropping, I thought to myself the words of the Beloved in the Ultimate Song by King David's son Shlomo, "I am dark and I am beautiful, you daughters of Yerushalayim, like the curtains of Shlomo's palace. Don't stare at me for it; it's the sun that darkened me." Glorious light made that one notable. Special. Maybe I was descended from David, from Shlomo, by that dark one. Anyway, Yosef's sisters were not even daughters of Yerushalayim. Only of Beit-Lechem. They should not worry me. They would, I considered, likely be appalled that I knew anything at all of Shlomo's Song—I, an unlearned Northern villager, and a girl. They might also be jealous. I had other relatives in the South—relatives connected to the Temple, and I had ways of learning more of the Tanakh—our people's holy writings—than some boys.

Maybe even than Yosef, who was surely no longer a boy. Him, I had met on more than a few occasions since childhood. On the day of our betrothal, and sometimes after it, he came to see my father and me. But he was a man with a business at home, and it was something to expect him to move up to a little village like Natzeret for a bride. So then, after the wedding I would go to him. I would be his wife and bear his children, and I was a little afraid I would even love him, if not his sisters. Well, of course I would. My family loved, and so it was in my nature. But I did not know this man—not really—and what if he could not be trusted, or took me for granted, or was cruel to me, and I loved him still?

On his visits he was always kind. He would eat the evening meal with my family, and I would steal glances at his face as he talked to Abba long into the night. I would fall asleep in the eaves to the sound of their voices, and never even hear Yosef leave to stay with an elderly aunt and uncle who lived in our village. Abba promised me to him on the condition he would not have me until our proper wedding night. I was his in all ways but that, and he honored the condition and me, and only asked to see me alone in the daylight. Some days he would ask to walk with me, and I would go with him torn with longing and hesitation, and the frustration that I could do nothing about either. Among my people, according to my people, I was born to marry and make more of the people of God. I did not know if this was what I wanted, because I did not know if there could be anything else. Yosef would lead me through fields and treat me with respect, but the last time, he turned to me and looked at me for a long time, and stroked my face gently with his rough carpenter's hands.

After that, I could not stop seeing Yosef's face and thinking about his hands. He had a dimple, just visible above his beard, in one cheek. His eyes were a deep, dark, warm brown, with enough depth, I thought even then, to merit their sparkle. He laughed a lot, not in derision—never that—but in a hearty enjoyment of life. His hands were large and rough and gentle like the wood he carved. I had noticed the veins coursing across the backs of them and marveled at the box those hands had made for me. It was very small, with traces of greenery carved into it and I had never seen anything like it. I also had nothing to put into it yet, but I kept it wrapped in the folds of my dress forever after he gave it to me. I would not have told him so, of course. I could not let him know so much yet. Shlomit knew.

A pebble dropped off the cliff. Somewhere in the middle of my thinking, the light changed, and then there was an angel looking at me—and I was looking at it. Later, Shlomit wanted to know how I knew it was an angel, and all manner of what it looked like, but I could never quite say for certain. What was sure was that no mere man could stand serenely with no turf beneath him, but as if there were. And there was so much light. But in any case, it didn't really matter what it looked like. I did not have to consider or wonder what it was. There was no question of its being anything else.

This was not good.

In the Tanakh when angels visit, humans wilt or become heroes. Either way, they always suffer. Surely Shimshon's mother suffered, watching her son take up with loose women. Shimshon himself suffered. He died for the people in the end—at the time when Adonai was with him most. I felt my chest grow tight, my heart drying up like a rivulet in a drought. I could not breathe.

Was the angel a sign of a drought then? It could be so, if Adonai thought somehow a drought would bring deliverance. I hoped that if that were what Adonai intended, he would at least leave us the water in our cisterns for a while. The spring, some way out of Natzeret, was our only living source of water, but perhaps we could survive for a time on the water we had stored up already . . .

I was also hoping, I realized as I began to breathe again, that the angel would excuse me for not falling on my face before it. This was the traditional response, I knew. But if I gave in to the impulse, I would surely fall off the cliff to my death after all. My vision blurred momentarily and I heard the sound of a thousand rivers rushing in my ears. I grasped onto a small branch above my head to keep myself from fainting away.

"Shalom, favored one!" said the angel, after the rushing sound stopped—or maybe through it. "Adonai—God the Lord—is with you!"

In the fear that poured over me then, like the sound had before, I almost lost hold of the branch. I tightened my grip. Adonai was with me? But why? I was only a girl—"not a child," did I say before? A child, surely, and one at the edge of a cliff. This wasn't the fear that I had of marriage—a delightful queasiness in the stomach. This was the fear that started with a prick in the toes, and a few moments later rushed over the whole body, leaving a chilly perspiration, even though the sun was so hot. Do angels have any idea how mortals feel when they say things like that? Do they realize how ironic their beatific greetings sound to us, who sin and are less accustomed to Adonai's direct presence than they are? There were curtains in the Temple in Yerushalayim because Adonai could not abide sin, and humans could not abide his purity. How was I still living, if Adonai were with me? I pulled my head covering about my face.

Whether or not the angel knew what its words sounded like to me, it clearly saw by my gesture—or perhaps by some other sign that angels alone can read—that I was troubled, for it said, "Don't fear, Miryam. I have said—you are favored of God. Look! You will bear a child—a son—and call him Yeshua. He will be the great one! Son of Ha'Elyon! He's the one Adonai promised to give the throne of his forefather David. He will rule Ya'akov's House—a never-ending kingdom."

I found that I was listening very hard to try to understand, and the harder I listened, the more the buds of twigs and leaves on the branch dug into my palm. Something was amiss in this announcement, surely. Was it possible that an angel could end up meeting with the wrong person?

"But that's impossible," I blurted out, "I'm a...well, I'm a virgin." It was absurd—even from the mouth of an angel such an idea was absurd. The world contains many mysteries, and I suppose that coupling between a man and a woman is a mystery itself, yet everybody knows it has to happen for babies to be made. Most of the smallest children know it. Homes in Natzeret aren't as large as all that, to keep such knowledge from anyone. What kind of woman did this angel think I was? I had never even lain with Yosef, my betrothed, and I certainly had not with anybody else. But the way this messenger of God was speaking, assuming it hadn't, in fact, announced its tidings to the wrong young woman, it sounded as if I were to get with child almost this very instant. If the angel were not so solemn, and if the implications of its message snaking into my mind were not so terrifying, I might have considered laughing.

The angel, still solemn and glad, answered, "It will be the Ruach HaKodesh coming over you. Ha'Elyon's own power will cover you. That is why the child you bear will be called the Son of God." Almost as instantly as I had wanted to laugh, I no longer wished to at all. I could not tell, precisely, what I felt.

"Miryam loves the Torah," old Z'kharyah had remarked to my parents time and again when we ventured to Yerushalayim for the feast of Pesach. Z'kharyah, the husband of my mother's cousin, was a priest, and educated and wise. He was right, too. My learning only made me feel smug when I thought of Yosef's sisters. It was my fortress against their thoughts about how Yosef deserved someone worthier than I. Otherwise, truly I drank up the stories Z'kharyah had told me from our holy writings as if they were water and I was dying of thirst. As a consequence, I had always considered Adonai to be very present—watching me. I wanted to please him, this very present God. But I had never expected him to ask me to try.

The wave of fear that had washed over me at the beginning of this exchange crested again, now buoying me up. I felt as if I were swimming in Lake Kinneret, perhaps, and as if, instead of drowning in the storm, I were walking on the water. This—Adonai with me—was more than I had asked for. Certainly it was more than I had bargained for. But it was favor indeed.

I had nothing to say, and the angel, blazing through my remaining doubts with its fierce light, continued. "You have a cousin, Elisheva," it said, and it was right. This Elisheva was in fact my mother's very cousin—the wife of Z'kharyah, of whom I had just been thinking. "She," the angel said, "is an old woman who everyone thought was barren. But she has conceived a son as well, and is six months along with him! With God, nothing is impossible."

I had not thought it was, really. And this God, for whom nothing was impossible, was calling me—Miryam!—to bear a child he was somehow to call his son. I found I was squinting, though whether at the news or at the angel, I could not tell. Was it the Messiah this angel was proclaiming? The one who would rule the earth and bring our people back to Adonai? The angel had not said so, but who else could be called the son of Ha'Elyon? It waited, while its words resounded, loud and strident in my head. "Favored one!" "Adonai is with you!" "With God, nothing is impossible!"

I shut my eyes for a moment because of the noise and brightness, and Yosef's face flitted before my mind. The beard and the dimple and the twinkling eyes. The rough, worn, caressing hands. Unwittingly, with my free hand I felt for his little wooden box in my robe. My fingers traced the carved flowers. I took it out to look at. It was easier to look at than the angel.

It occurred to me that I could say no to this astounding announcement, although I could not think of anyone who had said no to Adonai and truly lived afterward. I could say no and marry my husband, and surely Adonai could find someone else, someone much better, to mother his son. I could not be the best person for this task, I thought to myself. It was impossible. Shlomit—even Shlomit would have been a better choice, if Adonai were looking for obscure maidens. Shlomit, at least, could keep house without requiring every ounce of energy and concentration. "With God, nothing is impossible!" echoed the angel's trumpeting voice in my mind again. Even my keeping house, then.

At that, my head shot up at last, and I knew for the moment that what Adonai wanted mattered more than even Yosef. Yosef, dear as I hoped and feared him to be, was still only a man, with his mannish wants and needs and concerns. But Adonai had chosen me for something I could not even understand, and it was exciting, and I was favored. I looked at the angel finally, dropping my hands from my shawl so that it fell away from my face. I said, "I am Adonai's servant; he may do as he pleases with me. Let it be as you have said." It did happen to me as the angel had said, but after all, it hadn't said much.

2
THE ANGEL DISAPPEARED

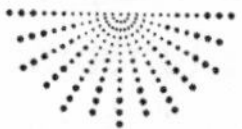

The angel disappeared completely as soon as I gave my consent to its message. I did not see it go—only suddenly it was there and again suddenly it wasn't. I remained sitting on my ledge, clinging to the tree branch, with considerably different thoughts in my head than had been in it only moments before. My limbs were shaking, and it took me a moment to pry my own fingers away from the branch. How would it happen? How would the Ruach HaKodesh come upon me? Would I know? Would it hurt? Would I...would I cease to be a virgin? I hugged my knees to myself more tightly than ever. Did I have to do something? Or was telling the angel "yes" enough? Had it happened already? Was I already now carrying the seed of a baby whose father was God? I curled my head down so my forehead touched my tightly clutched knees. Two tears leaked out of my eyes. I wasn't unhappy. I was only terrified.

The village lay behind me, down the slope leading to the cliff. When the shadows began to lengthen, I straightened up and hurried home. Shabbat was coming to an end, and no matter what had just happened, Shlomit would need me to help ready the evening meal. I tried to walk with my head high. I had seen an angel. It had told me I was favored, and that Adonai was with me. This was nothing to cry about. Nothing for which to be ashamed. Meantime, there were my father and my sister and my brothers.

"What happened?" asked Shlomit, as soon as I had ducked into the house.

"What? I—I was on the ledge this afternoon. You know I go there. Did you need me for something?"

"No, no." Shlomit peered at me closely. "But your face is different. Something happened. What happened?"

The tears would come if I told her. I would not be ashamed. I was favored, and I myself had told the angel I was willing. But there was so much to think and so much to feel, I would never be able to say it all, and it would come out of my eyes. I also knew that, while I could, at least eventually, tell Shlomit what had happened, our father would be another matter entirely. And the boys could never know—or at least not outside of even more extreme circumstances. If I started crying now, it was unlikely that I would stop for quite some time, and then there would be questions from Abba which I could not, at present, bear to answer. I shook my head at Shlomit.

"Tonight," I said, gritting my teeth to hold back the tears. "I promise I'll tell you tonight."

Shlomit took one more doubtful look at my red-rimmed eyes and shook her head. She clicked her tongue on the roof of her mouth. But she did not say anything else. Shabbat was over. We set to work on the evening meal in silence. We cooked flat bread on hot stones around the fire we had lit outside. There were vegetables from the garden, and olives from the tree that hung over the door, and water from the cistern. It was a simple meal.

I tried not to think about anything in the quiet between Shlomit and me. I tried particularly not to think about Yosef. He came to mind as soon as I began considering what it would be like to tell Abba. Now I was trying to drive him out of my thoughts, but having little success. I fingered the wooden box in my pocket once more to make sure it was there—that it hadn't fallen out. A shadow of the cold fear I had felt when the angel first spoke, passed over me again as I touched it. Telling Abba my story would be easy in comparison to what I would tell Yosef. What could I ever say to him so that he would believe I was still faithful? For truly, I had never been with a man. But Adonai was with me now. That didn't make me adulterous, did it?

The menfolk came in when the meal was almost ready. They had been sitting with the other men of the village all the afternoon, I supposed, having gone to synagogue in the morning. I found it difficult to look at them.

"Daughter, are you well?"

My head shot up, startled. I looked at Shlomit, who pursed her lips and looked away. My face spoke to everyone then. I would not even be able to hide. How could I lie about Adonai? But how could I tell my father any of it?

"Yes, Abba," I said. "I am well." Adonai was with me. I was favored. But I did not feel well, and so I sensed I was lying, maybe, after all. My stomach was woozy, and my shoulders ached with the weight of Adonai's presence. I couldn't live for days like this, I knew suddenly. "Elisheva is going to have a baby," I said, as a plan began to form. "I was thinking to go to her to help her."

Abba looked startled, and a little stopped up, as if too many questions had popped into his head at once and none of them could now find an exit. Shlomit suddenly became very still, over my right shoulder. At last Abba said, "Elisheva?"

"Yes," I replied.

"Your Imma's cousin."

"Yes."

"Is having a baby."

"Yes."

"How do you know this? Who has been talking to you? Traveling on Shabbat? Why did he not come directly to the house? Is it a reliable person?"

I paused a minute. I didn't think it had been a person, exactly, and I hoped Abba would forget the Shabbat detail immediately. But I did not truly imagine an angel of Adonai could be unreliable, in spite of my earlier concern that it had found the wrong woman. "Yes," I said, finally. "A messenger met me on the hill and told me. I think I should go to be with her."

"It's a very nice idea," Abba said approvingly then. "You always were one to think of others. We can arrange for you to travel with a caravan to Ein Karem so that you'll be there just in time for the birth."

"I don't—" I began, and then began again. "I'll need time to get there, and then time to help her prepare. The messenger said she is already in her sixth month."

"Miryam," Abba protested in his unhurried, unworried way, as truly I had known he would. "It is too far for you, and too close to your wedding day. It takes more than an afternoon to find a respectable band of travelers with whom to journey all that way. I should go with you myself," he added under his breath.

"Oh no, Abba," I protested. That would never do. Perhaps —well, surely—I would have to tell him eventually, but I needed some time myself to get used to the idea first. "Your health...But please, let me go. I am sure Elisheva needs me. And I think I need her, too. How can I prepare to marry without Imma? But Elisheva and Imma loved each other. She can help me."

I hated using my mother's memory in that way, but all the same, in this I was not lying. Although my mother had had a hand in the choice of Yosef as my betrothed years before, I did feel a lack of wiser womanly counsel as I entered the last months before my wedding. I had aunts and female cousins aplenty in Natzeret, but none of them were Imma, and they were all so prying. In that village, as in all villages I reckon, everyone knew everything about everybody, and I didn't want my friends' mothers, for example, gossiping about what I thought of Yosef, as they surely would have done, had I gone around confiding to the aunts I had at hand. But Elisheva was different. And she was far away. And now I had this even bigger secret, and Elisheva was, I knew, the only person who could tell me what to do about it.

Abba's face softened when I mentioned Imma, and I saw he understood—at least the part I was giving him to understand. "Maybe your cousin Yitz'chak can accompany you," he mused. "It is not so late in the year, and you will still be back in time for your wedding. And Shlomit can go. You can take her for company."

"Shlomit needs to stay and keep *you* company," I said firmly, and in this I was truly thinking only of him, because I would certainly have loved to have my sister's presence on such a journey. "Someone needs to take care of you. She's better at it than I am anyway."

"Miryam, you have always cared for me very well," Abba said, pulling me toward him for a rough hug. But we both knew I was right.

The boys were noisy during the meal because they had not yet learned to listen to things that were not being spoken. When we had guests, we two sisters fed the men first and ate when they had finished, but when the family was alone—which was never a foregone conclusion—Abba had us eat all together. So we sat there, our fingers mingling in the food between us, the three boys chattering and elbowing each other, we three elders keeping our thoughts to ourselves. As soon as Shlomit and I retired to our sleeping quarters for the night, however, she began the questions.

3
SHLOMIT WHISPERED

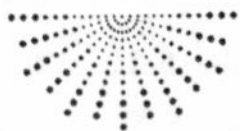

"Now, Miryam," Shlomit whispered from our corner in the raised part of the house. She turned toward me on the blanket. "What's happened, then?"

"You won't believe me," I muttered, facing the wall. "You can't."

"I can do anything I want," she retorted. It reminded me, oddly, of the angel's saying that all was possible for Adonai. But Shlomit was, of course, decidedly not Adonai, and I was no longer certain I could tell my story to anyone but Elisheva.

"I don't think so," I said. Then I turned toward her after all. "I saw an angel," I said. "It told me I am to mother a child for Adonai."

I could sense my sister's eyes widening in the darkness as a hand suddenly gripped my shoulder. "What does that mean?" Shlomit asked. "Is this the Messiah? You and Yosef? Truly?"

"No," I said, my voice shaking a bit with some sort of nervousness. "I mean, Yosef is not the father."

Shlomit was quiet for a long, long time. I didn't say anything either. I would let her ask the questions. I knew already what she was thinking, though I also knew she was wondering how it could be that I had been with a man other than Yosef, when I slept by her side every night, and we spent most of our waking minutes together, too. Only on Shabbat could I have committed an indecency, then, for only on Shabbat was I ever alone. "You are with child already," she said finally.

"Yes," I said, suddenly certain this was true. I did not know when it had happened, but it had been at some time on the hillside. I was carrying already the son of Ha'Elyon. It never occurred to me to doubt that the words would come true after I accepted them. I never thought once, in that long and troubling afternoon, that perhaps I had just imagined everything.

Shlomit did not seem to have thought of any of those things either, but then, I had not yet told her the whole story. "What really happened to you today, Miryam?" she asked, sounding, as she often did, more like the older sister than the younger. Her voice shook a little.

"An angel from Adonai came to me," I said. "It told me I was to bear a child for Ha'Elyon, but not by Yosef or any other human father. A child that Ha'Elyon would plant in me himself."

"Miryam, are you sure about this? Did someone violate you? You aren't just trying to protect someone, are you? Or yourself? Did he threaten you if you told?"

I felt as if a stone had dropped into my stomach, and I wondered to myself why I had only considered a few of the misunderstandings that could arise from my story. I had not thought of the charge that someone might have lain with me against my will. But surely, if people resisted questioning my own fidelity, rape was exactly what it would look like, because Yosef could not be considered the father. He was back in his hometown of Beit-Lechem arranging living quarters for his bride, and had not been to Natzeret in quite some time.

"No," I said, but I heard my voice trembling again. What had I agreed to? I was supposed to be favored by Adonai, but I felt instead as if I were going crazy. As if everything were going crazy. How could Adonai not just allow, but in fact cause his son, if he had to have a son, to come into the world looking like a bastard? Why would Adonai, even the God who brought deliverance from someone as disappointing as Shimshon, make a good Jewish girl look so shameful?

"Miryam," said Shlomit. She still did not believe me.

"Shlomit," I said, my voice steadying in determination to be understood by at least one person. "Listen to me. I have not lain with a man. This is what happened."

I told her the story of my afternoon from start to finish. I did not hide anything. "But now," I moaned as quietly as I could, "now I wonder. How could this be Adonai's will? What if it was not his angel?" I had known so much fear when it spoke to me at first. What if it were not the fear of Adonai after all, but the fear of malevolence? It had seemed such a bright and glorious being, but what if I were deceived?

Shlomit wrapped her arms around me and held me while I wept. She was afraid, too. I could feel it in her. But she said, "Whether from Adonai or the Adversary, you told it you are a servant of Adonai. You only agreed to the plan as Adonai's servant. Surely he himself will protect you if it isn't true. And if it is, we will see for ourselves. How can the Adversary create anything? And how can he make a child in your womb? Only Adonai could make a virgin with child, surely?"

I did not say anything. I needed to be with Elisheva more than ever.

4
MY FATHER CHANGED HIS MIND

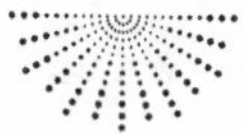

In spite of his early acceptance of my plan, my father seemed to have changed his mind in the night, or to have forgotten why he had agreed in the first place. He continued to argue mildly that I did not need to see Elisheva just yet. "You can wait until you are married," he said. "You will be more help to her after the baby is born, and you will be closer to her as well. The wedding is soon enough."

But it was not soon enough for me.

"She needs Elisheva before the wedding," Shlomit reminded him firmly. "Abba, I'm her sister, not her mother. I can't prepare her as an older woman could. Let her go. She's strong. With Yitz'chak, she'll be all right." To me, later, she said, "You could probably go on your own. If you're truly carrying the Messiah, Adonai won't let a thing happen to you."

As if he hadn't already.

I smiled wanly and went off to find Yitz'chak. If I were truly and already with child, I would soon, I knew, feel ill in the mornings. I did not want anyone in Natzeret to see me in that state, nor did I want to travel in it. Fortunately,

Yitz'chak, with whom I got on well enough, was agreeable to a sudden trip to the South. He was young, but the eldest of five brothers, and it was universally whispered that his parents had let him go utterly to waste. To be the eldest son was an honor to be sure, but, said the people who were prone to talk about such things, the honor came in part from whether or not such a child bore the position well. Strange as it was in an industrious village like ours, Yitz'chak had managed to avoid making himself useful for most of his life.

"When the Messiah comes," our old rabbi used to say, "he'll have something to say about young men like that." These comments were always made within hearing of somebody in the family, but never of Yitz'chak himself, or of his parents. "They are the disgrace of our holy people. If these men would take on the mantle of their own authority, given by Adonai, Adonai would not hide his face from us, and we could have an army to rout the Romans, be it as small as Gid'on's."

I never liked it when the rabbi talked like this, but even within myself I couldn't really argue. Yitz'chak had never applied himself to any study of the Torah, was lazier than anyone I knew and there was some talk that he was better acquainted with some of the women of the nearby city of Sephoris than any Torah-abiding Jewish man had a right to be. But he was sturdy, and likely to be able to hold his own in a fight if he needed to, or at least to intimidate, which might be just as good. One hoped, of course, for no trouble from armed Roman officers. But from fellow travelers, Yitz'chak would be protection enough. The other convenience about his general uselessness was that he had very few obligations to fulfill. Poor thing. He was probably bored with his existence. At any rate, he readily agreed to come with me, and all that remained was for me to prepare myself.

It did not take so long to gather things for travel. I only needed a few articles of clothing and some gifts for Elisheva and Z'kharyah. I chose some of the fabrics I had woven. I did some weaving sometimes, for the village, and I always felt an odd sense of pride and satisfaction in the work, though the cloth was simple enough. Well, so were we. Now, preparing to bring gifts to a priest and his wife, everything seemed woefully inadequate. But they were my family, and they would understand that I had nothing to give them truly befitting their status and means.

"You should take something for Yosef's family, too," Shlomit said, the day before I left. "You will be that much nearer to Beit-Lechem. Someone may hear you are there, and then what would you do?"

In fact, I had already considered that, and the idea made me feel sick enough even without the child who was growing in my womb. This journey, I thought, would keep me away from prying eyes at home. But it would also be the journey in which I would have to tell Yosef that I was chosen. What would he say? What would he do? I imagined the smiling eyes growing dark with wrath. It was an angry husband I feared, but I had not even been given a chance to love this man before knowing his anger.

Some other part of me remembered that Yosef was known to be, and had always shown himself to be, an honorable man. He would not want to hurt me. But the twinkle in his eyes turning to pain was an almost worse image than that of his anger. His very honor would make it impossible to marry me. Yet I would have to face him, whatever his response. And in facing him, I would, in some measure, have to face his family. Sighing, I added dresses for Yosef's sisters and blankets for their families. He was some older than I, and neither of his parents still lived, but his sisters most certainly did. I doubted even the finest robes on earth would repair their opinion of me when they found out what had happened, but at least I could make an effort.

And so began the first journey I was ever to take for my

son. In all of the things I had imagined for myself, so much traveling was not a part of it. In the end, I suppose this particular journey was not very eventful, although at the time it seemed tremendously exciting and I thought I should remember every tree we slept under and every hill we climbed. There was a constant underlying suspense, occasionally lurching into the stomach and shoulders, that we would encounter Romans. But in the entire journey, we only saw one band of soldiers, and they were evidently otherwise occupied, for they ignored us and gave us no trouble.

Yitz'chak and I had only just joined the travel route South when we came upon a caravan, and, since Abba had given me some money in the event that we came across a group like this, the leader seemed willing enough for us to swell their ranks. Most of the people in it, though they did not all know each other, seemed to be kindly folk, and I took heart that there was a matronly woman named Rut among them who I thought could look after me if I needed that sort of looking after.

"Yitz'chak," I ventured, after our first night with the caravan, "these are good people. I can stay with them until Yerushalayim, and I am certain someone will see me to Ein-Karem at the end of the journey. You can return home if you like."

"We don't know them," Yitz'chak protested mildly. "How do I know they will continue to treat you properly if I am not here?"

"That Rut won't let anything happen to me, I'm certain of it," I said.

"Rut will not be able to fend off Roman officers. Or outlaws, should we see any," Yitz'chak intoned. "And," he sighed, "what shall I do when I go back? Everyone will see that even my cousin didn't need me."

I felt chided and astonished. "Oh, Yitz'chak," I said. "I'm sorry. I'm sure you're right—I'm sure I need you here very much indeed." I was not lying, because as I spoke, it dawned on me that if I returned to Natzeret obviously with child, there could be some talk that I had been molested by a man in the caravan, or by a soldier or a bandit on the way, and that the child was that one's. This would be easier to explain than who the child's father really was, but all the same, I could not bear there to be any obvious reason for Adonai's child to be considered the child of a rape. Yitz'chak did not look much comforted, but he did not go home either, and in the morning his countenance was brighter as he helped the men pack up the camp.

Because of the number of us, the fact that we were all on foot and the additional fact that we skirted Samaria completely, it took us over a week to reach 'Ein Karem. Only particularly penny-pinching merchants went directly through Samaria as far as I knew, and I was glad that we had fallen among more sensible people, particularly as I was going to stay with a priest. It would never do to bring some sort of uncleanness into his house, when what I was bringing already was so strange.

Sometimes I felt sure that Samaritans were not really as bad as everyone said, but still, I did not want to find out. You never knew what to expect from people who were only half of something—half Jewish and half something else, with only half (if as much as that) of the understanding of the Tanakh. As a child I had grown up imagining that the Samaritans' strange and suspect views about God would contaminate me in spite of my best efforts. But now, as we skirted their territory to the west, I thought that I would also never have believed God would get a woman with child without the aid of a man, and now here I was—living proof that he had. This was probably the strangest and most suspect idea anyone had ever spoken of God. Perhaps these good people in the caravan would send me to live with the Samaritans if they knew. I made sure I told no one. Not even Rut. She suspected, I knew, that I was with child, but I did not take ill on the journey, and she never uttered a word about it; nor did I.

Our caravan had missed the hot, drying wind earlier in the season by just about a week, and now the air was warm and the sky was blue and the Galilean flowers blazed us South. Once we reached the South, there were not so many of those flowers, so you noticed the short, scrubby trees more, and swathes of green and brown. The landscape looked like a serviceable blanket or rug I might weave for the house. I thought of my own scrubby tree—the one under which I had sat when the angel came. I clutched Yosef's box in the folds of my robe and became more silent than ever.

Most of the travelers were going on to Yerushalayim. We did not enter the city with them, though we did catch glimpses of its shining buildings. Yitz'chak's eyes lit up at the first glimpse of it, but he composed himself when the leader of the caravan directed the two of us beyond the city. We arrived at Z'kharyah and Elisheva's house just at sundown, and suddenly I felt nervous. They did not know I was coming. Would they even recognize me? I had been only a child when I saw them last. Now I was a woman with child, and no father of that child immediately evident.

It turned out Yitz'chak was even more nervous. I had thought he would stay a few nights, out of good manners and to enjoy the couple's hospitality. Apparently, however, manners were other things he had not acquired as the spoiled oldest son. He seemed slightly overawed by the grandeur of the house, and made to leave as soon as the servant had disappeared to let Elisheva know of our arrival.

"But Yitz'chak," I protested, "they will let you stay here tonight at least."

"I don't know them," he said.

"It's manners, silly. How can you come all this way and then not accept their hospitality? It's rude." Even I knew how odd it was that I was now trying to persuade him to stay when earlier I had wanted him to leave.

"Let them think you came yourself. Or tell them I have urgent business back home and I can't stay."

"You?" I laughed, trying to make light of our debate days earlier, and Yitz'chak grinned.

"Oh, I don't know," he said. "I don't know them, and they are not my family—not really—just yours. And I...I look too much like I'm from—the Galil."

"You're being absurd," I told him. "If we're family, they're family, and I'm just as much from the Galil as you. Besides, it's getting dark. For heaven's sake, just stay tonight. You can leave first thing in the morning. Where on earth are you going to sleep instead?"

"The same place I've been sleeping the last eight nights," he answered. "Out of doors. Under the stars."

I remembered then that he was used to getting his own way. He had already gotten it once this journey. I also remembered, in a sudden flash, his women of Sephoris and the look on his face when he saw Yerushalayim. I did not think he would be going directly home—or sleeping under the stars either—and I could not say I approved of what I imagined he wanted to do in our nation's largest city. On the other hand, I wasn't going to reform him standing on the steps and arguing. Besides, I considered how nice it would be to be able to start speaking to Elisheva about everything right away, instead of having to wait until he left.

"Well then," I said, my sudden change of mind once again altering the argument awkwardly. "Good journey to you. Please tell my father and sister and brothers that I am well."

Yitz'chak grinned again and set off. "Well," I said again, to nobody really, "He didn't need telling twice!" He had scarcely disappeared around the corner, when Elisheva appeared in the inner gloom of the house, approaching the dimly lit entryway. She was aging, but she carried herself well. Also, perhaps on account of never having had children before, she had always been quite slender. That, in combination with her straight posture, made her seem tall and regal. She still walked that way, but she was less slender in the light of the lamp she was carrying, and there was a definite bulge around her middle.

She got halfway to the door when I saw her pause and suddenly put her hand against the bulge. Then she rushed forward and gathered me in her arms, after which she held me out at arm's length in front of her almost as impetuously. She was like a girl, this older cousin of my mother's. Perhaps it was because she was going to have a baby. But why didn't I feel like that, then?

It took only a moment. Elisheva's baby, it seemed, was a prophet, and inside her, he made her a prophet, too. "What a fortunate woman among women you are!" she shouted, much more loudly than necessary on a doorstep in the gloaming. I had been hearing that more often than usual of late. But at last, the instant she said it, something about it began to settle, and I started to believe it. I had believed Adonai was with me. I had believed he had given me a child. I could acknowledge I was blessed, but I had not yet felt it. Maybe I needed to hear it from a woman rather than an angel in order finally to be certain. People clamor for miracles—I have seen it in my day. But there's nothing like homegrown revelation from someone who has all her life walked closely with Adonai. I have seen that, too.

Still, I hadn't seen much of either at the time, as a young pregnant virgin standing hopefully outside of her cousins' house. Now, with Elisheva's exclamation—proclamation, really—I knew without doubt I was favored. I saw it: I was chosen—out of all the women of Isra'el—out of all the women in the world—to bear the Messiah. The one God had promised to our people in order to deliver us at last. The one for whom we had been waiting thousands of years.

"And the child in you is blessed, too!" Elisheva went on, aware of my baby but clearly unaware or unconcerned about what I was thinking just then. "But how have I deserved for the King's mother to come to me? Do you know? As soon as I heard you, my own baby inside me jumped for joy. Truly, you are fortunate, because you trusted that Adonai's promise to you will come true."

Had I? I was afraid. But I realized then that, in spite of the fear, I had indeed trusted. I had trusted enough to consent. Now I knew I was honored and glad. More than glad. By the time Elisheva had finished exclaiming over me and my unborn baby and ushered us into the house, I, too, was caught up—into something more and higher and better than emotion, which I've experienced a few times since then, but never had before it. It was the Ruach HaKodesh in that house with us, and under that inspiration I sang—maybe like my ancestor David, the poet-king. I had never sung poems out of my own head or heart before, but this one came almost unbidden, like when birds seem unable to contain their joy. I sang about how unworthy I was, but how blessed, Adonai having found it in himself to honor me by making me the mother of the one who would defeat kings and set up Adonai's own kingdom.

I was like Hannah when Adonai gave her Sh'mu'el. I was like Le'ah when Adonai gave her Y'hudah. I was like Rachel when Adonai gave her her Yosef. I was like all the mothers of Isra'el, rejoicing in the power of God to give them sons for deliverance. But I was unlike them, too. My son was to be called the Son of God. It was true I could scarcely bear the honor. Adonai would have known this, too. Yet he had chosen me regardless of my own worthiness, because of his.

5
WE WEPT, ELISHEVA AND I

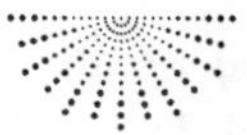

We wept, Elisheva and I, and she brought me to a room in the house which I was to have all to myself. "Dear young favored-among-women," she said. "You have travelled far—and who brought you?"

"My cousin Yitz'chak," I said. "He was afraid to meet you, I think." I grinned. It was funny, I thought then, that the person I had brought along to protect me was more frightened than I was. It was also amusing to imagine anyone being afraid of Elisheva and Z'kharyah. I left out the bit about what I imagined he was up to in Yerushalayim.

Elisheva chuckled. "As indeed he should be, no doubt. We are terribly fearsome, Z'kharyah and I."

"And how is Z'kharyah?" I wanted to know. I was a little surprised he had not come to greet me. It wasn't that I felt I was anything special—except I did, a little bit now, not by virtue of my own self, but because of Ha'Elyon's child growing in me. Even Elisheva's baby had greeted us in a way, and I had always imagined Z'kharyah looked on me with some fondness.

"He is well," Elisheva replied, still grinning rather irrepressibly.

I looked at her. "Shall I tell you?" she asked. "Shall I tell you about the announcement of my baby?"

I nodded, tucking my feet up under my robes, and remembering in the process that I had gifts for my hostess. The servant had taken my things during the commotion with Elisheva in the doorway. I would have to look for everything in the morning. Meanwhile, I enjoyed plumping myself into the cushions on the raised platform bed on which I would be sleeping later. No one had anything like such beds in Natzeret. Elisheva settled down, too. I was used to Z'kharyah telling the stories in this place, but I supposed some of his ability would have rubbed off on his wife. Now she was going to tell me a story that had never been written into the Tanakh, and yet sounded so much like it. I imagined fleetingly how amazing it would be if our holy scriptures could be added to, after all these years.

"Yes, Elisheva," I said. "Tell me about your baby." I thought maybe her telling would help me know something more about my baby, too.

"Well," she began, "you know how the priests are chosen by lot to serve before God."

I nodded.

"Some months ago, Z'kharyah himself was chosen. You can imagine how he felt about it—it's an honor, and a fear as well."

I could imagine very well indeed. "Did you go?"

"Yes," she said. "In the court of the women, of course." Her eyes glowed with pride.

"So," she said, "he went in there to burn the incense before Adonai, and he was gone a long time. Also the bells had stopped. The people became concerned and were just readying themselves to pull the cord and drag him out, in case he had seen a vision and died of it." Our people believe—because it has happened in our history—that the holiness of Adonai can kill a person. A priest sent into the Most Holy

Place wore bells at the edge of his garments so those outside could hear him and be certain all was well with him. He also wore a cord around one ankle. If those bells suddenly went silent, the men outside would know something was wrong, and pull on the cord to drag him out.

I could have died of my vision, too, I thought, though in that case the vision would have defeated the purpose. I supposed killing Z'kharyah with a vision would have defeated the purpose as well, unless Adonai gave Elisheva a child the same way he had given me one.

"He was certainly startled enough," Elisheva went on, "When he came out from burning incense, he could no longer speak, and we all understood he had seen something very wonderful indeed—although of course he couldn't tell anyone about it.

"All the way home, he did not speak. I did not question him, for what could I say, and what could he say to me? Even had he not been robbed of speech, the very experience of going into that holy place would surely have made him quiet and pensive. But after dinner he...he came to me..."

Elisheva was blushing now, like a girl. Like me. We were both grinning. I thought of Shlomo's Song—the Song I was not meant to know any of—and giggled.

"At any rate," Elisheva cleared her throat and laughed, "now I am with child. As you see."

"But can he still not speak?" I asked. "Has he found no way to tell you what happened?"

"He has told me something," Elisheva said. "He keeps a writing tablet to hand all the time now."

I had forgotten my Southern cousins—even the women—could read. It was a good thing, I thought, that I was not struck dumb after speaking with the angel that came to me, because I would be completely at a loss at how to communicate anything. It might have come in handy, I supposed, when my belly began to show signs of a baby—perhaps people would understand that I had had a magnificent experience and that the baby was special and I was therefore to be exonerated for having a child out of wedlock.

On the other hand, people expected priests to have visions and visitations. But young village girls had no such things. They just went mad. Probably if I had been rendered speechless, everyone would simply think I had been raped and gone mad with the distress.

"So what did he tell you?" I said.

"He had indeed seen a vision of sorts," Elisheva answered. "The great angel Gavri'el came to him—to Z'kharyah! He told him that at long last, we were to have a son!" She paused for a minute, as if still astonished at the news—and at the fact. She put her hand on her belly and I noticed that her eyes had reddened.

"Our boy is to be a nazir—dedicated to Ha'Elyon, and he is...he shall have the spirit of Eliyahu."

My eyes widened. Our writings did say that Eliyahu, one of the greatest prophets in the history of Isra'el, would return. This was not as great a promise as the Messiah, but still, our people had longed for that strong, stern, inspiring righteousness for many hundreds of years. Now my own mother's cousin was to give him birth. The thought made me shiver with wonder.

"This Gavri'el told him that our son would go before Adonai and turn the hearts of this people back to God."

I smiled. Elisheva's prophet-boy, and my Messiah-one. They were both coming—within just a few months!—and the world would be utterly changed. Isra'el would worship and serve Ha'Elyon truly again, and the Romans who occupied our holy land would be defeated. It was coming! Adonai had chosen us to bring it!

"But why cannot Z'kharyah speak?" I wanted to know. "Will he ever be able to again?"

On the one hand it was not too surprising if someone

were to be startled into muteness by talking to an angel. On the other, there was something mildly ironic about a prophet being sired by a father who could not speak.

"He doubted, a little," Elisheva said. "He asked the angel for a sign—as if an angel in the Temple's most holy place was not sign enough...So the angel gave him one: speechlessness until the baby is born and we name him Yochanan."

"Yochanan," I repeated. "I am to name my baby 'Yeshua.'"

"Yeshua," Elisheva repeated, too. "Tell me about Yeshua, Miryam." She had suddenly become very solemn—still with the joy of her first greeting, but a quieter joy all the same.

"He is the one promised through the ages," I said, simply. I felt suddenly, after my song-burst in the entryway, as if I should have known this all along.

"And his father?"

The question wasn't one of doubting. Elisheva believed wholeheartedly, but her prophet-baby clearly had not given her knowledge of all the details. I knew, too, that she would believe whatever I told her. But it still seemed so startling and almost disrespectful that it took me a good few moments of silence and opening and closing my mouth before I finally said, "The Ruach HaKodesh has come over me, and now I am with child."

Elisheva drew in her breath sharply at that. But she did not ask me if I were sure, as my sister had done. She was well aware that I would never say anything like that if I were not sure.

Neither of us said anything for some time. Then finally she stood. "My dear," she said, putting her hands on either side of my face, "you are a beautiful, brave, obedient woman, and Adonai is with you. You are so favored. I do not think you will feel that way at first. You will have a lot of explaining to do, and it will take a miracle almost as great as either of ours for anybody to believe you. I do not understand the workings of Ha'Elyon, such that giving me a child brings me such honor, and giving you one brings you such shame. But you are here, and for the time that you are, we will celebrate that Adonai has chosen you to bring the Messiah into the world."

I felt my eyes pricking. It was gift enough in this strange new world I had entered that at least one person believed me utterly and understood what I was about to face.

"Sleep now, Miryam," Elisheva said, taking the lamp. "You will need the strength that it can give." She kissed me on the forehead and went away.

6

THEY PASSED LIKE A LOVELY DREAM

I stayed with Elisheva for three months, and though for part of that time I was plagued in the mornings with the sickness, in my memory now, they passed like a lovely dream. And dream we did—about our sons and what they would look like, and what they would be like, and most important of all, how Adonai would lead them and what they would do to deliver Isra'el.

"He will be tall like you," I said of Elisheva's son. "And pale. With a beard like Z'kharyah's. Only dark." It was hard to imagine our unborn babies growing old.

Elisheva nodded. "With Z'kharyah's steadiness and my fire. At the same time." She chuckled. "Isn't it funny how we are only discussing the elements of his parents which we find appealing?"

I grinned, but said, "But he's a miracle child! Would Adonai allow your faults to commingle, if he has such great things in mind for your boy? Not," I added, looking up slyly, "that either of you have any faults." Z'kharyah, who had made himself known in his newly silent way at the end of my second day in the house, raised his eyebrows but laughed without sound. I was quite sure I would never have spoken to either Elisheva or her husband in this way even a week ago, but now she and I were sisters in some kind of strange divine spectacle, and the more time we spent together, the more I felt we were on an equal footing. I wasn't being forward. I was simply speaking as it came to me to speak. I didn't remember ever having felt so free before.

"And what of your son?" Elisheva read from the tablet on which Z'kharyah had just scrawled something I could not begin to understand.

My son was more difficult to imagine. A combination of two human parents provided a readier catalog of possible characteristics. But when the human parentage only came from me...well, how could it possibly be? Would my son share all my physical characteristics? Would he simply be a male version of myself? And would he share my personality and character, or would he exhibit something entirely different, coming, as it did, from Ha'Elyon?

"Surely," Elisheva said, "Ha'Elyon must have seen something in you that reminded him of himself, to choose you to be the mother."

Z'kharyah tisked, something he at which he had become rather adept after the loss of his voice.

Elisheva rolled her eyes with a slight smile and handed him back his tablet.

"Adonai is not a man," Z'kharyah wrote. "Through the prophet Yeshayahu he tells us that his ways are not our ways and his thoughts are not our thoughts."

"I should have thought that was self-evident," Elisheva answered. "Not one of us would have thought of his getting a good Jewish virgin girl with child."

Z'kharyah looked worried, but his wife just smiled. I wasn't sure whose side to fall on. Both of them had a good argument, it seemed to me. But then, I was not really an educated person, and what did I know about it?

Nevertheless we debated like this nearly every day, and

instead of the discussions turning into arguments as I often heard among the men in the street in Natzeret, these were seasoned with laughter—and silence in strange places while we waited for Z'kharyah to write. In between times, Elisheva had arranged for a loom to be set up for me, and the servants brought home armloads of yarn, finer than anything I had woven before. After I got used to new textures, my fingers flew over the colors as I made a long winding wrap for Elisheva's baby, and blankets for him, and cushions for his mother.

I was going to need swaddling cloths for my baby, too, I thought, as I wove and wove and wove. I didn't know what of myself Adonai was going to choose to put into this son of his, but I tried to put into the weaving something of whatever small amounts of love I was already beginning to feel for this little child growing inside. In the rhythm of the work, I kept remember the words I had said to the angel, "I am Adonai's servant. Let it happen as you have said. I am Adonai's servant. Let it happen as you have said. I am Adonai's servant. Let it happen as you have said."

I forgot my fears, those three months. I forgot the shame, and Yosef's inevitable disappointment, and father's inevitable anger. I even forgot, for a time, that those chosen by Adonai must suffer. At the moment, I was discovering that those he chooses also know great joy.

But as the third month closed, Elisheva said, "Miryam, it is time for you to go back. Soon we will be able to see the child within you. This should be a glory to you, and not a shame. But in order for it to be so, you must tell them about him first."

I knew she was right, and a bit of the old dread settled back into my heart. It had become so foreign a feeling, that at first I couldn't even tell what it was. "But," I protested after understanding it, "you will be having your own baby soon.

Let me stay with you and help you deliver him. That is why I came after all."

"Miryam," Elisheva looked at me. "That is why you said you came, but truly you came to receive strength for the next bit. You may stay until after you have gone to Beit-Lechem and told Yosef what has happened to you. This is not the kind of news that you should send to your betrothed by messenger."

In that case, I thought, it would be nice just never to go to Beit-Lechem at all. I could stay with Elisheva and Z'kharyah until their baby was born, and then I could stay until my baby was born. It would be safe, and so much lovelier, to stay always with people who believed me—even if there were only ever two of them until my son grew up.

But during those three months, in the talking and the weaving, I had thought over and over again about what, exactly, being a servant of Adonai meant. Among other things, I thought it meant that I was to be bold and not afraid of what any human thought. Not even my father. Not even my husband. I was no one else's servant now. When I had chosen to let the Ruach HaKodesh come over me, I had also chosen to follow wherever Adonai's will led me—for he himself had, apparently, chosen me.

Therefore, next morning I saddled up a donkey and went. Elisheva's child was too big inside of her now for her to accompany me, and Z'kharyah was too old for the journey, even though it was a relatively short one to the southeast. It was unlikely that anyone would have accosted a young woman and a very old man. Still, if there had been any trouble, Z'kharyah would have been unable to say anything, nor would he have been able to defend himself, let alone me. So Elisheva sent the servant. He was not so young himself, but he was young enough for foot-travel, and old enough not to look amiss escorting a young woman on a donkey.

We reached Beit-Lechem in good time, and I managed to find Yosef's family dwelling without too much difficulty. It was quite some while since I had been there. In fact, I didn't think I had visited since the last time our family went down to Yerushalayim for Pesach and saw Elisheva and Z'kharyah, before Imma died. Whenever I saw Yosef these days, it was because he came North to us, to continue to set wedding preparations in place, to visit with my father, to speak with me.

I remembered the last time he came to visit. It was perhaps two months before the angel's appearance, and so now we had not seen each other for nearly six. I wondered if he had traveled to Natzeret at all in the last three months, only to discover I was not there. He must have done, surely. I wondered if he wondered why I had not been to see him yet, and I wondered a little bit why he had not tried to see me. He could not have heard rumors about me—just about Elisheva. Only Shlomit knew my secrets there, and she would never have told them.

On that last visit, Yosef and I went walking in the fields, close enough to be seen by village busybodies, far enough so they couldn't hear what we said. The sky was overcast, but there was no rain, and the stalks of grain were dry. That was when he gave me the carved box. I had brought it with me to Ein Karem. I had thought I might find some trinket from the South to put inside it, but later I changed my mind. I would keep it empty until after my wedding night—if there was to be a wedding night.

Yosef stopped me in the middle of the field that day and held my hands below the tall grain stalks. "You are lovely," he said. "Do you think anything like this of me?"

I was so shy. I had nodded, but hadn't been able to bring myself to say anything about it. I wanted to squeeze his hands, to kiss them, for all I was so afraid of him and of life with him. But I simply looked at the ground and nodded. Perhaps I whispered yes. Now I wished I had said something more—done something more. If I had, he would have had more assurance that somehow I loved him, or thought I could one day. He would know I would never have gone with another man instead of him, and that this baby was none other than who I said he was—the Messiah, and the son of God.

But I hadn't. So now I was approaching his sister's house, and everyone would think how unsuitably overeager I was, coming all the way down from the Galil like this to see their Yosef. They would laugh behind their hands and talk about how uncouth we Northerners were. And then, after I left, they would think what a harlot I was, when really, I was nothing of the kind.

"I am the servant of Adonai," I whispered fiercely to myself—and to Adonai, since the angel had said he was with me and I had to hope he was listening. "Let it be to me as you have said."

I glanced at the old man walking beside me. He was mostly silent throughout our journey, though unlike Z'kharyah, he could have spoken had he chosen to. He knew my story—at least the basic details. His demeanor and lined face were completely inscrutable; I had no idea how he felt about what he had been told. Seeing no more expression there now than when we set out, I shrugged, took a deep breath, and was about to rap on Yosef's sister's door when I remembered the carpenter's shop.

How silly I was! Yosef would be there, of course. Perhaps I would not need to see his family at all.

This thought itself seemed silly, in a way. After three months with Elisheva, I was frustrated that I had to be so secretive about this baby. It was a glorious thing, not a shameful one, to be carrying the child of Ha'Elyon. Partly, I wanted to announce to everyone I met, "Do you know this Messiah you've been waiting for? Well, he's coming! I know. I'm his mother." But every Jewish woman who hoped for a

Messiah at all, also hoped to be his mother. Probably more than one had been convinced she was. Thus, I was still left looking shamed and possibly crazy. So I slunk around to the back of the house where Yosef was sure to be at work in his father's shop.

In this I was not disappointed. It was another mercy to observe that he was alone. The afternoon sun was falling in sleepy rays through the windows, wood-dust floating in the light. Yosef's head was bent over a plank, the dark hair with flecks of gray curling all over his scalp. I suppose he was studying the plank, although at first glance it looked like he had nodded off for a bit. In fact, he very well could have, as he had of late, I knew, been working day and night to make a home for us after our wedding, while yet keeping up with his usual business. My eyes began to well up, and I swallowed. The gulp was louder than I expected, and Yosef looked up.

Our eyes met, and I saw the mix of bafflement and delight in his turn to concern when he saw the tears in mine. "Miryam," he said, and one of the tears spilled down my cheek. "What are you doing here? Are you all right?"

"Yes," I said. "I am favored. I am the servant of Adonai, and it is with me as he has said."

Yosef looked even more worried at these statements, and I could not blame him. "What are you talking about?" he whispered. "What has happened to you?"

I did not even know where to begin. Finally I said what I had been wishing I could say to everybody all along: "Yosef, you know how we—our people, my father, you, me—you talk about it with my father sometimes—you know how we have been longing for the Messiah for centuries?"

He nodded, his brows knitting more and more tightly together, like a fist in the middle of his forehead, he was trying so hard to understand me. "Well," I said, "the Messiah is coming. In our time. I am his mother."

The brows unraveled just a tiny bit, but really, I hadn't

said anything very relief-inducing. "Of course, Miryam," he said. He looked at me the way one might eye a street dog whose mouth looks suspiciously foam-flecked. "Every Jewish girl dreams of being the mother of the Messiah. We can certainly hope..." A faint smile played around his lips in spite of his scowl. Clearly he thought I was using this as a rather exaggerated excuse to talk about having children. I had never broached that subject before, and here he was, supposing I had always been too shy to bring it up, as I was too shy to bring up so many other things.

"No Yosef," I said firmly. "I did not say, 'I hope to be the Messiah's mother,' nor even 'I will be the Messiah's mother.' I said I am his mother."

The smile fled from Yosef's lips, but he still spoke tenderly. "Please, Miryam," he said. "Speak plainly."

I spoke as plainly as I could. "Yosef," I said, as if saying his name over and over again would bind him to me, would keep him from breaking our betrothal. "I am with child."

His face drained of color so instantly that I thought he might collapse, but the muscles in his jaw tightened and his voice became cold, instead. "Who did this to you?"

Bless him. He wanted so desperately to think the best of me, but even though the truth was even better than the best, I knew he would think the worst soon enough.

"Listen to me, Yosef," I said. "I will explain everything, but you must listen and not say anything or ask any questions until I have finished. Please." I gazed into his eyes and missed the sparkle I was so used to seeing when I looked at him. The Messiah's mother should not have such a heavy heart, I thought.

"I am listening," Yosef said.

"You will think I am crazy," I said. "But I swear to you I am not. I wish you would talk to my cousin Elisheva. She believes me and she is even a sign that what I say is true...But never mind.

"Some months ago—four months ago...Four months!" I said, "I was sitting at the edge of the hill in Natzeret. You know, at the spot where I showed you. I was taking a moment's rest and thinking. I was thinking about you, Yosef. But then suddenly an angel appeared to me, and it told me Adonai was with me. This frightened me. I have always wanted to be pleasing to Adonai, but I never thought he would have noticed, you know? You do understand me?" I looked at him hopefully, pausing although I had commanded him not to say anything.

He nodded, looking baffled again. His expression had taken on a strained aspect, as if he were trying very hard to understand a native of one of the farther reaches of the Roman Empire, who had a fair grasp of Greek but no knowledge of Aramaic at all. Yosef knew some Greek words and phrases, but clever as he was, he was no scholar.

"The angel told me," I went on, "that I would have a son named Yeshua, who would be called the son of Ha'Elyon. I said, 'But that's impossible—I'm a virgin!'" I felt it was very important that I add that detail for Yosef. "But the angel said that the Ruach HaKodesh would cover me and make me with child—and so I am. I swear to you, Yosef. I am telling the truth."

By this time, Yosef was staring at me. I thought I had never seen so much of his eyes before, but there was no glint of any humor to be found in them anywhere. "How can you speak of Ha'Elyon in this way, Miryam? How can such a thought have even entered your mind? What kind of monster are you defending, that you would think you had to go to such lengths? If there is someone else, just say so, and be done with it!"

I had thought when it came to this, that I would collapse in weeping and beg Yosef to believe me. But now, in the moment, even in spite of the desperation I had felt just moments before, I knew I did not need to weep. I had told the truth, and I did not need to apologize for it.

I put my chin up and looked Yosef in the face. "How can you," I countered, "imagine I would lie with another man in the first place, and then concoct such a story to protect him? You should believe me. Have I ever given you reason to doubt me before? Or have I ever startled you with impiety? There never has been anyone else for me but you, Yosef." There. I had said it. "But if there is, it is Adonai himself, because I told the angel I was Adonai's servant to do with as he wished. The will of Adonai must always come first, before mortals, I think. Don't you?"

"I should believe you," Yosef acknowledged, somewhat under his breath and echoing my own words. "You have never given me reason to doubt you. But," he looked up and spoke a little more loudly, "please understand me, too. I am only a man, and I cannot grasp news like this. Give me some time while I think what to do."

My heart dropped a little, even though a request for time was far better than the outright rejection I had feared. "Yes," I said. "Take all the time you need."

The servant was waiting outside with the donkey when I parted from Yosef, and I left Beit-Lechem that afternoon. Though I am certain I ran across some of Yosef's relatives in the streets, either coming or going, I didn't recognize anyone, and I kept my head covering close round my face so that they could not recognize me. I left no gifts for Yosef's sisters.

7
AFTER THAT ERRAND WAS ACCOMPLISHED

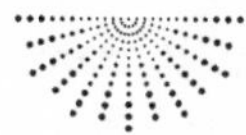

After that errand was accomplished, Elisheva said she had no further use of me. She was kind in the saying of it, of course, but there was no use arguing with her about it either. No, she did not need my assistance to deliver her baby. That was why there were midwives. If I stayed much longer, I would not be able to hide my pregnancy at all by the time I got home, and if I stayed longer than that, it would become dangerous for me to travel. The servant who had accompanied me to Beit-Lechem was dispatched to bring me to the Galil now. I could not imagine this pleased him very much, although by the end of the journey he was more talkative than he had been when we set out.

Who can resist the beauty of the Galil, really? It would make even the dourest person cheerful, I thought, as the landscape grew greener again and I began to recognize landmarks. I knew we were backward country folk. Southerners made fun of our accents and our ways, but I still loved my Northern village more than anything I had ever seen in the South. Except Yosef...I pushed him out of my mind and tried to listen to the man's description of how he had come to work in for Z'kharyah's family in the first place.

Our traveling companions on this journey, whom we joined a little further along in our passage than the caravan Yitz'chak and I had joined in the opposite direction, were friendly enough, but not overly remarkable. There was no matronly woman to help me feel safe, and the women there were, seemed to me somewhat dubious. I kept close to my guardian and let him tell me his quiet stories in his quiet way. I could glory in the sights and smells of the nearing North during the daylight hours, but when night fell, I wished to be back with Elisheva. I could not say I wished to be home sooner, because I still could not imagine what I would find there.

We left the caravan at Salim, and carried on the rest of the way to Natzeret ourselves. When we at last reached the outskirts, I dismounted from the donkey. "Thank you kindly," I said. "I haven't got money for you at all." He knew this, and I knew Elisheva and Z'kharyah would make his efforts worth it to him on his return, but it didn't keep me from feeling somewhat ashamed. "But here are some blankets that perhaps you and your wife can make use of." I gave him the bundle of blankets I had meant for Yosef's sisters. Anyone can use blankets. It was funny that I had taken them all the way from Natzeret to 'Ein Karem, only to bring them all the way back, only to send them back to 'Ein Karem without me. Life was full of strange little jokes, like that, I thought. We probably need them, or all the other things would drive us mad.

"Would you like to stay the night with our family?" I asked the servant. "My father would be more than pleased for you to do so." This was only polite and, under normal circumstances, my heart would have been fully in the invitation. But I was expecting an awkward if not outright disastrous evening, and so I rather hoped the man would decline the offer, as my cousin had months before. It did seem a little much to hope for, but then, these were unusual circumstances.

"Oh no," he declined, as custom also dictated. "I could not bear to trouble your family."

His refusal looked as genuinely sincere as my invitation had been the opposite. Unfortunately for both of us, we had not finished the prescribed routine. "Please," I said, "You have come with me so far. My father would like to thank the man who has looked after his daughter as if she were his own."

"It was nothing and a pleasure," said the servant. "I should return to my own family as soon as possible."

"Yes!" I wanted to say, "You should, and all the best to them, as well!" But I didn't. Instead I invited him one more time, and this time he accepted.

We continued into the village, both of us, I expect, looking utterly miserable. Accursed convention! Why couldn't one of the two of us have defied it for once?

As we entered the village, I passed one of my cousins, a girl younger than I, who glanced at me and smiled, and then dashed off, doubtless to tell her family that I had returned. I wondered how on earth I was to manage the people. Telling my father about my unexpected child was one matter. Somehow convincing an entire village I was still virtuous would be another matter altogether. I hunched over as much as I could without looking either infirm or unnatural, so that the folds of my robes would hang as straight as possible.

Abba was sitting in the sun, his back against the outer wall of the house as we approached. When he saw me he stood, his face beaming.

"Miryam!" he exclaimed. "Welcome home!" A few women cooking outside their homes looked up and called out greetings. Fortunately, none of them approached just then. But Abba rushed forward to embrace me, and this was the last thing I wanted. I hadn't wanted him to feel the small growing bulge in my abdomen before I told him about it. Then again, he was aging, and maybe he was not the most observant man, either. He wrapped his arms around my shoulders and kissed my hair, and I wrapped my arms around him, too, and hoped he would not say anything yet.

"Did you help Elisheva deliver her baby?" he asked conversationally after he had released me and I had introduced him to Z'kharyah's servant.

"No," I said. "Please, Abba. Can we go inside?"

"No?" Father was surprised. "Why not? Did something happen? Everything all right there? Go into the house? Has something happened that the neighbors cannot hear?"

"Elisheva is fine," I said, ignoring the last question and hoping said neighbors would, too, tugging gently on Abba's arm. "Her baby is fine. Z'kharyah is fine." I did not tell him about Z'kharyah's having lost his power to speak. Then I added, "I am also fine," but my voice quavered a little. I tugged the arm more insistently, and finally Abba followed me into the dim light of the house.

I had not wanted to cry. I had not cried for Yosef, and now I thought it would make it look as if I had indeed done something wrong if I gave way to tears. I had done nothing wrong. I was a favored lady, I reminded myself for the thousandth time. Adonai was with me. The angel had said it. I was blessed among women, and the child in my womb was blessed. Elisheva had said that. And I myself had sung three months earlier that the Mighty One had done great things for me. Me, his simple servant girl, whom he had no reason to notice.

But when Abba looked at me, loving concern all over his face, and said, "Miryam?" I burst into tears anyway. He and Yosef were so like in some ways. But this was my Abba, and I had known him since I was born. He was the one to whom I had run when I fell and cut myself on the gravel in the pathways as a child. He had held me when I had needed to be comforted. Now, I knew, I would need to be comforted from his very disappointment, and who would be able to help me with that?

Shlomit came into the room then. She had been at the cistern washing clothes, but someone had evidently seen her and told her I was returned. Her glance fell on the servant and I saw swift alarm flit through it. Then she came to me and embraced me as Abba had done, and kissed me on both cheeks. I noticed her look down at my belly and then look up at my face with a hint of tears in her own eyes. Then she set to work preparing food for our guest and serving him. Both of us knew better than to hope he wouldn't notice the scene which was surely to unfold, however.

This time my story blurted out in such a jumble of words that, even if it had been a sensible story in the first place, I would not have blamed Abba for not understanding it. In the end he had to grip me by the shoulders and say, "Miryam!"

I looked up.

"What are you saying?" His voice was hard, like it got when he was angry or afraid and trying not to show it.

"The Ruach HaKodesh has come to me and I am with child," I said.

He stared. "The Ruach HaKodesh..." he said. And then he hissed—loudly, if such is possible, "The Ruach HaKodesh is not a *man.* He does not come and seduce peasant girls and leave them with child! This is something like blasphemy, daughter, do you hear?!"

I heard. I only wished the neighbors couldn't hear as well. As they were still just outside and we had no window coverings up, I imagined that even with Abba's attempt to keep his voice down, they would have heard everything.

"Better," Abba continued more quietly but not more calmly, "you should say who the man was and have done with it, than to try to defend him by blasphemy. It wasn't Yosef, was it? Did you see him while you were there?"

"No," I said. "It wasn't Yosef. I did see him while I was

there, but only a few weeks ago. I told him everything I have told you. He said just what you did. It wasn't Yosef," I reiterated, though it would have been so much easier and less upsetting for everyone if I could have placed the blame there. "It was the Ruach HaKodesh."

"Or you!" shouted my father, rounding on our visitor as if he were not also a grey-haired man deserving of respect, and as if he had not already greatly inconvenienced himself in accompanying me home. Someone, it appeared, was now about to defy convention after all. No one would make the accusation my father appeared about to make without couching it in subtle terms and tricking the accused into a confession. But Abba so rarely got angry that when he did, he wasn't very good at dissembling.

"Abba!" snapped Shlomit, before he could shame himself and us. "This man has traveled far with my sister to care for her and we owe him our gratitude that worse did not befall her."

"Worse?" said Abba. "Worse? What could be worse than an unmarried, pregnant, blaspheming daughter? If this man has not put her in this condition himself, then surely he should have been more vigilant in keeping someone else from defiling her! What were your cousins thinking, sending someone so old he could not protect you?"

"Abba!" Shlomit and I shouted together. The servant rose, affronted, as well he should have been, for the insult itself and the fact that Abba was surely older than he.

"I shall return to my master and tell him you have no further need of me," he said. Shlomit tried to run after him, but her entreaties clearly did not prevail, for she returned shortly, looking like a storm over Kinneret.

Now that I was angry it was a bit easier to manage the situation. "Abba," I said. "You are the one speaking nonsense. How dare you insult that man! He was very faithful and good to me, and in any case, none of your accusations make any sense, because I have been with child since the day I left Natzeret. See here, if you must!" I grabbed his hand and placed it on my belly, in spite of not wanting him to feel it when I arrived.

He looked at me uncertainly then, and I suddenly saw he was, indeed, growing old. "But whose is it?" he whispered.

"I have told you," I said. "I am with child by the Ruach HaKodesh."

Then I saw fear on Abba's face as I had never seen fear. "You should be killed, daughter," he said in his fear. "Even for adultery, you should be killed. For blaspheming the Ruach HaKodesh, I am surprised he hasn't stricken you dead already. But, God forgive me, I cannot kill you myself. Oh Miryam!" He hugged my head in his arms then, as if I were a little girl, stroking my hair and sobbing as if he were a woman. I was comforted after all, but it was more by something he had said than something he had done. He thought the Ruach HaKodesh should kill me for blasphemy. But that, I suddenly realized, would never happen, just as my sister had said nothing would happen to me on my journey to and from 'Ein Karem. For my story was true, and I was not blaspheming. And if the Ruach HaKodesh would not kill me, nothing much worse could happen. I might even expect protection. I was carrying Adonai's child, after all.

On the other hand, things still could get considerably less pleasant.

8

I WENT OUT

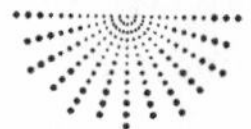

I went out after I spoke to Abba, and Shlomit made to follow me, but he stopped her sternly. That was when I knew that the embrace he had given me was the last one I would receive for a very long time, and that in spite of the weeping, things might yet become as difficult as I had feared. I felt the heaviness of his fear and of my sister's thwarted longing to follow after me.

I strode toward my sheltering tree at the edge of the cliff, trying hard not to hear the people. Already the story was getting about, and I had scarcely told it. The nearest neighbors—those who had heard my father's shouts, and those whom they had told already—whispered amongst themselves and stared at me, though people nearer the edge of the village who had yet to hear the news still called out greetings to me. It went against my nature not to acknowledge people, but I just did not know how I would talk to anyone anymore. I thought maybe the angel would come back if I waited for it. Maybe it would give me a message from Adonai about what to do next. Maybe it would tell me how to convince everyone about what had happened to me.

I suppose angels don't really come with wishing, though.

That is something for the pagan religions, and brings trouble with it, I suspect. I sat in the sun and stared at the hard blue sky and prayed as well as I could, but nothing happened except the sun going down, and I had to return to the house. I made sure I returned after dinner, although my youngest brother ran to me with a small bucket partially filled with water at the end of the afternoon. Shlomit must have sent him. I drank the water gratefully and waited until the air began to get cool and the stars began to come out. Then I stood, picked up the empty bucket by its rope handle, and slowly trudged back to the house. I felt as if I had been working in the fields for a whole day instead of sitting quietly by myself.

Abba did not speak to me when I entered. It seemed that, though he was not willing to bring me into the village for stoning, he thought he would try to make up for it by shunning me as completely as if I were already dead. Shlomit looked up when I came in. I started to ask her something, but she shook her head and inclined it slightly. My eyes shifted to the place she had indicated. My bed had been moved out of the loft to the section of the house occupied by the goats. I wondered how long it would be before I was turned out altogether. I would have to move into the abandoned house at the edge of the village, and I would become the scandalous woman, the crazy woman, living alone, raising a son everyone believed to be a bastard. Surely the Ruach HaKodesh would not allow this for his own son. Would he?

But already his choice of circumstances seemed foolhardy, so who could say? What did Ha'Elyon really know about human beings and our ways anyhow? "For my thoughts are not your thoughts, and my ways are not your ways," Adonai had said to the prophet Yesha'yahu. He could not have said it any truer. Why, then, could he not leave us alone? I forgot I had ever wanted a Messiah, let alone that I had even for a moment felt blessed to be his mother.

I went to my sleeping mat and lay down on it, with my face to the wall. The wall was damp and black there, from the goats rubbing up against it. The goats themselves nudged me a bit and nibbled at the edge of my scarf. I pushed at them with my arm and eventually they grew tired of me and gathered companionably together in the far corner of their pen.

The tears trickled silently out of my eyes, across the bridge of my nose, making the mat damp under the side of my face. Father had been my comfort as a child, but now he was rejecting me. That, in turn, made me think about Yosef. In fact, I could not stop thinking of him. I should never have told him to take his time. That was surely just putting off the inevitable. If he were going to reject me, too, I wished he had just done so outright. All the quiet of that day and that night had given me far too much time to think, and now I felt like I had given up the world for a burden I could not bear.

What if I had said no to the angel? I could have married Yosef and had the life of the usual Jewish woman in the Galil. All would have been well. But then, is anything ever well, truly, when one denies the demands of Adonai? I felt cheated, somehow. How had Adonai even noticed me, and why had He? His presence with me meant, apparently, that I could enjoy the presence of no one else. I knew that I should feel favored, but one becomes accustomed to measuring favor by the people one loves, and now there were none to love me. I belonged to Adonai now, and I was miserable.

9
THE NEXT DAYS BLURRED

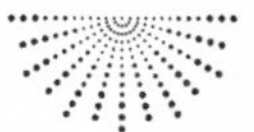

The next days blurred. I spent a long time on the mat with my face to the wall, getting up in the middle of the night to eat something to keep the baby alive. Shlomit tried to speak to me sometimes when Abba was outside leaning against the wall in the sunshine. It was very quiet out there for a number of days after my news broke, but as the days went on, I heard people stop to speak to him. Everyone would ignore me now, for the rest of my life. I could not decide if it were a mercy or not, that no one had threatened to stone me to death.

With so much time to think and so little to do, I convinced myself that, along with everything else, I would lose Yosef—and that he was the one thing in the world I wanted for myself. Never mind that I had been half afraid of him and of what he was to me before. Now that I thought I had to give him up utterly and forever, I did not want to. But I was the servant of Adonai, and so I steeled my will and fought with him in my mind as I lay among the goats with my face to the wall.

I do not know how many days passed before I felt a rough hand on my shoulder, larger than Shlomit's, and

Abba said gruffly, "Well then. You cannot expect to have a healthy child if you carry on like this. Get up, girl, and eat." I squinted at him, a human face suddenly seeming like a light I was not used to looking into. I realized later that Abba, at last deciding the Ruach HaKodesh had inexplicably spared me, was trying to make the best of a bad situation, and was reinstating my position as his daughter, if a besmirched one. I returned to my daughterly duties with determination and not much pleasure, but as the days progressed I gradually began to notice sunshine and early morning birdsong, and soon life seemed at least tolerable. I heard nothing from Yosef. I wouldn't, of course. Why would he even condescend to send a message to me to tell me the marriage was off? What would be the purpose? He was an honorable man, but I was no longer an honorable woman in his eyes, and why should he send a message when one did not need words to know that he was not going to marry me now?

I had kept his carved box with me in the folds of my clothing the whole time I was living with the goats. But now that I was allowed to live again, and life was not likely to include a husband after all, much less Yosef, I decided it was time to put it away. I considered throwing it off the precipice where the angel had met me. I further considered I might have done well to do that in the first place. But I could not quite relinquish it even then. It was so beautiful. So I climbed up to Shlomit's and my sleeping quarters and hid it under some blankets in a corner. Then, as far as I was able, I forgot about it.

More weeks passed. My growing abdomen was becoming harder and harder to hide. Had I been able to, people still would have stared and whispered and tutted, but as I grew, all such mutterings did, too. One of my cousins, a young woman around my age who might have been like a sister to me, had I not had Shlomit, faced me directly.

"Miryam," she said. "Truly—whose is it? I know you are a good girl."

Although she meant well, I had no patience, and her assertion that she knew anything about me at all—although she did—rankled. No one could know what I was feeling, because no one had ever experienced what I was experiencing. No one ever would. She wouldn't believe me anyhow, so what was the use in speaking of it? I told her as much, trying not to mind the wounded look in her eyes as she stalked off. She did not speak to me again until many years later. I cannot fault her for this.

One afternoon I was clearing up the few remains of our midday meal, when a shadow blocked the light coming in the doorway. It was not a woman's shadow. I looked up. "Lady," said the silhouette standing in the sun, light playing over the curls, "may I speak to your father?"

My heart dropped. Why did he have to come at all? Why did he have to let me hear his voice again, when I had tried so hard to forget it? I had felt sure it was decided between us—that he did not need to send any message. That I understood. That I would be quiet and raise this child myself and leave him alone.

But that was foolish, I thought, wondering with a start why I had not considered that of course he would have to officially break the betrothal with me so that he could marry someone else. Silently, I rose. I wished Abba were sitting outside our house in the sun as usual. Then I wouldn't have to find him and could have as little to do with Yosef as possible. Let the men revoke the agreement. It had not so much to do with me in the end, after all.

I ducked passed Yosef through the doorway, trying very hard not to touch him as I did so. Still, I felt the hem of my robe brush against his, and I flinched. "Miryam," he said, his voice reaching out to me, though his hands stayed at his side. But I did not look up or pause. I couldn't.

Abba was sitting with some of the other older men in a pathway; they were discussing whatever it was they always discussed to no apparent purpose. Rome, or deliverance, or the Messiah...or the price of fish. "Abba," I said, unable to raise my voice above a whisper.

The men stopped talking. I felt their eyes on me as I finally raised mine. I looked at each of them in turn. They had various shades of curiosity or disapproval on their faces. Abba looked embarrassed. Suddenly I decided I no longer cared. I could not live my life in the dark forever. They might try to stone me after all, I supposed, but I remembered Shlomit saying they couldn't hurt Adonai's baby, and in any case they had tried nothing of the sort so far. Therefore, I was going to have to face up to things. So I faced the men, and then I looked at my father. My voice became stronger.

"Abba," I said. "Yosef has come." Someone cleared a throat. Abba stood up and walked with me.

Yosef was standing next to my father's accustomed seat outside, and I disappeared into the house as soon as the two men began the accustomed, but in the moment rather stiff, greetings. I had hoped to hide in the shadows and listen. But Yosef called, "Come, Miryam, for this concerns you."

He was not playing by the rules I had established in my head. If he indeed had to come and break things off officially —and as I had only just conceded to myself, surely he did— could he not just get it over with and leave me out of it? I had thought Yosef a considerate man, but this was cruelty. Even having decided to face my bleak future, how could I bear to see Yosef tell my father he would have none of me?

"Sir," Yosef said when I reemerged into the sunlight. He suddenly sounded nervous as a boy, and this made me look at him. He looked nervous, too, but his eyes were smiling. I thought to be indignant about this, but instead the sight of that glinting laughter made my stomach leap in response to a hope I could not even articulate. He coughed. Then he said, "I would like permission to marry your daughter."

"You are already betrothed to her," said Abba. He watched Yosef as if he were some strange new sort of being whose habits were totally unpredictable. I could imagine the questions going through his mind: Was Yosef crazy? Did he even know the story? Was he up to some unimaginable mischief?

"Yes," said Yosef, and finally the smile on his face caught up with the one in his eyes, "I am. What I mean is, I would like to marry her now."

As I couldn't see myself just then, I am not certain who looked more surprised, Abba or me.

"You know," asked Abba, clearing his throat, too, "you know her condition?"

"Yes," said Yosef. "And I have eyes to see it." He chuckled. "And," he concluded, "I believe her story."

"You do?" asked Abba and I.

"I didn't," he confessed, "but I do now; I have to. An angel came and told me the same news Miryam brought me herself."

I felt the beginnings of my own smile forming—perhaps the first real smile since my return from Elisheva's. In the preceding days I had thought and thought and prayed and prayed, and after fighting had tried to submit myself to the will of Ha'Elyon. Perhaps two days before, I finally confessed my willingness to bear his promised one alone—alone forever, if necessary. At last I was trying to believe Adonai was enough.

But now—the hope that had made my bowels leap a moment ago turned into a seed dropping into my soul. I could not allow it but maybe—perhaps—I would not have to bear the promised one alone after all. It was not just Yosef being kind, though Yosef was so, so kind. It was that Adonai had sent him an angel, too, just as he had sent me one.

"Speak, man," Abba was saying brusquely. "What are you talking about?

"I didn't know what to think when you came to see me, Miryam," Yosef began. "I am so sorry I left you with no word for so long." He lifted my face towards his, and I saw him seeing my pain. I saw him feeling sorrier than I could have hoped. I felt myself blushing that Abba—and naturally one or two scandalized onlookers—should see us like this, but I felt so happy that I did not mind enough to pull away. "I simply could not believe that what you said was true. Except for the fact that I have never known you to lie before, and I know you fear Adonai too much to make up a story about his Spirit lightly.

"But you understand my position. If the child was yours by another man, I would doubt your faithfulness if I brought you under my roof. And if the child really was from the Ruach HaKodesh, then how dare I take you home and violate you, and how dare I think I could be a father to the Son of the Most High?"

Yes. I understood his position. I had understood it, more or less, almost from the time the angel appeared in the first place.

"I was—" he admitted, "—I was going to break our engagement. I didn't see anything else for it. But I could not bear to lose you, God forgive me, and I waited. And I thought. And I prayed. One night I could not sleep at all. It was time for a decision, I knew. I thought, though it nearly killed me to think it, that I would break with you once and for all. I would not have made a spectacle. I would have done it quietly, but I thought I had to do it. Then, just before dawn, I finally fell asleep. And I had a dream. A dream of an angel.

"The angel spoke to me and called me by name! 'Yosef!' it said. Then it called me by our ancestor's name: 'Son of David.' It said, "Don't worry to take Miryam home as your wife.'" His eyes were closed now as he spoke, remembering exactly the words the angel had spoken. "'For the baby who is conceived in her,'" he went on, "'is from the Ruach HaKodesh. She will bear a son, and you shall name him Yeshua, for he will save his people from their sins.'"

By the end of the week, I was Miryam, wife of Yosef, and, because we had not had the usual loud and festive wedding, if there were anyone left who had not known before, they all now knew I was with child. We did not try to explain. I had worn myself out telling the story to the few people I had considered worthy and able to hear it, and I would not tell it again for many years. The people would find out soon enough that the Messiah was here. In the meantime, he would just be Yosef's and my boy. It was enough that I knew whose child I bore, and so did my husband. And I had a husband, whom I loved and who loved me and loved the child inside me. I could take neither of them for granted. They were part of the unmerited blessing of Adonai.

In relief and gratitude, sometimes I laughed to myself over how much the people supposed, and how far it was from the truth. They thought Yosef and I had been intimate before our wedding. The truth of the matter was we did not share a bed even now. "Wait," Yosef said, kissing me on the forehead. "Wait until you have borne your son, and I have named him Yeshua."

I fingered the wooden box I had returned from its corner in the loft to my pocket. We waited, and the time grew short.

10
TO MOVE SOUTH

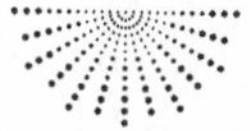

It grew even shorter as the time came to move South. Yosef had had to halt his carpentry business as well as preparations for our home in Beit-Lechem due to his journey North to marry me ahead of schedule. Given the change of plans, we would have just stayed put in Natzeret for a while. However, some time before, Caesar Augustus, our distant overlord, had issued a census, and heads of families were meant to return to their hometowns to be counted. Our people's little portion of the Roman Empire was soon to be inundated with census-takers who knew nothing about us, and though we might have resented the interference, there was really no good reason not to cooperate. Unfortunately, we had not known we would have to relocate immediately, until I had very little time left indeed to carry my son unborn.

So it was that Yosef and I loaded his donkey and set out to the south sooner than we had expected. It was a very different journey than when I made it the first time. In spite of how much heavier I felt in my body, I felt lighter in my soul. Adonai had proven himself truthful in giving me this baby and protecting him, and he had also provided me a better husband that I could have imagined. What other man could be expected to marry under such strange conditions? Yosef was as solicitous of me and my unborn child as if the child truly were his.

We did, however, find people to travel with again. There were many more travelers on the roads this time, as everyone was moving about to make sure they got to their own town in good time for the census. No one wanted to cause any trouble. Well, doubtless some did, but we encountered no bandits or rabble-rousers on the way.

Because I was so much greater with child this time, we journeyed very slowly with lots of stopping and resting. We kept company with no particular traveling band, but joined any who happened to be passing for as long as they would have us or as long as we could keep up. "It's a shame you had to journey with such a burden," most people said. "It's a shame the census had to happen just now."

"Never mind," I said, though it was true that the travel was becoming more and more exhausting for me. "We'll be there soon enough." I hoped I was right in this. My back felt liable to break some days, and the store of food we had brought with us had to be rationed carefully. "We should have gone through Samaria," Yosef murmured to himself one night. He was hungry. I wondered if it would have been acceptable for the mother of the son of Adonai to eat Samaritan food in an extreme situation like this. But surely it would have been acceptable for his seeming father to have done so. It would not taint the baby.

I just hoped we would have a place to stay when we got to Beit-Lechem. Yosef's hometown it may have been, but the house was unready, and we were not the only family members who were sure to want to stay with his sisters. Besides that, Yosef's brothers-in-law's families would take precedence even over these.

"What did you tell your family?" I had asked Yosef almost

immediately after we were married. None of them had come up to the Galil to acknowledge our nuptials, so I gathered either they did not know about them, or they disapproved.

Yosef looked a little uncomfortable. "I had to tell them you were having a baby, Miryam. How else could I explain my haste, and the fact that we were not going to have a usual celebration?"

"It's all right, Yosef," I said. I had expected as much, and really, what else could he have done? "But what did you say? What did they say?"

"I told them I was going to marry you, and they, like your father, said, 'But of course you are. You're already betrothed. Do you mean you're going to marry her up there?'"

We both laughed at that. Although our two families had some history, as well as King David as a common ancestor, it quickly became something of a joke between us how Yosef's family, like most people in Y'hudah, considered Northerners to be somewhat uncouth. How could those sisters, who had scarcely moved from Beit-Lechem in their lives, imagine how wonderful the North could be, with its clear air and Lake Kinneret so nearby? Now that I was Yosef's and he was mine, I felt less intimidated—most of the time—by his sisters, and so I didn't mind joking about their prejudice. I knew better than any of them what they were missing.

"So I said, 'Yes. I'm going to marry her now.'" I grinned, imagining the uproar that one statement must have made. "Then," Yosef went on, "I had to tell them somewhat why." I nodded, still waiting to hear exactly how this news was presented and received.

"I said, 'Miryam was visiting her cousin in 'Ein Karem the last few months. I have seen her. She is with child, and I would like to marry her before evil tongues start spreading false information.'"

I raised my eyebrows. It wasn't bad. It certainly was

ambiguous. But I couldn't imagine Yosef's family leaving such a statement without asking some more questions.

"Everyone got even more excited then, of course," Yosef admitted. "Faces began turning red and all that. Then Hadassah said, in that stone-cold way she has, 'And just whose child is it, Yosef? Is it yours?'

"So I looked her straight in the eye and said, 'As soon as I marry Miryam, he will be. His name is to be Yeshua.' Not that *Yeshua* is at all uncommon of course, but I think it startled them enough that I was that sure the child was a boy, and that I had a name for him...anyhow, they couldn't seem to think of any further questions right then. The ones they thought of later, I just didn't bother to answer."

I smiled a little wryly. It would do. They never would have believed him if he had said he was going to marry the mother of the Messiah, and that she was already the mother of the Messiah. And if they had thought he himself had lain with me before our marriage, although surely they would have forgiven him soon enough, it would have been a little disappointing to them. On the other hand, if they thought he was marrying a woman who had been unfaithful to him, they would be totally disgusted and possibly never speak to either of us again. The way Yosef spun the tale, they had no real answers to any of their questions, and they weren't likely to get any, so they would just have to decide how to respond based on hunches.

"They'll recover," Yosef assured me, equally wryly. "But when we return to Beit-Lechem, they might give us the cold shoulder for a while. Will you be all right, Miryam? Would you like us to live in Natzeret instead?"

He had, of course, asked that question before we knew we would be required to return to Beit-Lechem anyway. Now as we journeyed Yosef said, "They will house us. They'll have to, because we are still family and the town will be too crowded for them not to. It would be disgraceful if any of their friends or neighbors had to put us up instead. But I don't expect it will be very comfortable for us until our own home is ready."

"We couldn't stay in it anyway?" I asked hopefully.

"It's too incomplete," Yosef said apologetically. "I thought I'd have more time, of course. And it's too cold now to stay there—the wind would cut right through. It's no place to keep a newborn baby."

I didn't say anything for a while after that. I was not relishing the time with Yosef's family. This made me a little bit sad, for in spite of having been intimidated by his sisters, I supposed I liked them well enough under normal circumstances. I didn't expect circumstances would ever really be very normal again.

Instead of the usual four or five days it would have taken to get to Beit-Lechem, it took us nine. Perhaps we should have left earlier. As it was, Yosef was right, and the town was overflowing with people. The reunions lent a festive air, but I was feeling heavy, tired and sore, and altogether ready to get the baby outside of me. I was also worried. I couldn't stop imagining Yosef's disappointed, disapproving family.

Although it would have been natural to go to Hadassah's first, she was also married to the brother-in-law with the most relatives outside of Beit-Lechem. This meant that all of them would be coming back, too, and that house would probably be so full as to be uncomfortable, even without the awkward circumstances we were bringing with us. So we headed to Rivkah's. It may have been fortunate that it was the end of the day and people were more concerned about the practicalities of where everyone would sleep than they were about who was actually there.

Even in spite of her husband's more local relatives, Rivkah's house seemed rather crowded as well. People were coming and going and a small group of men stood outside, presumably while their wives tried to sort out the sleeping arrangements. Rivkah's six-year-old son saw us first.

"Imma!" he cried out through the open door to his mother inside the house. "Yosef is here! Yosef and Miryam!" Happily, he loved Yosef. Also happily, it appeared that no one had yet told him not to.

Rivkah came out to meet us, which also surprised me, although she seemed distracted. She kissed her brother with a real smile, though it dampened when she looked at me. Then she shrugged almost imperceptibly and turned back toward the house. "Come in, then," she called back over her shoulder. "I must warn you, though, that we have no room here. Absolutely no room. We've been packed full since yesterday. You'll have to sleep with the animals."

She said it so nonchalantly it was difficult to tell whether she were punishing us or just being practical. Yosef and I looked at each other. If I hadn't been so tired I probably would have laughed. As it was, I could scarcely whisper, "It's all right. It's not like I haven't slept among the animals before." And the animals, as I knew from my previous experience, would not judge us the way the people would.

Yosef chuckled, put his hand on the small of my back, and ushered me in.

11

THE MAYHEM

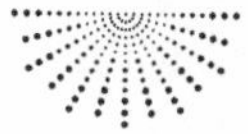

The mayhem was greater inside than out, even though the men and children, who comprised the greater part of the mob, were still outside. Women were staking out their territories in the upper living quarters. Rivkah's husband's cousin's wife had, apparently, just come down from the roof, bringing all her family's bedding with her. "It's too cold yet," she blustered, even though the sun was shining warmly. "I mean, it will be. Sleeping on the roof in summer is one thing. Not this time of year! Too early."

Naturally I kept quiet, but I was sure I would not have argued with her in any case. It was springtime, but temperatures still dropped at night, and I would not have wished to brave the chill either, even if I hadn't a nearly-born baby to worry about. But I did want a place to settle. I felt as if I were about to collapse.

"Here," whispered Rivkah's eldest daughter, tugging on my sleeve. She was a rather thin, nervous-looking girl with a hopefully helpful face. I suppose she was only a few years younger than I, really, although I thought I felt so much older. "I knew you would come here. I wanted you to come.

So I made you a place. I'm sorry it's by the cow—but it's soft. It will be all right for the baby when he comes, won't it?"

I glanced at Yosef, startled at his niece's kindness. He looked nearly as surprised as I did. "Thank you, Tamar," he said. "That was so kind of you."

Tamar's face glowed as if he had set a lamp alight, making her look somehow softer and less waif-like. "I made it just for you," she said again. I found myself staggering as I followed her through the crowd of oblivious women, but I did not sink down until there were straw and blankets—and Yosef—to catch me. "Thank you, Tamar," I said in the sinking, and I meant it.

The hubbub did not subside until quite a bit later that night, and I slept through some of it. Yosef went back and forth between me and his relatives, trying to make certain I was all right—and trying to make certain they were. After the men ate the evening meal, they went up to the roof while the women ate theirs. Yosef looked rather torn, but I nodded that he should go with them. "Tamar is here," I said. "She will look after me."

She did. She brought me the best that she could of what was left, and although I saw her mother eye her a little askance, everyone was too polite—or something more uncertain than politeness—to protest. After taking as much as she could for both of us, the girl sat down with me and we chatted a bit. We had just finished eating, and she was saying something about young men in Beit-Lechem, when I felt the wetness. I looked up at her. For all she seemed so naive, she knew exactly what had happened. "I'll get Imma," she said, jumping up instantly. "And Aunt Rachel. She's delivered plenty of babies."

Now that my time had arrived, nobody bothered much anymore about where this child had come from. The women all seemed, in that instant, to decide that no matter what the circumstances, a baby was coming into the world, and they had better do something to make his arrival as easy as possible. I doubt that many children have had quite so many midwives, but it was probably a good thing, because the birthing took a while.

I don't think I expected there to be so much pain. I knew there would be some, surely. I had seen women give birth before, and I knew what HaElyon had uttered to our first parents in Gan 'Eden after they ate fruit he had commanded them to leave alone. Havah would have pain in childbirth, and so, therefore, would all her daughters after her. But perhaps I had supposed, unknowing, that as I was bearing Adonai's son, that agony would be spared me. Now I can think about that time calmly, having borne more children and more pain in the years that followed. But then I was still a new mother, and I had never known a man. I was untouched, and in the excruciating pressure and tearing, I thought, when I could think, which was never very clearly during that ordeal, that Yosef might have to raise the Messiah on his own because I surely would not survive.

I shrieked, and Yosef came running. I saw his eyes widen and the blood drain from his own face as he saw the blood that was issuing from me. Rivkah, her face set and determined and almost angry, tried to shoo him off, but he would not leave the place where I lay. He babbled a little bit about the Messiah coming into the world and how he had to be there to see it and to name him. The rest of the time he just repeated my name, rocking back and forth as if he were praying. Perhaps he was. Rivkah shook her head and set her mouth even tighter, and Tamar's eyes were round as she wiped my face with a cloth she had dipped and wrung out in the water bucket.

Then all of a sudden there was a cry, and it wasn't mine. I didn't realize how hard I had been listening for that cry until I heard it, and then I stopped screaming and panting and pushing. I fell back. I could still feel blood, but I knew it would stop flowing and I would be all right. Some of the sisters-in-law bound me up with cloths, and Tamar and Rivkah bound up the baby and I began to cry, myself. They were different tears than the ones I may have shed during the birthing. There was a baby here, and he was the Messiah, and he was...he was mine.

Rivkah put him in my arms, and I stared and stared at that face. He looked like...a baby. The same way any baby looks when it's just born: red and wrinkled and astonishingly beautiful and homely all at once. Then I looked at Yosef. His eyes were moist, too. He had not quite lost the look of fear on his face. I looked back at the baby. "Yeshua?" I said.

"Yeshua," said Yosef. He sounded as if he had just been swimming in Kinneret when the waves were rougher than a swimmer might have expected. "For he will save his people from their sins." I continued to stare at the baby. He would? This baby? But it had to be true. I could not have imagined it, because until that night, I truly was a virgin.

Tamar already believed Yosef's words to be true. When I looked at Rivkah's face, I saw she had become convinced some hours before. She was not a stupid woman. She could tell I had never known a man.

"Come," she said. Her voice sounded different. "Let me put him in the manger. That way he can rest. You can rest. We all can rest."

She took Yeshua out of my arms and placed him in the feeding trough. Well, it was as good a place as any. It was sturdy and secure, and the cow, though likely to be confused at finding a human child lying in her food, was unlikely to eat him. I lay back down, but kept my head propped up a bit, just so I could see him if I needed to. The children, who had been sent outside to play as soon as my labors began, trickled back into the house, as did their fathers from the roof, and everyone assembled in their respective corners the living quarters for the night. The children gathered around the manger on their way up, and stared at the baby as if they had never seen one before. Eventually the house settled, and everyone began to sleep. It was finished.

The house had settled to near-silence, when there was a commotion outside. Yosef, being the man closest to the entrance of the house, got up stiffly and went to see what was going on. Before he could open the door, however, it was shoved open from the outside, and the commotion turned into a great woolly bundle tumbling into the room. Eventually the bundle disentangled itself and I could see that they were men—shepherds—with bushy beards and curly shocks of hair and bits of grass and earth sticking to them in places. They had obviously just been running, for they were panting, and their words came out in a jumble, with great gasps for air in between. Something about *baby,* and *angels,* and *feeding trough.*

Probably Rivkah would have turned them all out if they hadn't managed those words first. There was, after all, a baby in the feeding trough. Eventually the shepherds recovered enough to speak, but by this time they had also discovered the baby they had been babbling about, and they craned round each other to get a good look, in near-complete silence. Some of them fell to their knees. I noticed this, because I had never seen men—any men, never mind shepherds—get so worked up about a baby before. I also wondered how they had learned about mine.

By the time they were ready to tell us, the entire place was quiet again, in spite of everyone's being awake now, from the animals on the ground with us, to the people in the raised living quarters. We were all curious about these shepherds, probably more curious than we had ever been about shepherds in our lives.

At last one of them coughed. "It was," he said after the cough, "it was an angel of Adonai told us to come here," he said. I felt a shiver—a good, confirming kind of shiver, run up my spine.

The people up above leaned forward so that even I, lying back where I was, still resting from the labour of bringing a child into the world, could see faces and hands peering over the edge. But the shepherd who had spoken was looking at me, his eyes asking for permission to continue. I smiled and nodded.

"Well, we were out in the fields," he began again.

"Just like any other night in lambing season," chimed in another shepherd. "We're always in the fields, nights. Some ewe might have a lamb. Lambs—you never know for sure when they're coming."

The first shepherd nodded and went on. "All of a sudden, there's this light, and it's brighter than that fire we had—and it isn't coming from the same place, either."

"It came from the sky," said a young lad, almost as if he were still seeing it.

"It came from the sky," repeated the spokes-shepherd. He didn't seem to mind being interrupted. "And it—it was—well, it was an angel."

"An angel from Adonai," said the boy shepherd, in the same tone of voice as before.

"Well, we were mighty afraid," said the first shepherd, appearing unashamed at his admission, "what with all that light and it's being an angel of Adonai and all. But the angel said..."

"To us!" piped up a shepherd who, until this moment, had been speechless.

"There wasn't anyone else for it to speak to, was there?" said someone else. "Except the sheep."

"But the angel said," repeated the first shepherd, now seeming rather more desperate to get his story back, "it said, 'Don't fear! I'm here to announce great good news to you, that will bring joy to everybody. Today, right now, in David's town, a Deliverer who is the Messiah was born—the Lord! You'll know it when you see it—you'll find a baby wrapped in clothes and lying in an animal trough.' And there he is, just like they said."

The shepherd fell silent, but one of the others spoke up again excitedly. "What about the last bit, Ya'akov? Don't forget the last bit."

"This is the last bit," said the spokes-shepherd, indicating his surroundings. "But you mean after the angel spoke to us. Well, all right. Suddenly—well, suddenly a great army appeared. An army of heaven, I mean—might've been all of heaven itself, for all we know. An army, fierce and furious, but they weren't fighting, they were singing. And they weren't furious either, really. They were glad."

"They were singing, 'Glory to God in the heaven of heavens! And here on earth, peace among good-willed people!'" said the boy.

"And then they disappeared," said Ya'akov, "and this lad here said, 'Let's go over to Beit-Lechem and see it—why else would Adonai have told us about it?' So we came straightaway, and it's just as the angel said. There you are and there he is—in the feeding trough!" He laughed.

"What about your sheep?" asked someone from the living quarters above us, but the rest of the family, amazed at the shepherd's story, hushed him up, and then it was very quiet in there for a while, as everyone gazed at the baby in the feeding trough.

"He's awfully small, isn't he?" ventured one of the shepherds at last. "He looks just like any old baby."

"Ah," said Ya'akov, looking at his friend. "But this one isn't just any old baby, is he? This one was told us by angels, and here he is, just like they said. You go look round the rest of Beit-Lechem and see if you can find any more babies in feeding troughs! This one may look ordinary, but the angel said he's the Deliverer, and so he is."

The shepherds left not long after that, and the people above gradually settled back into their places and to sleep. Yosef sat up with me for a while, watching over the baby as if he were his own, but finally even he got tired and drifted off.

I should have slept, too, then. I wasn't sure if I moved that I might not start bleeding again, and my body ached from delivering my son. My son, the Deliverer. But I could not stop thinking about the shepherds. I could not stop thinking about what they had said. Who was this baby, this boy, this son of mine? This Deliverer? He was the Messiah. The shepherds said the angels had said it. He was heralded by angels. An angel had come to me and said he would be called the Son of Ha'Elyon. An angel had come to Yosef and said he would save his people from their sins. And now an entire army of angels had appeared to a field of shepherds I had never seen before, and prophesied to them great joy for all the people. They told them he was their Deliverer, their Messiah.

But why an army of angels? And why shepherds? I had no argument with them personally, but everyone knew they were dirty and smelly and probably immoral, and their occupation kept them from observing the religious regulations properly. The leaders of our people called them "unclean." But Ha'Elyon had sent his angels—a host of them—to shepherds. Even I, the mother of this child, had only ever seen one angel.

Many, many years later, I remembered the shepherds. When Elisheva's Yochanan grew and started calling my son "the Lamb of God," I remembered them. When Yeshua began calling himself "the Good Shepherd," I remembered them, too. But that night, the night he was born, I had heard none of those names. That night I began to build a treasure-store in my heart—of all the names I knew so far for my son—of all the events that had surrounded his birth. The names were bold and strong and full of promise. The events were bright and shining. They filled me with wonder, and all I could think as I mulled them over—treasured them—was, who is this child?

I got up feebly and dragged myself over to the manger to have a look at him. There was a small tuft of wool on the ground next to it, having dropped from one of the shepherds' garments. I picked it up and fingered it. Then, gingerly so as not greatly to disturb my wounded body, I took Yosef's wooden box out of the folds of my robe. It had returned to its rightful place there as soon as Yosef had married me, and there it has remained, but until the night of Yeshua's birth, I had not put anything in it. I took it out of my robe and opened it. The inside was smooth and the light-and-dark veins of the olive wood were just distinguishable in the moonlight from the window. I fingered the tuft of wool again. Then I put it in the box and shut the lid.

Yeshua began to cry, just like an ordinary baby. I took him out of the manger, eased back into my place with him, and suckled him again. He was tiny and warm. He looked and felt utterly helpless. Just like an ordinary baby.

12

NO ONE KNEW WHAT TO MAKE OF US

It was clear that no one knew quite what to make of any of us in the morning. Most of the adults in the household tried to act as if nothing strange had happened in the night at all, although the very attempt made everything stranger. Some of the children, however, ventured closer to Yeshua and me and asked about him. "He's the Messiah, isn't he?" asked the nephew who had greeted us on our arrival. "He's going to make Eretz-Yisra'el into the kingdom again, isn't he?"

"Yes," I said, "he is," even though at the same time I felt as if I hadn't the faintest idea what I was talking about. Tamar sat with me quietly for a while in the afternoon. "I welcomed him," she said quietly and happily. "I didn't even know who he was, and I welcomed him."

"You did, Tamar," I said. Then it sank in just how much her welcome had meant to me, and once again I said, "Thank you."

Yosef went out. He had determined to set to work on our house again immediately, so that we could move into it as soon as possible. It was hard for him to see me resting with the beasts, even though I told him I was comfortable, and I was, too. Also, we were not intending to return to Natzeret any time soon. The other families staying with Rivkah would move on as soon as the census-taking allowed. He did not want us encroaching on his sister any longer than we had to.

On the eighth day after the birth, my baby was officially given his name. He had his b'rit-milah and Yosef formally named him Yeshua, just as the angel had said. Yeshua —"Adonai saves"—because he would save his people from their sins. Yosef told everyone that was why. Everyone tried, as well as they could, to ignore this explanation. For one thing, no one, including Yosef and me, exactly knew what it meant. Also, the idea of my baby being the Messiah was still something of an awkward topic for everyone. Nevertheless, they had got over the scandal of his questionable origins enough to have a proper party for his b'rit-milah at least. Rivkah prepared a modest feast, and even the neighbors came. They said what a beautiful child he was, even though at eight days this is a difficult statement to make with much accuracy. They said he would do great things, even though they truly had no idea. In return, Yeshua fussed, but everybody knows that the eighth day is not only the prescribed day for a b'rit-milah, but also the day that the baby feels the least pain, so no one worried about him. The aunties tutted over him and tried to catch his eye with baubles, and everyone did what was expected of them. It would have been hard to do the expected if anyone thought too much about Yosef's utterances, so they simply didn't.

I had thirty more days after Yeshua's b'rit-milah to ponder what it could mean, that my baby would save his people from their sins. The thirty days more were a mitzvot for us, which Adonai gave us through Moshe. The law said a woman had to wait forty days after giving birth, and then offer a sacrifice for purification.

The law also said that firstborn sons must be redeemed to Adonai. It had something to do with God rescuing our people from the Egyptians and killing all their firstborn sons, and with the subsequent practice of dedicating every first-born and first yield to God. We were commanded to sacrifice an animal in our firstborn's place. In this way we enacted saving the lives of our own firstborn children (unlike the Egyptians') and in a different way set them apart for God at the same time.

Yeshua, as my firstborn son, somehow belonged to Adonai already in any case, and so I was excited about consecrating him properly. We were much closer to Yerushalayim than we would have been in Natzeret, which made observing this mitzvot much easier. The morning was cloudy and somewhat brisk as we set out for Yerushalayim and the Temple.

The journey was brief. The city was crowded and noisy, as Beit-Lechem had been when we had arrived there. The difference was that Yerushalayim was bigger, and busy all year and every year—the holiest of cities in our holy land.

It was easy to find the Temple, gleaming majestically at us from its hill. "Look at it!" I said to Yosef. It wasn't that I had never seen it before, but Abba and Shlomit and the boys and I had not been down to Yerushalayim for Pesach or any of the other customary holidays since Imma had died.

"You know it's not as splendid as the first one," Yosef said. He was teasing me, man of the world that he wasn't. Our Scriptures say that when the second Temple was erected after the first one was destroyed, half of the assembled gathering wept because it didn't measure up. This one wasn't even that second, but the third.

"Everyone knows that," I said. "But I've never seen Shlomo's Temple, or the one that came after, and nor have you! This one is quite grand enough for me. How could the first one have glowed any brighter?" It glowed even when the sun was behind the clouds, I thought. It was impossible not to feel a surge of pride at the sight of it. This was our

Temple. Our Temple to our One True God, who made heaven and earth and chose us as his very own people. It was beautiful.

As well as the city itself, even the Temple was bustling, we saw as we got to it. The outer court was full of money changers and animal vendors; the money was special Temple currency, and the animals were for the sacrifices. My sacrifice was meant to be a lamb for a burnt offering and a young pigeon or dove for a sin offering. In his mercy, however, Adonai had made an allowance for people who could not afford a lamb. This was a particular mercy to us, because we couldn't.

Yosef's carpentry business did well enough to support us, or at least it would when he was able to resume his work. But he had been working less of late, in order to prepare the place for our family after our marriage. Also, he had been away from his workshop for over a month now, and we had spent much of our savings on the trip to Beit-Lechem. Finally, everything in Yerushalayim seemed very expensive. So we bought two pigeons for the sacrifice instead, and went to offer them to Adonai.

We had scarcely done this when a man came hurrying toward us. He was very, very old, but I saw, through his great beard and his great wrinkles, that his eyes were lit up with an irrepressible joy. Later we learned that this was Shim'on, a tzaddik—a righteous man, a holy man. He had been told by the Ruach HaKodesh that he would not die until he had seen the Messiah. He had been hoping for the Hope of Isra'el for many years.

At the moment, however, we did not know this. At the moment he was simply a strange, joy-filled old man, who took Yeshua from my arms and blessed Adonai. Children are blessings—everybody says so. They unite people. Any person would talk to someone who had a child with them. I was not afraid to give Yeshua into the old man's hands. But he seemed so overcome that I did feel something like suspense. Something was about to happen.

The man held Yeshua to his chest and stared and stared for a few moments, tears running from those bright eyes into that thick beard, Then he lifted the baby gently, but high in the air. "Now, Adonai," he said, his voice quavering but certain, "I have seen your salvation—just as you promised—a salvation you enact before all the world, to enlighten the goyim and glorify Isra'el. I am ready now. I am at peace."

It was more treasure—more words about my son. The newest surprise was the bit about revelation to the goyim. Was God going to bless the people who were not part of Isra'el, as well? Yosef and I looked at each other, eyes wide.

The old man spoke again. He saw our astonished faces, and laughed, blessing us. But then, almost in the same breath as the blessing, he spoke something which chilled my heart, and reminded me of the fear I had felt on first seeing the angel who had announced Yeshua to me, and then again of the fear when I thought I would lose Yosef. This tzaddik looked intently into my face and said, "This child will be the exaltation and downfall of many in Isra'el. People will speak against him, and you will not be spared, either—a sword will pierce your very soul. Through this the essence of every person will be revealed."

The words were not a curse. In fact, the man's remarkable eyes, as he stared at me and spoke, looked as if he thought he was still speaking a blessing. It was rather like the angel calling me favored because Adonai was with me. It was a great honor and a great good, but for a mere woman like me —how could I bear it?

It sounded almost as if this Shim'on were telling me I couldn't bear it at all. What did it mean, that a sword would pierce my heart? Somehow, once I had got over the dread and aftermath of telling Yosef I was pregnant with a child he had not begotten, once Yosef had said he would marry me anyhow, once I had borne the child in question, I had forgotten that any other trouble might be ahead. *Who is this child?* I wondered again, as Shim'on put him back into my arms. *What will he do? What will happen?*

I did not have long to wonder about this just then, however. At that moment an old woman came up also. She was certainly just as old as Shim'on. Someone said she was Hannah Bat-P'nu'el, a widow and a prophet. They said she lived at the Temple itself and was constantly worshipping, fasting, and praying. They were not sure whether she lived like this because she was a prophet, or whether she was a prophet because she lived like this. They were certain, however, that she became a prophet not long after her husband died. She had been married to him only seven years.

Whatever the case, she was certainly prophesying at the moment. She lifted up her voice and thanked God loudly, and then called out to anyone waiting for Yerushalayim's deliverance. By this time she had drawn quite a crowd, and then she began speaking words about Yeshua—wonderful, exhilarating, sobering, frightening words. Yosef and I stood next to her, where we had been before the crowd gathered. I held Yeshua tightly, and Yosef held me tightly, as the words flowed over and around and through us, and the faces staring at us three mixed awe and respect and skepticism.

I wanted to put something in Yosef's box—something to remind me of the day and the strange words that had been spoken again about my son. I glanced about me and noticed a thread on the flagstones. It looked like a thread from a tzit-tzit, the tassel of Shime'on's prayer shawl, perhaps. And perhaps not, but it would remind me. I bent down and picked it up.

"What are you doing?" Yosef asked me.

"Remembering," I said. I smiled as I drew out the box he had carved for me. It seemed long ago now, though I supposed it wasn't really. I opened it and put the thread inside. The ball of wool was in there, too. "Just remembering." Yosef raised his eyebrows but smiled back.

By the end of the day, Yeshua was dedicated. I was purified. We were heading back to Beit-Lechem, to our own home—the one Yosef had prepared for us. I pondered all the things that had been said about Yeshua that day. I talked to Yosef about them on the way, fingering the box at my side, and he pondered with me. We agreed we had never heard such things—that the things we were hearing kept getting more and more wonderful until we could not even imagine what this child would do.

"But Yosef," I asked, "What about what the old man said? What does it mean that a sword will pierce my heart?"

Yosef put his arm around my shoulder, and when I looked at his face it was troubled on the surface, but deeper, in his eyes, was peace.

"I don't know what it means, Miryam," he said. "Except that such seems always to be the case with those who are chosen. But it is also the case with them,' he added, "that Adonai is with them; he will help you to bear it, and all will be well."

He was silent for a bit, and then said, almost under his breath, "I only hope I live to help you bear it, too."

This did not comfort me, and I told him so. He laughed and said he was sorry, and kissed me, and we forgot about it for a while. But it was not really all that long afterward that one of the other prophecies of that day began to come true.

13
IT WAS PAST THE TIME FOR COMMOTION

It was past the time for commotion. Usually there was a fair amount of noise in the street outside our home in Beit-Lechem. Yeshua had completed his first year and was halfway into his second, and was just beginning to speak a little, and to walk on his own. I was always having to make certain he didn't toddle out the door, which I usually kept open for air and light.

But at night the air grew cooler. Yosef came home and shut the door behind him. The noise in the street died down. We had supper together—a quiet family of three if we weren't visiting the sisters. While we ate, Yosef would tell me what had happened at his shop, and I would tell him what funny little things Yeshua had done that day, or what new words he had learned. Sometimes Yeshua would say the new words—even entire sentences—himself. I thought he was very clever. No other child learnt to speak so well, as young as he, surely.

Then one night, the street's commotion began again, after having died down already. This was very unusual, and Yosef went to the window to look. In a moment he said, "Miryam, come see. Yes, bring Yeshua, too."

Yosef held Yeshua so he could look out of the window, and I peered round him. Coming down the street was the strangest and most magnificent procession I had ever seen. It was as if Caesar Augustus himself had come to visit—except there was nothing Roman-looking about the procession at all. There were camels and horses and banners and canopies encrusted with gold. Someone was playing music, and people followed after and in and out and among the legs of the camels. It was something out of a story, and probably a pagan story—surely not one of our Hebrew Scriptures, unless perhaps it was the story of Hadassah, after whom Yosef's sister had been named.

Suddenly a cry went up, and the whole procession stopped. Then there was a great bustling about as the camels sat and people helped other people to dismount. Someone detached himself from the mass of activity and came running straight to our door. The next thing we knew, he was knocking on it.

I clutched Yeshua to myself tightly, as Yosef went to answer the knock. The man at the door said something, and Yosef said something back and then opened the door wide, though not without a slightly bemused look on his face.

Then there was a moment when I felt like I was back on the pile of straw at Rivkah's, having just birthed Yeshua and with a crowd of shepherds tumbling through the doorway. Only these people weren't shepherds. They didn't tumble, and they weren't dropping tufts of wool everywhere, though they looked as if they might be capable of dropping flakes of gold off of their garments without noticing or minding much. They entered the room, took one look at the little boy in my arms, and suddenly they were all face down on the floor.

I gazed at them in silence for a moment and then thought to look at Yeshua, who was being unnaturally quiet himself.

He, too, was staring at the people on the floor before him, with a smile on his face. It was the sort of smile very small children have when they take an immediate liking to someone—a look of pure childish delight. It could have been for anyone. Yeshua was particularly fearless around people, even strangers—a fact which worried me at times. But something about this smile seemed significant. These people were clearly worshiping my son, and of course a child as young as he could not be expected to understand that, but I couldn't get over the feeling that he was smiling about it.

Or maybe it was just that he liked the bright colors and shimmering materials. The people rose from their faces at last, and one of them said something to another in a language I had never heard before. The person spoken to disappeared for a moment, and it was then that I realized that some of the people in the house with us were simply servants. To me, each one looked like royalty.

While we were waiting for the vanished servant to reappear, I cleared my throat and ventured a question. "Of which countries are your lordships kings?" It sounded polite to me when I said it, as I never spoke like that, not having the opportunity. It was only later that I realized I should have offered them refreshment first, and that I had forgotten my true manners.

The company laughed. One said, "We are not kings of any country," and I noticed that the speaker was a woman. I reddened. She saw this and smiled warmly, saying, "We are not royalty at all, but we serve royalty."

"We are magi," said another, who was, in fact, a man. Seeing my blank expression, he added, "Astrologers."

The entire situation was becoming more and more overwhelmingly bizarre. A group of gloriously-dressed foreigners, who also happened to be astrologers, under my roof? Adonai frowned on star-searching, and most of my people and I had an idea he frowned on foreigners, too, though it had to be admitted there were concessions made for them in our Law. On further consideration, I also had to admit to myself that this was not any more or less scandalous than my becoming a mother out of wedlock, through the work of Adonai himself. But still, it made me uneasy. Then I remembered Shim'on saying that this boy of mine would be "enlightenment to the goyim." These goyim may have been astrologers, but here they were, clearly seeking Yeshua who would, Shim'on had said, be a light to them. Somehow.

At the same time as I remembered this, I remembered my manners. "Here," I said, holding Yeshua out to the woman, "would you like to hold him, while I get something for you to eat and drink? You must all be hungry and thirsty after your travels."

The woman took the little child from my arms gingerly and with wonder. The rest of her companions gathered round with much the same manner. As I scurried about, trying to prepare something plentiful and suitable enough for our grand guests, I could hear them clucking and cooing over Yeshua in awe-filled voices.

As they ate then, Yosef talked to them. I sat with Yeshua on my knee in the corner and watched, and listened.

"So," Yosef was saying, "how, if I may ask it, did you know about—about the newborn King of the Jews?" Those words were theirs, and Yosef, trying them out, was finding them almost too astonishing to say. There was a king of sorts already, after all. King Herod. He had done many things for our people, but everyone knew he was not a Jew at all, and was still under the thumb of Rome. Everyone also knew he had a violent, evil streak. Some said he was mad; he had killed immediate family members before this. If word got about that there was a "newborn King of the Jews" lurking somewhere in his kingdom, we could expect trouble.

"From the stars," answered one of the men, as if it should have been obvious. "From the movement of the stars and planets we saw that a new king was to be born in Y'hudah. And not just any king—a great one."

"We went to Yerushalayim first," admitted another, "though I can't say why. That star had been leading us from the beginning, but it didn't point us to that city. Still, I suppose it is natural to expect a king would be born there."

"Not so natural once you've met the king," muttered the woman in some disgust. "After that experience anyone would know that no great king would arise from his family."

"You spoke to King Herod?" Yosef asked sharply. He had clearly been thinking along similar lines to mine.

"We did," answered one of the men. "He was very helpful." From the set of the man's teeth, I guessed he was being ironic.

"Well," said another, "he did set us on the road to Beit-Lechem—he and his little seers."

I bristled a bit at that. I supposed he was referring to our priests—our cohanim—and our Torah-teachers. Many of our cohanim belonged to the sect of the Tz'dukim, a group of Jews who seemed to wish they were Greek instead. Not all of us were overly happy with this set who ruled the Temple; nevertheless they were, in some sense, the cohanim of God, and how dare this goy insult them? But I said nothing, and another of the magi spoke instead.

"Yes," he said. "That king didn't know where the new king was to be born—the Messiah, he called him. So he asked the priests, and they knew all right. They quoted a prophecy running thus:

"'And you, Beit-Lechem in Y'hudah, are certainly not the most unimportant place in Y'hudah; for from you a ruler will come who will shepherd my people Isra'el.'"

My annoyance at the goyish slight to the cohanim dissipated and turned to amazement that this foreigner could recite a prophecy he had probably only heard once. "And they were right," he continued. "We set off for Beit-Lechem, and there was the star again, leading us until it stopped right here—right over this house."

"And here he is," said the woman softly, gazing at the child who by this time had fallen asleep in the corner. "The King. He will be great."

"And so," said a man. "We have brought him gifts." One of the attendants came forward with some bags full of something. "There are more worthy gifts than these," said the magus. "But for a king, these are all we know to give."

The bags were opened, and we were presented with gold, frankincense, and myrrh so that our eyes nearly fell out of our heads with staring. "Now we can go back to Natzeret," I whispered to Yosef with a grin, "and have something left over so that you can start your business there instead." Sometimes I missed my family, particularly my sister. Sometimes I teased Yosef about returning. He did not ignore me when I did this, but he didn't relent. He didn't relent this time, either.

"They're for Yeshua," he grinned back, but said nothing when I put a small gold coin in the box at my side.

"We must away now," said one of the magi, presently. "But we thank you for your hospitality, and we thank the Most High God for this young King." At that they all prostrated themselves again, and then rose and went out into the night. I urged them to stay a bit longer, partly according to custom and partly because I was sure I would never see the like again. But they turned away east, and I at least, never did see them again.

Yosef was tucking Yeshua into blankets when I came back inside and began to tidy up the remains of the food. "Leave it, Miryam," he said gently. "There is nothing there which cannot wait for the morning. It is late. Let us sleep."

I gave one rather despairing look at the mess, sighed at it, and then agreed with him. But it never did get tidied up.

I woke groggily to find Yosef hurriedly throwing things into saddlebags—the ones we had not used since moving down to Beit-Lechem. One lamp was lit, and it was dark enough in the house for me to know that it was still black as soot outside. I squinted, more out of confusion than because of the dim light of the lamp. Yosef saw me sitting up and said, "We've got to go, Miryam, and it's got to be now. I'll explain once we've started."

"What are you talking about?" I asked.

"I told you," Yosef snapped at me. "I'll explain it all once we've started. Now get Yeshua and come!"

I knew Yosef must have a good reason for getting us all up at midnight and putting us on the back of a donkey. He had a good reason for most things. But I certainly had no intention of leaving my comfortable bed and home at that hour until I knew what the reason was. I told him so.

At last Yosef stopped his frantic packing and said, "All right then, listen. Those magi went to Herod before coming here, and now Herod thinks someone's out to usurp his throne. We both know the magi couldn't have meant any harm, but harm's been done in any case." He then told me he had seen another angel. Angels, I thought, were not meant to become commonplace. But on the other hand, it did not seem to be advisable to ignore one when you saw it.

"It came to me in my sleep again," said Yosef. "It told me to get up and take you and Yeshua to Egypt because the mad king is coming to kill him."

"Thank you," I said, getting up immediately. "I now understand perfectly, and yes, I will get Yeshua ready and come." And I did. I wasn't worried at all, and this was strange. Usually I was the one who fretted while Yosef remained calm. Maybe, now that Yosef was fretting, I didn't feel the need to. Or maybe the sense of peace was from Adonai. This child we were rushing to protect was his child. This plan to go to Egypt was, apparently, his plan. He would help us escape in time, and he would keep us safe in Egypt. He would not let his Messiah die.

But many others died instead.

14
EGYPT WAS HOT

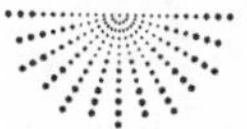

Egypt was hot. We lived with other poor families from many other countries in Alexandria. But it was, after all, Alexandria, and so even being a poor family there was not too uncomfortable. There are many Jews there, and many learned people among both Jews and goyim. First we lodged with a family at the outskirts of the city, but eventually Yosef was able to get us small quarters closer to the center by doing special carpentry work for the citizens.

Still, it was a city. It was bigger even than Yerushalayim. We had to stay there longer than we had ever spent at one time in Yerushalayim, though still not more than a year. I felt cramped and longed for someplace clean. I also longed to hear a familiar language. We were among Jews, and many could speak Aramaic. But most of the families had been in Egypt for so long, they now spoke Egyptian exclusively, and the Aramaic was halting and accented. Yosef picked up quite a bit of basic Egyptian, and I used a few words, but it was difficult for me and made me feel anxious. I felt as if I were constantly struggling to communicate anything of meaning. It was hard to settle when I supposed we would be moving home soon, and yet without knowing what "soon" was. I was grateful for Yosef. And for Yeshua.

Yeshua grew into a little boy in that strange, great land, where our ancestors had slaved under the Pharaohs, and from which our greatest leader, Moshe, had led them to freedom. His hair grew curly there, and his eyes grew bright. My favorite moments of any during our stay in that country were when he had just woken from sleep and would let me hold him. We sat quietly, Yeshua on my lap, the fingers of one hand in his mouth, those of the other tangled in my hair. Mothers and children sit like this in afternoon sun the world over, no doubt. In Egypt, too.

Later we realized even this sojourn in Egypt and our return out of it had been prophesied. It was a prophet named Hoshea who had said, for Adonai, "Out of Egypt I called my son." Unaware of this connection at the time, however, we brought that son out of Egypt at last, when Yosef saw an angel for the third time. This time the angel told him that the king and those who wanted to kill Yeshua were dead themselves, and that it was time for Yosef to bring us back home.

When we returned to Y'hudah, we learned that King Herod had indeed tried, and tried very hard, to take Yeshua's life. Not long after we escaped, the king, in one of his rages, had sent soldiers to Beit-Lechem to slaughter all male babies under the age of two. They had done it, and now, passing through the City of David, I saw deep sorrow still etched on many faces—especially those of the women. Perhaps it was how all the mothers in Egypt had looked after the angel of death had passed over and killed all their firstborn sons. Was this a reversal of Adonai's mercy to our people, all those centuries apart? How had we been safe in Egypt, of all places, when the children of our people were being slaughtered?

All the fear I had not felt when we had left for Egypt came over me then, as I imagined the scene and what could have happened to my beautiful boy had we stayed. It hadn't happened to him, all praise to Adonai. Only, couldn't Adonai have kept these other little ones from dying, too? Couldn't he have kept these mother's hearts from breaking?

Of course he could. But he hadn't, and that thought chilled me more than any fear of his lack of power. Where was the sense in this destruction of innocence? Where was the deliverance? How was Adonai any different, then, from any of the idols other peoples worshipped, who required children as sacrifice? Our Scriptures said our God required no such thing. But now here was a town—among his own chosen people—still reeling from carnage, and he had not done a thing to stop it. I covered my face as we rode through and wept and wept and wept.

Eventually I came to see that no one is innocent. I learned that Adonai never requires anything of anyone which he is not willing to give himself. This is the difference between Adonai and the idols. Adonai gives, and gives his own heart, his own life, to disobedient and ungrateful mortals, whether we return the favor or not. But it took me a long time to see this.

In the meantime, though Yosef had first considered resettling in Beit-Lechem, under the circumstances and given that the lately deceased Herod's son Archelaus now sat on the throne, we decided to keep traveling back up to Natzeret. "Just as you wanted to," he grinned. "We can sell the house in Beit-Lechem, maybe. Hadassah's husband can arrange it. You've been away from home long enough, my love. We can go back now."

After the initial excitement of returning home, things settled into a sort of pattern. Yosef set up his work right in Natzeret, and I once more had a house to make into a home. After the time in Egypt, this was not a privilege I took lightly. Nor was living near family. It was wonderful to be with them again. Shlomit was married now. I had missed her wedding, lost in Egypt as I had been. But now we could visit each other every day, and we did, too.

I began to forget Egypt and the slaughtered babies in Beit-Lechem. To help me forget, Yosef and I began to have a few more babies of our own, without the direct intervention of the Ruach HaKodesh.

But Yeshua was always the special one—even to Yosef. Everyone in the village was now convinced Yeshua was Yosef's son as well as mine. They seemed to have conveniently forgotten the strange, hurried wedding and the way they had gossiped before we left for Beit-Lechem. Meanwhile, Yosef treated Yeshua just as if he were indeed his own. It wasn't as if he were trying to lie about Yeshua's origins. It was just that he loved him. He gave Yeshua small tasks in his shop which increased as Yeshua grew older and stronger. "He has the makings of a fine carpenter," people would say. "You must be proud of him." And Yosef would smile and say, with something like pleasure and something like wonder, "The child is God's, and yes, I am."

Yeshua was just as willing to help me in the house as he was to help Yosef in the shop. He loved to look after his younger brothers and sisters, and he showed an uncanny knack of knowing just what to do in a given situation. In fact, although wisdom is scarcely if ever attributed to a child, that is the only way I can describe what Yeshua was like. He was wise. Oh, he was still a child. He still laughed and shouted and played with the other children. He still cried when he hurt himself. But he was wise. And then we took him to Yerushalayim again.

As it happened, we took him—and all the children, when we could—to Yerushalayim for Pesach every year. But the first year of his manhood was different. For one thing, he acted as if he had never been in his life. Maybe it was because we were to celebrate his bar-mitzvah there, and he was so excited about his new status that it seemed to him as if he were a new person going to a new place for the first time. I still do not know. I never asked him.

Whatever the truth of it, from the time we told him we would celebrate Pesach and bar-mitzvah there at the same time, he could scarcely contain his delight. "Really?" he kept asking, even though he knew we always tried to be truthful to him, and certainly would never tease him about such a thing. "Really really?"

To everyone else he said, "Guess what? Give up? No—you'll never guess it—I'm going to become a man in Yerushalayim this year!" After everyone in the village had heard this four or five times, it was no longer a question of guessing. They just laughed and rumpled his hair, although he was soon supposed to be a man. He didn't mind; by that time he was partly joking, too, though his excitement was still genuine. His eyes would light up with a mischievous gleam when he saw someone approaching. "Guess what?" he would grin.

"I know, I know," the person would say, "you're going to 'become a man' in Yerushalayim." They usually laughed at the innocence of his words, but no one got annoyed. Everyone liked Yeshua.

When he wasn't teasing, he would ask details of people who had made the pilgrimage before. He asked about the journey, how long it took, what there was to see along the way. He asked about the city itself, the gates, the buildings, what the people were like.

"You've been there before," people would protest, puzzled.

"I know," he would say. "But I want to hear how *you* see it."

Especially he wanted to talk about the Temple. But usually he only asked me about that.

"I ask you about the Temple because I know you'd notice," he said once. "And you understand about Temples. You're one yourself."

When I asked what he meant by this, he replied, "You let Adonai in." He did not explain any more, and I felt a shiver run up my spine. We had not really talked much to him about the circumstances surrounding his birth, Yosef and I. Sometimes we told him about a crowd of shepherds coming to see him when he was born, and even he had the very faintest of memories of the magi. But we found it difficult to tell him that Yosef was not actually his father, and even more difficult to explain who was. When he made statements like this, however, sometimes I wondered if he knew already. I sometimes wondered if he knew more about it than I did.

"We won't see Yochanan this year, will we?" Ya'akov asked. He was my eldest with Yosef. The little girls were trying to help me pack things for our Pesach pilgrimage, and Ya'akov had come in to help. He could be bossy, but he was a matter-of-fact, practical child, and he was usually willing to help with tasks that some of the other children might have balked at.

"No," I agreed. "Yochanan went to live with the people in the desert."

"Why, Imma?" asked Little Elisheva, named, naturally, for the mother of the very Yochanan we were discussing.

"His imma died," I said. These things happened, and were best not hidden from children.

"Like his abba," Ya'akov added, in an almost unkind tone of voice, although he was right. Old Z'kharyah had died a few years after Yochanan's birth, and never did get to see the greatness he had sung about when his power of speech was restored.

"Imma, are you going to die?" Little Elisheva asked, her voice quavering a bit.

"Someday I will," I said. "Someday everyone will die."

"Even Abba?"

"Yes, Abba, too."

"Even Yeshua?"

Little Elisheva well-nigh worshiped her eldest brother. He was, to her, in a different league from her other brothers entirely. Of course, he truly was, though none of them understood how. I was about to say "Even Yeshua," but then I realized I wasn't exactly sure. Everybody died. All the deliverers died, eventually. But somehow I had a hard time imagining Yeshua's bright soul ever being extinguished. Also, thinking about it filled me with more dread than I had felt as a child asking these same questions my daughter was asking me now. I didn't know the answer, so I changed the subject.

"This year in Yerushalayim, we will celebrate Yeshua's becoming a man, as well as Pesach," I said.

"His bar-mitzvah," Ya'akov said importantly. His own would be approaching in another few years.

"Yes," I said, "his bar-mitzvah." This shift of topic seemed to have taken Little Elisheva's mind off the gloomier one we had just been discussing, for she began to dance about, forgetting the blanket she was trying, rather awkwardly, to fold. "Yeshua's having his bar-mitzvah, Yeshua's having his bar-mitzvah!" she sang.

"But anyway," said Ya'akov, going back to his original question, "Won't Yochanan at least celebrate with us? Those caves aren't so far from Yerushalayim, are they? He's healthy, and he's had his bar-mitzvah already. He can walk."

"He can," I admitted. "But I don't expect they'll encourage it. Those people out there think they are more righteous than the rest of us. I imagine they think he will be contaminated if he celebrates Pesach with the likes of us."

Ya'akov snorted. "That's stupid," he said. "Isn't it better to live with everybody else and help them than to snub your nose at them and live with only people who think like you?"

He was a thinker, this one. "I expect so," I said, and turned to Little Elisheva to help her sort out the blanket.

"So now," Ya'akov persisted in the background, "we are celebrating with Abba's family?"

"Yes," I said.

"Fine," he said. "I like them better anyway." He trotted out of the room, presumably to find his brothers. I shook my head. I could have been offended by his preference of Yosef's family over mine, but he was still just a child. And I could see the appeal. Yosef's sisters had many children and grandchildren to play with already, while the first Elisheva had been a soft-spoken old woman, with Yochanan her rather strange only son. The rest of my family lived near us in the Galil, and so even when we also celebrated Pesach with them, the festivities did not have the sense of novelty and distinction for the children as they had when their Southern cousins were included.

"I'm glad, too," Hannah, my other daughter whispered. "Yochanan scares me."

"He doesn't mean any harm," I said. But I could understand this, too. "He didn't have a father for a long time, and his mother was old. He never had other brothers and sisters. He didn't get to learn how to play with other children very well." Besides, I added to myself, he's going to be a prophet or some such. No one could expect one of them to be normal.

It was rather less enjoyable for me celebrating with Yosef's family, however. They were loud and boisterous, and at the same time, I never got over the feeling that they still somehow disapproved of me and Yeshua. Although I knew Rivkah and Tamar believed the truth about us, it was a difficult truth to accept, and though Tamar remained quietly friendly, Rivkah seemed to have decided simply to ignore the knowledge—and usually us, too. The rest of the family had heard the shepherds and things had eased when we lived in Beit-Lechem, but after our sudden departure to Egypt I could never feel certain that they didn't secretly think—and even say—uncharitable things about my first son and me behind my back.

"They don't mind anymore," Yosef assured me, but for once I did not believe him.

"Look at the difference between how they treat him and how they treat the others," I protested.

"But they haven't seen him in a while," Yosef said. "And he's a man now. They're helping us celebrate that well enough, but it's hard to change the way you treat someone when he was a child the last time you saw him and a man the next."

I supposed he was right, or at least partly, so I gave up my objections and gave myself over to the Pesach festivities. In any case, Shlomit and her family had come down with us as well, and whenever I felt a little awkward with Yosef's sisters, I could relax in her company. We sent all the children scampering about to clean the hametz out of the sisters' homes, and then all of us worked together to prepare the seder meal. We traveled into Yerushalayim for the final day of the feast, and for Yeshua's bar-mitzvah, and the children's eyes widened as they always did at the glowing Temple. The time seemed to fly, actually, in spite of my unease around the sisters, and soon it was time to return North once again.

With all the family from both Yosef's and my side, however, the leave-taking dragged on a bit. Finally I bundled up the bedding we had brought. Yosef was helping the other men break camp. The children had all bounded off again sometime during the farewell proceedings. Even Yeshua. I sighed. He was a man, it was true, and more mature than some his age, but he still had a lot to do before his behavior was truly that of an adult.

Having bade all of Yosef's family farewell at last, Shlomit's and my family made our way to the agreed-upon meeting place for the rest of our caravan North. Once the group had all gathered, we set out in earnest. I walked with my sister and our friends. No one was riding, but no one minded. It was a beautiful day and we were all used to walking. We travelled far in a day and Yosef and I only saw each other at the end of it, when we stopped to set up camp again.

"So," I said, as we all sat down to eat. "Where is Yeshua?" The girls had been close to hand all day, and the other four boys had appeared as soon as the caravan had stopped. Shim'on was never one to miss a meal, and his ability to find us when we had one for him was unfailing. The other boys simply followed. But Yeshua was not with them.

"With friends, I expect, since he isn't with you or his brothers," replied Yosef placidly. "I haven't seen him all day."

"Really?" I said, feeling a faint twinge which would, I knew, grow into panic if I gave in to it. "Well, I expect he will turn up in a minute. He's bound to be hungry." But he didn't.

The twinge was turning into panic anyway, despite all my efforts not to attend to it. I tried to eat, but my stomach was too woozy with worry for anything else to fit in there very well. Everything suddenly tasted very dry, as if someone had mixed wood shavings from Yosef's shop in with the dinner. At last I got up. "I have to look for him," I said.

"He'll be fine," said Yosef. "He's heady with the thought of manhood and is trying out being on his own. There are enough of us here to look after him."

"Yes," I snapped. "If anybody actually knew where he was!"

"Someone will." Yosef's mouth was full of bread and he seemed altogether too comfortable with the disappearance of our son. My son. Sometimes, in dark moments, I imagined Yosef actually resented Yeshua—having to claim him for his own. He never in fact demonstrated any such thing, but wives have their intuition, or at least we tell ourselves that we do.

"Yosef!" I began, intending to take him to task about this.

"What's wrong?" asked Shlomit. She had been sitting next

to me, but was busy attending to her own brood. She looked at me in that way she had, though, and I knew she thought she was forestalling a public marital spat.

"Yeshua's missing," I said. I tried to say it calmly, but I'm sure she heard the tension in my voice.

"Missing?" said my sister. "Nonsense. He must be somewhere. Not everyone is around the fire. Look about. You'll find him."

"Don't take his side, too!" I hissed. "That one," I nodded at Yosef, "has already pointed out that he must be somewhere. Of course he must be somewhere!"

"Miryam," said Yosef soothingly, which he should have known by this time was certain to grate, "he won't be found more quickly with stewing, nor with empty stomachs. Let us trust him to God, eat our dinners and then go look for him if we must."

"Trust him to God!" I repeated scornfully under my breath, and then felt foolish. Doing anything but trust that one to God was surely opposed to his purpose for being in this world. On the other hand, God had trusted Yeshua to us. What sorts of parents would we be if we left him to be torn apart by wild animals? Well?

I squatted on my haunches and stared at Yosef while he ate, resisting, however, all urges to remind him that it was getting later and every single person in the caravan was now eating so how could Yeshua still be with the caravan if he weren't with us? I didn't eat anything myself. As soon as Yosef licked his fingers for the last time, I stood up.

"We've got to go back," I said. "We've got to find him without delay. Where will he sleep tonight? Who will look after him?"

"He's a man now," said Yosef again, but his lips were white, and I could tell he was beginning to worry, too. In the next breath he said, "Come on then—let's go."

"Where are you going?" our friends protested. "It's night

now and you're tired—you won't be able to do anything until morning anyway." Oh the people who could find reasons to wait! But at least we would be back in Yerushalayim by morning, maybe, where we needed to be if we hoped to do anything then. I remembered the conversation with Little Elisheva before the start of our journey about the possibility of Yeshua dying. One part of me was sure he had to be all right. He was the Messiah. He had been given to me. And he had done nothing yet to save his people. But I couldn't bear the thought that something might happen to him in the meantime.

"Are you joking?" I asked the next person who told me to wait until morning. "I won't be sleeping tonight, will I? And neither," I added, glaring at Yosef, who nevertheless had maintained his new air of genuine concern, "will you!

"Shlomit," I turned to my sister. "Please will you look after the others? We really must go back!"

"I have plenty of help," she agreed, smiling bravely and nodding in the direction of the assembled crowd. Given the crowd's general spirit of apathy at the thought of a missing child—or young man—I was not greatly comforted, but I knew we'd never get anywhere or find anyone if we brought the rest of the children with us.

"Thank you," I whispered, kissing her. Then I kissed the children. "We have to find Yeshua," I told them simply. "But Abba and I love you, and so does Aunt Shlomit. She will take very good care of you until we get back."

"Are you going to die, Imma?" Little Elisheva whispered, her eyes large. "Not just yet," I whispered back. "Not for a very long time." I hoped I was right. I tried once again to tell myself this was Ha'Elyon's Messiah we were frantic about, and there was no need to be frantic at all. Ha'E-lyon would protect him. He had done it so many times already. But all I could see in my mind was a curly-haired twelve-year-old.

Of course it took us just as long to travel back to Yerushalayim as it had taken us to travel away from it. Longer, in fact, because in the end, worry and lack of sleep exhausted us and we did have to stop somewhere and rest. "We won't be able to look for him properly in this state," Yosef had said. "Better to get some sleep and be fresh in the morning." I still thought I would be incapable of anything remotely resembling sleep until Yeshua was safely back with me. But to my eventual surprise, I fell asleep as soon as I lay down.

We needed that rest, because worry did keep us up the next two nights. We stopped in Beit-Lechem briefly first, though both of us were sure the family would have sent someone to bring Yeshua to us if he had somehow lingered there and been missed. After that, we combed Yerushalayim from top to bottom for two days, and still there was no Yeshua. Some people thought they had seen a boy of the description we gave, but they were never very clear about where. Others looked at us as if we were mad. "Sounds just like most of the other Jewish boys around here," they laughed. We did not find this funny. One person was even insensitive enough to say, "Give up and go home, friends. Once you've lost a boy in a city like this one, chances are good you'll not find him again. Or if you do," he added ominously, "you'll not recognize him."

By this time, I was so exhausted and panicked that the comment nearly knocked me off into a faint. Yosef was busy holding me steady and steering me away from the man who had said this, which is probably a good thing, because I would say that from the set of his jaw, he would have preferred to have hit him.

After that came the second sleepless night. On the third day, I finally thought of the Temple. I don't know why I had not thought of it before. When we got to the Temple court, we saw a small knot of people sitting and standing among the pillars. Yosef went forward to see what was happening. He stood and listened for what I thought was far too long a time when we had a lost boy to find. But then he said something, the crowd broke up, and there was Yeshua, walking out of the middle of it. I noticed next that the crowd had largely been made up of rabbis.

As Yosef returned, his hand on Yeshua's shoulder, I could see from his badly disguised grin that he was prepared for me to be angry with the boy, but that he himself was not upset any longer. Well, I was angry. We had been given a terrible fright. I did not care what Yeshua had been up to—nothing could justify such thoughtless treatment of his parents.

Before I could open my mouth to express this, Yosef said, in a voice which could have sounded proud or angry, "You'll never guess what this one was up to. Arguing with the rabbis about God!"

I did not care. "Child!" I almost shouted, forgetting he had just been made a man. "What did you think? Why have you terrified us like this?"

Yeshua stared at me then, his eyes puzzled. "Did you really not know where I was?" he asked. "Didn't you know I had to attend to my Father's business?"

I could not understand what that meant, and when I looked at Yosef I saw that he couldn't either. If Yeshua had been concerned about his father's business, he would have come home with his father—and me—at the appointed time, so the two of them could get back to work in the carpenter's shop.

It was only later that I thought I might know what he meant. Afterwards I heard in more detail how Yeshua had been listening to the rabbis and challenging them. Afterwards I heard how those rabbis listened to him and were amazed. Afterwards I saw Yeshua at home again, obedient to Yosef and me as he had always been, growing tall and wise. Then I heard him in my head, asking that question again in the Temple court, "Didn't you know I had to attend to my Father's business?"

The emphasis had been on the "you." Didn't we—Yosef and I, of all people—understand that our son had to be concerning himself with his Father's business? His Father's business. Which father? I already had some suspicions that he knew more about his birth than I had ever told him. But how did he know? Had his Father—his true Father—God, his Father—been communicating with him somehow? And why not? Why would a father not want to find a way to speak to his son?

15

SO YESHUA GREW UP

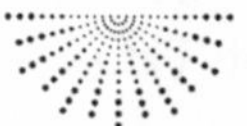

So Yeshua grew up—taller and stronger, and all the people loved him. He never gave us any more serious trouble after that Temple incident, although he continued to make oblique references to "his Father" from time to time. He wasn't making any effort toward being a Messiah, however. Instead, he took over more and more of the work in the carpentry shop, which was helpful for Yosef, who had been tiring more easily of late.

Yosef's fatigue seemed strange to me. He had always been a strong man, I thought. A true man, too. We sat together in the early evenings, and I held his carpenter's hands, which had grown rougher and more vein-y over the years. Sometimes he held them to my face and gazed at me, his eyes twinkling.

"We're not old enough," I said. "You are leaving me, Yosef. I know you are. But we aren't old enough."

"I will go when Adonai calls me," he said. "I haven't ever been able to do otherwise, have I? But I don't want to leave you, Miryam."

It was one of the things I loved about him, I thought. He had seen angels. He had heard the commands of Adonai. And he had always obeyed them, whether he had wanted to at the time or not. But because of that, and for so many other reasons, I couldn't bear the thought of letting him go.

"You have done it, too, Miryam," he said, when I told him this. "You have to obey, too. You started it. You said you were the servant of Adonai, and so you are."

I was feeling frightened. I wanted Yosef to gainsay me, to tell me that he wasn't going anywhere. I loved that he always obeyed Adonai, but at the same time it frustrated me, and I didn't know how to talk about it, so I began complaining about Yeshua. I loved Yeshua. He was the special one. But there he was, dutifully working in the carpenter's shop . . .

"To what purpose?" I spat. "I agreed to bear the Messiah, and there he is, still, not delivering anyone of anything."

"Have I been with you all these years just to find that you think carpentry is so ignoble?" Yosef asked, a grin playing in and out of his beard.

I put my face down in his hands between our laps and shook my head. His hands smelled of wood shavings. It was one of my favorite smells.

"You know that isn't what I mean," I moaned. My voice was muffled through his hands and my skirts, but I knew he understood me. I sat back up and looked at him pleadingly. "It's the noblest of professions, creating things for people with such love as you do." I took the box out of the folds of my robe—that box he had made for me when we were betrothed, and before everything else.

"Did you know I carry this with me everywhere?" I asked. "Ever since the day you made it for me. You made the box and I put my heart in it and it's been there ever since."

Yosef swallowed in a way that made me think I had moved him and I couldn't look at him for a while. It seemed he couldn't say anything. Then I went back to talking about Yeshua. He was in that box, too. Somehow he and my heart had become inextricable, and we were both in

Yosef's box. "I love that you are a carpenter," I said, "and I love that you have looked after Yeshua all this time and that he loves you as...a father." I realized with a little surprise that I couldn't say "as his father," because I didn't think that would be quite accurate. But I knew Yeshua loved and respected Yosef and was close to him. "Carpentry is good work. But the angels said Yeshua was to save our people, and I just don't see how spending his life in the shop is going to accomplish that."

"Nor did we see, either of us," said Yosef, after acknowledging what I had said with a brief nod and the set of his mouth, "how you could be his mother without my intervention, or how I could marry you then, or how we would survive in Egypt, or how . . ." He stopped. I understood him.

We went to sleep that night as if we were a new bride and groom—in the way we hadn't gotten to be a new bride and groom in the first place. In the morning, I could scarcely bear to send him to the shop. I packed something for him to eat as I always did, for when he got hungry midday. He wasn't even going anywhere—just closer to the center of the village. I could walk down there and eat with him if I wanted to. I wondered why I hadn't done so every day of our married life. Why had I never considered that I might run out of days? I put the small loaf of bread into his leather pouch and thought I was going to be sick with grief. "This is ridiculous," I told myself. "Yosef will be fine. This is what we do every day." Besides, Yeshua was already down there. If, by some unlucky chance, something were to happen, he would be there and know what to do.

I handed Yosef his pouch. I had trouble looking at him, but I knew I had to. I could not imagine forgetting his face, and I never wanted to. He embraced me again, and kissed me, almost as he had when we were younger, and then set out, his eyes twinkling. But sometime in the afternoon, Adonai called him. Yeshua was at a neighbor's, delivering a bench he had made for him. Yosef was found, as if sleeping over his work, by a customer later in the day.

I wasn't surprised, but I was devastated. He had been such a good man, and he had seen angels. What was more—probably less, really, but I couldn't help its feeling like more to me—he had loved me. I had loved him, too. I still loved him. The mourning period was prescribed, but I did not care anything about that. I wept long afterwards.

Of all my children, Yeshua, the only one who could not actually claim Yosef as father, comforted me most. Maybe it was because he was the only one who could. The rest of us wept, hoping the P'rushim were correct—that a person's soul did live on somehow and somewhere after death—but not being sure. But maybe Yeshua was beginning to know the certainties behind these things already. Maybe his Father had told him.

In any case, he always seemed to know when I was feeling particularly morose, and he always knew what to do about it, so that when I was away from him again, I felt such peace inside me I nearly gasped with it. It was a bracing peace, like the air on the top of a mountain is to someone who lives in the valley—so pure that you want to take it all in at once, but so somehow different as well, that you can only take it in small amazed gulps. When Yeshua left me peace like this, I forgot I was his mother, and I marveled at him. He had to be the Son of God. No other man could do what he did simply comforting me in my grief. He was astonishing. In thinking about this later, I realized the peace had always come when Yeshua had succeeded in getting my mind off of my deceased husband and my grief, and thinking instead of him, and of his Father. Gradually, my heart began to heal, and then one day Yeshua came to me and said, "I am going to the Yarden. I am off to my cousin Yochanan."

That was when I knew his time had come. It was also when I realized how deep the tie between Yeshua and Yosef had been. Had Yosef lived longer, would Yeshua even now be setting out on the mission for which Adonai had given him to me? I didn't know why Yosef's presence would have held Yeshua back. Certainly Yosef never would have kept him back of himself. I wondered about this more as my grief over Yosef began to fade, and then I would tell myself that such thoughts were better debated by rabbis and other men of God. All I had to know was how to be the mother of the Messiah, and I realized with a start I still had very little idea about that, after thirty years. I hoped it would become clear to me as Yeshua's ministry began. Perhaps there would be more angels. Perhaps Yeshua would tell me himself.

Now would begin the deliverance of Isra'el—and, remembering the magi all those years before, deliverance of the goyim, too, perhaps. I wanted to go with Yeshua, to see what would happen. I had the right; I was his mother. I wondered if perhaps he would worry about me, and I would get in the way, and so inhibit the very deliverance I had helped to birth. But I packed a small bundle anyway, and kept it in the corner. He had to have known about it, but he didn't say anything. I would let him go off on his own of course, but maybe I would follow a few days later, to see what happened.

Both my daughters, young though they were, were married now, with their own children. But my sons had something to say about Yeshua's leaving the carpentry shop.

"Well, why not?" I asked. I had never talked to them about Yeshua's origins, and if they suspected that his Father and theirs were not the same, they never said as much. I certainly couldn't bring it up now. "None of you were so keen to take over the business. Yeshua has always been about the work of Adonai, even when he was building things." I could say this now that he appeared to be finished building things and all my trouble of the early years looked as if it was finally going to have accomplished something. "And people are calling

Yochanan a prophet. Why shouldn't he go see what his cousin is doing?"

"They were close when we were children," Yosi conceded. "I suppose he might be curious."

"Just so long as he comes back," muttered Ya'akov. "How many other sons have we heard of who have gone off in the name of Adonai and left their widowed mothers?"

"Oh, well, if it comes to that," I said, somewhat sharply, irritated that this son of mine was now making me the problem, "I have got four more sons, haven't I?"

"It isn't that," said Y'hudah, placatingly. "It just seems disrespectful, that's all."

"I don't feel slighted," I said. In fact I did, but not by Yeshua. I had intended to see if one of my sons wanted to accompany me to the Yarden, but after this conversation, I doubted it. In the end, I took Shlomit with me. Her children were all grown now, too, and her husband was an easy-going soul. So long as his wife wasn't off galavanting entirely on her own or with complete strangers, it was all one to him what she did. Besides, he knew she had a soft spot for her eldest nephew. "Just take care of each other," he quipped as we set out. Shlomit tisked at him but grinned. They were always teasing.

It wasn't hard to find Yochanan. Word of mouth got more and more prolific the closer we got to the River, and once we did get there, all we had to find was the crowd. It was enormous, spreading out all over the western bank, and a little on the eastern side, too. Yochanan had found a tranquil spot in the River's route, and he was immersing people in it. He had broken with the Essenes, those people in the desert, some years before, and as far as I could make out his message was brief and to the point: "Turn from your sins! Turn to God—his Heavenly Kingdom is near!"

"You know how people talk," Shlomit said conversationally, as we approached the crowd. I nodded, anticipating some understated wry observation and getting it. "I didn't think they really meant he wore camel skin."

I looked up. There were quite a number of people in the water, presumably all of them waiting to be immersed. Then I noticed the man who seemed to be the focus of the attention of the people on the bank. He was tall but wiry, and his arms were bare, as were more of his legs than I would have expected. The covering he had was indeed a light brown and appeared to be very heavy and very hairy. His own hair had some of the same properties, though it was much longer and more disheveled. To add to the effect, he was waving his arms about and yelling. Thus far the rumors had held true. People also said that he subsisted on a diet of locusts and wild honey. Apart from any personal reasons, for I had loved Elisheva, I often thought it a shame she had not lived longer when I heard reports like these. Yeshua, at least, knew how to eat a proper meal, and what was more, he liked to. He also dressed decently. No one could say he had grown up without a mother.

I wanted to find Yeshua and learn what he made of all this, but I couldn't see him in the immediate vicinity. Then Shlomit suggested that at any rate, maybe we should watch the proceedings for a little while first. "That way we can find out what we make of it ourselves," she said. This did seem a reasonable course of action, and so we sat down among a group of congenial-seeming people and looked around.

I suppose I expected more bellowing, based on the rumors I had heard. Although Yochanan did call to the crowd on the bank, he didn't do it as persistently as I had imagined. On the other hand, there was still a fair bit of that going on. I thought of the prophets of old—Yesha'yahu walking about naked for a year, Yirmeyahu in floods of tears, Yechezk'el lying on his side for months and eating food cooked on animal dung—and I wondered if all prophets were required to be slightly mad.

In that case, my Yeshua would not be a prophet. But he hadn't come to be a prophet anyhow. He was the Messiah—the promised one anointed of Adonai—and I thought he was probably the sanest person I had ever known.

But Yeshua was still nowhere to be seen, and meanwhile, here was this Yochanan. Like those other prophets, he did not mince words. Clearly he thought his message too important to waste time with niceties.

"Vipers!" he growled once. "Who told you to escape with your skins? If you're really sorry for your sins, live like it—prove it! Don't make excuses about Avraham being your ancestor! God can give Avraham descendants from rocks if he wants to! Trees are about to be felled; if they don't produce good fruit, they'll be chopped down and burnt up!"

People near us shifted uncomfortably. Even I was startled. It was one thing to counsel repentance, and something else again to question the people's heritage. But prophets had said more scandalous things before now, and there had not been a true prophet for centuries. I supposed it wasn't surprising if we weren't used to it.

"I think if I didn't know his origins," I whispered to Shlomit, "I would doubt his authority."

"He is rather...bracing," she agreed. "Listen—someone is asking him something."

"How do we prove it?" someone hollered at the man in the water. It was difficult to tell, from his words and his tone, whether he were heckling or sincere.

But Yochanan began to answer his questioners, one by one. "For a prophet, he's very practical," said Shlomit.

"Mmm," I nodded. "Ya'akov might find more in common with him than he thinks."

More people, obviously having heard answers to their satisfaction, descended the bank. It was quiet for a while, except for the sloshing of water, and an occasional confession heard over the general hum of the crowd.

Then, out of nowhere, Yochanan began shouting again. "Pay attention!" he called, "Someone else—more powerful than I am—is coming next! I don't even deserve to get down and untie his sandals. I have baptized you in the water, but this next one will baptize you in the Ruach HaKodesh." I felt a chill of recognition run up my spine and down my arms, and I gripped the box I still kept in my robes, as if it would steady me. I glanced at Shlomit, who raised her eyebrows. "The time is coming," she whispered, and I felt the chill again. I wondered if Yeshua and Yochanan had met and discussed these things already. Perhaps this was the moment when Yeshua would emerge.

But he didn't. Nor did the people stop coming to Yochanan in the water. Nor did he stop them. He may have realized that he wasn't the one to whom the times were leading, but it appeared he still thought he had a significant role to play. "Turn from your sins! Turn to God—his Heavenly Kingdom is near!" he called, just as we had been told he would. He put his hands on another person's head, pushing him down under the water somewhat abruptly. The newly immersed man came back up, spluttering, dripping, and with a look of relief on his face.

The sun began to go down, and we decided we needed to find a place to stay. "Perhaps," I said, voicing what I knew had been in our minds since we set out, "we can find Yeshua and stay in his camp." The crowd was beginning to disperse, and we got up, too. Yochanan stood alone in the River.

Then, out of the corner of my eye, I saw a flash of movement. This was strange, because, with all of the people packing up to return home, there was quite a lot of movement. But this one made me turn my head. Maybe it wasn't so strange after all. A mother would know her son. I saw him. It was Yeshua.

No one else seemed much concerned with him, so evidently he had not been made known before our arrival.

But he was walking in the opposite direction of the crowd. His stride was purposeful. This was the moment. He was going to speak with Yochanan. I grabbed Shlomit's arm and began pulling her back down the slope toward my son. A few of the people around us stopped and stared. Some of them put their packs back down and watched.

When Yeshua got to the water, we were not far behind, but something in the look he and Yochanan gave each other made us both pause. We could just see the side of Yeshua's face, but Yochanan's registered immediate recognition, twice. First I saw him recognizing his cousin, even though it had been so long since they had seen each other. His face lit up, but then, almost immediately, his eyes filled with wonder as it dawned on him who his cousin really was. He hadn't known, then. Except for when he was a baby still inside Elisheva, the Ruach HaKodesh had not told him ahead of time.

Yeshua stepped into the water and stood before his cousin. Yochanan looked surprisingly ill at ease. "Why are you coming to me?" he asked, in a voice we could hear, but which was unusually small in comparison to the way he had been speaking all afternoon. "I should be baptized by you instead! Not the other way round!" A few more in the departing crowds stopped and turned to see what was happening.

"This is the right way," Yeshua assured his cousin. "God's goodness requires it." He crouched down. Yochanan, obviously emboldened by the reminder of Adonai's demanding goodness, put his hands firmly on Yeshua's head and thrust him under the River. Then something happened which is very difficult for me to understand or explain. Shlomit saw the dove but did not hear the voice, and various other onlookers saw and heard other bits of the experience. What I saw was the sky being ripped apart, somehow, and out of the void beyond flew a brilliantly white...something...that of all things I had ever seen before looked most like a dove. It landed directly on Yeshua's head as he rose out of the water, and then there was a voice. It wasn't like a voice, really, but I understood words anyway, and they said, "This is my deeply loved Son; I am delighted with him."

In that moment I knew, more than I had at the beginning of everything, that I was in the presence of the One who had given Yeshua to me. All of Ha'Elyon was there in that instant, and somehow my son was a part of it. The next thing I knew I was on my knees, with Shlomit next to me. It was an experience we have never forgotten.

We stayed among the followers of Yochanan that night, but we didn't see where Yeshua had gone after his baptism. In the morning, both Shlomit and I were baptized, since even Yeshua had been. Yochanan, who was silent and terse around us, but not unkind, agreed that with such an endorsement from his Father as he had received the day before, Yeshua would likely begin his deliverance of our people almost immediately. Shlomit and I searched for him for some days. But he had disappeared.

16
NO ONE SAW HIM

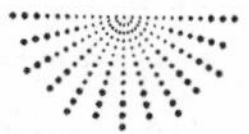

No one saw him again for over a month. And then I myself did not see him again for some time after that. In fact, I did not know he had returned to the Galil at all until some grapevine rumors let slip that some of Yochanan's followers—*talmidim*—had chosen to follow Yeshua instead. I confess that I felt a little put out. Of course he needed to begin the deliverance, but why had he not come home first? Surely it would not have set him back so much to come and pay his respects to his own mother. Not after all the time he had spent simply working with wood.

Then another rumor began—one which hinted that Yeshua had had an encounter with the Adversary. When I first heard it, I wrapped my arms around myself and had to look up at the sky to decide whether or not the light had actually changed. We do not call just anyone "the Adversary." As far as I was aware, the only real Adversary we as a nation had was the fallen servant of God who deceived us into sinning and then accused us before God when we had succumbed.

I supposed I should have known the Messiah would ultimately fight with the Adversary. In the beginning, Elohim had told Hava our Mother that her offspring would crush the Serpent's head. Some rare scribes believed this was a prophecy about the Messiah. But if such it were, I had not actually ever completed the thought. I had not considered the possibility of Yeshua, my son, fighting in person with the Adversary. After the coldness had passed, however, and I did consider it, I was hurt that he hadn't come home to his mother for rest and refreshment before setting off to save our people. If I couldn't support my child through something so harrowing, what was the purpose of being his mother? I wondered.

"Well what would you have done?" Shlomit asked me pointedly. "How does one refresh someone who has looked the Adversary in the face? And if that person manages to look the Adversary in the face and survive it, let alone triumph, what have the rest of us got to offer him? We succumb to the Adversary in little ways every day."

She was so often right, this younger sister of mine. It was irritating, particularly as the things she was right about had more and more often to do with my son, and not with any of hers. How did she get to know so much?

"Well perhaps," I said, "he could have come back and comforted his mother, then." I still felt some tremors sometimes when I thought of what he must have endured.

"That would have been considerate," Shlomit acknowledged. "But didn't you say he always felt his greater responsibility was to his Father?"

I knew she did not mean Yosef. This, I thought to myself, was another time when the nearness of Adonai did not truly feel like a favor. Why would he demand that I bear him a son, only to take that son away from me? But he had not demanded, I knew in my heart of hearts. And I had also known that this son was not mine to keep. No child ever truly belonged to his or her parents, and this one...he belonged to no one but Ha'Elyon, even from the start.

In any case, we all saw Yeshua again soon enough after all. There was a wedding. It was in Kanah, also in the Galil. Nothing is too far from anything else in the Galil, and eventually you find that anyone you meet is related to someone you know—or maybe even to you yourself. As it happened, the bride was the daughter of the cousin I had snubbed all those years ago when I was carrying Yeshua in my womb. It was maybe remarkable, therefore, the my whole family had been invited to this wedding.

"Yeshua will be there, I suppose," said Ya'akov, less drily than he might have some months before, but still not with anything that could have been described as warmth. He was rolling up a bedroll, his littlest son, Yirmeyahu, hanging onto his legs.

"Well, naturally," I said, doing my best not to sound annoyed. "He is their family, too."

"Ya'akov means, doesn't Yeshua think he's too important now for such considerations?" put in Yosi.

Yosi was most lately married himself, of all my sons, and although the wedding had happened before Yeshua's baptism and the struggle with the Adversary, ever since Yeshua had abandoned the carpentry shop, Yosi had taken it into his head to imagine some slight that had occurred at the wedding some time before. I thought this was more than absurd, since Yeshua had taken great care to help construct the quarters on the house that Yosi and his bride were now occupying.

"That's not what I said," Ya'akov said, through gritted teeth, shooting his brother a warning look.

I shook my head. "Really," I said. "I was looking forward to celebrating the marriage of two lovely young people and enjoying the company of all my sons in one place. Is it too much for a mother to ask that they allow her this? Is it too much for her to ask that they put aside stupid squabbles and give her the joy of their presence? Is it too much to ask that we all be a family again?"

"Not exactly our fault we're not all together all the time," muttered Yosi, at the same time that Shim'on, who had come in for the second half of my diatribe, said, "It still won't be the whole family—the girls aren't coming."

Both of them had a point, but I still thought I had one, too. I sighed. "The girls," I glared at Shim'on, "would be a blessed addition. They don't resent their older brother. But it's between them and their husbands whether they come with us or not."

I meant to say more, but Yosi cut in, "They aren't affected by their older brother's absence from the family business, either."

"Oh put it to rest," said Ya'akov, for once not fueling the fire of discontent. "Imma's right. This is stupid. He is our brother."

"Please," I said, "you're all my boys. I love all of you. Please can't you get along with each other?"

"You love Yeshua and want us to get along so you don't have to feel bad about it," said one of them. I couldn't, in fact, tell which one of them had said it. The room became very quiet and cold and still, almost as I had felt when I had heard about Yeshua's encounter with the Adversary, even though sunlight was streaming through the openings in the walls and pushing the dark into corners.

"I—" I said, "do you honestly believe that?" Still no one said anything.

"I am living with you," I said. "I have provided you with a roof over your heads for all of your lives...or your father did, which amounts to the same thing. I haven't demanded that any of you follow in his footsteps—it's you yourselves who resent the shop. I look after your children and cook your dinners and...honestly!"

Yosi looked down at his feet, and Shim'on went into the

basket of bread and pulled out a piece that had been left from the day before. I was waiting for the ever-practical Ya'akov to point out that of course I did those things because that's what good Jewish mothers did and I wasn't likely to have known what to do instead, and also that his wife and the other ones also helped me cook and look after the children. But he didn't say anything at all. I supposed that was as much satisfaction as I was going to get on the issue, so I returned to my own preparations. We left soon afterwards.

It was a very quiet journey down—particularly for a party going to attend a wedding. I kept thinking about the argument that morning. I wanted to love my children equally, but even I knew they were right that I loved Yeshua differently. I couldn't help it. I did love these boys—powerfully. They were a testimony of the love Yosef and I had had for each other. They were a reminder of him. Still, Yeshua—he was a testimony of Adonai's having chosen me—maybe even of his loving me, if I could dare to think it. The more I knew of Yeshua, the more I realized I did not know him at all but wanted to, and the more he reminded me of Adonai himself.

But I was trying: I wanted these sons to know I loved them, too. So it worried me a little bit that, the closer we got to Kanah and the wedding, the more excited I felt. Yeshua would be there. This was the first time I would see him since his baptism. When we arrived, he was indeed there already, with a boisterous group of the men who had begun to follow him about. They were his talmidim—his disciples, his students. In a very short time, merely by walking around K'far Nachum and preaching, "Turn away from your sin; turn to God, for his Heavenly Kingdom is near!" like his cousin, he had already collected quite a following. But he was Yeshua. Why was I surprised?

"Imma!" he exclaimed when he saw me, kissing me on both cheeks. He did not act like he hadn't seen me in months. He did not seem surprised. He did, however, seem delighted, and any remaining slight I had felt from him melted away. I wondered how all the other people present did not turn their heads at the light of his smile. He greeted his brothers with equal delight. They laughed and clapped him on the back, but their smiles were not as bright as his, and I saw they were still only half-pleased. Yeshua saw it, too. I wondered if his talmidim were clever enough to see things like that. Would it matter to them that there were tensions in our family—even in the family of the Messiah?

But they did not notice, apparently, and nor did I soon, for I was whisked off to the women to help with the bride's finishing touches. She was a little thing, and rather dark, like me. "You are dark but beautiful," I whispered to the bride, remembering Shlomo's Song. She smiled. It was unlikely, but maybe she knew the Song, too.

Eventually the wedding festivities began in earnest, and I was talking and laughing and dancing along with everyone else. There were my sons, all of them together, just as I had wanted, and they all—each of them—seemed to be genuinely enjoying each other's company. I raised my voice in ululation like the rest of the women, and everyone thought it was because I was celebrating the marriage, but I was celebrating the reconciliation of my sons. Truly weddings were wonderful things. But then the unthinkable happened. Halfway through the days-long festivities, the wine ran out.

What an embarrassment—a wedding without wine. "They would have done better not to have invited so many," I muttered, mostly to myself, "if they could not afford the wine." I flushed then, realizing the serving girl had overheard my murmurs. I hoped she would say nothing, because I could not afford for my cousin to hear I was criticizing her again. The girl turned red herself, and I realized I had just belittled her master, and felt ashamed in full.

I did feel sorry for the groom, too, however, and even sorrier for the bride. It was her wedding—the moment of all moments that would change her life forever. At least she was having a proper one, unlike the rushed and hushed promises Yosef and I had made to each other. But now no one would remember her wedding except as "the wedding when they ran out of wine." Unless something happened... But what could alter such a thing?

So far, not many people had noticed the state of affairs. I had only heard the servants whispering, and seen the groom's face suddenly cloud over.

Then I had an idea. I don't know what made me think it, but in a flash I remembered the dove and the voice out of heaven the last time I had seen Yeshua. For some reason, that memory made me think the absurd: Yeshua could help them. He was the Son of Adonai, and Adonai had often provided drink for his thirsty people in the past. It was true, he had always provided water, but it couldn't be a hardship to provide wine this time, could it? Wine for a wedding—for a celebration. There were scores of feasts and joyous occasions in our Scriptures. And Yeshua had always enjoyed a celebration himself. I went to look for him. He was off to one side with his friends and his brothers. I smiled, remembering: They usually only forgot they really loved him when they were apart. For the last few days the men had been laughing and talking and having, apparently, a wonderful time. I went over to interrupt them. Yeshua looked up, smiling.

"The wine has run out," I said to him simply.

"Imma," Yeshua replied with gentleness in his voice. "Is that my business? Or yours? It isn't time yet."

I looked at him, not understanding. I still do not understand it, really. Of course his time had come. He had gone to the River and been baptized by Yochanan. The Ruach HaKodesh had landed visibly upon him and his Father had audibly called out his pleasure. At least, I had heard it and seen it. He had gone to the wilderness and struggled with the Adversary. Now he was living in K'far Nachum and preaching repentance and the Kingdom of the Heavens. I still did not know what I expected him to do, but I was sure the Kingdom of the Heavens was more than words, and I could not believe his time had not come.

So with a touch of annoyance because I couldn't understand, and because I was his mother, after all, even though he was the Son of God, I said to the servants, who really were excellent eavesdroppers, "Whatever he says to do, do it."

They must have been eavesdropping on Yeshua for some time in fact, and have seen something in him which they trusted, for they came forward immediately. Yeshua looked around at all of us and suddenly burst out laughing. Then he looked around again, his glance falling on six stone water jars which stood nearby. These jars were for our ceremonial washings, and they were at least waist-high for most men. "Fill those up with water," Yeshua ordered the servants.

Just as I had told them, those servants did everything Yeshua said. But their faith was maybe greater than mine, for they filled those jars right to their tops, so that they were on the verge of overflowing. "Now," Yeshua said when they had finished, "take some of the water to the man in charge of the wedding." One of them lowered a pitcher into the first jar. It came up full and dripping, but the drops were still the clear drops of water. All eyes turned to Yeshua, questioning. He did not look worried at all, nodding to the servant who had the jug in his hand.

It was at this point that I began to have second thoughts. What had I just asked these servants to do? What if, for some reason, it wasn't Yeshua's time? What if nothing happened? What if the servant took that water to the master of the banquet and got beaten or dismissed for insolence?

The servant had to be considering all of these eventualities himself. But he looked up, his eyes met Yeshua's, and in that moment of boldness, I saw them fill up with confidence from Yeshua's own stare. He smiled slightly and, taking the jug firmly in both hands, started off in the direction of the banquet director. The other servants, clearly eager to see what would happen, followed closely behind. The rest of us stayed where we were, to see what we could from a distance.

The banquet manager, ever since it had first dawned on him that no more wine was forthcoming, had been looking extremely gloomy. He brightened slightly as the servant approached with his jug, although his manner still indicated a bit of skepticism that anything could really transpire that would improve the situation.

The servant obviously said something then, for the manager nodded, and another servant proffered a cup, into which the first servant poured something. What was it? Instinctively, all of us craned forward to see. All of us did, except Yeshua. He was leaning back, utterly relaxed, and smiling his bright smile.

Noticing this, I almost missed the moment of the transfiguration of the banquet director. He sniffed the liquid in the cup, and then took a sip from it. He closed his eyes and tilted his head back, licking his lips. Then he took another sip and beamed.

There was a sudden croak of surprise near our heads then, and we all, my sons, Yeshua's talmidim, and I, turned to see who had made it. It was Kefa, that most boisterous of Yeshua's K'far-Nachmi friends. He had peered into one of the vats when he saw the change on the director's face, and he seemed to be startled by what he saw there. He put his finger in the vat and then stuck it in his mouth. A look of delight spread over his face and he stared at Yeshua in wonder.

"It's good!" he exclaimed in a scarcely modulated bellow. "How did you do that?"

The others peered into the jars now, too, and soon our corner of the yard was full of crowing, backslapping, and once again, loud laughter. Yeshua, it seemed, laughed loudest of all.

But one of the other fishermen, named Yochanan just like Yeshua's cousin—a man as quiet as Kefa was noisy—had turned back to the scene with the servants and the banquet director. The director summoned the groom, who had been looking glummer and glummer, in spite of his bemused bride's best efforts to charm him into a smile. Clearly fearing something else was amiss, the young man shuffled up to the director, and looked bemused himself as soon as he noticed that the man was smiling. The man said something, and the groom grabbed the cup from his hand. He peered into it, sniffed it, sipped it, and his eyes widened. The director said something else, and the groom stumbled back to his bride, grinning dazedly. I happened to notice that he smiled sincerely at her for the rest of the evening.

Meanwhile, the servants had returned to draw more wine for the guests. They were beaming, too. "They have no idea where it came from," one of them chortled gleefully. "The manager told him most people save the worse wine for after everyone has gotten drunk, but that he had saved the best for last. He thinks they planned this all along!"

"This is the Messiah, you know," said Kefa, clapping Yeshua on the back for the millionth time. "I believe he is, sir," said the servant who had brought the wine to the manager in the first place.

"See?" said a talmid called Natan'el to his cousin, a man named Philip. "I told you he was the Messiah!"

Philip opened his mouth to say something and shut it again. Yeshua winked.

I did not understand all of this. These were Yeshua's friends and already they had their own jokes and private understandings. But what I did know was that these men believed now. And, already knowing and believing, I trusted again—that this man Yeshua my son was the promised one of God.

The party finally broke up in the wee hours that morning. Yeshua and his talmidim were heading off or K'far-Nachum again. "But come with us," he said. "All of you—Mother, Ya'akov, Yosi, Shim'on, Y'hudah—come stay with us for a while."

This idea occasioned a good deal of discussion, with me protesting at the trouble we would cause, and people like Kefa generously offering the roof over his mother-in-law's head. In the end we went to see, as Yosi put it to me under his breath on the way, "what it is, exactly, that a Messiah does."

"Besides make wine," I added.

17
ON SHABBAT

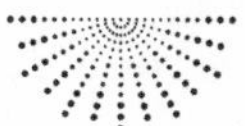

On Shabbat, our weekly holy day, all of us went to synagogue. It was strange going to synagogue so near home, but yet not the one I always went to. The familiar rituals comforted, as did the presence of my children. But at the same time, I felt a little ill-at-ease. This meant that I listened to every word. It didn't hurt that most of the words were my son's—my Yeshua's. He taught, and I sat enthralled. I shouldn't have been surprised that he could speak so wisely and so well the words of Adonai. Adonai was, after all, his Father. But I suppose we—any of us—get used to what we know until we can't imagine anything else. I had grown up loving the Torah and the prophets, or at least revering them. But I had never heard them spoken as compellingly as this. It was as if Yeshua had thought of those words and those teachings himself—as if our holy writings found their origin and home in his mouth.

If I were tempted to think I was only being biased because the speaker was my son, the women around me dispelled that worry. Distracted and chattering at the outset, they were now completely silent, their eyes widening as they listened.

Suddenly there was a bit of a commotion. Someone at the other side of the room stood up noisily and said in an unnaturally loud voice, "What do you want with us, Yeshua from Natzeret?" I had heard voices like that before. They only meant one thing. A demon. Or perhaps more than one thing, if by that one meant many demons.

There were a number of people in the Galil at that time who were home to demons. In fact, such people could be found all over Y'hudah as well. Some folk suggested it came with the forsaking of Adonai and the Torah, but whatever the reason, almost everyone knew at least one family who was saddened or terrified by the touch of such a spirit.

For those families who weren't, it was important to avoid all contact with people who carried unclean spirits. One wouldn't, after all, want somehow to become unclean oneself. Most people inhabited by these beings looked like it, but I couldn't remember having seen anyone who looked out of the ordinary when we had entered the synagogue. I craned my neck like everybody else to see. This man shouting now was one of the rare few who carried demons but didn't show it on the surface.

"Why are you here? Have you come to wipe us out?" he shouted at Yeshua. "I know you—Holy One of God!"

It was true, everything that man was saying, but hearing it in that voice, in that way, made me nervous. Others squirmed uneasily where they sat. Who had let this man in the synagogue anyhow? K'far Nachum was not so large that its inhabitants wouldn't know who the troublemakers were.

"Silence!" ordered Yeshua, "Come out of him!" His voice was not loud, but firm and strong, full of authority and peace.

The man fell to the floor, shuddering and writhing. Then there was a loud, eerie shriek, and he lay still. The demon was gone.

We all—everyone in the room—sat in stunned silence for

a moment after this. Then the man got up, a little shakily. He shook his head. He looked at Yeshua for a long time, his mouth hanging open and, quite frankly, looking rather more foolish than he had before the demon was cast out. As if he somehow knew what I was thinking, he closed his mouth, and then he opened it again and I thought I saw him shape the words "thank you" with his lips, though no sound came. Then he turned and walked into the sunshine.

Although the man's spell had been broken some moments before, the one Yeshua himself had cast on the rest of us onlookers only shattered after the liberated man had gone. And maybe even then it continued; the hum that began as people filed outside soon turned into a low roar of amazement. "What's this?" people asked each other. "Something new! This man teaches as if he actually has business saying it," said one. I saw the speaker's mouth quirk upwards slightly when he said it. Everyone knew that none of our Torah-teachers taught like Yeshua had just done. It wasn't just the teaching, either, but the miracle which confirmed it. "He even orders about the unclean spirits and they obey him!" people cried. Some of our leaders carried out exorcisms, but they were far more complicated endeavors than what Yeshua had just done. Nor were the results so certain. I expect everyone went home thinking they had never had a Shabbat like this before. But the first miracle of the day was not the last one.

"Rabbi," ventured Yeshua's friend Yochanan, the quiet one, "Kefa's wife's mother is ill. That's why he's not here this morning, I expect." One of the other men snorted in a way that implied Kefa's synagogue attendance would have been unlikely in any case. But Yochanan continued. "I was wondering...well, I thought, after this morning and the wedding and everything, maybe you could do something about it."

I looked at Yeshua, expecting the usual smile, but it did

not come. "Let's go," he said gravely. Only then did I notice that his eyes were twinkling. It reminded me, suddenly, of Yosef. He had learned the trick even without the bloodline. I felt for the wooden box I continued to keep with me, and my throat turned thick for a moment. It was maybe fortunate we were off to visit the sick, or I might have begun brooding, missing the one who had been such a good father to the son he had not fathered. As it was, there were other things to think about.

The house was a large one of unusual shape. I knew Kefa and his brother Andrew had a fishing business; I had not known until now that it was quite so successful. Yochanan and his brother Ya'akov, I had heard, were partners with these two. I wondered if their house was as grand. It mattered less, I supposed, that Yeshua had no home of his own when he had friends like these with plenty of room to house him.

Andrew answered the door when the group of us arrived, looking slightly sheepish but even more relieved. "Come in, Rabbi," he said. "And everyone else," he then added with a tired smile.

We all squeezed into the dim room, and Yeshua went straight up to the living quarters, where Kefa and his wife sat hunched by the side of the bed.

It seemed all I did was blink, and suddenly a woman, just about my age, was climbing out of the bed and down the steps, smiling. "Thank you, Rabbi," she said with quiet gladness. "Now let me do something for you." Immediately she began preparing a meal for us all.

It was early for meal preparation. Shabbat had not ended yet. I shifted uncomfortably. I could hardly sit by and watch a woman, who had only moments ago been sick with fever, prepare us a meal all by herself. But regulations were regulations, and here we were before the Son of Adonai...who didn't seem to mind at all. I saw some of the others stealing sidelong glances at him as if they were having similar thoughts to mine, but Yeshua settled himself right down as if it were any other day of the week and began to talk to Yochanan and his brother Ya'akov.

It was nearly dark, I reasoned to myself. Nearly the end of Shabbat. And this was food prepared for the Son of Adonai, so perhaps exceptions were allowed in such cases. Besides, I was beginning to feel out of my element. So I joined the woman's daughter, Kefa's wife, and the two of us helped her with the meal.

When we began to feel comfortable with each other, I asked, "What happened? I mean, what did he do to you up there?"

She smiled with a sort of amazement at the back of her eyes. "He just took my hand, and suddenly I felt cool again. And then he lifted me up and I felt better." We three women were all quiet for a little while again, and then she asked, "And you? He must have done something for you, too. What was it?"

"Me?" I returned. "He's my son."

"Your son?" both women gasped, eyes glistening.

"Yes," I answered.

"How blessed you are!" sighed the mother. I smiled. What did one say to such things? Yes? No, not at all? But I thought I did agree with her.

In the beginning, Ha'Elyon had blessed our first parents with the work of caring for his creation. This day began the glimpses of how being blessed with Yeshua also entailed the work of caring. Yeshua could not do two miracles in one day, with the rumor of one in Kanah as well, and stay in hiding.

The sun had scarcely gone down when we began to hear the voices. At first I thought it was the hum of people going to and fro, preparing for their week now that Shabbat was over. Then Kefa's wife, Jemimah, said, "What was that?"

"A moan, in fact," I said, moving to the window through

which the sound had distinctly come. I backed away almost as quickly and grasped Jemimah's arm. "Look!" I whispered.

She and Avigail, her mother, tiptoed to the window. We behaved as if we thought we could convince those outside that no one was home if we were quiet. But it was clearly already too late for such charades. The entire town seemed to have converged on that one house. All the area surrounding the house, including the street that ran past the door, had suddenly become paved with sick mats and people lying on them. "Where do they come from?" I wondered. "Does K'far Nachum truly have so many people?"

Yeshua and his talmidim had been talking all the afternoon long and into the shadows. I had caught snatches of their conversation but not really attended to any of it. Did he even know what was now transpiring outside of the house? And if he did, what would he do about it? Surely he was the reason all those people were here. Surely invalids and the demon-owned did not normally assemble outside of the house of this fisherman's family, relatively well-off though they were. Last night he had said his time had not yet come. But he had performed three miracles in the hours since then. I watched his face. I thought he knew. I saw him readying himself. I turned my attention then to my hostess's face to see how she was reacting to this intrusion.

If anything, Avigail seemed to grow gladder and stronger, seeing the people crowding round her door. She and Jemima pulled out mats and blankets and all such things as they could to make the people outside more comfortable.

"Yeshua," I said. He was the Messiah. These were the ones he had come for. And if there was liberation to be had but he could also liberate them from their ailments, then it seemed fit he should do one before the other. Where would his army come from, if not these people whose lives he had transformed?

I did not need to say more than his name this time. He

rose and gathered the men around him, and then walked into the flood of people. Jemimah and Avigail and I followed with the blankets and other comforts we had managed to find, and we distributed them to as many of the people as we could. Jemimah ran off to the wives of the other talmidim to see if she could gather more. I looked into the faces of those people who had come to see my son. There was so much pain, and such longing. I saw in them a longing almost deeper than their afflictions. If anyone could help them, even with this other longing, Yeshua could. I knew it in my bones—the bones that had absorbed all the promises given to me about Yeshua, from his birth until now.

One by one, he touched the people. He looked at them—into their eyes—and I saw nothing less than hope meeting fulfillment. If he spoke, it was but little, and only enough for the healed one to hear. The sounds of the crowd itself changed; where there had been moaning and even weeping or raging, there were sighs of relief and cries of amazement. Some even laughed. I never saw so many miracles before that night, and I suppose I might say I had seen quite a few. The crowds didn't seem to thin much, however, until finally, long after dark, Yeshua went back in the house and closed the door behind him. I thought he would be glad of sleep then, but when I rose next morning, he was nowhere to be found.

"He does that," said Kefa, in a voice that faintly suggested surprise that I, the Messiah's mother, didn't know. "We've found him off praying by himself before now."

"Let him be," suggested one of the others, a man named Bar-Talmai. "If he wants to pray, who are we to stop him?" But when he looked outside, he clearly thought better of his idea. "Everyone's back again," he whispered, face ashen. "It looks like they've brought their friends. We'll never be able to deal with all these people without him."

"We'll go get him," said Kefa. "I reckon I know where he

went. Come on, men. Oh, and madam," he added, nodding to me. "That is, if you'd like to."

"I'll stay with your wife and mother-in-law," I said. "Thank you." I wanted to go find Yeshua myself. I wanted to know where he talked to his Father. I wanted him to let me be his mother again for a day. But the men looked relieved not to have any women tagging along and set off before I or the other women could change our minds. As they waded through the crowd which was already swarming the door, I heard Yochanan's brother Ya'akov calling, "Yes—we're just going to find him for you. Wait right here."

But the day wore on and they never came. The crowd gradually trickled away. I began to wonder if I should think about going back to Natzeret myself. It was not so far. Surely a son or two of mine would catch up with me on the way, and we could continue home together.

But Avigail was pleasant company, and as I kept waiting to see if something else would happen, I never did start back by myself. It was late afternoon when any of the men returned at all. The ones who did were my sons—my other sons. "Come, mother," said Yosi, with scantly disguised irritation in his voice. I didn't think he was irritated at me. "Let's go home."

"What happened?" I asked finally, after we had been walking for a while in unfriendly silence. "Didn't you find him?"

"Oh, we found him," muttered my Ya'akov, without any sort of happiness in the telling. "There he was by the lake with his prayer covering over his head, looking ever-so-holy."

"So Kefa goes to him and says, 'Everyone is looking for you!'" Yosi contributed.

"And then he says, 'Let us go to some other villages near here, so that I can preach in them, too, because that's why I am here,'" Ya'akov ended, his voice sounding both affronted and triumphant, as if just uncovering an enormous indiscretion on the part of his brother. I failed to see it.

"And where is the crime in all that?" I asked sincerely. But my sons, brothers to the Messiah of God, all sighed and groaned. One of them muttered, "As always—completely blind to any faults when it comes to her precious Yeshua!"

I thought about this. Was I? But was it blindness not to see faults when they honestly weren't there? And what if they honestly weren't?

Finally one of my boys—for that is how they seemed to me at that moment, mere boys—said, slowly and patiently, as if I were perhaps a doddering crone instead of his mother, "It isn't really a crime, of course, mother. But don't you see how this is all going to go to his head? A little conjurer's trick at Kanah that hardly anyone knew about is one thing. And I suppose if he's decided to settle in K'far Nachum, it's nice for him to do a little something for the local populace. But there's no need for him to go gadding about the countryside like a common wonder worker, just to make himself look impressive—him and his bunch of fishermen friends."

I stood still and stared. I would have liked to give all four of these boys of mine a talking to as if they were still little children. If Yosef were still around to administer it, I would have recommended a thrashing. I thought my words might only make matters worse, as the boys were already inclined to think I was playing favorites. Still, I just couldn't keep quiet.

"Conjurer's trick?" I exclaimed, using the words of theirs which had shocked me most. "A little something for the local populace? Is that what you think all that was?"

"Come, come, mother," said Shim'on. But I would not be placated.

"Is there any such thing as a 'common' wonder worker?" I went on. "And why would Yeshua need to make himself look well for anyone? When has he ever done anything on the basis of what other people think?"

"Well, he certainly doesn't care what we think, at any rate," grumbled Yosi.

"He doesn't need to make himself look good because he is good!" I concluded, over the interruption. I began to walk again, determinedly, lips pursed and face set toward Natzeret.

"But don't you see?" Ya'akov asked, in one last attempt to bring me to reason. "Once he attracts a following—a large one, from all the Galil—it will be too easy for the crowds to convince him he really is the Messiah. I know he's strong and I know he doesn't care what people think, but that's a lot of pressure for one man. He'll succumb to it one day, and then everyone will be disappointed in the end, and he will be shamed—and disappointed, too. It's only for his own sake that we worry about this."

I almost laughed. Did he truly believe his own words? Did any of them? But I restrained the laughter and said seriously, "Maybe no one will be disappointed. Maybe he is the Messiah after all."

18
STAYING FAITHFUL TO MY SON

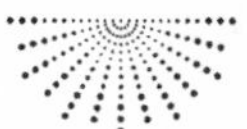

Staying faithful to my son and what he was doing became increasingly difficult, however. Even I began to feel that perhaps my other sons were being taken advantage of. Yeshua had now been away from the carpenter's shop for two months. I had known that he couldn't stay there forever, of course. I hadn't wanted him to. It was what I had discussed with Yosef that last evening together, and other times before that. I fingered Yosef's box in my skirts—the box with the signs of all the words I had learned about my son when I was younger—and reminded myself that deliverance would never come for anyone from planks and blocks of wood. But, afraid of the rivalries which already existed among my sons, I had never been able to mention this to any of them, and so they had all remained ignorant of the fact that one of them would one day need to take over their father's business.

To anyone who didn't know the story of Yeshua's birth—and now my sister and I were the only ones, in the Galil at least, who really did—it appeared that Yeshua had abandoned the family trade. There were complaints. Yeshua's brothers, though true sons of Yosef, seemed to have inherited none of the carpentry skills Yeshua had mastered. While they were still arguing among themselves about whose family should be burdened with the shop, reports kept coming to Natzeret about Yeshua's new successes.

"Now he's healed a man with tzara'at!" said Ya'akov. Tzara'at was what we called any skin ailment which the cohanim declared unclean. People with this condition were sent out of the towns and villages to fend for themselves as best they could. Everyone pitied them, but few ever got close enough to do anything about it. As with demons, there was no reason to risk becoming unclean oneself.

"Isn't that a good thing?" I asked innocently. "What has happened to your compassion, that you would begrudge the happy man this release?"

"It's compassion for all those deluded followers of my brother that makes me say this," Ya'akov returned. "What if he had been unable to cure the man? He would have put all those crowds in danger. He has no business risking the lives of others for one person."

I thought this was a bit of an overstatement, and anyhow it did not seem that Yeshua was unable to heal anyone. The next report, coming right on the heels of the one about the cleansed man, was about Yeshua's having healed a centurion's servant from miles away.

Apparently the centurion had come requesting healing for his orderly. When Yeshua had offered to go to him however, the centurion balked, saying something about how he understood authority: when he told a servant to do something, the servant would do it. It seemed he was implying that diseases themselves were under Yeshua's authority.

Yeshua had then proven the point in a burst of pleasure which I could all but imagine—that smile!—for when the report came back from the centurion's home, it was that the servant was healed at that very same moment.

I had heard the story from my sister, who always seemed

to be somehow better informed about Yeshua's doings than I was. I was still marveling over the idea that Yeshua could heal even at a distance, and trying to forget that Shlomit had heard the story before I had—again—when Y'hudah stormed in.

"Healing goyim, too, now!" he growled. "Goyim! If he is the Messiah, what business does he have healing any of them?"

"The orderly may have been a Jew," I said, hoping to pacify him.

"Not likely," Y'hudah mumbled. "And if he was, he didn't deserve the healing, working for a Roman like that. Besides, did you hear what he said?"

"Who? The orderly?"

"No, Yeshua." I thought I had heard, but I asked anyhow. "What did he say?"

"He said," Y'hudah paused for emphasis, "'I'm telling you, I have never found an Israelite with so much trust. In fact, people will come from all the corners of the world to feast in the Heavenly Kingdom with Avraham, Yitz'chak, and Ya'akov, but those born for it will be thrown into the night, where everyone's moaning and grinding their teeth!"

It was almost exactly what I had already heard Yeshua had said. Y'hudah had obviously memorized it very carefully so that he could spit it out in just that way. If Yeshua had, in fact, spoken those words, they would need no embellishment to make enemies for him. I had to admit it seemed possible that he had said that very thing.

I thought of the magi, those strange and ardent people who had followed a star all the way to Beit-Lechem just to see my son. I thought of old Shim'on, praising Ha'Elyon for a child who would bring revelation to the goyim and glory to Isra'el. Perhaps this centurion and his orderly were part of the promise, too, just as the magi had been. But I could not tell my other sons about this. Not now that I had waited so long to tell them anything already.

Besides, the reports about Yeshua were starting to put me out of sorts in spite of myself. It was one thing for the Messiah to be big enough to help the goyim as well as bringing glory to his people Isra'el. It was completely different for him to start saying the goyim would enter the Kingdom *instead* of the people of Isra'el. Perhaps he hadn't meant it the way it sounded. Perhaps someone had exaggerated the telling. Perhaps only some of "those born for the Kingdom" would be thrown outside. But how were we to know which ones? In any case, he should never have said such things. They would only antagonize people.

However, from all reports, it did not seem that Yeshua minded antagonizing people. One might even have supposed he was trying to do that very thing. He preached that those who were persecuted were blessed, and those who laughed were in a woeful condition. He told people their goodness needed to be as perfect as that of the Torah-teachers and the P'rushim, but then he told the Torah-teachers and P'rushim to stop being hypocrites, praying and fasting in public without sincere hearts. He said that he had come to complete the Torah and the prophets, not to abolish them. But after that he told people to ignore the laws which spoke "eye for eye and tooth for tooth" in favor of loving enemies.

I should have known it would be like this. Perhaps I was wiser when I was young. Then, at least, I had understood it was a fearsome thing to be told by an angel, "Adonai is with you." Then, I had known that the presence of Adonai in my life would turn everything topsy-turvy.

But now that his son was walking about in our very own Galil, explaining just what "topsy-turvy" would look like, I found myself forgetting all the promises and warnings I had stored up about him for years, Yosef's wooden box notwithstanding. I forgot that Ha'Elyon had never been a simple household god who could be manipulated to my wishes. I see now that I was trying to make my son into exactly that. He was my son, after all. Why shouldn't I want him to be at home? He could come back and work in the carpenter's shop and preach from there if all he was to do was be a preaching-Messiah. People would still come to hear him, when they brought him work to do. His brothers would be appeased, able to return to their families and preferred occupations instead of worrying about the carpentry shop. Our home would be happy and tranquil again.

It was a very small dream, and when I first began to dream it, I couldn't help laughing at myself and it, for its smallness. But I couldn't help wishing it all the same, and the more I thought of it, the more reasonable it seemed to be. Then came our Pesach festival again.

Even with Yosef gone and all the children with families of their own, we still made the journey to Yerushalayim most years. "Are you sure you want to go this year, Imma?" one of my children would always ask me.

"I'm not ancient yet!" I would retort. Well, I wasn't, either —only in my mid-forties. I guessed sometimes one or more of them was looking for an excuse to avoid the journey, but they wouldn't be getting one on my account.

I was excited about this Pesach, because I was sure we would see Yeshua again. He would come and celebrate with us, and preside over the celebrations as he always had since Yosef's death. We would see for certain that he was not the disgrace we were all dreading that he had become.

Then we learned, by messenger and not from Yeshua himself, that he would not be joining our family festivities that year. He was taking his talmidim and going to Yerushalayim with them instead.

"But we'll see him, of course," I said, more for my own benefit than anyone else's when I told my sons the news. "We'll all be in the same city, and I'm sure he'll stop to see us."

"I'm not," grumbled Ya'akov darkly. "If he can't take the time to come with us, clearly he won't be stopping to see us. And Yerushalayim isn't the Galil, Imma."

"No," I replied. "It's smaller."

"With all the same amount of people crammed into one place," Shim'on added. I had hoped no one would mention that, but I wasn't surprised that someone had.

"It's probably about time he heads down there," Y'hudah mused. "The big city will swallow him up. He'll find out he isn't quite the sensation down there that he is in these parts. Then he'll come home and behave like a proper son and brother."

I couldn't admit it to myself right then, but the thought had occurred to me as well. Later, lying in bed with my thoughts as I always did, I felt a little ashamed at wanting the Messiah to behave as a proper son and brother at all. But how could he lead all the people to deliverance when he couldn't sway his own family?

In truth, I thought to myself, turning over on the straw pallet, if Yeshua had come with us that year, it would likely have been a very unpleasant Pesach indeed, because by this time his brothers were so resentful of him they could never have contained themselves in his presence. Still, I was disappointed. Yeshua always performed the parts of the ceremonies reserved for the head of the household, and he had always made them come alive. Besides, as Pesach was, like many of our other festivals, about such a defining moment of deliverance in the history of our people, I couldn't help but wish that celebrating it all together would help reunite our quickly deteriorating family. But instead, his brothers now just had one more thing to resent.

I couldn't think of a time when Yerushalayim was quiet, exactly, but sometimes I hoped that was because we only went there for feast days. Surely sometimes there were spaces of calm. Ya'akov went ahead and scouted out one of the houses perched on the way up to the Temple. It wasn't the same one we usually stayed in; someone had claimed that one already. But we were still early enough that we found a suitably large place to stay. The grandchildren ran about, scouring the place for yeast so their mothers and I could begin to make the unleavened bread. I listened to their shrieks of laughter with delight. Only, then they reminded me of Yeshua, and his chuckling in the same game when he was a child, and I felt unhappy again. The Messiah, I thought, setting my lips firmly, should not be the cause of such heartache. It was one thing to be uncomfortable with the presence of Adonai. It should have been something else again when dealing with one's own son. But in this case that son's presence was lacking, which was part of the problem.

The next day, we joined the swarm of others up to the Temple itself. It was a steep climb, and a sunny day, so we were hot. But we sang with the crowds the songs of Ascent, and the Temple glowed at us with its otherworldly splendor. "I'm tired," Little Elisheva's son, Adam, complained on the way up.

"But look at how beautiful it is," I said to him. "This beauty reminds us of Adonai. He meets us here. It's not so very much, is it, for us to climb and struggle just a very little bit to meet him?"

My grandson gazed at me with big dark eyes but said nothing.

"Is it?" I asked again.

"No," he said in a small voice. No doubt he was just agreeing with me, his elder, to placate me. It is true he was so very small. But I wanted my children and my grandchildren to think like this. I wanted them to feel that no burden was too much for the sake of Adonai.

Eventually we reached the base of the compound, and then the Court of the Gentiles. The place was a hubbub as usual, with the vendors and moneychangers providing the wherewithal for people to offer sacrifices and gifts of money to the Temple. The people were noisy enough, but the bleating and lowing and chirping of the animals and birds was nearly deafening. I wondered how people could do any sort of transacting at all, with all that ruckus.

But then, somehow, the din seemed to grow louder.

There were so many people there that at first, I had spent all my energy trying to make sure all the family was still together and not getting mixed up in the crowd. I had not forgotten the one other occasion of losing someone in the Temple at Pesach. Although I occasionally scanned the pilgrims for a glimpse of Yeshua on our way up the mountain, I had left off doing that once we reached the Temple precincts.

It appeared I did not need to search at all. The increased commotion had begun in the central area of the business transactions. It affected the crowd a little like a wave. No one exactly got quiet, but the people closest to it noticed the uproar first, and then those closer to them, and so on outward like a ripple when a stone is thrown into a lake. By the time I was aware of what was happening, all I could do was watch in horror.

The commotion was my son—my eldest son, Yeshua. His arms, still muscular from the carpentry shop, even after all that time away, were bared, and he was grabbing tables and tossing them in the air like so many twigs. Money scattered everywhere. Then he began to let the animals loose. People screamed, gathered up children, tried to scurry out of the way. They were only farm animals, but there were a lot of them, and they were terrified. A flock of doves flurried over my head and then over the Temple ramparts. I felt the breeze of their wings lift my head-covering. The frightened, flapping mass was so unlike the single dove descending on my son all those months earlier, that I never even thought of the two events together until later. All I knew was that Yeshua had gone mad.

For over the screaming people and yelling businessmen, Yeshua rose up in a rage. He had improvised a whip and was swinging it about him wildly, bellowing as I had never heard even his cousin do.

"Get out of here!" he cried. "How dare you turn my Father's house into a business?"

I couldn't bear it. I grabbed Adam—the grandson to whom I had talked about the beauty of Adonai in the Temple—exchanged a stricken glance with his mother, my daughter, turned tail and fled the premises. I did not know what else would happen. I did not want to know. I couldn't bear to see what was happening to my son. I had thought Pesach would make all things right. I had thought we would see him and talk and we would see his perspective on things, and he would see ours. But now I thought I would never see what he was about.

I put the child to bed when I got back to the house, even though it was midday. Then I went down to the living quarters, but when I got there I could not contain myself any more. I collapsed on the floor and sobbed, loudly and with abandon. I had momentarily forgotten that there was anyone with me in the house at all until I felt a small hand patting my face. My grandson had gotten up again and toddled down the stairs. He said nothing, only looking at me with concern in those big eyes of his.

"Let me cry, little one," I said, tears still streaming down my face, for the comfort of a child only served to remind me of Yeshua's own comfort of me when he was small—and when he was bigger, too.

"Your uncle does not know what he is doing. He has taken away the beauty of the Temple." I sat up and gathered the little boy onto my lap. I held him tightly and rocked him, as if he were the one needing comfort, but I continued to grieve. I sobbed for a son who had come to me as a miracle, whom I had been told would be the Messiah, but who was now attacking his own people with a whip. To make matters worse, he was doing all this in the name of his Father—Ha'E-lyon, the one who had set aside this people and commanded them to meet with Him in the Temple in the first place.

It is true: there are passages in the prophets where Ha'E-lyon himself rails against his people as Yeshua had just done. But I was not thinking of that then, whether because I didn't want to or because I had forgotten, I do not know. I simply wept for the son who had grown up so well, whom I had thought so perfect, and who was now, I suddenly knew, not perfect at all.

"He'll succumb to his popularity one day," Ya'akov had said, "and then everyone will be disappointed in the end." It was true. Ya'akov was right. Surely the end had not come yet, and I was disappointed already.

19
HE ISN'T EVEN EATING

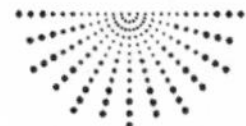

"He isn't even eating properly anymore," said Yosi.

"It's true," said Y'hudah. "There are too many people. They crowd him all the time so that he doesn't have time to eat."

We were back in Natzeret, and no one spoke of the incident in the Temple at Pesach. By the time the rest of the family had returned that night, close-lipped and tense, I had already retired to my sleeping pallet and was lying on it with my face to the wall. I had not gotten up for anything, and had not responded to any of my children's expressions of concern.

I had thought that it would be best for me if no one ever mentioned Yeshua again, but it was impossible to escape the sound of his name. After we had all returned home, he also had returned to his travels about the Galil, and we still heard stories about him. The people of Natzeret looked on me pityingly, and even Shlomit seemed troubled, but it was clear that no one was going to pretend he had died or anything. So in the end, we simply pretended the Temple incident had never happened. This gave my sons the freedom to continue to whine about their brother's other goings-on whenever they wanted.

I continued to think about the Temple on my own of course. Gradually the idea began to form in me that perhaps worship at the Temple really was not all that Adonai had intended. The Sanhedrin was made up of those Jews who seemed not so proud of their heritage, caring more for Rome's favor than God's. Everyone knew the money changers charged exorbitant fees...It was during this time that I began to remember the prophets who had prophesied against the earlier Temple so many hundreds of years before. Still, Yeshua's display of rage had been upsetting, and surely excessive. Besides, hanging onto that incident in my mind made me feel that I had some reason to begrudge Yeshua his freedom, as my other sons were doing.

"How can he not have time to eat?" asked Shim'on, who loved to eat and was also less concerned than his brothers with following news about his oldest one. "What about the time he fed five thousand men with only five loaves and two fish? Didn't he eat then?"

"Oh probably," said Yosi, "but that was ages ago. The crowds have been even worse since then—they all want to be fed like that."

"The crowds have been more than five thousand men?" asked Shim'on skeptically.

There was a pause while Yosi collected himself, and then he said, "Well, all right, not always, but they've been more persistent. Didn't you hear about that one time in K'far Nachum? The house he went to filled up so fast that they were spilling outside and listening through the windows. Then a paralyzed man appeared, brought on his bed by four of his friends, and when they couldn't get in the usual way, they went up on the roof, dug a hole in it, and lowered him down to Yeshua that way."

"No, I didn't hear that," yawned Shim'on. "Did he heal him?"

"Forgave his sins, too, they say," snorted Y'hudah. "As if anyone but Adonai has the right to do that! Honestly, Shim'on—he's your own brother! How can you care so little about what happens to him?"

"You don't care either," said Shim'on. "You only care how it affects—or might affect—you. Which I must say I don't see is any better than being indifferent. It might even be worse."

Y'hudah made a lunge for him, I started to cry out, and then Ya'akov finally spoke up. "Peace, brothers," he said. "There's no reason to let it get to this point. We're brothers. And Yeshua is our brother, too, who, whether he knows it or not, is in trouble. Surely you now see, too, Imma, that he is a danger to himself?"

I nodded, but didn't say a word. I had agreed with this idea ever since Pesach. I simply hadn't wanted to talk about it.

"Then I, for one," Ya'akov continued, "mean to bring him back."

"I'll go," said Yosi. "He just needs to come back to his family and rest . . ."

"And eat," Shim'on interrupted.

"...and recollect himself," Yosi finished.

In the end we all went. "You come, too, Mother," Y'hudah had said, "if you like. He will listen to you." I was not at all convinced he would. On the other hand, I was indeed his mother, and now that I was no longer lying on the floor and sobbing over poor uncomprehending grandchildren, I had a piece of my mind I wanted to give him. So I went, too. I thought about inviting Shlomit and then decided it would be easier to lecture my son without her.

As usual, he was not difficult to find. Everyone knew who Yeshua was, and where he was as well. By the time we reached him, he was sitting in a house, teaching again. Just as all the reports had claimed, the place was full to overflowing with people.

"Maybe we should cut a hole in the roof," Y'hudah said.

The others offered a few wan smiles in the twilight by way of response. I, on the other hand, was trying to hear what Yeshua was saying as it drifted out of the open windows.

"If a kingdom is divided within," he was saying, "it can't last. And if a home is divided against itself, that home can't survive either . . ."

His first statement about the kingdom had smacked of hypocrisy. How could a kingdom not be divided when one of its own sons was desecrating its most precious location? But as soon as Yeshua mentioned the household, everything seemed to shift a little inside me, as if the ground had shifted on the outside. If a household is divided..."What's he talking about?" I whispered to a woman who had edged her way toward us. She looked faintly familiar to me, but I could not think where I had seen her before.

"Some of the Torah-teachers accused him of casting out demons by Ba'al-Zibbul, the ruler of demons," the woman explained. "He's telling them that if Satan casts out Satan, his entire kingdom will topple. He also said," she added with a chuckle, "'If I drive out demons with the help of Ba'al-Zibbul, who helps you drive them out?'" She laughed again, a clear, free laugh. I hadn't heard such a laugh in a long time. I certainly hadn't laughed one myself. I thought it would be nice to laugh that way again. But now her words only made me wonder if I myself thought Yeshua was driving out demons by Ba'al-Zibbul. I would never have said so, but I certainly had not thought that his actions in the Temple were from Adonai. And I had conveniently forgotten, really, about the good he was doing for people.

We were all silent again for a moment, and I heard Yeshua saying, "Listen. People will be forgiven anything, but not for continually blaspheming the Ruach HaKodesh. You can say what you want against the Son of Man—you'll be forgiven—but if you keep on speaking against the Ruach HaKodesh, you can never be forgiven—not in the present age nor in the next one."

The woman to whom I had spoken before interrupted my reverie. "You're Miryam, aren't you?" she asked. "You're his mother."

"Yes," I said, startled.

"I'm certain you won't remember me," she said, "I'm Jemimah, Kefa's wife."

As soon as she said it, I recognized her indeed. "Yes!" I exclaimed. "Jemimah! Forgive me for not recognizing you before. How is it that you are here? Are you traveling with them to look after your husband?"

Jemima laughed again. "Well yes, him too. But mostly when I travel, it's with the other women; we look after Yeshua mainly. We're his talmidim as well, of course."

Of course. Of course? Other rabbis never had women followers. "How many are you?" I whispered, as I let this new and strange idea sink in.

"Oh, it varies," Jemimah said. "As the number of male talmidim varies, too. Yeshua has his special Twelve—the ones he stayed up all night praying about before he chose them, they say. But everyone else comes and goes. Mostly they come, though. Mother is here; after Yeshua healed her it was as if she never wanted to get back into that bed where she'd been sick, again. And she's found a purpose in her life—much more than being a mother."

More purpose than being a mother? I had built my life around being a mother. I thought all women did—except for the poor souls unable to bear children; then they usually built their lives around trying to become mothers. But I had to admit that motherhood had seemed less than fulfilling of late, with one son striding up and down the Galil and shocking people—shocking me—while the other four squabbled about him in his absence.

"Perhaps," suggested Ya'akov, "Jemimah could go and inform Yeshua that his family would like to talk to him."

"Certainly," agreed Jemimah, seemingly indifferent to the tone of Ya'akov's voice. She made her way through the small crowd gathered by the door and managed to disappear into it.

A moment later, the sound of Yeshua, still teaching, stopped. I could imagine Jemimah, or maybe one of his famous Twelve, whispering our message to him.

Then suddenly his voice rang out loud and clear. But what he said chilled me. "My mother?" he asked. "Who is that? Who are my brothers?" Then he paused, and I could guess he was pointing to the people who had followed him since he began his "Father's business," as he called it. "Oh there you are! These are my mother and my brothers! Whoever does what my Father wishes, that one is my family."

A woman's voice spoke up then, loud and staunch, defending me and mothers, "Blessed is the mother who bore and nursed you!" Avigail had said that to me once. I wondered if it were she who spoke now. But Yeshua replied, "More blessed by far are the ones who hear God's word and obey it!"

My sons—my other sons—were livid. "How dare he say such things about us? About you?" they growled. "Come, Imma—we will leave him here, if he no longer wants us." They placed their hands on my shoulders, turned me, and led me away. I was too stunned to say a word.

But we had not gone far before I regained my voice. "Stop. Let's stop," I pleaded. "It's too late to travel home now, and I want at least to see him before we go."

"That's all very well, Imma," said Y'hudah, "but he apparently doesn't want to see you." He doubtless meant this as another criticism of his brother, but I felt as if all my sons were dismissing me now, and all I could hear was Yeshua's voice saying, "More blessed by far are the ones who hear God's word and obey it!"

I had obeyed the word of God. I had borne his son. I had not known it would extend this far, and there were still so many things I could not understand. But I knew I had been holding onto the Temple incident in my soul, as I had once held onto the words about my son. Perhaps I needed to remember those words and forget the Temple in order still to be Adonai's servant, so that it could be with me as he had said.

I was about to burst into tears, but before I could do so, Shim'on said, "But Imma is right. It is late. We should find some place to get food and sleep."

Someone made a derisive sound at Shim'on's mention of food, and I said, "I'll go speak to Jemimah, to see what she recommends." With that, I marched straight back in the direction from which we had come.

Jemimah was standing outside again. I found her at the edge of the crowd, searching for us, her face showing concern when she saw me. "You heard him?" she asked.

"Yes," I said. I started to say something else, but suddenly I found myself finally sobbing. Jemimah put her arms around me and led me away again. People craned their necks around to stare at us, but I could not stop weeping. I did not see my sons.

"This is where we're staying—mother and I," said Jemimah, leading me into a house. No one was there.

"Who lives here?" I asked.

"Some relatives of Levi—the one some people call Mattityahu. They've gone to hear Yeshua like everyone else."

"What does this Levi do?" I wondered. The house was grand indeed, making Kefa's home look like a hovel.

"Well, he's one of the Twelve now," Jemimah replied, rather evasively I thought. Having stopped crying for the moment, I took the opportunity to stare at her hard, until she said, "He used to be a tax collector."

A tax collector. Truly, Yeshua chose the most inappropriate friends. Tax collectors were thieves and traitors, Jews who worked for the Roman government and lined their own pockets with the extra money they collected. I thought I remembered hearing about this man. Yeshua and his talmidim had gone to eat with him, maybe, and when the P'rushim had protested, Yeshua had said . . .

"Yeshua says the ones who need a doctor aren't the healthy but the sick," Jemimah said into my thoughts. "He says he didn't come to call the already righteous people, but sinners." Her voice was tentative, as if making excuses she wasn't certain I would accept, for her hero. I probably wouldn't have accepted them, either, but now my world felt topsy-turvy again, and so I just sighed. I was in the home of the relatives of a tax collector. It certainly was spacious and well-furnished. Ostentatious, I started to think, but stopped myself, first because it wasn't kind, and second because it wasn't even true. The house was finer than any I had been in besides Z'kharyah and Elisheva's, but it was not extreme or excessive. I sighed again. "Yes," I said.

We were quiet for a bit. Jemima sat me down and disappeared to get me something to eat and drink. After a few moments, another woman appeared. She looked to be somewhat older than Jemimah and somewhat younger than Yeshua. Her eyes were wide and serious. She looked at me and smiled out of her serious eyes. "Who are you, mother?" she asked.

"A mother," I said simply. "Just a mother."

The woman narrowed her eyes slightly, guessing. "You're his mother, aren't you? They said you were here." She was not hostile, but she seemed wary.

"Yes," I replied. "I'm his mother."

Jemimah returned with bread, olives, dates. "Miryam!"

she exclaimed, and I saw she was addressing the other woman and not me. "And...Miryam," she laughed. "We'll have to go back to calling you Magdalit," she said to the other Miryam. "At least for the evening."

Magdalit smiled. "That's my name, too," she said.

I thought that perhaps I had heard of Miryam of Magdala before, but not in connection with Yeshua. Many people had demons, but she was better known than some of the other possessed, for her demons had made her wander. There were few villages in the Galil in which she had not been seen at one time or other, noisy and lewd. I thought I had seen her once myself. But his woman, though abrupt and startling with her large black eyes, did not seem mad.

I must have been staring. "The demons are all gone now," she said to me, a sigh of deep gratitude still fresh, in her voice. "They were seven, but they are all gone now. He sent them away. Do you know who he is, your son?"

"He is Yeshua," I answered, "Son of Ha'Elyon." I did not explain anything else. No one asked me to.

20

I'M GOING TO STAY

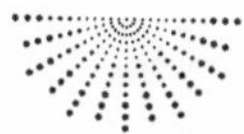

"I'm going to stay," I said. "I'm going to become a talmidah."

My sons shot glances at each other. "Everyone has been very kind," Ya'akov conceded. One of the Twelve, another Shim'on who was one of the Zealots, had found them. After ascertaining that I was being well cared for by the women, he had taken my sons under his wing, feeding them and allowing them to share his campfire. "But," said Ya'akov, "we still haven't been able to talk to Yeshua. They won't even let us near him."

"It's all very well to want to follow him now," added Y'hudah. "Things were quite comfortable for you last night. But what happens when he moves on again and you have to sleep outside? You are not a young girl anymore, Imma, and you deserve better conditions than this. And what if you give up everything and he still refuses to see you? What then?"

Their tones were harsh with concern, but they did not know what I knew. They had not been told by an angel that Adonai was with them. I had. Certainly, I had somewhat forgotten it in the last year. But now I remembered. I suppose, as a young woman just out of girlhood, it had not occurred to me that Adonai's call would continue on me when I was older. Frankly, I rarely remembered then that I would grow older. But the call was on me again, if it had ever left, and I was going to say yes to Adonai once more. "He will not refuse," I said.

"Because he is your son?" asked Yosi. "He already has refused, don't you see?"

"He said people who do the will of his Father in Heaven are his brothers and sisters and mother," I said. "I haven't been doing his Father's will, and so I have no claim on him. Maybe I never shall, but by following him at least perhaps I may be near to doing what his Father in Heaven requires."

"Surely you don't believe all that, Imma," Y'hudah protested. "It's all very convenient for him to go round saying God is his Father, and it's uncanny how all of his ideas seem to be 'his Father's will.'" He chuckled and then grew serious. "But isn't that dangerous, Imma? Isn't that blasphemy?"

I was silent for a long while, looking at my boys. I wanted to see if they could bear my story, the story of their elder brother. But if they thought Yeshua was blaspheming, they would surely think I was, too, to say their brother had been given to me by the Ruach HaKodesh. They would think I had gone mad, that I was blaspheming, that I had been unfaithful to their father. I had not expected the story with its potential shame to pursue me this far, any more than I had expected it of the call of Adonai to be his servant. I had not expected it to divide me from my sons.

In the end, I ignored Y'hudah's question and kept the story silent. Instead I said, "Adonai was with me once. I know this. He was with me when Yeshua was with me. But now Yeshua has gone, and I feel that Adonai has gone with him. If Adonai will not longer come to me, well, I must go to him."

Y'hudah opened his mouth for one more protest, but closed it again without speaking. "Stay, too," I said. "Forget he is your brother, and learn from him. We can all be together. Bring your families. Someone will buy the carpenter's shop." None of them wanted the shop for themselves, really, but they stared at me now as if I had just deeply insulted their father.

"He would want it," I said. "Your father would want it. He saw more clearly than any of us who Yeshua is."

There was silence, until Yosi said, "It is impossible, Imma."

"Very well, then," I said. "Do what you must do. And let me do what I must do. I am staying with Yeshua. I am going to become a talmidah."

So I joined the talmidim and began to follow Yeshua. There were many other women who followed him besides Jemimah, Avigail, and Magdalit. Even Yochanah, the wife of Kuza, the current Herod's finance minister, was among us. At first I hid myself among them, rather uncertain about approaching Yeshua, content simply to follow and listen. He was my son, and a mother has rights to her son—a right to expect a certain deference and behavior from her son even when he is a grown man. Yeshua, however, was also the Son of Ha'Elyon through the Ruach HaKodesh. God himself was his Father, and for the first time in many years, I began to glimpse the magnitude of what that meant. It meant, first of all, I believed, that I had no rights whatsoever. So I hung back.

And Yeshua came to me.

It did not take so long for him to come, after all, either; he sought me out in the evening, the start of my second day as a talmidah. "Imma!" he said. It was an exclamation, but a quiet one. Tender, perhaps.

I hadn't expected, I noticed as he said it, to hear that word from his lips again. I had never, I realized now, deserved to be the mother of this man, and I certainly didn't deserve to be called such. Hearing him say that word to me, therefore, felt like such an enormous, unmerited gift, that for the third time in a very short period, I burst into tears.

"Imma," Yeshua said, taking me in his arms. "Imma. I'm so glad you came. I've wanted you here so badly."

"You have?" I sniffled, looking up. "But I—but you—" I stopped.

"Shalom, favored one," Yeshua said softly. "Adonai is with you." When he said it, it sounded as if the words had been his, and not the angel's, from the beginning of time. They also sounded much more comforting than the first time, and I knew that once again, they were true. The sword had pierced my soul, as ancient Shim'on had said it would, but I had lived.

21
A FARMER WAS PLANTING SEED

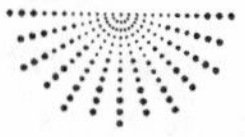

"A farmer was planting seed," Yeshua said. He didn't seem to be shouting—he rarely seemed to be—but his voice carried from the fishing boat where he stood, across the water to the ears of those of us sitting or standing on the shore. It was the first time I had heard him tell one of his well-known parables, and I didn't want to miss a word. Fortunately his voice across the water was so clear, I had no need to worry.

Shlomit had come down from Natzeret as soon as my sons returned and told her what had happened. "I've been wanting to join him for months," she said when she arrived. "Even after hearing what happened...you know. In Yerushalayim. But I thought it wouldn't be right to be here without you."

"I wish you had said," I said. "You are so clear-sighted. I wish you had talked to me about the things I couldn't or wouldn't see myself."

"Well, never mind," she said. "We're here now." She held my hand as Yeshua began his tale.

"Some of the seed he was throwing," Yeshua continued, arcing his arm out like a farmer seeding his field, "landed right in the middle of the path; the birds came and ate it." People chuckled. "Some more of the seed," he went on, "fell on stony ground—not much soil there! Up came the plants right away, on account of how shallow the soil was. But then the sun came out and the seedlings got scorched—no roots!" The people nodded. So it is with rocky soil. We would see what would happen to the other seed in this story. "Still other seed fell into the thorns. The thorns grew quicker and choked the seedlings. But," he said, and paused, and smiled as if he were about to tell a great secret, "other seeds fell into good, rich, moist soil and produced food--one hundred or sixty or thirty times more than that farmer had planted! Can you hear what I'm saying? Pay attention!"

I began to feel vaguely despondent again. I had heard everything well enough. But I could not understand it. Perhaps it was because I was not accustomed to Yeshua's stories yet. "What does it mean?" I asked Magdalit, who stood near my sister and me. It was embarrassing to be asking for instruction about my own son from a younger woman who was not even related to us.

But Magdalit only said, "I don't exactly know. We can ask him when he comes back in."

Yeshua taught some more, but I could not, after all, pay attention. I spent the rest of the afternoon wondering about seeds and soil. In the evening the crowd dispersed so that only the Twelve, the women, and a few others were left. At last, after much other talk, someone asked him about the parable.

"You are the recipients of God's Kingdom secrets," Yeshua answered. "Everyone else is given the parables, so they are always looking around, but never actually seeing; always hearing but never understanding. If they could actually see and understand, maybe they would even repent and be forgiven!"

He was quoting the prophet Yesha'yahu, I knew. I had

heard such words before. Adonai had chosen the people of Isra'el for himself out of all the peoples of the earth, but sometimes it seemed almost as if he wished he hadn't. We certainly had been a disappointing, unfaithful people for most of our history, and he had every right to want to destroy us, I supposed. Still, it had always struck me as somewhat odd that he would send so many prophets to plead with us to return to him, only in the next breath to say something like Yeshua had just quoted. It made him sound, I thought, something like a jilted lover, which didn't seem quite the right impression to have of Ha'Elyon. The words didn't sound any less puzzling when Yeshua said them, and besides, he still hadn't explained the parable. I thought this was worrying. If I couldn't understand it, did it mean I was still an outsider, one of those who would be always hearing but never understanding?

Just then Yeshua said, "You really don't understand the parable? If you can't fathom this one, how will you be able to understand any of them?" At first I thought he was speaking directly to me since I had been wondering that very thing. Only then I saw that nearly everyone was looking as bemused as I felt, and Yeshua was looking round the room at all of us.

"Look. The farmer plants the message of the Kingdom," he explained at last. "When seed falls on the path—those are people who the Adversary steals the message from as soon as they hear it. So then, the rocky soil is those people who accept the message with joy, but then something bad happens to them, and because they have no place for the seed to take root in them, the seedlings wither. The thorny ground is where people hear the message, but the every day worries of life choke out the hope it brings, and nothing happens. But people of the rich soil hear the message, receive it, and bear fruit in their lives—far beyond what they could ever have accomplished alone."

After he explained it, the meaning seemed perfectly obvious, and I wondered how I hadn't seen it myself. But the meaning was also uncomfortable. Which sort of soil was I? I had been given the message—the most concentrated form of message possible: a baby—Yeshua himself. "Shalom, favored lady," the angel had said. "Adonai is with you." Old Shim'on had fairly sung to Adonai, "I have seen your salvation—just as you promised—a salvation you enact before all the world, to enlighten the goyim and glorify Isra'el." Shepherds and magi had worshipped him. Yeshua himself had asked, "Didn't you know I had to attend to my Father's business?"

I had received this message. But like the soil that was full of stones, I hadn't allowed it to take root in me. Trouble had come on account of him: a divided family, the stares of a community who found his words and actions preposterous, my own dashed mother-hopes of seeing her son accomplish great things as respectably and with as little cost as possible.

I was the rocky soil—I, the mother of the Messiah. Full of shame, I kept to myself that evening and pondered. Did one always have to remain the same kind of soil one was at first? What if the farmer came back and cleared the stones, after the land had lain fallow for a time? What if he sowed new seed? Would I be able to bear fruit for him again? Yeshua had not turned me away, at least. I would stay, no matter what future hardship would come, and see what sort of fruit I might bear for Adonai.

22

I WASN'T EXPECTING TO GO HOME

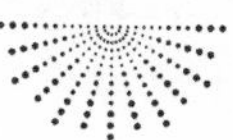

I wasn't expecting to go home so soon. It seemed I had scarcely joined the band of talmidim and already we were packing up our few belongings and heading to Natzeret. Not that I minded. I was excited, in fact. Already I had heard my son say things to make my head spin. I felt younger, exhilarated with the surprised but heady feeling that comes with the new impression that Adonai, God of Heaven and earth, was maybe more knowable and approachable than even I could have guessed. Now Yeshua would go back to the town of his childhood and share the same message with our family and friends. They would hear and finally understand, and then all of them—even his brothers—would see that he was for them, not against them, and they would become his talmidim, too.

Indeed, the way things began, it appeared that this was exactly what would happen.

On Shabbat, Yeshua went to the little synagogue as always. Most of his talmidim who had followed him to Natzeret followed him the rest of the way to the synagogue. Having stayed the night with my sons, who had also taken in Shim'on the Zealot for his previous kindness, I took it upon myself to bring them to the synagogue with me as well. I had to do very little convincing. The entire village had every intention of going to hear their famous young man preach, and his brothers certainly did not want to be left out of the occasion.

The synagogue filled up quickly, full of craning necks and straining ears. Would Yeshua speak? At last he stood. He was handed the scroll of Yesha'yahu, one of our great prophets.

"The Spirit of Adonai is on me," he read, when he had found the place he wanted. His voice was rich and resonant —not loud, for it did not need to be in that small place. But when one heard it, it struck deep. As I had noticed before, when he read the Scripture it sounded as if those words were his own words, his own thoughts. If he read that the Spirit of Adonai was upon him, one could be certain the Spirit of Adonai was really upon him, himself. But of course it was. I knew that.

He read on, "He has anointed me to tell good news to the destitute; to declare freedom for the prisoners and sight for the blind, to release the oppressed, to proclaim the year of Adonai's favor!"

He rolled up the scroll, handed it back to the one who had given it him, and sat down. Everyone was quiet, staring at him, waiting to hear what he would say about this passage. Eyes were shining in anticipation. The passage was a good one. Everyone wanted to hear about the year of the favor of Adonai.

"Right now," Yeshua said, "as you listened to it, this passage was fulfilled."

A murmur of approval went up then. Yes. Yeshua was going to tell them that he was the Messiah, about to break the bonds of poverty and Rome. If he had said so, or even if he had simply stopped speaking right then, probably a large portion of the populace of Natzeret would have followed him that day. But, as Yeshua explained to me later, they wouldn't have followed him long. In any case, he did not stop speaking right then.

"I'm certain," he went on, "you will quote me that old saying—'Doctor, heal yourself!' We've heard about everything going on over there in K'far-Nachum; but this is your hometown! Do those things here, too."

I thought he was right; this was probably exactly what people would expect. It did not seem unreasonable. I listened with growing dismay as he continued to speak. "But truly—prophets are never accepted in their own hometowns. Believe me—when Eliyahu was prophesying, and there was a rainless famine for more than three years, there were plenty of widows, but Eliyahu was sent to one outside of Isra'el in Tzarafat, in the land of Tzidon. Also plenty of people suffered tzara'at in Isra'el during Elisha's time, but only Na'aman the Syrian was cured."

To this day, I do not know whether he intended to say more. The crowd in the synagogue rose with a roar and, united like a storm wave of Kinneret, thrust him out of the building. Hands grasped at his garments, dragging him from his place and toward the door. I stared desperately across the expanse of people at the men—the Twelve. Yochanan and Kefa were struggling to get through the press, but all my townspeople—family, most of them—kept them out. They tightened in a knot and continued to surge forward, and even once they had got Yeshua out of the synagogue, they did not let him go.

I knew where they were headed now. They were taking him to the crest of the hill. My crest of the hill, where I used to sit and think, and where the angel had met me. I could scarcely believe it. These were my family, my friends, my neighbors. But they, those people who had seen Yeshua grow up and who had loved him, were driving him straight to the edge. I began to scream. What were they thinking? Had they gone mad?

One red-faced man at the edge of the crowd heard me above the clamor of voices and turned to me with a snarl. "Not us, woman," he growled, and I could have wept to see it was the husband of one of my own childhood friends. "We've not gone mad; it's him! How dare he speak of his people this way? He's not fit to live!"

It was the ultimate conclusion to all the sorts of thoughts and feelings I myself had had just weeks ago, before I became Yeshua's talmidah. If I decided that my own needs and prejudices were more important than what he claimed Adonai his Father had said, then the logical end to it all would have been to kill my own son. I was discovering that no preconceived prejudice could survive long in Yeshua's presence. Either it had to die or he did.

Now I knew I would rather die myself, and all my silly, easily offended notions with me, than to see this man, who was so much more than simply my son, tumble over the cliff. I lunged toward the crowd, not really expecting to be able to stop them, but not wanting all of this to end without my having tried.

Only then I noticed something strange. The crowd had already stopped. There we all stood, at the brink of the hill, just above the scrub tree under which I used to sit. No one was moving except Yeshua. He had been shoved to the very front of the mob, to the very edge of the cliff, right to the precipice. I couldn't imagine how it was possible he wasn't either still teetering on the edge or hurtling off of it. But he wasn't.

Instead, he simply turned around and faced the frozen mob. The look on his face was one of deep sadness, a sadness that looked as if it had existed since before there were stories. Then he began to walk. The crowd, all those neighbors and relatives and friends who had just now tried to do away with him, parted as if they had no choice. The air was heavy, and I had the sense that all creation had stopped for us, for this moment. Yeshua passed through the aisle between the people, down the hill, and out of sight. We didn't see him again that day.

All the Nazratis shuffled off back to their homes, as did I. I found my sons, and we walked back to the house in silence. Their faces were white under the darkening of the sun, and I could see they were as shaken as I was.

When we returned to the house, no one said anything for a long while. Finally Ya'akov said, "He's my brother. He says stupid things, but he's my brother. I didn't want them to kill him."

I said nothing about my earlier realization that I'd either have to give up my own way or Yeshua would have to die. There was another long stretch of silence until Yosi said, "What if he really were the Messiah? Did you see how the crowd was powerless before him?"

Someone snorted quietly, but then Ya'akov said, "That was more than a simple stunt. Those people were murderous. They really wanted to kill him. They really would have."

Y'hudah said nothing at all.

The rest of the day passed quietly, as Shabbat should. I would have liked to have spent it with my sister, but I couldn't bear to find out that her husband, too, had tried to push Yeshua off the cliff. I didn't know whether he had. I could not remember having seen him, but everything had been confusing. Then, just as I was thinking these things, she appeared in the doorway. She approached me seriously, and we embraced in the same way.

"Is he here?" she asked after a moment.

"No, not here," I replied. Then I added, "Someone will find where he is tomorrow, and we will follow him there. I do not think he will stay in Natzeret." I could not have smiled then even if I wanted to.

But in the morning, when I got up to help my daughters-in-law cook something for the day, there was Yeshua, in our house. He had gotten the cook-fire ready. I took one look at him, remembered the horror of the day before, and felt like a mother. I couldn't help it. Messiah and Son of Adonai he was, but he was still my son, too. I hurried to him and cradled his head in my arms, and he let me.

23

YESHUA STAYED IN NATZERET

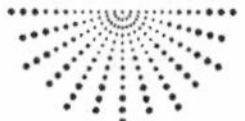

Yeshua stayed in Natzeret longer than I had expected. He healed a few of our neighbors' minor ailments, but not many. He said there was so little trust in our village. It was a quiet time, and many talmidim went back to their homes to wait until Yeshua was ready to travel and teach again. After a few weeks he began to travel about the Galil once more and the crowds increased again, but he did not go south to Judea. He said the people there wanted to kill him. I thought they couldn't have wanted to kill him more than those of his own town had wanted to, but I said nothing, preferring to listen and learn and try to trust that he knew what he was doing.

Before long, the celebration of our festival Sukkot drew near. This festival had its roots in the earliest days of our people, when Moshe was leading us out of Egypt to the land God had promised. Our ancestors had all lived in tents then, and we still celebrated today by setting up makeshift tents and living in them for the week. It was a reminder of our history, but it also had the effect of making me feel like a child playing at house-making. I loved this festival. This year the people of our village, as well as those of many others, began to make preparations to observe this feast in Y'hudah, and to begin the journey south.

Ever since the day when Yeshua had almost gone over the cliff, his brothers had been much kinder to him. It was as if suddenly a wall crumbled between them and they were able to see him as truly their brother again. I thought they even were beginning to get a sense of his true greatness. Perhaps I saw it simply because I wanted to. Nevertheless, though they still could not bring themselves to call him Messiah, or to become his talmidim as my sister and I had, they tried to be supportive of his endeavors.

One day just before the festival, they approached Yeshua, all of them together in a group. "You should go to Yerushalayim," one of them began abruptly, though not unkindly, "Then your talmidim can see your miracles."

Clearly they had realized Yeshua's miracles were limited in this place. The fact that they were now encouraging their eldest brother in what before they had thought so deplorable was somewhat amusing. I almost burst out laughing when I heard Ya'akov's next suggestion. "If you want people to know who you are," he said, "you don't act in secret. Show the world!"

My Ya'akov. In truth, I first had to look at him intently to be sure he wasn't just making fun. When I realized he wasn't, I had to chuckle at least.

Yeshua smiled, too, his eyes as much as his mouth. "It isn't time for me," he said. "Any time is all right for you. The world can't hate you. It hates me, though—I keep telling it how evil its ways are."

My other sons looked at each other and nodded and shrugged. I think I might have seen one of them roll his eyes, but perhaps I only imagined it. That last statement of Yeshua's was true, at any rate. No one had to mention the Shabbat on the cliff's edge to know we were all thinking of it.

"You go on ahead to the festival," Yeshua urged them. "I'm

not going now, because it's not the right time."

After a bit more discussion, Ya'akov eventually agreed to this, and my boys packed themselves and their families, following the rest of the inhabitants of the Galil down to Y'hudah. After some indecision on my own part, I went with them. It seemed strange, after following Yeshua all about the countryside, suddenly to leave him behind and follow my other sons. But I thought he wanted it, maybe, and I knew I would see him again soon enough. The worried feeling I sometimes felt as his mother was not altogether vanished. Still, as Yeshua's talmidah, I had a strange assurance of our belonging together that I had not known before. It made me feel free to go on without him. This is how I discovered that Yeshua's reputation extended far beyond the Galil. Everyone, it seemed, was looking for him.

Yeshua himself like to stay in Beit-Anyah with friends when he was celebrating in Yerushalayim, but as he was not with us, my sons and their families and I set up our makeshift tents in the hilly park near the city under the olive trees. Sometimes Yeshua's talmidim stayed there when the crowd following him was big enough. I had heard this even though I had not been a talmidah for long enough to have been there myself.

A man I slightly recognized as one who had joined our journeying in the Galil for a time, some months before, approached me. He scanned the faces of my children and grandchildren and said, "You're his mother, aren't you?"

I supposed I knew who he meant. "Yes," I said.

"Isn't he here? Where is he?"

"He told us to come down to the festival without him," I said.

In the evening, people built fires and sat and ate around them. The man who had addressed me first clearly lost interest after finding out Yeshua was not there, but I heard people talking about him round every fire, nonetheless.

Clearly, everyone expected him to be at the festival. In all the jostling crowds, we kept overhearing talk about him.

"Where can he be?" the people asked one another.

Some said, "What a good man!"

"You see?" said Ya'akov to us in the morning, as the sun clambered up over the hills and turned the silver olive leaves to gold. This practical son of mine was still unaware of how ironic it was for him to be talking like this. "He should have come. He would have amassed a great following."

But I was not so sure. I had noticed that for every person who spoke well of Yeshua, there was another, or maybe more, who disagreed, saying, "No, he's a liar." I remembered how sentiments like that had almost ended in Natzeret, and I shuddered. I also noticed that most of the people we overheard speaking about Yeshua spoke about him in whispers. This was especially true if the religious leaders were about.

It had not taken long, as Yeshua's talmidah, to learn that the cohanim and other religious types were not too fond of him. It had taken me slightly longer to accustom myself to it. "They're the leaders," I had said to Shlomit one evening in our travels. The men were seated around one fire and we women, having served them already, were finishing up our final morsels of food, licking our fingers and talking about our sore feet. And about the cohanim.

"They're the leaders," Jemima answered, "but Yeshua would call them manmade, wouldn't he? Don't you think? They speak about the Torah, but when I hear him speak about it instead, I always wonder how it was I ever thought their interpretations made sense. His make so much more."

"But they spend their lives studying the Torah," I persisted. I wasn't sure exactly why I was standing up for them since, even as a new talmidah I had seen enough to know that these men were, by and large, my son's enemies. I guess I was just trying to put words to my own bafflement. I had been thinking of this for some time. "It seems to me it shouldn't be possible for someone to read and study and learn the words of Adonai like that every day of his life and then never understand them…or never obey them. How can that possibly be? And how can anyone become a leader unless Adonai ordains it?"

"Why would he ordain such pompous fools?" asked Magdalit. We looked at her, and I, for one, wasn't sure whether to laugh or shush her.

"They must mean well enough, surely," I said. "Even if they somehow don't understand the Torah after all? I mean, not all of us immediately understood Yeshua's purpose." A few heads jerked toward me. I didn't often talk about my doubt of my own son. "I used to object to his teachings, too. But here I am following him. They have to realize who he is sooner or later, I think?"

"That might be true," Shlomit said, "if they only objected to his teachings. I don't think it's that simple, though. Do you? I think they object to *him*. I think they're jealous."

"Yes," agreed Jemima. "They're constantly sending someone to follow Yeshua around, and if he makes us, his own people, look bad, he makes those men look the worst. 'Hypocrites!'" She laughed.

That was Yeshua's favorite expression to describe these fountains of religiosity. I had never heard anyone use the word this way before, but we all knew exactly what he meant when he said it. "Hypocrites" were Greek actors wearing masks to hide their true identities and emotions. In spite of my initial misgivings about defying the religious authorities, after watching their spies and listening to Yeshua long enough, I began to think his description of them was just about right.

"Hypocrites," echoed Magdalit. "He's right. He is our Messiah, and they have no idea. They can't be true to the Torah and not see it. Such men do not deserve their authority and he more than deserves his. When he speaks it makes me wonder how I ever thought the words of the P'rushim and the Tz'dukim meant anything at all." She stopped and then said, almost to herself, "Then again, I suppose I never did. Perhaps that's why there were demons..."

Her voice trailed off and then she spoke to us again: "Besides, Yeshua makes me feel Adonai cares for us again—that if we draw near to Yeshua, we will be nearer to Ha'Elyon himself. I've never felt anything like that before. Have you?"

Now it was Sukkot, and if anything, the tension between these people and my son had only deepened. With Yeshua's authority and popularity, the cohanim and mitzvot teachers seemed very weak. But they were angry. I saw it in their faces as they passed in the city streets. Anger has made many a weak man stronger, and those looks frightened me. I was only glad Yeshua had not come with us after all.

Then, halfway through the feast, he appeared in the Temple courts. Ya'akov was there already. I had stayed behind under the trees. The Temple, while still a glowingly majestic building on the top of its hill, did not enthrall me as it had before Yeshua had run through it like a scouring fire. One of my older grandsons came panting up the hill where we sat in the shade and gasped out, "Yeshua's in the Temple. My father thought you should know."

His father was right. I gathered up my robes and, forgetting myself a little bit, ran after my grandson.

It had not taken long for Yeshua to draw a crowd, and among all the unfamiliar faces of the Judeans, I did also glimpse many more of his talmidim. There were the Twelve, of course, and my friends the women, but also talmidim we had traveled with and encountered in other times and places. As the crowd gathered, Yeshua taught, and as he taught, the crowd kept gathering.

"I thought he said his time hadn't come yet," muttered Ya'akov, obviously put out at having had his suggestion rejected and then taken up again as if he hadn't made it.

"It seems it has now," Shim'on grinned. "But it won't make much difference whether his 'time has come' or not if he doesn't do some miracles again soon. That's what they're all after."

"Oh do hush!" I said. "I want to listen."

So, it appeared, did the crowd, in spite of no miracles and Shim'on's cynical assessment of them. I thought to myself he was probably the one who wanted the miracle. He had missed the one where Yeshua fed all the people.

Then I stopped worrying about my son's wry remarks, because I began to hear more ominous rumblings. "How can this fellow possibly know so much without having studied under a rabbi?" murmured someone near my head. I turned and glanced at the person and realized that one of the Tz'dukim was standing right next to me. Then I looked around and saw that both Tz'dukim and P'rushim were scattered neatly throughout the crowd. My stomach dropped. I looked toward Yeshua again quickly, pursed my lips, and didn't say a thing in response. But under Yeshua's voice, I could hear more whisperings and mutterings.

I don't know how Yeshua knew what they were saying. They weren't heckling him but simply whispering doubts into the ears of already fickle, miracle-greedy people. I suppose he knew in the same way that he was able to heal a paralyzed man or cast out a demon. I suppose his Father told him. It was certainly his Father he talked about when he answered the charges.

"I'm not teaching my own ideas," he announced, as he was always announcing—so often that more people really should have known and believed it by now. "They're from the one who sent me. If you wish to do what God wants, you'll know whether my teaching comes from him or whether I am just inventing it myself. Anyone speaking on his own authority just wants the glory for himself—but if that person tries to gain the glory for the one who sent him, he is honest and trustworthy."

He spoke of Moshe and of the Torah, but the attitude of the crowd was already shifting. They are good at sowing doubt, our religious leaders—these men meant to increase our faith—I thought. I began to listen to the murmurings of the crowds instead of to Yeshua.

"Isn't this the one they mean to kill?" someone asked. I shuddered. He had already said they wanted to kill him.

"But look," responded the companion to the first speaker, "he's speaking freely, and they're leaving him alone. You don't think they've concluded he's the Messiah after all, do you?"

"Of course not," said the first man. "We know where this one's from. When the Messiah comes, no one will know where he's from."

I almost laughed then. Even that Herod all those years ago had known that the Messiah would come from Beit-Lechem. They knew nothing, these men. They probably didn't even know that Yeshua really was from Beit-Lechem, and not from the Galil. As for the other thing—that I had been a virgin at Yeshua's conception and birth because his Father was Ha'Elyon, well, of course they were ignorant of all that, too. I turned to these men and opened my mouth to tell them all this, but then the implications of it all returned to me. I closed it again and turned away.

But Yeshua seemed to have heard them, too, for he was answering them instead. "Ah yes—how well you know me!" he exclaimed. "As well as where I'm from!" A few, but only a very few, people laughed. Then Yeshua got as serious as death. "But truly, I haven't come alone. The one sending me is real, and I know him and am with him. You, however, don't know him at all."

This was too much, obviously, for many. I saw the Temple guards, standing in their places at the edge of the crowd. But at this word, one of them must have gotten a signal from one of the P'rushim or someone. The guards moved forward and the crowd shifted nervously. An arrest. They were going to arrest him at last, and then what would become of us?

Everyone became very quiet, and then someone in the crowd whispered, "When the Messiah comes, how will he possibly do more miracles than this man?"

It was surely a comment not intended for anyone but the speaker's friend, but with the hush that had fallen, everyone heard it. The guards halted, and first I thought they were going to arrest the one who had spoken and then capture Yeshua. They could have done so, as Yeshua was still standing in His place, looking entirely at ease and making no move to escape. But then I looked at the face of the leader of the Temple guard. He was not looking for the speaker. It was as if the whispered words had struck something within him and he knew those words to be true. He was looking at Yeshua, and Yeshua was looking at him and smiling.

Then Yeshua began to speak again. He said something about not being with the people much longer, and the people were asking questions, and I even think there was another half-hearted attempt at arresting him, but I was no longer paying attention. I had just remembered something and was astonished I could have forgotten it and been so faithless.

Of course they would never arrest Yeshua. Or if they did, they could not do much worse. Of course Yeshua would not have gone over the cliff that day. I remembered my felt assurance, thirty years before when we had been running to Egypt. He had not been an ordinary child, nor was he an ordinary man. He was Messiah, and the Son of Ha'Elyon, and Adonai would not let his Messiah die.

And he didn't. On the last day of the festival, Yeshua cried out to us all, "If anyone is thirsty, let come to me again and again! Let him drink and not stop! If you trust in me rivers will flow from your very soul, just as the Tanakh tells you."

I'm certain only Yeshua himself had any true idea of what he meant then. I know I only had the vaguest notion. But I also know that everyone in that crowd heard Yechezk'el's prophecy to which he was alluding. The fulfillment was coming. With a rush, Adonai would finally flood the city with his divine River, just as he had promised, and we would all be washed righteous and follow Yeshua, the slaker of our souls' thirst, to deliverance. One could almost hear it beginning; a muted rustling sound passed through the crowd as the people turned to each other in excitement, their whispers building like water rushing close.

"This man can only be the Prophet."

"This is the Messiah."

But, as usual, someone was bound to disagree. "But the Messiah can't possibly come from the Galil," the dissenters grumbled. "Doesn't the Tanakh say that the Messiah comes from King David's line, and from Beit-Lechem where David lived?"

I wanted to scream at them, "You stupid people! Yeshua is from Beit-Lechem! I should know! I'm his mother!" But I didn't. I, too, had once been one of the "stupid people," and I was beginning to see that it took much more than a recital of the facts for people to really see who Yeshua was. In the evening, we who followed Yeshua all camped out together again in our shelters under the stars, but Yeshua went off on his own soon afterwards. He climbed to the top of the hill and disappeared into a more secluded place.

"He goes to speak with his Father," said Jemimah. We had run into each other in the Temple after Yeshua had appeared teaching. After she said it, she looked at me a little startled, as if realizing what she had said and the implications if Adonai were literally Yeshua's Father.

I smiled but did not enlighten her. "Yes," I said. "I know." The River did not break forth that day.

24
YESHUA WAS STILL MISSING

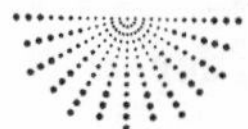

Yeshua was still missing when we woke, but in a few moments a talmid came running up the slope to the camp with the message that he was back at the Temple already. The celebration had run its course, but evidently, having arrived in Yerushalayim late, Yeshua did not intend to head back north again immediately. When we got to the Temple, we saw that a crowd had gathered already, too, and Yeshua was teaching them.

It was not long before a commotion began, and I don't suppose anyone was too surprised to see that the cause of it was a group of P'rushim and Torah-teachers. They all came together in a bunch, and they seemed to be dragging something, or someone. On closer inspection, it appeared to be a woman. She was disheveled, weeping, and looked utterly terrified.

"Rabbi," said one of the P'rushim in a nasal voice which sounded used to ordering people about or accusing them of things, "this woman is no better than a harlot. We caught her in the very act of adultery."

The crowd shifted uneasily. No one liked the P'rushim

much these days, but everyone knew that according to the law handed down by Moshe, adulteresses should be killed. Adulterers should be, too, however. Even I knew this—I, a woman, though likely these men would have been annoyed to find out I knew. I wondered where the man in this adulterous situation was. If this woman had been caught in the act, surely he had been there, too. He must have paid the religious leaders plenty in order to be let off. Or maybe he was one of them.

I was startled by my own thought. Even in my mind I would never have accused our P'rushim and Tz'dukim of such a thing even a year ago. I thought how I would have viewed this scenario then, before I had begun to follow Yeshua and travel with his friends. I would have been uncomfortable for him, of course. These men had set a trap which, blatant though it was, would not be easily dodged. Now, however, I was also outraged on behalf of the woman. In the past I would have avoided even looking at her, for the shame she had brought on herself, and on all women. Before, I would have resented my connection with her. Now I felt drawn to her because of it. I thought of the woman to whom Yeshua had given such dignity and even favor, in the house of a Parush just like these men. She had been a prostitute. I still squirmed when I thought of sins like theirs. I did not understand how Yeshua would answer his accusers in love and justice together, but I knew now that these women were people he loved, and that if he loved them, it must mean Adonai did, too.

"Now," the nasal-voiced Parush continued, bringing me and perhaps others back from our reveries, "according to our Torah, Moshe ordered that such a woman be killed by stoning. What do you say?"

Our Torah. As if Yeshua had a different one. Or lacked one altogether. I looked at Jemimah and rolled my eyes. She grimaced, too, but looked nervous. Either Yeshua would uphold the Torah, which surely was just, for how could adultery be allowed to go unchecked? Or he would grant this woman mercy. One way he could be accused of defiance to Rome, as our people are technically not permitted to issue the death penalty. Or he would be accused of defiance to Adonai, whom he was forever declaring his Father. They were clever, our religious leaders. I thought, not for the first time, that I was beginning to detest them.

But Yeshua did not answer. Instead, he bent down and began writing in the dust with his finger. I could not see, above the heads of others, what he was writing. To this day I do not know. But just the sight of him doing it, and his apparent nonchalance in the face of such a test, was enough to make me want to cough out a startled laugh.

The P'rushim and Torah-teachers did not find it so funny. They kept questioning Yeshua until finally he straightened up. He didn't even look at the woman they had brought, who had stopped crying but not stopped looking terrified. Rather, he looked at her accusers, one by one, and then said, "Are any of you sinless? Let that one be the first to throw a stone at her." After that he didn't look at them again, but bent down once more to write in the dust.

There was a silence. Then one of the elder P'rushim turned slowly away and left. He was followed by another and another. As they were leaving, we in the crowd backed away as well. None of us had accused the woman. None of us had picked up a stone to throw. But we might have, had it come to that. There was something holy happening that we were not yet a part of, and I think it was for that reason that we backed away.

After the last Parush, a young, red-faced fellow, had turned on his heels and stormed off, it became very quiet again. Yeshua stopped writing. He looked up at the woman and then stood and looked at her more intently. "Where did they go?" he asked her. "Is no one here to condemn you?"

"No one, sir," she replied, a little shakily.

"Then I don't condemn you either," Yeshua's voice was so gentle, so tender even, that I found myself wanting to weep, though I did not know why. "Now go home. Don't sin anymore."

25

TO HAVE FORGIVEN AN ADULTERESS

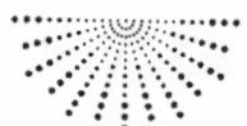

It was, of course, all very well for Yeshua to have forgiven an unknown adulteress. She went, as he had directed her, and it seemed likely that she even refrained from sinning anymore. You didn't very well forget or ignore an encounter with Yeshua like that one. It was also true that I had felt something of a bond with that woman, just on account of being a woman. But sometimes, even as a talmidah, I was still just Yeshua's mother, and sometimes I really did wonder about his choice of friends.

"Do you suppose," I asked my sister Shlomit, a few days after the incident with the adulteress, "that Yeshua chose the Twelve simply to keep an eye on them? They seem to need extra prodding so often." Yeshua had been staying in Beit-Anyah throughout the whole Sukkot festival, coming into Yerushalayim each day. The rest of us had dispersed to stay with friends and family, too, but now Yeshua was getting ready to move back north, we thought. Those of us who had remained in the city were heading off to meet him in Beit-Anyah that evening.

Shlomit smiled at my question. Jemimah appeared around a corner just then and giggled.

"I'm sorry," I said to her quickly, although I don't suppose I was, really. It was just embarrassing to have been caught out by the wife of one of the men I was talking about. "I didn't mean to offend you. Kefa is..."

"Kefa is in need of more watching that most," Jemimah laughed. "As you see, though, I stayed behind to travel with you, not with him. Since following Yeshua, I've walked more than I ever thought I would walk in my life, and I certainly expected to spend more time with a roof over my head. But it's worth it for the help he gives me in keeping Kefa out of scrapes." I laughed with her. When she put it this way, following Yeshua sounded much less high-minded than the way probably most of us thought of it—as if Yeshua were spending all his time minding children.

Magdalit approached then. Her arms were nearly empty, as usual. It seemed she never brought anything with her when she traveled, and yet she never seemed to require anything, and she was always able to help those who needed it. "That," she said, "is why I keep away from husbands. They are altogether too much work." We laughed companionably, but I thought I knew better. I thought there were other reasons Magdalit was still unmarried, and it wasn't the demons. After all, those were long gone. If you didn't know she had had them, you would never be able to tell. I thought she would have married my son, if he'd have had her.

There were other women who probably would have, too. Those two sisters in Beit-Anyah, for example—Marta and Miryam. Yeshua was great friends with their brother, El'azar, and it was with them Yeshua stayed when he came to Yerushalayim. Everyone felt honored when Yeshua paid a visit, but these sisters...It was different with them. I am a woman, and what's more, I was Yeshua's mother, and I could see things. Also, I had heard the story about the first time Yeshua and his Twelve had dined with that family. Apparently Marta, the elder sister, had created a feast fit for a king, while little Miryam had sat at Yeshua's feet with the men and listened to him teach. This was before everyone had got somewhat more used to the idea of a rabbi who had women tagging along among his talmidim. The two sisters had had words, apparently, and Yeshua had told Marta that Miryam had chosen better. I couldn't imagine Marta taking that very happily. I had met her since, and she struck me as highly capable, with high expectations of herself and everyone else. Still, she was always gracious, and she seemed to hold no ill will against her sister, or Yeshua, either.

But women, I noticed, did not long hold grudges against Yeshua. And sometimes I wished he would just choose one and settle down. I sighed about this now. It was not the thing to be talking about in public—not with Magdalit right there. But then Jemimah herself said, "Miryam-Imma, do you not wish you had grandchildren by Yeshua?"

I felt myself reddening as if I had been asked another sort of question entirely, and when I looked up, I saw a faint flush on Magdalit's face, too. She was very studiously not looking at any of us, or even around at her surroundings. Her eyes were carefully focused on the ground. She kicked a pebble. I did not want to make her uncomfortable.

"Sometimes," I said. "Sometimes I wish he would just choose a nice girl and settle down with her."

"Yes," Shlomit mused, allowing the idea to take her, even though we had spoken of this before, she and I, and had agreed that in reality Yeshua could never have a family. "Imagine what his children would be like...so beautiful and good. The world could be transformed that way."

I smiled to myself, imagining just that.

But then Magdalit looked up. Her large dark eyes filled with flashes of fire almost, and she said fiercely, "It wouldn't do at all. Don't you see? Not at all!"

We stared at her. I suppose we were all surprised she

would think like this, but also that she would speak so heatedly about it.

"Yeshua can't marry," she said. "He's different. And besides, then he would belong to someone—to that one person. It would separate him from the rest of us. He came to deliver the whole world, and how could he do that, settling down, not teaching the people, not loving us, just focused on his one little family? But as he is...just himself and his Father as he is...well then, he can be for all of us, and we can all be his family, And maybe we're not so beautiful and good as any children he might have naturally, but maybe we're becoming that way, by getting to be with him. And then maybe, isn't it a better way to change the world—by fixing the people who are already in it, instead of just making more all the time?"

I wanted to retort, "But I made more, and look, here he is, making the world better!" I had never heard another woman say something so outrageous. All the Mothers of Israel had spent their lives mothering Israel, bearing and raising children, even at great cost. I thought of Elisheva, and I glanced at Shlomit to see if she felt as I did, that the role of mother had just been denigrated. Still, I couldn't say anything like what I wanted, because I myself had not made Yeshua. Adonai had given him to me.

Shlomit either did not notice my look or was ignoring it. We had all stopped walking as Magdalit went on, and now my sister laid a hand gently on the young woman's arm. "Magdalit," she said, "we didn't mean to upset you."

Jemimah, being young like Magdalit and feeling the need for words where maybe silence would have been better, added, "But it could be you, couldn't it? He could marry you."

I drew in my breath involuntarily. These were conversations to which I did not want to be privy. I was Yeshua's mother. Although I certainly would have had the right—nay, the duty—to find a wife for my son, I was not sure that was my right in the case of this particular son. Therefore, I had no desire to look like I was either encouraging or discouraging hopes about him in any direction.

"No," said Magdalit. "It would never do. He cannot marry anyone. Ever. Because he is for all of us."

Jemimah spent a little more time trying to tease more words out of her. I could not tell if she wanted a confession of infatuation from her friend, or if she wanted to understand better what it was that Magdalit meant. I would have liked to understand it better, too. I am a mother—and a grandmother, too—and I would have loved nothing more than to see my eldest son devoted to a woman and raising children with her. But perhaps Magdalit was right. He was the Messiah. While it might have been possible for his talmidim to travel with their wives, I was not sure that the life of the Messiah himself could truly allow for a family.

"Whoever does what my Father wishes, that one is my family," he had said. Magdalit was right somehow. He was for everyone. He could not take a wife.

26

THE BATTLE WAS AGAINST BLINDNESS

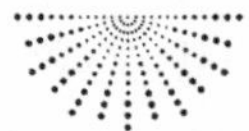

The Twelve and we women who had stayed near Yerushalayim after Sukkot, all spent one evening at El'azar's with Yeshua. In the morning, he said, we were going to travel back up to the Galil. "It's like wandering in the desert with Moshe," I said to the women as we set to bundling up our belongings yet again. "Adonai led them in the cloud and the fire and every time he moved, our people had to break camp and follow."

"Yes," said Magdalit. "Following Yeshua is just like that—except for our already being in Eretz-Yisra'el of course."

"Yes, except for that." I chuckled. "One day, just as Moshe led our people here to Eretz-Yisra'el, so Yeshua will lead us to victory over our enemies, and this land will belong to Adonai and the people once again!"

But not the day we moved again. This day, the battle was against blindness.

It was Shabbat. Of course, it had been Shabbat the evening before; we had all rested together, even in the evening meal, which Marta and Miryam—or at least Marta—had prepared for all of us beforehand. But in the morning it was still Shabbat. I dare say there were more than a few of us who felt a little guilty about traveling at all on that day. I dare say all of us knew some Parush or other would find fault because of it. But we did not go far. We left Beit-Anyah, it is true, but then we stopped at the next nearest synagogue. As we made our way there, however, Natan'el caught sight of a blind man. There was some discussion amongst a few of the Twelve, and by the time I was aware of it, they were bringing Yeshua into it.

"Rabbi," Natan'el asked, not bothering to keep his voice down. One didn't, I supposed, around blind people—as if their lack of sight meant they couldn't hear either, when very often it was the opposite. "Who sinned—this man or his parents—to cause him to be born blind?"

We wonder about such things, our people. When Adonai gave us the teachings of our Torah through Moshe, he said that if we followed those teachings, we would be blessed. If not, the curses visited onto us would be terrible. After centuries of our ancestors' disobeying the very laws that should have blessed us—after centuries of wars and famines and other discipline at the hand of Adonai—finally we made the association. Now, although we were captive to Rome in our own country--and this, too, was a result of our people's sin, most thought—we were much more careful about obeying the laws in the Torah. The P'rushim saw to that. They and other scholars pored over the words of our Scriptures and drew out meaning, and built up a series of interpretations around the commands that were already there, so that, by keeping those, we would be well-protected from breaking the ones at the center of it all.

But someone must have broken through the rules in this poor man's case. In that event, there was no need to lower our voices in discussing his sins, since he—or someone—had obviously brought this affliction on himself. Yeshua answered back just as loudly as Natan'el had asked. "He is blind," Yeshua said, "not because either he or his parents sinned; he is blind so you can see God's power in him. While there is opportunity, I have to keep doing my Father's work. Night is falling, and no one can see to work when it's dark. But as long as I am in the world, I am its light."

Suddenly there was a sound of someone spitting. It was Yeshua himself, making mud. He bent down and put the mud on the eyes of the blind man. "Go," he said to the man as we watched. "Rinse your eyes at Shiloach!" Off the man went, scarcely stumbling, and I marveled again at the fact that blind people could go anywhere by themselves. I was certain I couldn't if I lacked my two eyes.

We went into the synagogue then, and I thought perhaps we had seen the end of that miracle. I did not doubt that Yeshua had healed the man. I was sure that, after the fellow washed in the pool as Yeshua had directed him, he would return home seeing. But it was rare in those days of traveling not to see the miracle completed. I sat with the group of women talmidim and wondered at a man being born blind so that God's power might be seen at work in him.

I confess I did not, therefore, attend very well to the things the men were reading and saying that day. I kept thinking about Adonai demonstrating his power through affliction. It was true, I mused, that sometimes our people had suffered through no fault of our own. The most obvious instance was when our ancestors were slaves in Egypt—the very event which led to our deliverance and the giving of Torah. Adonai had shown his power in so many ways, over so many years, during that time. If we hadn't been in captivity, we never would have needed deliverance, and if we hadn't needed deliverance, we would never have known how magnificent Adonai is. We would never have known how he is the source of our lives and our livelihood and our purpose.

I supposed maybe there was some sense in afflicting an entire nation, because then when the affliction was lifted, an enormous number of people would know about it and thus be able to bring glory to God. Still, when I thought about the poor blind man, the whole situation did seem rather out of proportion. Although my mind shrank from thoughts of blasphemy, I couldn't help feeling that afflicting a man with blindness for a lifetime was a little cruel, when probably only he and his family would ever know about the results of his healing. It wasn't as if the nation would be saved because of it.

So lost was I in my reverie that Shlomit had to shake my shoulder when everyone got up to leave. "Miryam," she whispered. "We're going. Were you praying?"

"Perhaps," I said. "I'm not sure what I was doing." My ankles were sore and wobbled a little as I stood, from having sat too long in one position. When we got back out into the sunshine, I felt a little blind myself. Then when my eyes focused again, I realized our whole group had stepped into something of an uproar. Yeshua, however, was nowhere to be seen.

A group of P'rushim seemed to be interrogating a few people. On closer inspection, I felt sure it was the man who had been born blind, as well as an older couple. The man himself did not appear to be blind anymore.

The older man standing near him was talking nervously. "Yes, he is our son," he was saying, "and yes, he was born blind; but we don't know how he can see now. We don't know what happened. We don't know who healed him." He sounded almost breathless with panic, poor man, and I could sympathize. No one wanted to get on the wrong side of the local P'rushim.

"Shabbat!" I heard the talmid T'oma mutter under his breath, as the reality of the situation dawned on me as well. "Why does Yeshua insist on healing on the Shabbat, anyhow? It's like he wants to rub it in their faces—but now he isn't even here, and look at these poor people having to take the blame themselves."

I hadn't heard any of the Twelve utter such skeptical comments about their Rabbi before, but I supposed maybe they did when I wasn't around. Everyone knew I was his mother. In any case, this T'oma had a point. The panic-stricken man and his family could quite possibly be barred from the synagogue for crossing the leaders. Even if one did not regularly attend, it would never do to have the choice taken away. It was a little like being banned from the community altogether. Not to mention that such a singling out of his family would reflect particularly badly on this old man as the head of it.

The older woman, who must have been the frightened man's wife, looked ill at ease, too. Still, it didn't prevent her saying in a rather loud undertone after her husband had finished speaking, "Ask him! He's old enough to speak for himself!" I looked at Shlomit, who raised her eyebrows and suppressed a grin.

The formerly blind man was still in the vicinity. He appeared, however, to be completely and utterly awestruck and distracted by all he was finally seeing. I felt sorry for him, that his first good look at people was at frightened and angry ones. I felt sorry that his indisputable good fortune had resulted in such fear and anger. Yet he seemed remarkably unperturbed by it all. I supposed even twisted angry faces would be fascinating to look at if you had never seen a face before in your life.

The P'rushim did not, to my surprise, berate the mother for her biting remark, but instead turned back to her son. It took them a moment to regain his attention. With all of them focused once again on the healed man, the two old parents slunk away. Talmid Yochanan, who had stayed closer to me and the other women like T'oma, while the others had gone off to find Yeshua, shook his head. "That was badly done," he said. "That man may not have been born blind for anyone's sin, but there is something wrong with that family."

Meanwhile, the P'rushim had regained the man's attention and were interrogating him for what I was sure was not the first time.

"Swear before God to tell the truth!" demanded a Parush whose voice brooked no argument. "Your healer is a sinner."

The formerly blind man, indifferent to the tone of the man's voice, said stolidly, "Sinner or not, I can't tell you. What I can say is, I used to be blind, but now I can see."

"But what did he do, this man? How did he accomplish this trick?" asked another leader.

"I've told you everything already," the man replied, "You're not listening. Why do I need to tell you again? Do you want to become his talmidim, too?"

At that Shlomit giggled. "Clearly he takes after his mother," she whispered.

"Good for him," I nodded.

"You yourself may be that man's talmid," railed a Parush, turning red and resorting to childish insult tactics, "but we follow Moshe! God spoke to Moshe, but no one even knows where this man is from!"

These religious people kept saying that. It was getting monotonous and starting to sound threadbare. I had half a mind, again, to step in and clear up the mystery once and for all. But, as at every other time, I held my tongue.

"How strange," the man said, looking at the P'rushim directly and unabashedly, perhaps unaware because of his long sightlessness that one did not address a Parush that way, "that you can't guess where he's from—given that he gave me my sight! I've heard Adonai doesn't listen to sinners, but if someone respects Adonai and obeys him—God listens to that one. Never before have I heard of someone's opening the eyes of a man born blind. If this man weren't from Adonai, he couldn't do a thing!"

I felt myself holding my breath with awe and admiration.

It seemed that perhaps Yochanan and Shlomit were doing the same thing.

Then the storm broke. "Why you scum!" the P'rushim shouted. They seemed to be shouting a lot these days. "Are you preaching at us?" Then they grabbed him by the elbows and threw him out of the synagogue premises.

After that there was no reason for the rest of us to remain either, so we left. The man had disappeared quickly, but Yeshua was just returning. "Yeshua's going to go find him," Yochanan's brother Ya'akov said. The rest of us followed at a distance.

We found the man fairly quickly. He was meandering down a side street staring at everything. Or maybe he was looking for something. Or someone. It occurred to me just then that he still had never seen Yeshua.

But Yeshua had seen him. He strode up behind him and placed a hand on his shoulder. "Do you trust the Son of Man?" he asked. "Son of Man" was what Yeshua liked to call himself. It was a name of mystery. He was my son, but not Yosef's. I never quite knew why, if he were going to name himself, he didn't insist on "Son of God," but surely he had his reasons.

"Sir," answered the man, looking intently at Yeshua's face, "if I knew who he was, I would trust him."

Yeshua smiled. "You are looking at him," he said.

The man fell to his knees with a "Lord, I do trust you!" Yeshua did not tell him to rise. He never prevented people from worshiping him. This usually still made me uncomfortable. I did not think I would ever understand it. But there was something about Yeshua, I knew, that truly was one with his Father, and as the man who was worshiping at his feet right now had said, God wouldn't listen to a bad man. It therefore could not be blasphemy in Yeshua's case, if he allowed people to worship him. This time, watching the seeing man worship my son, I felt nothing but the rightness of it.

Only immediately after that, I felt the tension of disapproval over my shoulder. In that moment I realized that the P'rushim, in spite of evicting the man from their presence, had followed him.

As if he were completely unaware of their presence—and as if he were fully aware of it—Yeshua said, "I came into this world to judge it, so that the blind might see, and the seeing might become blind."

"So," said a Parush, "are you calling us blind, too?"

"If you were blind," said Yeshua, glancing up but then turning his attention back to the worshiping man, "you would be guilty of nothing. But you are still convinced that you see how things really are—and given that, your guilt remains."

As usual, I spent the evening wondering. No doubt God was glorified by the giving of sight to a blind man. But it seemed I had heard more dissension and anger that day than praise. Yeshua had made the P'rushim angry again, healing on Shabbat and calling them blind. The seeing man's parents had essentially left him to fend for himself. Those of us following Yeshua surely glorified God in our hearts—or at least we would after the questions abated. It was dreadful to suspect that the healing miracles were starting to feel routine and unsurprising—except, perhaps, when the talmidim performed them, which we sometimes did. But whether this were the case or not, none of us talmidim needed another miracle to persuade us of who Yeshua was.

From that perspective, the only new person giving glory to God because of Yeshua was the seeing man. Had he truly been born blind only so that he—one lone man—could meet the Messiah and give glory to God?

I was starting to expect to think new thoughts whenever Yeshua did or said anything, but the thoughts themselves continued to surprise me. Did Adonai require glory from individuals, and not just our chosen race?

It was true, he had shown interest in individuals when he chose me to bear his son. I still could not fathom why, however. I supposed sometimes he just needed to settle on someone, all of us imperfect and marred. He, in his separateness and goodness, could still, by his might, express something of himself through us if he wished. I supposed something like this had been behind his choice of me. Someone had to mother the Messiah, strange as it still seemed, given what I was coming to understand about the Messiah.

But Adonai's choice of this man was different. It could, I realized, have happened that we not witness the end of the miracle. In that case, the man would still have defended Yeshua to the P'rushim, without ever seeing him. After that he might very well, I supposed, have perished in obscurity, the only one to ascribe glory to God over the incident.

Was it possible that Adonai had sent his Messiah, not just for the Jewish people as a whole, not even also for the Gentiles as a group, but for individual people as well? Was the Anointed One anointed to deliver men and women from the sin and sorrow of their lives, as well as to deliver nations from oppression?

I pondered these thoughts for many days. And I gave glory to God. But the trouble with individuals is that they can reject you.

27

HOW THE TWELVE SAW IT

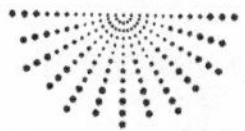

We were on the move again for a time. In one town a gaggle of mothers accosted us with their children. At least, that was how the Twelve saw it. And it is true that it is more difficult to move with any sense of purpose if children are suddenly frolicking about one's feet. But who said we had anywhere to go, really? Yeshua quite clearly always had a destination in mind, but it was never very clear what or why it was, or even when we were meant to get there.

And there were these children. All we women, except for Magdalit, who had held herself a bit apart from us since we had talked about marrying off Yeshua that day, and who sometimes seemed a bit afraid of children, smiled at the newly arriving mothers. We held out our arms to the little ones. But the Twelve frowned and sighed and huffed and tried to shoo them away. "He has more important things to do," grumbled the one called Y'hudah from K'riot. "We're traveling."

Just because that Y'hudah said it made me want to bring all the children with us wherever we went for the rest of the day. Or better yet, to sit down with them and not go anywhere. On the other hand, I would not have liked to subject any child to too much of the presence of that one from K'riot. There was something not right about him, I thought. I knew my son had lived more than thirty summers and he could take care of himself. But when it came to the one from K'riot, I felt like the mother who worried because her child had taken up with the wrong sorts of friends. I could never say why, although when I tried to describe it to Shlomit, she agreed with me.

"Maybe it's because he's clever," she suggested, still trying to be charitable. "He has more learning than all the rest of them combined. Than all the rest of us. He has more learning than Yeshua. But Yeshua has wisdom, and he has his connection to his Father. We needn't worry about Y'hudah, I think. Yeshua knows who he's got around him." As usual, I could not argue with her, but I still felt something like revulsion over that man. And Shlomit could not argue with that.

Meanwhile, there was this problem of the children. Although I wanted, if it would not have somehow irreparably damaged the child, to make Y'hudah from K'riot pick up one of the toddlers and carry her, I did not feel I could speak up. I did not feel I could truly say anything to any of them—those Twelve.

Even though Yeshua treated his female talmidim quite as equals to the men, still, the Twelve were the ones for whom he had stayed up all night praying. They were the chosen of the chosen. Not to mention that most of us women were not accustomed to being allowed to speak up to a group of men. Nor were the men so accustomed, for that matter. You had to earn the right to do that. Sometimes I felt I had. I was older than most of both the men and the women, and I was mother to the one we were following. They called me Imma—mother—out of respect. But at the same time, I wasn't really mother in the way in the way most women get to be mothers to their sons. I had grown heartily tired of hearing that

Yeshua's time for whatever it was I had told him to do, had not yet come, and of not being able to predict when "his time" would come, or when he would find what I was saying eminently reasonable as I always thought it was. This lack of authority and a firm footing was worse than any argument between two parents, because the Father in this case was invisible to me, and who was I to say what he had or had not actually told our son?

Then there was the simple thought, "our son." When Adonai himself is the other half of the "our," I suppose it should not be surprising that even decades after the event, I sometimes hesitated and stumbled in my mind as to what my role was. Adonai had chosen me as his hand-maiden, and so did that not give me some right to tell Yeshua what to do? Yet Adonai was still Adonai, and who can instruct him—or his son? I would not counter his talmidim simply because I did not want to be contradicted by this man I had borne in my womb for nine moons and borne in my heart for much longer. This day I settled for glowering at the K'riot and saying nothing.

But then it turned out that today was a day when Yeshua would have done what I said, thereby still rendering it useless for me to say it. I wondered briefly whether Yeshua ever contradicted me just for the delight of it. For example, if I had said, aloud, "Look at the children. You were once one of them, son. Don't send them away without blessing them," would he have said, "My time for children has not yet come"? I would never know, because now he rounded on his Twelve like the stubborn mules they were and said, "Stop pushing the children away. Let them come here! The Kingdom of God is for them in the end."

The men parted, muttering, embarrassed. In spite of my rather cynical musings about Yeshua's contrariness to his own mother, the chance of his turning children away was, in reality, small. Yeshua was so frequently telling us of our need to be like children, I couldn't understand why the Twelve had such difficulty remembering this. But then, no man that I've ever heard of likes to be called a child, even when he acts quite a bit like one. And it wasn't just the men, of course. One time Yochanan and Ya'akov's mother, who sometimes traveled with us, had tried to cajole Yeshua into making both her sons his second in command when he came into possession of the Kingdom. That didn't settle so well with the rest of the men—or with their wives and mothers who were among us. That was the first time Yeshua had told us all we needed to be like children. I had thought then that everyone was behaving more childishly than usual, but I don't suppose that was what he meant.

Perhaps that was why it was so difficult for us all, and for the Twelve in particular at this moment, to take seriously his command to be like children. Perhaps all we could think of was pettiness. Or perhaps in some way we didn't think Yeshua really meant it. But Yeshua never said anything without meaning it. Meaning it again this time, he said firmly, "Honestly! If you can't accept God's Kingdom like a child, you can't even get in!" He seemed rather stern about it, and I had another sort of moment that I'd been having lately —where sense of motherly rights dissolved and I felt like a child indeed, whom he was teaching. It didn't matter, in those times, whether I had ascribed to the prevailing view which he was correcting. I was a talmidah, and we were all included in the rebuke together.

In this particular case, his rebuke meant that we did, after all, let the little children go to him. This meant we stayed there for a while, as the children approached him—some timidly, some boisterously—and he blessed them. However they approached, you could see in their small faces that they wanted to be near him. They wriggled in delight under his gaze, and under his hands on their heads.

I found myself wishing again, and then glancing guiltily at

Magdalit for thinking such things, that Yeshua would, in fact, marry. He would, I thought to myself for the thousandth time, have made a wonderful father. And then I thought, in a flash that only stayed with me a moment, that he really was a wonderful father—to us, the ones he kept calling children. Even though there were times, as now, when I felt more like a child in my son's presence than like his mother, I had never thought of us in quite this way—as really his children. It gave me a start and I gave up thinking about it almost immediately. Yet still, it stayed somewhere within me, like the names given to Yeshua by the prophets in the Temple, all the way up to the things I had learned from the blind man about giving glory to Adonai.

Eventually the last child received Yeshua's blessing. The mothers collected the stragglers and herded them away, and we rose and began to move onward, too.

The remains of the crowd that had gathered but was not accompanying us, began to disperse. But suddenly a figure pushed through the departing people and approached Yeshua. It was a young man. He was dressed in such a way as to exhibit that he was wealthy without looking like he was exhibiting it.

"Good Rabbi," he said, addressing Yeshua politely, but more as an equal than people usually did, "What good work do I need to perform to gain eternal life?"

"You do know," Yeshua asked, "that only God is good, don't you? But if you want everlasting life, keep the mitzvot."

"Which ones?" asked the young man.

"No murder," Yeshua recited the familiar words to him, "no adultery, don't steal, don't slander, respect your parents, love your neighbor as much as you love yourself."

The man suddenly looked very like a boy—the kind of boy who always knew the right answers to give the rabbis at shul. "I have kept these mitzvot," he said, confirming the impression.

It was hard to read Yeshua's face. It was hard even for me to know at the best of times what he was thinking, but now it was nigh impossible. Yeshua never said anything he didn't mean. He obviously was telling the truth: following the Torah led to life. But there was something behind his words. He was telling the truth. He was acknowledging that the man knew the right answer. But perhaps there was more to eternal life than the right answer.

The young man's face displayed anxiety, as if he were aware that something was missing. "What else have I got to do?" he said, the anxiety leaking into his words.

Yeshua's face changed then as he looked at him. He looked as if he knew this young man at the depths of his soul and enjoyed what he found there. He looked as if he would have loved nothing better than to add this man to his group of talmidim, to talk and laugh and break bread with him. But behind Yeshua's eyes was sorrow, too.

"If you really mean it," he said, "if you really wish to live forever, sell everything, give your wealth to the poor, and you will be wealthy in heaven. Then come with me!" His eyes shone with the welcome of his offer. His voice was warm.

But the man cast a stricken glance at Yeshua's face and turned back the way he had come. He did not hold his head up as he had at his approach. His understated elegance hung off him now, awkwardly and no longer like a birthright.

Watching him go, Yeshua sighed. "It's so difficult," he sighed, "for the rich to enter the Kingdom. It would be easier for a camel to squeeze through the eye of a needle than for a rich person to enter the Kingdom of God."

This was a fairly vivid illustration of impossibility, and Kefa burst out what we were all thinking, "But who can be saved then?"

If not the rich, then who? The rich—and those with the correct answers—were the ones with privilege in our world. Doors opened for them which would be slammed in the face of a fisherman—even a successful one like Kefa—or of a hill-country mother like me. This man had both qualifications, and yet Yeshua was saying he could not enter the Kingdom of God. It was true that our Scriptures have some choice words to say against the rich, but still everybody thought that in the end wealth was a blessing, not a curse, and that anyone who had it was particularly favored by Ha'Elyon.

I chuckled to myself as the truth dawned on me. I was the favored one. The angel had told me I was, because Adonai himself was with me, not because wealth was. I had never been wealthy—not ever—but Yeshua was greater favor than anyone could ever have imagined being given. After chuckling, however, I felt as if someone had struck me in the stomach and I thought for a moment that I might become ill. That man. That poor young man. No wonder Yeshua had looked at him like that. Yeshua himself was the treasure, and the man had blindly chosen the wrong thing. He had missed the right answer after all.

I thought about the earlier hours of the day—all of those children, all of those mothers, laughing in the sunshine, but laughing more in Yeshua's presence. Children, I remembered—remembered from seeing them that day and from having had my own and also from the dim memories of having been one—don't know about wealth, and they know very few of the answers. But they loved Yeshua. The children this morning couldn't get enough of him. They would have followed him anywhere if they could have. The young man, on the other hand, had chosen his wealth instead. He was boyish, but he wasn't enough of a child anymore to trust Adonai with giving it up. I began to understand why Yeshua kept telling us to be children. "Humanly," he said now, "it's all impossible; but God makes everything possible."

"Look," said Kefa, boasting like a child. "We've left everything behind so we can follow you. What will we get for that?"

"You have, indeed," Yeshua agreed. "Anybody who gives up home or spouse, brothers and sisters, parents or children, for God's Kingdom's sake, will get that much more and then some in the present world, and in the coming age, they will get eternal life."

That sensation of having been struck still gaped in the pit of my stomach. The feeling was, I knew, the terror of truth. It was almost something like I had felt on that rock, on that hillcrest, all those years ago when Yeshua was conceived. I was beginning, as I had then, to live out the terrifying truth. I had left my home and quarreled with my boys over this, my son whom I could scarcely anymore call (but still so deeply loved as) "my boy." But family and country are everything to my people. Do you see? "My people." It was easier to give them up if I closed my eyes and jumped, as it were. It was harder to do if I thought about it. But Yeshua seemed to require decision, commitment. One could be born a Hebrew. One could not, apparently, be born a talmid or talmidah of Yeshua.

I thought of the seeing man of some weeks before. The parents of his birth had essentially disowned him for his good fortune and his decision of loyalty toward the one who had brought it to him. In the end, it came down to people one by one, I thought. Everything narrowed and narrowed until a person was left all alone, face to face with Yeshua. And he would look into your soul and ask you to give up the thing you most cherished in the world.

If you said yes, you might find out he had kept for you what you had given him all along. I had given up the dream of Yosef in order to bear this child—this man. When I did, he gave me Yosef back. I had had to give up my rights as his mother in order to follow him, but when I did, I was granted the privilege to stay with him for, evidently, as long as I lived. If the rich young man had, in fact, given up his wealth, I had no doubt he would have found himself the richer, somehow or other. And when we gave up our community, our leaders, our sense of identity, for Yeshua, suddenly we found ourselves enveloped in a new community, with him as our identity. After passing through the needle's eye, we lone camels entered a land of depth and breadth and fullness and communion. Approaching it, we each had felt it was impossible. Who could really choose such a narrow way? But with Adonai, as the angel had said when I first began squeezing through that small space, nothing was impossible.

28

MOTHERS' CHILDREN DO DIE

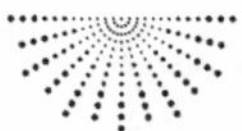

Except it still did seem impossible that Yeshua could die, and he kept talking about it.

Maybe it's just that a mother can't bear to think about her child dying. But mothers' children do die. It was a soul-rending reality. Everyone knew someone who had lost a child, though of course no one wanted it to happen to her own. These are things you learn when you are young. No one tries to hide it from you. Yet I could not imagine Yeshua dying. More than the fact that I was his mother, I think this was because I had never known anyone who seemed more alive. It was almost as if, somehow, he and life were inseparable. But after the incident with the young man, Yeshua began talking more and more about having to die.

"He speaks in metaphors," said Y'hudah, the clever one from K'riot. Not all of us knew what metaphors were until he told us. "This is another metaphor, of course."

In spite of the fact that it was the K'riot who said this and there was still something about him that made my skin crawl, this seemed a likely explanation. Yeshua never said anything without parables. But if this were a parable, he was suddenly getting very stuck on the same one, and he never explained it so that it became clear. The other problem was, I myself never heard him talk about it.

The only reason I knew anything at all about Yeshua's talk of dying was that some time after I became a talmidah, Kefa told me. He came to me quite shaken one afternoon, sniffling a little in his beard and calling me "Imma." They all called me that eventually, but I was still new enough among the travelers at the time that I wasn't completely accustomed to it. I supposed he called me that because his own mother-in-law had gone home for a bit, and Jemimah had gone with her.

"Imma!" the big fisherman burst out, rubbing his eye a little bit. "He said I'm Satan! He just called me Satan!"

For a moment I felt as if I were mediating a squabble between children. Sometimes I intentionally forgot about who Yeshua was proving to be, and I just wished he would mind his tongue. I wanted to say, "I'm sure he didn't mean it," but with Yeshua, that was never the case. Even if it were, no one would call someone the name of the Adversary in jest.

I didn't know what to say after all, and I'm sure my face showed my bewilderment. I simply held out my arms to the distraught young man and he buried his face in my shoulder, just as if I really were his mother. He was slobbery, for a man. But then, men so rarely cry it always does turn to slobber with them. "What happened?" I asked, after he stood up properly again.

"We were out with him, just us, you know, like sometimes?" He paused, as if to make sure I was listening. I nodded. "And he started talking about dying. He said he was going to go to Yerushalayim and the elders were going to make him suffer. He said he had to be killed."

I felt a chill run through me, unlike anything I had felt before. "Killed?" I whispered. "He can't be killed..."

"That's what I said!" Kefa exclaimed. "I only said that. 'By heaven, no, Lord!' I said. I even invoked Heaven, you see?

'There is no way this will happen to you!'" At this point, the big hearty fisherman burst into full-fledged sobs. I could see why. The very idea of Yeshua's being put to death at any time, by anyone, was enough to melt a heart of stone, I thought. But Kefa still hadn't told me about the Adversary bit. So I kept my own eyes dry and waited until he could continue.

"Then," he sputtered, trying his hardest to compose himself, "then he turns on me—you know those eyes! You know how they look when he's displeased...well, maybe you don't; I don't suppose he's ever displeased with you, being his mother and all..."

"Oh, I think I know," I said, chuckling a little in spite of myself. "I don't believe I have any exemption from anything as his mother. But," and this I genuinely could not understand, "why was he so angry?"

"I don't know!" Kefa cried. "He just turned and stared at me, and that was when he said, all cold and like we weren't friends and never had been, 'Get behind me, Satan! You are blocking my way with your merely human thinking. You can't see the way God sees things at all!'"

How was this even possible? First, the fact that Yeshua would ever say such a thing to this man, who was, I knew, one of the best friends he had, was completely baffling. But second, I could not begin to imagine how Kefa's simple horror at the idea of his Lord's death could be such an offense. How was such thinking not from God's perspective? Yeshua was himself from Ha'Elyon—directly from Ha'Elyon. God was his Father, for goodness' sake. How could God's perspective, then, be for him to die at the hands of enemies? I thought I would never understand it.

"Can you talk to him?" asked Kefa.

So I did, but when it came down to it, I was too afraid to ask him myself about this dying-talk. I merely addressed the problem of a rift between friends. Yeshua, however, did not seem to think there was a rift at all, and when I watched the men interact, it really did not seem to me that Yeshua treated Kefa any differently than he ever had. "Well, but talk to him," I urged my son. But that was silly. Yeshua was not afraid to address problems among us.

After a time, things seemed back to normal, but after the encounter with the rich young man, I began to hear rumors again. This time it was Yochanan, the brother of Ya'akov, who told me. I liked this talmid. He, along with his brother and Kefa, was one of Yeshua's three closest friends. Whatever I thought about others of the Twelve, I had full confidence in the three. This Yochanan especially.

"But why doesn't he talk to all of us about it?" I asked Yochanan when he brought it up.

"I don't know," he said, wrinkling up his nose in puzzlement. It was a way he had. "I don't know why he talks about it at all—that's why I asked you. I thought you might understand him, being his mother and all."

"Sometimes," I said, "I feel like that makes me even less qualified than others to understand him. I certainly didn't at the start of his ministry, did I?"

"But you're with us now," Yochanan laid a comforting hand on my shoulder. "Y'hudah from K'riot says he must be telling parables, and I confess that's all I can imagine, but parables usually become clear after some time or other. Or he explains them. I'm not making any headway with this one at all."

I talked to the K'riot myself later, to see if he had any idea of how to interpret this particular parable or metaphor, as he called it. But his interpretation was long and confusing; I felt more in the dark than ever, afterwards. I told myself I shouldn't have been surprised. I did not want to worry the other women, so I said nothing. I suppose they knew something, too, though no one broached the subject to anyone else, so it was difficult to tell.

Under this cloud of perplexity, things really did begin to take a take on a serious cast. Yeshua's encounters with the leadership became more and more difficult—like the time he healed that brave blind-but-now-seeing-man—and more frequent. Our travels had always had a purposeful direction before, though I never fully understood what that purpose was. But now I began to catch glimpses of it, and the purposes seemed to be avoidance. Yeshua would not go to Yerushalayim. He would not even visit his friends in Beit-Anyah for some little while. Then we got news that El'azar had fallen sick.

"He's very sick, apparently," Magdalit said, bringing us women the news. "I suppose we'll be going down soon. We'd best ready the supplies."

"But he doesn't want to go south," protested Shlomit. "At least, he hasn't wanted to, and I can't imagine he has risen in anyone's favor down there yet."

"I don't suppose he has," I said, "but he wouldn't leave his friend, would he? He has healed so many before this; surely he wouldn't leave his friend to die. Or he could heal him the way he did that centurion's servant, perhaps. His Father will protect him. He always has. If it were not for that, Yeshua could have been arrested any number of times now." I spoke as if I knew all about it, when really, I was feeling less and less certain about anything. I could not imagine that all this time of traveling and ministry and learning and teaching and goodness would end in a death. Not Yeshua's death. At least not until he had delivered our people, truly, because otherwise, what was the purpose of a Messiah, and why had Adonai given him to me?

Still, a sneaking suspicion had been growing in my mind and heart. The K'riot was wrong in spite of all his learning and all his words and ideas about metaphors and such things. Everything I heard from the Twelve made these words about dying sound like a warning. If they were a warning of something to come, and if Yeshua really was to return to Yerushalayim to die, then perhaps the time was coming now. Beit-Anyah was so close to the city. Perhaps this journey down would be the last.

I tried to remember all the other things about Yeshua I had stored up since he was born, but now I had to add this great fear to them all, and it overshadowed them so that I couldn't think straight.

And then we did not go to Beit-Anyah. At least, we did not go right away. When Yeshua received the news about El'azar, he seemed completely unconcerned. "What is wrong with you?!" I shouted in a moment of abandon. He never treated his friends and family the way I expected, the way I wanted him to. "Are you afraid to go down there? Aren't you always telling us to lay down our lives for each other?"

It wasn't that I wanted him to die. I didn't. Part of me couldn't believe the words had come out of my mouth. But I did want him to be the noble son and friend and brother that I knew he could be. I had not brought him up to be selfish and calloused. And he was usually such the opposite of those things. All he said was, "Death won't be the end of this illness. It's to bring glory to God, to the Son of God."

This sounded so much like what he had said when he healed the seeing-man that I knew I should have been heartened. But I was worried. I did not feel better at all.

Then suddenly, two days later, he changed his mind. "Let's go back to Y'hudah," he said. Shlomit and Magdalit and I, after raising our eyebrows at each other a little, joined with the other women in bustling about to make sure we had provisions after all. "Do you ever get tired of his changing plans like this?" Shlomit asked Magdalit one day.

"It's Yeshua," Magdalit said, as if that explained everything. "He can go where he likes. Whom else would I follow?" I wished yet again that Yeshua would take a wife. For all Magdalit had some strange ideas, perhaps a Messiah needed a wife who was a little different than the usual Jewish housewife.

The men, however, who had been closer to the animosity surrounding Yeshua down south, and who had also been hearing from his own mouth the words about dying, protested differently. "Rabbi!" they exclaimed. "Practically yesterday the people in Y'hudah wanted to stone you to death. Are you sure you should go back there?"

"Twelve hours in a day," Yeshua said, apparently not worried in the slightest. "When you walk in the daytime, you don't fall down because you can see by the light of the sun. But if you walk at night you're going to stumble, because you haven't got any light."

I did not see how this had anything to do with stoning or Yeshua's arrest or really anything. But then he said, "El'azar has fallen asleep—but I'm about to wake him up."

"Lord," suggested Andrew, "if he's sleeping, he'll get better."

This was, many of us considered, a good observation. Besides which, we had a bit of travel ahead before we would get to El'azar's, at which point he might already have woken up on his own. Going into a hotbed of trouble now that the danger to his friend had evidently passed seemed like a waste. Why did Yeshua always do everything backwards?

Then Yeshua sighed and said, "El'azar is dead. For the sakes of all of you, I'm glad I wasn't there, so that you can learn to trust me. Come on. Let's go see him."

"Yes," T'oma said, firmly, staunchly, "Let's go—so we can die with him!" There was a rousing chorus of assertions from the men, the heroes. We women were left to pack and wonder and worry in our hearts.

In the gloaming a woman marched towards us. I thought both sisters would have come out to meet Yeshua, and if only one had, I expected it to be Little Miryam. But it was the elder sister, Marta. She was dignified even in her grief, but I saw her face was haggard as she said to Yeshua—only to Yeshua, for he was the only one of us who mattered to her, really—"Lord, if you were here, my brother would not have died. Still—I know God will even now give you whatever you ask him."

"She is brave," whispered Magdalit. "She is still hoping, even though her brother has been in the grave for four days."

"She is angry," I said. "But she still loves him." Perhaps, I thought to myself, all the women who have ever known Yeshua have been angry and still loved him. Mother, aunts, sisters, friends. He never did what we expected, but he always seemed to love us back.

Shlomit shushed us. She was right, as usual. This was an important meeting. Everyone was still, listening.

"Your brother will rise again," Yeshua said to Marta.

The woman's eyes flickered with hope, and then she pushed it down again. "I know," she said stolidly, grateful for the hope that she believed, not wanting to acknowledge a hope any more impossible than that, "He will come to life at the Resurrection at the end of things."

"I AM the Resurrection and the Life!" Yeshua burst out then, like a trumpet. It was a pronouncement. It was for everybody. He was using the name of God which we never speak, and he was calling himself life. This conversation was not just for Marta anymore. But it was still for Marta. "Anyone who trusts in me will live—even if he has to die first. Everyone living and trusting in me won't ever die. Do you believe it?"

I thought, what if *you* die? But in the echoes of his trumpet-like pronouncement, that seemed a very faithless thought indeed.

"Yes, Lord," Marta answered, "I believe—that you are Messiah, the Son of God, who was promised to the world." She couldn't quite say the words about her brother. She couldn't say she believed he would rise again right then and there, that day. But she did believe, as I think most of us did then, that Yeshua was truly God's Son, and that where he was, was life, and that he had her good at heart and would see to it that it happened.

Her eyes welled up and she put her hand over her mouth, staring her Hope in the face. Then she turned and dashed back to the house. We could have followed, but Yeshua waited.

Soon there was another woman coming. She had an entourage of other people following her—mourners and family and friends. Perhaps they thought she was going to the tomb to grieve. This woman I expected to see running, as she had to Yeshua so often in the past. But she did not run. She did not march like her sister, but she came very slowly, as if she were dragging something, though nothing was to be seen. She is angry, too, I thought. She is angrier than Marta, and she has not the hope.

When she got to Yeshua's feet, she collapsed. "Lord," she gasped, "if you were here, my brother would not have died." Here was her Lord, and she still called him such. But where had he been when she needed him? She loved Yeshua more deeply than she loved anything or anyone, and she did indeed love deeply, this girl. But the one she loved so, had disappointed her, and she was afraid to trust him, and maybe also afraid not to. If I could see this, Yeshua surely did. His own eyes grew moist as he knelt down next to the young woman. He lifted her up against him. "Where is he?" he asked.

"Lord," said the people who had followed Little Miryam out, "come—look." He straightened himself and steadied the young woman. But then, when she was back on her own two feet, we all noticed to our surprise that Yeshua—Yeshua himself—was weeping. He did not try to hide it, or try to stop. His tears were silent, but his face did not look hopeless. It looked angry, too.

"How much he loved him!" the rest of the mourners marveled. But I heard a voice ask, "He healed a blind man. Couldn't he have prevented this death?" It was not a surprising question. The sisters had already, each in her way, asked it.

No one said anything, but when we got to the tomb, Yeshua let out a roar of grief. It startled everybody, though probably not so much as the tears had at first. It echoed off the exposed rock of the cave and there was silence after it for a moment. Then Yeshua said gruffly, "Take that stone out of here!"

Marta, who had joined us again on the walk to the tomb, protested. Sensible Marta. She was probably trying to overcome her lapse into hopefulness a few moments ago. "He's going to reek," she whispered. "He's been dead four days."

Yeshua turned to her. I thought I could almost see a faint smile on his face. "What did I tell you about trusting me? Don't you want to see the glory of God?"

Marta didn't answer, but at a sign from her, some men moved forward and pushed the stone away from the front of the tomb.

Then Yeshua looked up. We had all heard him pray before, and it was always sort of a shock, because he never postured or used special fancy words. He just spoke to God as a man might speak to his father. This time he said, "Abba, thank you for listening to me. I mean, I know you always do; I'm saying this because of this crowd here, so they can believe you've sent me." Then he roared again, but now it was words: "El'azar! Come out!"

We all stared at the tomb. Yeshua had raised a dead man before, but never this long after he had died. Never someone who had been embalmed and buried for four days. People say after a person dies, the soul lingers for three days. You could imagine it might even re-enter its body, given the right set of circumstances. But the third day had passed. No one would expect El'azar's soul still to be hovering, waiting for this very moment. We were all very quiet. If Yeshua could summon a soul back from wherever they go after the waiting-time, well then!

We heard a rustling sound after a moment, and then a sort of shuffling, and then sure enough—out came a figure. Little Miryam let out a cry and rushed toward it.

"Unwrap him," Yeshua said, laughing. "Let him out!"

By this time, Marta had also run toward the stumbling figure, and both sisters were fumbling desperately with the cloths wrapped around his head and his hands and his feet. They got the wraps off of his head first, so he could breathe. When they had done it, he looked around with some surprise at his sisters crying over him and the crowd of people standing, wonder-struck, in the background. Then he smiled, and kissed his sisters. "I feel better," he said. "Marta, with what shall you feast this lot today?"

Marta stared at him, stared at Yeshua, sobbed out a laugh, and led her brother back to the house.

29
THE MIRACLE DID NOT SIT SO WELL

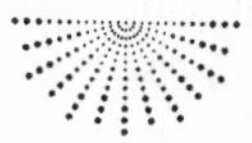

The miracle of El'azar flabbergasted everyone who was there, and plenty more people decided to make Yeshua their Lord. But that did not sit so well with the P'rushim and the Tz'dukim. This was just one more thing to turn the people over to Yeshua and away from them, and it was beginning to look like it was the last thing needed.

Yeshua took the Twelve and a few more of us off to a town called Efrayim, near the desert, and we stayed there for some days. I wondered if this was the "dark" he had mentioned, when it was not safe to go about at all. But six days before Pesach, we all returned with him to Beit-Anyah, to El'azar's. El'azar had a feast for us all, yet again. I suppose it was some way of thanking Yeshua for what he had done for him and his sisters. The place soon filled, because Yeshua had brought us, and meanwhile a number of southerners who had heard he was back, came and packed themselves in, too.

Marta served probably the finest feast she ever had, which was saying something. Miryam sat with the guests as usual, but after the meal was well underway, she disappeared. No one noticed she was gone until she was back again, with an alabaster jar in her hands. She walked directly over to Yeshua with it. At first I thought she might offer it to him. Instead, she broke the stopper and began to pour it all over him—over his head, his shoulders, his hands. When she got to his feet, she unbound her hair, and wiped them with it.

The room got uncomfortably silent. I looked at Magdalit to see how she was taking this display toward a man I knew she loved deeply. Her look was inscrutable, but I thought I would have recognized jealousy had I seen it. The men, however, were squirming. It was one thing for a woman to forget her place and sit with the men while a rabbi was teaching. It was something again for her to give one of her most prized possessions to a man, and to let down her hair for him—in public, no less. I was embarrassed for her. Everyone knew she loved Yeshua. Did she have to make an exhibition of herself? This, I thought, was what happened to women who remained unmarried too long. They became unbalanced.

The K'riot broke the silence. "This oil is worth a year's work!" he exclaimed into the quiet. "If it was unnecessary to you, why didn't you sell it and give the money to the poor?" Shlomit and I glanced at each other. He would say something like that. He kept the common purse for our traveling band, but sometimes we had to get money from him to buy food for us, and it seemed to us that there wasn't always quite the amount in there that there should have been. After he said that, I began to feel a bit kinder toward Little Miryam, even though the awkwardness had not changed any.

"Leave her alone," Yeshua said, quietly but firmly. "She has been saving this for my burial. You will always have poor to look after. You will not, however, always have me." I looked at Shlomit again. I felt the fear in my stomach once more. Now we had heard him say it for ourselves. His burial? I wanted to think he was speaking in stories still. Clearly he was not dead, and if he was comparing Miryam's sacrifice to our embalming process, then he could not have been speaking literally. Could he? No one embalmed anyone before they had actually died.

I saw then that Miryam was crying, quietly, over Yeshua's feet. At least one other woman had done something similar in the earlier part of Yeshua's work as Messiah. But that one had been a harlot, and this one, apart from the provocative display of her hair, was, as far as I knew, a good girl. What was she crying for? She had no sins to hide. Did she know something about this burial herself? And why was I, his mother, still so in the dark about it?

30
IT RAINED IN THE NIGHT

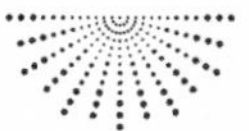

It rained in the night. By morning, the sky had cleared, but everything was still wet and now sparkling. In the kitchen as we prepared the morning meal, I thought Little Miryam looked something like the day itself. Her eyes were still bright, and maybe even a bit swollen, from her tears the night before, but her face was serene now. It was as if the offering of the perfume had released her.

"He is going to Yerushalayim today," Marta said, all business and practicality. We bustled about preparing packets of food that could be eaten in the city without having to stop to sit down. No one spoke of what might happen in the city. A few of the women stayed behind to keep Miryam and Marta company, and to help them with the evening meal for when everyone returned. But, "Go with him," Marta told me. "You're his mother."

It turned out that most of the people who had attended the previous night's feast were also coming with us. As we walked, more and more people joined us. All of us had been waiting. For better or for worse, something was about to happen. In the beauty of the morning, however, it looked as if everything was, after all, going to be for better.

As we reached Beit-Pagei, going into the city, Yeshua said to two of the Twelve, "Go into the village up ahead. Just as you enter, you'll find a donkey tied up with its colt. Bring them to me. If anyone protests, just tell him I need them, and he will let you have them.'" The animals must have belonged to another talmid, one who did not travel with us. Shortly after the men had gone, they were returning again with the animals, just as Yeshua had said.

Now the sense of anticipation was almost palpable. Maybe, finally, Yeshua was going to usher in his Kingdom. None of us truly knew what to expect or how to expect it, but here he was, getting ready to ride a donkey—an animal of peace—into Yerushalayim. True enough—the elders of our people were not likely to appreciate the idea, but no one could deny that, from all appearances, Yeshua was finally claiming his kingship. And why not? He was the son of Adonai. And he was my son, too. I am a daughter of King David, to whom God had promised perpetual kingship. Yeshua was going to fulfill the prophecy at long last. Yeshua was going to fulfill all the prophecies.

The men had begun stripping off their outer garments and placing them on the donkey and her colt. No one could expect her to go anywhere without her colt, of course, when it hadn't even been weaned yet. Some of the other men started tearing branches off the nearby trees, or cutting at them with their knives. Women laid hold of these, giving the smaller ones to their children. Someone started a cheer, and then someone started a song, and then someone else started a chant. The donkey had begun to move, her colt close beside her. I thanked heaven she wasn't a horse—skittish animals. This donkey seemed utterly unperturbed. She had her son with her, and so whatever else was happening, she was content.

I had my son with me, too. With him, I also was content. There he was riding on a donkey—a simple animal, with which I suddenly felt a strange bond. But no one else could have been thinking like this. They were all waving their branches and layering the street with their outer garments, with bits of head-coverings. It was a parade. It was a festival. It was the king, riding down to claim the city for himself.

"Please!" shouted someone in the crowd, loudly, above the rest of the noise, "Deliver us!"

"Son of David!" the people cried.

"Blessed is the one who comes Adonai's name! From the highest heaven—please! Deliver us!"

At first I thought we were bringing the crowd with us, but then I realized we were simply walking into it. Whether people had congregated because they had heard the noise up on the Mount of Olives, whether someone had run ahead and told people or whether there had been some other, more mysterious, more miraculous signal bringing them together, I do not know. In any case, the road was lined, rows thick on both sides, with people. The path under the donkeys' feet was also lined, with the people's clothing. "Please! Deliver us!" they shouted over and over again.

My heart soared. I couldn't help it. It was as if that Dove that had descended when Yeshua was baptized, had descended on everybody now. It was as if that Voice that had boomed from Heaven to tell some of us, at least, that this was Ha'Elyon's beloved son, was crying out from the people themselves. It was as if they couldn't help but sing who Yeshua really was.

This was how I thought about it then. The sky could not have been bluer. The waving branches, the flying colors of the women's shawls and the men's cloaks, entranced me. We were walking in a dream. It was a good dream. The Kingdom was coming. This was why I had borne this boy—this Man. This Son of Man. He was going to make us a people to be reckoned with, but we would be a good people—a people of God once more.

"Shalom in God's realm!" shouted the crowds. "Glory in the heavens!" That was what the angels had said to the shepherds, I thought. All the way back when Yeshua was born, the angels had said that and I had listened to those words, and I had treasured them, and I had remembered. I did not, however, remember Yeshua's words about dying. I did not want to remember those. Perhaps I supposed if I did not think about them, they would not happen at all.

Yeshua could not leave me to my fantasies, however. At last we were in sight of the entire city. Yeshua had wept over it before. He had mourned over wanting to gather its people to himself as a hen gathers chicks. But now, it seemed the city was gathering to him, and it seemed odd that he would weep. He halted the donkeys and let out a wail, so that the singing crowd nearest to him stopped in their tracks and their songs to listen. "If only you had any idea what is needed for shalom!" he wept. "But you can't see it. For the time is coming that your enemies barricade you and smash you on the ground—all of you, and all your walls, too—just because you missed your opportunity when God presented it to you!"

"How is it," I whispered irritably to my sister, "that he always manages to find the worst moments for everything?" She only looked at me. She did not say a word. She knew as well as I did that I was speaking out of fear. Yeshua never was one to leave us comfortably in error, and he would tell the truth, whether anyone wanted to hear it or not.

Still, the truth did sound a little incongruous on a day like today. Surely the people singing his praises—worshiping him, no less—were proving that our people knew very well what made shalom. They knew it was found in Yeshua. They were choosing him. Weren't they?

At any rate, their spirits did not seem dampened by his doleful pronouncement. After a moment of awkward silence following his outburst, they picked up their songs and shouts again as if he hadn't said a word. They picked up their branches and their scarves and shawls, and they danced Yeshua into the city.

At last we reached the Temple. Everyone always did reach the Temple in the end. It was not much different than it had ever been—a glowing glory on a hilltop, filled with the cries of animals and the exchange of money. At the entrance, Yeshua dismounted from his beasts. He caressed their heads for a moment, and then sent them off with Andrew with instructions for their return to their owner. Andrew would be missing the rest of the day's activities, then.

But he had already seen something like them. We—Yeshua, the talmidim, the crowd—squeezed through the gate and into the court of the Gentiles. It was strange to me. I never saw the Temple anymore with the same eyes that I had seen it with before Yeshua's outrage there. But the same commerce went on there. It was as if he had never done anything there at all. Perhaps he thought the same thing. At any rate, in one fluid motion, he stripped off his outer garment and handed it to the K'riot. Then he strode, once again, to the tables of the money changers.

I suppose it was not so shocking a second time. My loyalty was with my son now and not with the Temple and its leadership. But you might still expect flying tables and loosened animals to cause something of an uproar. "The Tanakh says," Yeshua roared, as he had done in the past, "'My House is for prayer,' but you've made it into a thieves' hideout!"

The only people who really seemed upset this time, however, were the elders, who were always upset about something, and the money changers, whose money was in disarray all over the flagstones. The former knotted together in a group, fuming, while the latter scrambled about on the ground, trying to gather their dubious earnings. The rest of the people—those of us who had traveled with him for some time, and those who had just joined us that morning—were enthralled. It was not like the first time at all. Now the people saw that their true King, the Son of David, was going to start everything over new and fresh. The people could not get enough of him. He taught them. He healed them. I think I saw more of his healings that day than I had in a very, very long time.

As the sun began to sink, the adults grew quieter and quieter. We were tired. So much excitement wearies as it exhilarates. But the children were still dancing. It seemed nothing would wear them out. Yeshua stood and moved as if to leave the Temple precinct. A group of children had joined hands and began singing and dancing around his legs. It was anyone's guess whether they had understood anything of what Yeshua had been speaking about that day. It did not seem to matter to them. They just kept singing.

Yeshua's face, which had been more somber than anyone else's all day, brightened then. He stood there and smiled, and then laughed.

This seemed to be all the sign needed for the elders to approach. They never could bear to see anyone happy, least of all Yeshua. Through the course of the morning, and then on into the afternoon, up until that very moment, they had been clustering and murmuring together like ill-tempered wasps. Now they swarmed in. The children, apparently oblivious, apparently unaware what it was like to run afoul of the religious leaders, kept singing their song to the Son of David. A few of the more daring parents, seeing the storm brewing, began once more to join in the song. Finally the group of P'rushim sputtered out, "Rabbi! Restrain your talmidim!"

"Trust me," said Yeshua, making his way out of the Temple, "if they go quiet, the stones will start singing."

But the P'rushim were evidently not satisfied, nor done spluttering. The children, who had stopped dancing when Yeshua broke through their circle, had not stopped singing.

"Don't you realize what they're singing?" the P'rushim gasped.

"Of course," Yeshua replied. It was like the night, so long ago, when the magi had come and bowed down to him and he, small though he was, had smiled. He was smiling now. He was smiling more than he had since he had mounted the donkey that morning. He continued, "Surely you've read, 'From the mouth of little children you have arranged praise for yourself'?" Then he turned on his heel and made his way back—down the hill, out of the city, back to Beit-Anyah where the day had started.

31

A DEEPENING, DARKENING BLUR

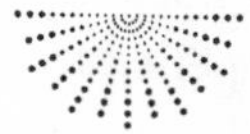

The rest of the week seemed to smear together in a deepening, darkening blur. Yeshua taught in the Temple every day. It was what we all would have expected. But the P'rushim and other elders asked more and more damning questions, and Yeshua's answers became both harder to gainsay and harder to bear. In the meantime, he kept telling parables about people unready, people rejecting God's gift to them. The stories got darker as the week did.

"Now here's a parable," he said one day. "A farmer planted a vineyard. He set it up just as a vineyard should be, rented it to tenants and went away. At harvest-time, he sent his servants to collect his share of the crop. But those tenants grabbed his servants, beat up some and killed others. The farmer sent other servants—more of them—and the same thing happened. Finally, he sent his son to them, thinking they would respect his son. But instead, when the tenants saw him, they said to each other, 'This is the heir. Come on—let's kill him and we can inherit!' So they seized him, tossed him out and killed him. Now when the owner returns, what will he do to the tenants?"

One bold man in the crowd that day answered gruffly,

"He will tear those men apart and rent out the vineyard to other tenants who will do their job and give him his share of the crop."

He was right, surely, this man. But this was my son we were talking about. I thought, I would destroy those men in the parable. I would rip their hearts out, woman that I am. But how would even that make up for the loss of a son? This son? I thought if that happened to me and I were the farmer, I would not care about the vineyard anymore after that. I would not care whether I had good tenants or not, as long as I had justice on those ones who had killed my son.

I hoped this was just a story. I knew beyond doubt that the P'rushim and Tz'dukim wanted to see the end of Yeshua. But that evil was in their hearts already. Yeshua had once said that speaking evil of someone was as bad as murdering them. Maybe this meant that these men had already killed my son in their hearts, and in that case, those of us who loved him could, I hoped, keep him still. Perhaps this was what his metaphors, as the K'riot called them, meant.

As for that one—the K'riot—he kept disappearing. First he was there, nearly hovering around my son, calling him "Lord" instead of just "Rabbi," and then he wasn't. No one but me seemed to find this very odd. It was true, he had always been more scarce than the other Twelve, what with having to make financial arrangements for us all the time. Still, something about his behavior now seemed even more sinister than usual. I tried to talk to my son about it, but he seemed preoccupied, and he did not really respond. Frustrated, I went back to the women, wondering what on earth was the point of being a mother anyway, when one's children would not listen. "I suppose he thinks," I muttered to myself, "that he doesn't have to listen to me, as he is the Son of God. But God his Father gave him to me, and I should think there must have been a reason for that!"

This sounded like very good logic to me, and so I said it

again to Shlomit later. But Shlomit, typically, only listened and nodded, as if she understood my feelings very well, but didn't necessarily think I was in the right. "Oh for heaven's sake!" I exclaimed, after a moment of her silence, "You should have been his mother, clearly, as you understand so much better what's going on!" Then, to my surprise, I burst into tears. I suppose it was only because I could no longer imagine not being Yeshua's mother. It was the strangest motherhood I had ever heard of, but I would never have traded it for anything.

32

HALFWAY THROUGH THE WEEK

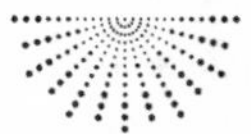

Halfway through the week, things began to muddle. Yeshua had never minced words in his teaching, but now it seemed one almost could not listen to him without feeling offended. Even those of us who loved him found ourselves cringing. I suspect it was more out of fear of what could happen than out of a true distaste for what he said, but feelings were getting muddled, too, and even now I cannot say exactly what mine were then.

Besides, Pesach was upon us. At least we could be sure that if the religious leaders hoped to try to harm Yeshua, they would wait until that festival was over, since they had not done anything so far. At first I thought we would all celebrate the seder together—Yeshua, the Twelve, the women, the family at Beit-Anyah. It was a larger gathering than usual for a seder, but the meal was to be eaten with family, and it seemed we were all family now. I felt we were. Even the K'riot. Who was I to say who should and should not be chosen? Yeshua had prayed about all the Twelve. He had prayed about the K'riot, too, then. I resolved to look at the man differently. It helped he had not been around as much the last few days. He had been so busy buying things for the seder feast. But I was going to try to think of him more kindly afterwards, too. I was determined.

Two days before the beginning of the feast, Yochanan came to me looking apologetic. "Imma," he said respectfully, "Yeshua wants the seder with just the Twelve."

This set me on my heels. "Oh," I said. "Oh."

The young talmid went on, "He says there are other families of his in the city. He said...well, he was talking of being killed again, and how he wanted to celebrate with his Twelve. I didn't understand everything. But I thought you should know."

"Oh," I said, for a third time. I wasn't really sure what to say instead. Then I said, "Of course. Thank you, Yochanan. We will find some other families in the city to celebrate with. We will see you during the other days of the feast."

"Yes," he said, though his eyes looked worried. "I expect you will."

I spoke with Shlomit almost as soon as Yochanan had gone. We talked about going to Yosef's family in Beit-Lechem, but decided it was better to stay right in Yerushalayim this year. Too much coming and going would waste too much time, and something was clearly going to happen very soon, though we could not really know what it would be.

I felt a knot in my stomach, and I could not tell if it was the fear of things to come, or feeling rejected by my son again. I decided it was probably a little bit of both. Something reminded me of the time he had said his family were those who did the will of his Father. Had I not done the will of his Father then, after all this time? I had borne his Son. I had followed him. I stayed near Yeshua for the rest of that day, but I could not speak to him. He felt very far away.

But there was the rest of Yeshua's family—the ones who still did not quite trust in him. My other sons and their wives and children had come down to Yerushalayim a few days earlier. The women were preparing the lodgings and getting rid of all the hametz, the yeast that symbolized pride and evil and which had to be evicted before we could celebrate Pesach. Shlomit's children came down, too. We had seen them all earlier in the week, in and about the Temple. My son Ya'akov had spent quite some time listening to his elder brother, although he didn't say much to me about it.

"Perhaps," I said to Shlomit, "we are to celebrate with our children. Other children I mean," I added, my heart still yearning after Yeshua.

"There is no question," said Shlomit. "These are our families, too."

And so we each made our way to the lodging houses where our respective children and grandchildren were staying. I felt undeserving, going there after the women had done almost all the preparations themselves, while I had been following one son up and down the countryside. But on the other hand, I could not, I knew, have done anything differently. Perhaps my sons would be out of sorts and not want me to join them. If that were the case, there were other talmidim of Yeshua's in the city, and I would just stay with them.

Y'hudah my son, not that difficult man from K'riot, was standing outside talking to someone when I approached the house. He looked up and, to my delight and relief, grinned. "Imma!" he exclaimed. "Are you coming here?"

"Yes," I said, still feeling a little like the youngest son in a parable Yeshua had once told, even though I knew I had done nothing wrong. "If there is room enough at the table."

Y'hudah's wife came out at that point with her hands on her hips. "Room enough?" she asked, almost as if she were angry, as was her way. "Are you mad? Come in, Imma. Everything will go more smoothly, now you are here."

That day was a happy one. The children ran about the houses, shrieking and laughing as they searched out all the remaining hametz and got rid of it. I cooked with my daughters-in-law. We sang while we worked. It was a holy time. I missed being with my new family—the other women and the Twelve—but I knew I was where I needed to be, and I found I had missed this family. I had not noticed until I was back with them.

The next day I continued on with my children. My oldest child, I thought, would have little time for me that day. Nearly all the preparations had been completed for the next one, starting that evening, but the day still went quickly enough. It was both strange and lovely to be surrounded by the family of my own flesh again. I had not been able to be a usual grandmother or mother in a very long time. Yeshua had said we had to give up these things for him, I reminded myself. But he had also said we would receive them back. Maybe my sons and their families would finally see Yeshua for who he really was. Maybe they would follow him, too. Maybe after all the sinister darkness surrounding the religious leaders had passed. For surely it would pass.

I thought how very much I wanted the family to be whole again. I knew it could only happen if everyone acknowledged Yeshua on his terms, and I was not sure I could imagine my headstrong sons being willing to do that, much as they now knew they loved him. But they had questions for me. Everyone had questions. Ya'akov had the most questions of all. In my great desire to have all my children together again forever, I answered them as best I could. And then the sun began to go down.

Ya'akov officiated, as Yeshua was once again not there. It had, I realized with something of a pang, been long years since I had celebrated Pesach with my eldest son. This, I thought, was why I had so wanted to celebrate with him tonight. For a moment I felt a surge of panic, as if I would never be able to celebrate with him again—as if this had been my last chance, and he had denied me it. Then I told myself such thinking was nonsense. I further told myself that even if it were true, I was the servant of Adonai, and it had to be with me as he had said. I did not know, in this case, what he had said. After all these years, however, I was finally beginning to realize that what he had planned to accomplish was always for the best. If I was never to celebrate this holiest of festivals with my son, my Messiah, again, who was I to say anything? So I kept silent and listened to my second son bless the wine. We all drank.

The ceremonies and traditions proceeded as they always have for centuries, but in spite of my best efforts to concentrate and not be distracted by my absent son, I began to feel increasingly uneasy. When the time came for the maggid—the recounting of our people's release from slavery—and the littlest of my little grandchildren asked, "Why is this night different from all other nights?" I practically jumped out of my skin.

Why? Why was it different? For something was truly different about this seder, this night. Reclining, I shifted uneasily on my elbow. "Is everything all right, Imma?" Ya'akov's wife, who was reclining next to me, whispered as quietly as possible. I nodded. I did not want to interrupt anything. In fact, I had the feeling I needed to pay extra special attention to this seder. There was something in it I needed to understand, and it had to do with Yeshua. But everything was not all right.

I listened to the familiar story of our people's captivity. Moshe and Aharon standing in defiance of the oppressive, evil Pharaoh, and Adonai's angel of death coming to kill the first-born Egyptians, but passing over our first born. I thought of the people I had known in Egypt. They had been Jews, too, mostly, but there were one or two Gentile Egyptians I had known. I imagined how they would have felt if the angel of death had visited them. I thought of the prophecies over Yeshua, how he would also bring blessing to the

Gentiles. I thought of deliverers. I thought of Yeshua riding into Yerushalayim on the donkey. I thought of the simmering, whispering hatred of the elders. We needed deliverance again, it was certain. I was no longer certain, however, that I knew precisely what we needed deliverance from. Most people I knew had always said we needed freedom from the Romans, and I didn't appreciate that nation's presence any more than the next person. But I was no longer sure that they were our primary problem. And if Yeshua were for the Gentiles in some way, too, then presumably Gentiles included Romans.

I felt woozy, and I did not think it was the wine. Yeshua. Adonai had given me Yeshua so that he could deliver our people, and now it was Pesach. We were celebrating deliverance before he had even set us free, I thought. But he was going to do it. I just didn't know how. And I felt a shadow over my soul, as if a sword were lofted to strike it. I had thought, over the last years, that old Shim'on's prophecy had already come true, numerous times. It had, I suppose. But now I had a hunch that those soul-piercings were really just pin-pricks.

At the end of the maggid, Ya'akov uttered another blessing and we drank our second cup of wine. It was very red. We washed our hands again. I am a mother. I raised a family and looked after a household for most of my life. All I could think was how difficult wine stains are to remove from clothing. Then I thought of how bloodstains are equally difficult to get out. I washed my hands very well. Ya'akov's wife looked at me again, concern in her eyes, but this time she said nothing.

Ya'akov spoke the next two blessings—over bread in general, and over the matzoh in particular, and then we ate some. It was dry, as matzah always is, and I found I had difficulty swallowing it. The maror and charoset, which came next, helped. They represent the bitterness of our slavery, but oddly enough, they seemed to be the only way for me to get the final matzoh crumbs down.

When the time came to eat the lamb we had sacrificed at the Temple that day, I could scarcely stomach anything. And when we opened the door to let in Eliyahu, as tradition states, I felt as if I were going to be ill. I was too nervous. Eliyahu would not come to us. Old Elisheva's Yochanan had been the returned Eliyahu, Yeshua had said. We had celebrated Pesach with him when he was a child. But now he was dead and the Messiah was due to reveal himself at any moment.

I heard something of a commotion outside. It was not in the immediate vicinity, but the night was otherwise too quiet for any sort of hubbub to go completely unnoticed. The seder traditions had been completed, and everyone was settling down to tell stories and sing hymns, but we all heard the faint sounds of shouting. Who would disturb the night of the seder like this? Everyone should have been quietly in their homes, celebrating and remembering.

"Yeshua," I whispered. "They are doing something to Yeshua."

"They cannot touch him," Ya'akov said quietly. "He has not done anything wrong. He has never done anything wrong."

I was surprised by this assertion, but I did not think now was the time to question him. "He said they were going to kill him," I shuddered, still whispering.

"They have to try him first," Ya'akov said. "They will not be able to find him guilty. They must make the trial public. They must have witnesses who agree." None of this was news to any of us.

"I am going," I said, and got up.

There was a general murmuring outcry, but I ignored them. I was their mother. They could not say anything. They could not keep me from my son in trouble. In the doorway, I slipped on some sandals and cloaked myself, and then I set out.

Shlomit appeared in the street behind me only moments after I did. Neither of us said anything. Neither of us had to. We both appeared to be heading toward the Temple. I was running, I noticed a bit later. Not very fast, and my breath was began coming in ragged gasps much earlier than it should have. "I am old," I thought, with some dismay, wondering when that had happened. I was not truly old—not like Hannah in the Temple at Yeshua's b'rit milah, for example. Not even like cousin Elisheva when she had borne Yochanan. But the girl who had traveled to Beit-Lechem great with child was long gone. I rather forgot why I was running for some minutes. Yeshua was the only person in my head, and I could not think why. I could not even realize that I did not know why. I just ran. Sounds in the night became louder, but I did not know if I were running to or from them.

Then Shlomit and I turned a corner and saw a procession. A week ago there had been a procession, but that one was in broad daylight and people were singing. There was nothing of singing about this. There were masses of torches and men, but in spite of the flares, everything seemed rather murky. Except Yeshua. He was in the middle of the darkness, and the lights reflected off of his robe—the seamless robe I had made him when he set off on his ministry to begin with—and he seemed like a light himself. He did not look afraid. But I was afraid, because when I searched the faces of the men surrounding him, I did not recognize a one. Where were his talmidim? How had they become separated? There were too many of the Temple guard around my son for any others to have taken the talmidim somewhere else. I made to cry out, but Shlomit put her arms around me.

"Let's just follow," she whispered. "We will see what they will do. We will see what we can do."

As it turned out, we could not do much. They led Yeshua

to the home of Caiaphas, who was the high priest that year. Caiaphas' father-in-law, Annas, also lived there. One of the two was bound to see Yeshua, and neither of them approved of him. I wanted to go in and speak for my son, but those men would never have listened to the testimony of a woman —even less of a mother. Still, two women had to be witnesses and here there were two of us. "Shlomit?" I asked, "Shall we witness?"

She looked doubtful, but I suppose we were both willing to try. I took my courage in my hands and followed the crowd up the steps. At the door, a guard turned back toward my sister and me and barred our way. "We have come to witness on behalf of the man you have arrested," I said.

"There are enough witnesses," the man said gruffly.

"On his behalf?" Shlomit persisted.

"There are enough witnesses," the man repeated. He seemed to lack both imagination and sense of humor. Then again, what was funny? "Anyhow, what good do you think you could do, woman?"

"There are two of us," I said. This should have been obvious, but sometimes one has to state that. "And," I added, "I am his mother."

The guard paused a moment. No doubt there were numerous reasons both for and against letting us in—even I could work out some of them—but eventually he only planted his feet more firmly and said, "Trust me, mothers. You and he are both better off if you stay out here."

I wasn't sure I believed him and toyed with the idea of trying to find a way to sneak into the house, but that, I knew, would be lunacy. Maybe even suicide. And what good would I be to Yeshua dead? The high priest's house was heavily guarded at the best of times, and I had already been reminded of my age. It wasn't as if I were a young lass who could clamber up vines and through a window or some such —or intrigue the guards with my hypothetical feminine wiles. I had never really been that wily. We descended the steps and retreated to a corner and a wave of futility washed over me.

"Where are the talmidim?" I sobbed quietly to Shlomit. "Where are they? They've deserted him, haven't they?"

"We don't know it," she said, her arms around me. But I heard the tremor mixed with steel in her voice, and I thought I knew what that meant. And then suddenly I saw Yochanan and Kefa. They were in the courtyard and conferring together, and hadn't seen us. Suddenly I did not want to speak to them, but just knowing they were there made me feel a little better. I watched them mutely, saw Yochanan approach the guard we had just been arguing with. He said something and obviously had better luck, for he was allowed in with no questions even asked. Kefa stayed by the fire. I remembered then that Yochanan's family had some connection to the high priest's family. Well then. That was good news. Perhaps Yochanan could do something. Still, the knot in my stomach did not loosen.

It was cold, but I did not want to go to the fire. I did not want to stand near Kefa, no matter how much affection I normally had for him. I think all my usual emotions and loves were wiped out of me that night, as if I were a clay pot that someone had thoroughly emptied. All I felt was fear. I did not want to know anyone in that courtyard. I wanted—I think—to feel my fear, to revel in the anguish of suspense. I don't suppose even then I really understood quite what I feared or that what I feared could not even begin to touch what was actually going to happen.

"You're cold," said Shlomit. "You're shivering. We could go stand near the fire."

"You go," I said. "I don't want to." My eyes were glued to the door through which Yochanan had disappeared. I don't think I broke my stare until sometime much later. Shlomit did not stand by the fire. She stood by me and wrapped her arms around me again, and we waited. For a while nothing happened. Nothing at all, either outside of me or inside of me. My eyes stayed trained toward the door, but I don't suppose I was really looking at it. And then suddenly everything was happening at once.

I was roused by a commotion over by the fire, but before I could look there or attend properly, I saw that there was also movement by the door where Yochanan had disappeared. People were coming out of it. Yeshua was coming out of it. I saw his face. He looked right at me. He did not look afraid, at least. Just sad. Sadder than I had ever seen him. I could not tell who the sadness was for. I thought he looked sorry—not that I was there, exactly, but that I was seeing something which was only going to get harder for me. But the sorrow also went deeper than that. I wanted to run to him—to hold him. Surely the guards would let his mother . . .

Then the ruckus over by the fire erupted and I heard a familiar northern voice bellow, "I tell you, I don't know the man!"

In that moment I felt almost as if I were watching someone else's life, and wasn't actually a part of the scene at all. Yeshua's eyes left my face and turned toward the voice of his friend disowning him. His eyes were not surprised, though I thought they did look hurt. I followed his gaze and saw Kefa look away from his own accusers and catch sight of Yeshua staring at him.

Just then a rooster crowed. I caught my breath. It had happened. Yeshua had said it and I had forgotten. Kefa had been terrified of denying his Lord, and now he had just done it. His face turned ashen even in the firelight, and looked far more stricken than Yeshua's. He covered it with his hands and a howl, and dashed out of the courtyard.

Hardly anybody else even noticed him. The guards surged around Yeshua and pulled him down the stairs. I heard something about Pilate. I tried to move in, to cut through the mass of armed men, but one of them shoved me to the side and that was all I saw of Yeshua for some time.

"Come," said Shlomit, taking me by the elbow. "We'll just follow them, that's all."

Yochanan suddenly appeared at my other elbow. "They're taking him to Pilate," he said, in case we had missed it. "We won't be able to get inside there, but we can wait outside and see what happens."

I nodded, suddenly feeling toward this young man as I would if he were one of my sons. "Thank you, Yochanan," I whispered. He was not one of my sons, but he loved the son of my soul and I thought it was good to have something like a son to lean on just then. So lean on him I did, and the three of us followed the crowd to where the governor lived.

Others have told what happened that night and that morning—how Yeshua was flogged within an inch of his life. How he was dragged back and forth between Pilate the governor and the Herod of the time. How Pilate could not fault him, but how he also could not resist the pressure of the people. How Pilate "washed his hands" of the affair, which was no better than condemning my son to death. How Yeshua was made to carry his cross-beam up to Gulgolta . . .

Others have told it, and it needs to be told, but even now, even after knowing a little more clearly what it was all for, I am his mother, and there are no words for a mother who has seen sights like this, this brutality inflicted on her own child. Also, as it turned out, I did not witness very much of it.

By the time we got to Pilate's the first time, I was a lioness. I was furious. What could they find wrong with my son? How could they think of harming him? I stopped leaning on Yochanan and pulled away from my sister's restraining arm.

"What do they think?" I hissed in protest when she reached out to me. "That this Roman will care? That they can do away with Yeshua at Pesach? What do they think?"

There was a crowd already outside the governor's palace, already waiting for him to come out with Yeshua and give a verdict. I forced my way to the front. It took Shlomit and Yochanan some time to reach me, by which time I had already begun crying out, "He's innocent! That man is my son! Give me back my son!"

I could not be shushed by the surrounding mob, partly because I refused to be, and partly because no one seemed to want to stand very close to me after they realized who I was. They were ashamed I think. Well, and so should they have been. But then a soldier came. He could have shaken his spear at me and I would have paid him no more notice than a gnat. But instead he cuffed me on the side of the head, and I knew nothing for some time later.

When I at last came to, the verdict, which was no verdict at all, had been decided. I was in a dark room, and Shlomit was sitting there, holding a moist cloth to a part of my head, which was throbbing. "Where is he?" I asked.

"Yochanan?"

I sat up. Why would I be asking about Yochanan? "No," I replied disgustedly, forgetting the knot of anxiety in my stomach and the pain in my head for just a moment, "Yeshua, of course."

Shlomit didn't say anything. Yochanan was, I saw, standing in the shadows in a corner of the room. He didn't say anything either. I looked at both of their faces.

"What are we doing here?" I fumed, pushing Shlomit's hand away. "What are you doing here? Something must be done. We can help him!"

Shlomit put out a calming hand for the millionth time that morning, and again I pushed it away. "You can sit here in the dark if you like," I said. "I shan't."

"But Imma," Yochanan protested respectfully, "you've been hurt."

"So has he," I snapped, sure of it, though I had as yet heard nothing of it. "Where are we, anyhow?" I wanted to know. "And where do we need to go?"

"Gulgolta," Yochanan whispered. "We need to go there."

It was then, I think, that my hope began to falter. All my life I had followed this son, worrying about him, loving him, proud of him, despairing of him. He was the son of a promise Adonai had made to me, and also that I had made to Adonai —that I was Adonai's servant, and it should be with me as he had said. But this. This was not about something happening to me. It was about something happening to Yeshua, and Yeshua was the son of Ha'Elyon, and Ha'Elyon, I had thought, would not let his Messiah die. I had been so certain of it. This, I thought—this assurance of Yeshua's deathlessness—had been promised me, too, hadn't it? But no angel had said such a thing to me, and the only promise, of all the words about my son which I had stored up over the years, that came to mind now was the sword of old Shim'on. The knot of anxiety in my stomach, which had come mainly from a sense of urgency to do something, melted away and flowed through my body in a wave of something like despair. "Oh," I said. I put my face in my hands then.

A moment later, however, I looked up. "Who is with him?" I asked, my voice still small. "Who is with him if we are not?"

"Let's go," said Yochanan, taking my arm. Shlomit followed us out.

33

THROUGH THE COURTYARD OF THE HOUSE

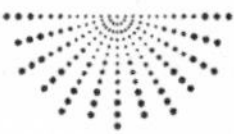

We walked through the courtyard of the house and out a door at the back. The streets were oddly silent. The sky was oddly dark. Ominously dark. The sort of sky you would imagine on a day that God died, just before the world ended. "Where are we?" I asked. It didn't matter. I just needed to hear a voice in that strange dark silence, even if the voice was only mine.

"At Mark's family's," Yochanan murmured, not really attending. "This is where we celebrated the seder last night."

I saw in my mind's eye my family's own seder celebration. I saw the lamb on the table, cooked and ready to be eaten. Sacrificed for us. Where was my family now? I wondered. Did they know what was happening to their brother?

Mark was a young talmid who had started following Yeshua in more recent days, along with his parents. He seemed a timid soul to me, but his parents were well off and had no apparent qualms about associating with and providing for Yeshua and his band of followers. Their house, conveniently, was near the old city wall, and it did not take us long to reach the city's true outskirts and Gulgolta, the

Skull Place. The hill was mobbed, and as we approached I could see three crosses, a twisted body on each.

Yeshua could not look so deformed. Even then, in the back of my mind, I harbored a tiny glimmer of hope that something would happen, because something always did happen, and Ha'Elyon had never yet let his Messiah die—even when his own townspeople had tried to shove him off the cliff, for goodness' sake.

As we drew even closer, however, I saw that Yeshua was indeed one of those men hanging above the earth, and when I saw it I screamed. I screamed loud and long and from somewhere below my gut, maybe below my feet. I did not know I had that place in me, that place from which the scream came. It kept coming and coming and a few moments later I discovered I was running. I reached the foot of the cross and collapsed in a heap. There was no more screaming. But I sobbed silently.

Soon I felt arms around my shoulders, and they were not Shlomit's. I looked up, and there was Magdalit, her face tear-streaked, but full of concern for me, nonetheless. Slightly behind her stood some of the other women—Miryam, wife of K'lofah, and Yochanan's mother. She bent down, too, and the two women helped me to stand up.

In front of me was a beam of savagely hewn wood. It was a strange color, having soaked in so much blood. I did not want to look up. I did not want to see the pain of my son. But also, after I had stopped screaming and my sobbing had abated, I thought it was hardly fair for him to have the pain of his mother as his last sight on earth. So I wiped my eyes, somewhat futilely, it turned out, as the tears continued to pour down no matter what I did, and I looked up.

There was a man above me, and he was almost completely red. They must have done terrible things to him even before putting him up there, because no cross had ever made its victim as horrifyingly bloodied as this one was. I searched his body with my eyes for one place—just one little place—that remained whole, but I could not find one.

"Yeshua," I moaned. He did not look like himself at all, but I am his mother, and I know my son.

Also, he was looking at me. He loved me, I saw. He had never given me reason to doubt it, but sometimes in the past he had felt so above me, so beyond me, that I couldn't quite believe or even imagine it. Now I saw it was true. It had always been true. It would always be true.

This, I realized in the next instant, was the thinking of someone on the verge of insanity. Yeshua's love—even Yeshua's love—could not be with me forever. Here he was, dying, and Ha'Elyon was not doing anything about it. I could feel the faintest flicker of rage deep within me, in the place from which the scream had come. I stopped thinking about it. I could not be angry right now. There would be time enough—the rest of a lifetime enough—to rage against the one who had given me this son. Against the one this son had served so faithfully and well.

Now Yeshua was looking beyond me. I turned slightly and saw Yochanan. He and Shlomit had caught up. Shlomit was standing with the other women, but Yochanan, perhaps feeling cowed by all of us, was off a little way to the side. "Mother," said a croaking and gasping voice above my head. I wheeled around again. That did not sound like my son. It was, though. "This is your son," he said.

I wasn't exactly sure what he was talking about. Himself? But then he looked back at Yochanan and continued. "This is your mother," he said. Yochanan nodded. He came close to me and put his arms around my shoulders. I thought of my other sons. I had other sons. But none of them loved Yeshua like this one. Yochanan had another mother. She was right there. But she did not move, and I did not protest. I did not know how we would go on together, this new son of mine and I, both of us mourning the same person for the rest of our days. But perhaps it would be better to mourn together than alone. Perhaps Yeshua knew that. Even now he was taking care of us.

I had successfully quenched the fire of anger in me for the moment. But then I heard a chest-rattling intake of breath. Yeshua was straining up on the nails in his limbs—those limbs which had worked the wood and the nails themselves before this, but only ever in implements of peace. A fresh ooze of blood seeped out of each of the nail wounds, and he cried out with more strength than I could have expected, and more anguish than I had ever before heard, "Eli! Eli! L'mah sh'vaktani?" Some nearby observer said foolishly, "He's calling Eliyahu, isn't he?"

But why would he have been? He was calling for his Father, his true Father, who had deserted him. He was asking why. If even Yeshua felt deserted and betrayed by Adonai, what hope was there in the world? I began to sob again. Yochanan gripped my shoulders hard so that I wouldn't fall, but I did not stop sobbing for a long time.

Someone came forward with vinegar on a sponge for Yeshua, but he closed his lips tightly and wrenched his head away. After the person has lowered the sponge, Yeshua gathered all his breath again. The sky was pitch black now. The world really was coming to an end, I thought. And just as I thought this, Yeshua cried out, "Finished!"

What? What finished? What had been accomplished? And why, ravaged as he looked and as his voice sounded, did the cry itself sound like a call of triumph? And why did the earth rock and tremble so that we had to grip each other to keep connected with the ground? Sometimes we have earthquakes, but rarely. Our people like the firm ground under our feet, and avoid the ocean if we can. Now the earth was bucking like waves on Lake Kinneret, and finally no one could stand anymore. We all surrendered and fell face-down to the earth. In the silence, I heard Yeshua whisper, "Abba, I give you my spirit."

All I could do was wonder why.

34
AFTER THE TREMORS FINALLY STOPPED

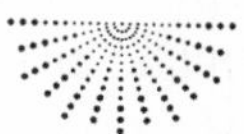

After the tremors finally stopped, we all picked ourselves up, and I saw the centurion staring at the body of my son, hanging above him. The man's mouth was hanging open, and I heard him say, just above a whisper, "This man really was a son of God."

I blinked and stared at him. He was just a Roman soldier, like any Roman soldier, and he had just killed an innocent man. That man had not resisted—had appeared powerless to resist. That man was a Jew. He had not done any miracles to free himself. He had just died, for Heaven's sake. And here was a Roman soldier—the only one with any power in this scenario, as far as I could see—who had just decided that this innocent, dead Jewish man was a son of God.

If it weren't for the fact that the soldier had just killed my son, I could almost have run to him and kissed him for saying it, because this day was the culmination of my own people having decided this man was not the son of God at all. If anyone who mattered had truly recognized it, my son would not have had to die.

Only...if it were true that Yeshua was the son of God, how was it even possible he had died? But if he weren't...my entire life up to that point had been a lie, and it couldn't have been, because where else had Yeshua come from? I had not begot him all by myself. Here, from this centurion's mouth, was yet one more word about my son. It brought me back to where I had started. Truly, Yeshua was the son of God.

As I continued to stare at the soldier, however, I saw in horror that he had lifted his spear; suddenly he thrust it into the side of the body which had been Yeshua. A gush of water and blood spilled out. He was dead. He had died some moments before. This was just the soldier's way of proving it. He and some of his underlings set to work taking the body off the cross.

It wasn't my son anymore, that body. His light and life had gone from it. And yet I had carried that body inside my own for most of a year, and I had watched it grow for thirty-three more, and I could not just walk away from it. I walked toward it, instead. The Romans stared at us women as we came forward. I would have to speak for us, I thought, and hope he would have mercy on a mother and let me have what was left of my child. Not that I knew what I would do with him. Take him back to Natzeret, I supposed. Bury him with Yosef. I had thought my time would come to lie there before Yeshua's did.

"Who is going to bury the body?" asked a man's voice behind us. It was a voice I faintly recognized. I turned round and saw that I faintly recognized the man, too. He was Yosef of Ramatayim, a prominent member of the Sanhedrin. I narrowed my eyes suspiciously. These interferers. It was as Yeshua had said—they murdered the prophets and then looked after their tombs.

"We will," I said, my chin jutting forward.

Yochanan put a hand on my arm. "Imma," he whispered. He had called me "Imma" for as long as any of the talmidim, but now it sounded strange, somehow stranger since Yeshua had given us to each other as mother and son. "He is a talmid."

I spat.

"He is," Yochanan insisted. "He has been too afraid of the others—he and Nakdimon, too. Can you blame them? Look what has happened."

I saw very well what had happened, and I thought that if the Sanhedrin had contained secret talmid, it was almost worse than if they were all enemies. Cowardly men, these talmid, who never spoke up to stop this disaster, but didn't mind cleaning it up after it had happened.

"Madam," said that one from Ramatayim, "Forgive me."

He did not say anything else, and I supposed—I hoped—he knew somehow what I had been thinking, and what I felt, and was apologizing for that. All the same, I was not sure whether I could forgive him. I was not sure I wanted to. "Forgive me." Such an easy thing to say. It did not even take any remorse to say it.

I simply stood there and stared at him, and he stood there and stared at me, and the other women and some guards stared at both of us. Then Yochanan whispered in my ear again, "This man can give him a decent burial. At least let him do that. We cannot do it. All the money we had was spent on the seder." I stared for a moment longer, and then nodded. I hoped the man did not think the nod meant I forgave him. It only meant he could have the body. The body which was, anyhow, bereft of my son.

"Sir," Yosef of Ramatayim said to the centurion, evidently taking my nod for what it was, "I would like to bury the body."

"Oh, sir," the centurion replied, "You'll have to take that up with the governor. But I will accompany you to his palace and vouch that the man has, indeed, er, deceased."

Deceased. As if Yeshua had died in his sleep. I wanted to spit again, but I could not quite get over the respect with which this Roman was speaking to a Jew, and besides, this same Roman had just acknowledged my son as the son of God. I turned to him, "Please, sir," I asked, my voice smaller than I had expected—smaller than it had been when addressing the member of the Sanhedrin at my elbow. "Could I hold him for a moment at least?"

The Roman looked at me—really looked at me, as one human being to another, and asked, "Are you this one's mother?"

For a moment I had a crazy thought that he was going to ask me if Yeshua was, indeed, a son of God, and how that had been with me, but he didn't. "Yes," I said.

"Yes," he echoed, and motioned for Yeshua's body to be brought to me. My people say that glory is what gives a person weight—influence and substance—and Yeshua's glory had certainly left his body behind. Still, I sank beneath what was left, though more from grief and exhaustion than from its own weight. I held a sack of bones, and many of them, I could tell, were not attached as their maker had intended. But this sack of bones was, nevertheless, all I had left of my son, and I cradled it for a while. I stroked his face and kissed it, and ran my hand along his punctured side, and noticed that I was crying again. Or still. I had not held this boy of mine for fifteen years—not like this—and now he was gone and would not come back and I never would hold him again. I had missed the last seder, and I had missed my son, it seemed, even though I had been following him for most of his life.

I looked up at the centurion and lifted the body toward him again. Now I was finished with it. If Yeshua had finished with it himself, I certainly had no more use for it. The Roman bent down and took it from me, and I thought maybe his eyes were glistening more than men's usually do. Certainly more that a soldier's. He was a good man, I thought. It was a pity he had never met Yeshua until now.

Yeshua with his love of Goyim. He would have loved this man.

Yosef of Ramatayim, who had retreated a step while I held the body, came forward again. "We will go to Pilate's?" he asked.

The centurion nodded. They both looked at me expectantly, but I turned away. "You go," I said, to whomever wanted to go.

"Come, Imma," said Yochanan, taking my elbow again and trying to turn me to follow the two men and the women.

"You go," I said again. "I have no use of that body. He isn't there."

"But wouldn't you like to see that he is properly taken care of?"

No one, I knew, except for maybe Magdalit, with all of her surprising ways of thinking about things, would be able to understand a mother who mourned her son by ignoring him, instead of by hiring people to wail loudly and make her grief sound all the more tragic. But my grief really was tragic. Part of the tragedy was that, either from shame or from misplaced hatred or from fear of guilt by association, professional mourners would not likely wail for my son, no matter how much I paid them. And when a man—an innocent, good man, who only ever lifted burdens from people's shoulders and healed them from their illnesses—dies in such ignominy, there is no grief loud enough to express his mother's agony. So she has to retreat to silence.

"Yosef—that man—will see to it," I said, wishing in an instant that my Yosef were alive again and there to help me carry this loss. "I cannot bear anymore." I was no longer crying, but I could not help but cover my face with my hands.

"So be it," I heard Yosef say, though there was a bit of uncertainty in his tone. After a pause I heard the shuffling of feet and the clanking of mail; the centurion and some of his soldiers, with Yosef and the rest of the women, were heading off.

"You go, too, Yochanan," I urged him. "You want to. It will help you."

"No, Imma," he said. "Staying with you will help me. You are all that's left of him." It was true, I thought. No other person in the world shared his blood but me.

35

ON SHABBAT, EVERYONE WAITED

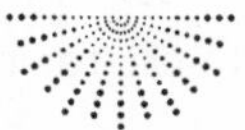

On Shabbat, everyone waited. It was probably the only Shabbat in the history of our people which was truly quiet enough for the P'rushim. Nobody went anywhere. From time to time I hauled myself up from the bed I had been given at Mark's house and stared from the shadows out the window at the street. Nothing happened there all day.

The city was stunned, probably. No matter what anyone had thought about Yeshua when he was alive, the implications of his death and how it had come about were somewhat mind-boggling even for the most detached person. A man who claimed to be the son of Ha'Elyon had been brutally killed on a cross. He was cursed then, obviously. The Tanakh says, "Anyone who hangs on a tree is cursed," and surely anyone who asserted that Ha'Elyon was his Father should be cursed anyhow.

Unless, of course, it were true. I knew it was true, but I did not know how I could know it, except that I had borne him without the help of a man. Certainly his death did not make it seem truer.

The men in the upper room did not think they knew what was true anymore. They were afraid. Mark's mother was less so, perhaps. She took us all in anyhow, although she knew that, come the morning, officials would probably come looking for everyone associated with Yeshua. Chances were good there would be a slaughter. Somehow this reminded me of the little boys who had died in Beit-Lechem, while Yosef and Yeshua and I escaped to Egypt. What good had the escape been? I wondered. He died anyhow, and now still more people would have to die for him.

I stayed in the main part of the house with Mark's mother and her servants, but the men—our brave Eleven, hid themselves away in the room above, where they had held their last seder with their Rabbi and Lord. They kept the door locked. They were no longer Twelve. That day no one had yet discovered that Y'hudah—the one from K'riot—had hanged himself and fallen to pieces in a field. Even without knowing that, no one expected to see him. If we had, we would likely have killed him ourselves. The fear did not extend that far. My fear did not. I would have killed him. I would have done it with my own hands, for I found I had been right about that man; Yochanan told me how he had offered Yeshua up to the Temple guards with a kiss. *Traitor* seemed a thin word for him. There were not words in my head dark enough to convey how I felt about Y'hudah from K'riot.

It was only later we found out what had happened to him. It was gruesome and appropriate although it would, I thought, have been even more appropriate if someone had been able to wreak vengeance on him before he did away with himself. My consolation might have been that Yeshua's Father, Ha'Elyon, would visit harsher punishments than I could have devised, now that Y'hudah had gone the way of all flesh. But I was no longer certain of Ha'Elyon's own goodness. If he had not stopped Y'hudah in the first place, who was I to suppose he would punish him in the life to come?

Occasionally Yochanan came down from the room above to look in on me, or to urge me to join the men up there. I declined. I would not stay with my own sons, partly because I did not want to endanger them and also because Yeshua had given me to Yochanan as his mother, and how could I deny the final wishes of my dying son? But I did not need a locked room. I was not afraid for myself. Perhaps the Temple officials would not bother with Yeshua's aging mother. But if they did, it only meant less time for me to live without him.

Meanwhile, those very Temple officials, those Sanhedrin and their minions, were doubtless enjoying a restful and completely self-righteous Shabbat in their own homes. They would be congratulating themselves, certainly, on getting rid of a troublemaker just in time for the end of Pesach and the beginning of Shabbat. They would be pleased with themselves at how holy they were keeping this day. It made me want to go to the window and scream. I wanted them to hear my grief and my rage and my perplexity. I wanted them to come find me and do away with me to shut me up. I wanted them to look at me and see a mother like their mothers, who had been deprived of a son. But, soulless men that they were, they would never see that. They would only see another nuisance.

I saw Yosef of Ramatayim's face in my mind then. His eyes were kind and sorrowful, but even he had not wanted to be troubled by his colleagues. Why had he never done anything to stop what had happened? Why had he and Nakdimon not argued with their associates? Why had they let them kill Yeshua? They were afraid, too. All these men. So afraid.

Thoughts circled like vultures in my mind that quiet day. I overheard one of the women saying that some of Yeshua's last words on the cross had been to his Father, to forgive his tormentors for not knowing what they were doing. I thought of this, but in the moment, the idea of a plea like that from him drove me even crazier with rage. Of course they knew what they were doing. Yeshua had always told everybody exactly who he was. He had never denied that Adonai was his Father. And so they had tortured and killed the son of God. It was like killing God. It was killing God.

They had killed God.

How was the sky still supported above the earth? How had the earth not crumbled to pieces? How had anyone survived at all? This was the end of the world. Even if it could go on without the hand of Adonai to keep the sun rising and setting, life had ended. Life could not go on without the breath of Adonai to give it meaning and light. It was as if we had descended to Sh'ol without having died. "Those in Sh'ol do not praise you," David had sung, and it was true. We did not praise him because we did not know we could. He was not here anymore, and in any case, he had not done anything worthy of praise. Not in this place of death.

I was angry. I knew it. I had known it since the day before. But was I angry at Adonai? Was I really angrier at Adonai than at Yosef of Ramatayim and Nakdimon? I was! I was angrier at him even than I was at Y'hudah of K'riot. Everyone looks after himself. Who could blame them? And, if those two in the Sanhedrin had loved Yeshua—I did not think I could ever suppose that the K'riot had truly loved Yeshua—well, who could help it? If they had not loved him enough to prevent his death, so, neither had Kefa.

But Ha'Elyon? He could not be called "Most High" for nothing. He had saved Yeshua in Egypt. He had kept him from being thrown off a cliff. He had kept the authorities from arresting him time and time again. And yet he had—according to anyone who knew anything about the choosing of the Twelve—guided Yeshua to choose Y'hudah from K'riot, and that one unsavory, crafty little man had undone everything. Could Ha'Elyon—the Most High—really not have prevented that? What kind of God was this, who let a human being have such power? What kind of God was this, who gave a woman a scandalous child, only to wrench him from her in the cruelest way possible, before her eyes?

Yeshua had said his Father loved him. But this did not look like love to me. I was his mother. *I* loved him. I knew what love was and I would never have allowed such a thing to happen to my son—any of my sons, but especially not that son—if I could in any way have prevented it. If only the soldier had not stunned me, I thought, and then dismissed it as futile. I would not truly have been able to halt the disaster in any case. But I would have died trying. The same could not be said for Ha'Elyon.

Could it?

Some whisper of another sort of thought came to me then, sharp and crisp, like a knife of a breeze cutting down from the mountains. If Adonai had truly died, in the form of my son...Well, Yeshua had said it would happen. He had spoken of it all along. He had gone to it willingly. He had known the K'riot better than anyone. And what if he had died because he was trying to prevent another tragedy? There had to be a purpose in his dying. There had always been a purpose in his living, and his death could not have been meaningless if he had known about it, could it?

If he and his Father were one, as he had always said, then the love he had lived among everyone he met must be the love his Father had, too, mustn't it? And if his Father had such love, he could not have allowed his Son to die like that...unless there was some dreadful thing that would have happened if he hadn't. If I would have died to save my son from this horrible tragedy, then he, knowing, must have died to save someone else from something else. Like the lambs at Pesach. We slaughtered them before Adonai so that our disobedience and guilt would be taken away. Yeshua's death —it was a sacrifice. Adonai himself had made a sacrifice at Pesach.

I saw the lamb I had eaten with my family at the seder,

that night which seemed so long ago. That lamb had been sacrificed to take away the guilt of our disobedience. Why had Yeshua been sacrificed? I couldn't understand it. But I could not stop seeing the lamb's eyes as its throat was cut. I could not stop seeing Yeshua's eyes as he hung on the cross. "Abba, forgive them. They don't know what they're doing." I hadn't heard him say those words myself, but all the same, I could hear him saying them.

The sun was going down. Shabbat would soon be over. My self-righteous Shabbat. My face was wet and my eyes were swollen, and I did not even realize I had been crying, let alone that I had been crying so hard. Yochanan came in then. "Imma!" he cried, taking me in his arms. "Are you all right?"

"Yes," I said. "I forgive him."

"Who?" Yochanan asked. "Who?"

"Yeshua," I said. There were other things I could have answered. But after I said it, I knew that covered all of them.

36

I WENT TO THE MEN IN THE UPPER ROOM

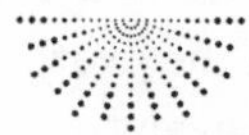

After it grew dark, I rose and went to the men in the upper room. Yochanan let me in. The others sat in small miserable clusters. No one had eaten anything. To a man, they looked as if every shred of purpose had been wrested from their lives, as, truly, it had. They stared at me with a strange combination of fear and dullness. Kefa shrank back into a darker corner. I thought I knew why.

What I didn't know was exactly what I was doing there. I just thought that finally someone needed to know the story.

"He is the son of Ha'Elyon," I said.

No one responded, which was maybe not so surprising, as the statement appeared to have very little to do with anything, especially now.

"He is," I persisted in spite of myself, and themselves. A ball of tears rose in my throat that might stop me speaking, or might come out of my eyes, or both. I didn't know why I was suddenly determined to tell stories—true though they were. Speaking of Yosef after his death had been sorrow enough. This grief and loss was beyond that. But I knew I would never understand anything about my firstborn if I did not start telling the stories, even if it were too late. I took

Yosef's box out of the folds of my robe. It had been there all along, though it was long months since I had taken it out to look at it. Now I held it in my hand and caressed it, as if doing so would release all the words about Yeshua which I had stored in there by my imagination. "He is the son of Ha'Elyon."

"Yes," Yochanan agreed. "We know he is, Imma." The respect in his voice was diluted a little bit with something like condescension, as if he were addressing a very small child or a woman too old even to remember her name.

"No," I said. "You don't know it. Listen. I do not know what he would have us do next. It doesn't appear that any of you know, either. But his life was not meaningless, and at the very least, we ought to remember it. You haven't been speaking of him at all, have you?"

"It hurts us, Imma," said Yochanan's brother Ya'akov simply. "We wronged him. We did not stay with him. How can we speak of him?"

At least, I thought, someone had a fair assessment of the situation. "Then," I said, "let me speak of him. Let me tell you of the son of Ha'Elyon."

I had scarcely begun when I realized how awkward this was. I had never been one to speak to men of the ways of women, although of course no one in that room was a stranger to those facts. But these men needed to know this story. They needed to know that they had not just spent the last three years pursuing a mirage.

So I began from the beginning. I told them of the angel and its message, and of my journey to Elisheva's. I told them of the birth of Yochanan, even though I was not there for it myself, and of the journey to Beit-Lechem with Yosef, and of his family's grudging hospitality. I told them of the shepherds, and of Shim'on and Hannah, and of the magi who came later, and of our journey to Egypt. As the story spilled out, I found myself reliving it, unearthing the treasure-store of words about my son.

I was tired when I began, but by the end I was exhausted. It was something of a relief finally to tell such things, but when I had finished, no one said anything. I could not tell if they believed or disbelieved me. I suppose it was because to them, it no longer mattered either way. I sighed.

Nothing was better. None of all those amazing names for my son—none of all that amazing story—diminished the fact that Yeshua was no longer there. He had been killed, and whether or not those stories were true, we were bereft, and who knew if we would ever learn why?

"I just thought," I concluded, "I just thought you should know, that's all. I don't think this is over, although I don't know what's next. I just thought you should know."

The men thanked me, but with no more light in their eyes than when I began. Without Yeshua there to tell the stories himself, a story was just a story. It might hold some interest, but it was not enough to live on. Not without him. I got up to return to my room.

It was still dark when I heard voices at the front of the house. Mark's mother was talking to someone, and then the voices got closer and they were talking to me.

"Imma," said Magdalit, who, it turned out, was the other voice, "Shabbat is over. We're going to care for his body. Won't you please come with us and help us to do it properly?"

I got up and pulled a shawl around me. It seemed like a formality now—this care for a dead body—but I had spent myself in a story for the men cowering upstairs, and now here were these braver women going to face their sorrow for themselves, and how could I not go with them, too? I would face my sorrow as well, and see if maybe I could find what it was that made me think the story was not over.

The tomb was in a lush garden, and although I still

harbored some distaste for the man of the Sanhedrin who had loved Yeshua but not defended him, I had to agree that he couldn't have been laid to rest in a more beautiful place.

"There are guards," said Shlomit. "I do not know how we'll get past them."

"Guards?" I asked. Who had posted guards, and what on earth did they think was going to happen, that they would need them?

"The elders told Pilate we talmidim would try to steal the body," explained Magdalit.

"Steal the body?"

"Yeshua said something about rising three days after his death," Magdalit went on. "Those foolish men think we would try to make it look as if he had done."

"He said that?" I asked, but none of the other women—almost all the women who had ever traveled with us: K'lofah's Miryam, and Ya'akov and Yochanan's mother, and Yochanah the wife of Kuza, and Susannah, and Shlomit, not even Magdalit—seemed to think that there was anything in it. Maybe not, but...he said that?

"There's a stone, too," Kuza's wife said. "They sealed it and it's heavy. Maybe one of us can convince the guards to help us move it. They could come in and watch us embalm him if they need to. Couldn't they?"

I pursed my lips. This woman's husband worked for the Herods. It surprised me that she was still willing to associate with the likes of us. But she had always been very generous, and I did not hold her own associations against her most of the time. Today I found it a little more difficult not to do so. Evidently complete forgiveness would take some time.

We stepped down into the garden and were suddenly lying facedown in it. The ground had lurched us toward the tomb of its own accord, and then we had to hold onto whatever grew out of that ground as best we could and wait until the bucking stopped. This was the second tremor of the earth to occur in three days. When the motion stopped, we all lay still for a few moments, and then got up cautiously, brushing ourselves off and exchanging glances.

It took a few moments really to understand what we were seeing as we rounded a bend to the tomb. There were, as predicted, two Roman guards—lying unpredictably prone on the ground. Probably they had fallen during the quake as well. We stood there for some time, watching them, waiting for them to get up and throw us out, but they didn't. Then we noticed that not only had the guards been knocked senseless, but the stone had rolled away from the opening to the tomb. We looked at each other again, and then Magdalit dashed into the darkness of the cave.

She wasn't in there for even as long as it took the rest of us to descend to the level of the cave-mouth, when she came bursting back out, sobbing. "He's gone!" she wailed. "Someone stole the body after all!" She pushed through us and was off, running back in the direction she had come.

"Magdalit!" I called after her. "Wait! Let's see if we can truly learn what has happened!"

But she did not pause or turn and soon enough she was out of sight. "She's probably going to see about the Twelve—I mean the Eleven," said Kuza's wife. "To make sure they didn't do something."

"I could have answered her that," I said. "They're too frightened even to think of doing anything. *Anything*."

"Miryam," whispered Shlomit. "Is that what it looked like?" I had to look where she was pointing to know what she was talking about.

This one looked more like a man than the one I had met on my cliff so many years ago, before Yosef, before I was a mother. But it was the same thing, I thought, this angel. "Yes." I said. It was sitting on the top of the rolled-away stone, even though it hadn't been there a moment ago. It had a fierceness in its eyes like the other one had had, but this time I realized that within that ferocity was joy. "Don't be so shocked!" said the figure on the stone. "I know—you're looking for Yeshua the Nazrati, who was killed on the cross. He's alive—he's not here! Go see where they laid him. Then go tell his talmidim, Kefa especially, that he will meet you in the Galil, just as he promised."

Yeshua was again being heralded by angels. Again. I felt a chill run through me, but it was a good chill. "It's true," I whispered. "He really is alive. Adonai wouldn't send an angel if he weren't."

I knew it, and yet I didn't know it. How can a mother—how can anyone—see an innocent person tortured and killed and then not twist around her own grief and thoughts so that she can even imagine that he is still alive? Or alive again?

Shlomit was ducking down through the entryway. "Well," she said, "it said to look at the place where they laid him. Let's look."

We followed her in silently. Certainly there was no one else in there. Light shone in through the doorway and the graveclothes were folded up neatly, just as I had taught him to care for his things when he was a boy. A robber wouldn't have left the clothes. The body had been all over blood and wounds, and unwrapping it would have served nothing. Unless, indeed, someone were trying to make it look like he had really been raised when he hadn't. In that case, however, how could they have got the body out without leaving a mess? And who would have done it? Not the Eleven—I had been with them all night.

What was Yeshua wearing now? I wondered with a shock. Surely he wasn't wandering about the countryside in the state of Adam and Havah before they ate from the Tree? Then again, I reasoned, he had just been battered and bludgeoned and crucified, and if he were alive again, I supposed he could do whatever he wanted. I would have to weave him another robe. His first one had been won in a bet by some of the soldiers at the cross.

"Quick, let's go tell the men, like the angel said!" suggested Miryam the wife of K'lofah. She sounded somewhat breathless, though we had all recovered from the earthquake earlier. "And Magdalit. She left too soon to hear or see the angel!"

"Poor Magdalit," I nodded. We tumbled out of the tomb again in a rush, and then began running as quickly as our old legs would carry us. We must have looked utterly ridiculous, a bunch of aging matrons, huffing and bobbing and lurching down the streets back to Mark's family home. None of us thought of that at the time, however, or if we did, we didn't bother about it. I think as we ran our certainty and hope in the angel's words increased, and by the time we got to the house and pounded on the door, we would have shouted the news from the rooftops—or better yet, Gulgolta itself—if the angel's instructions hadn't been rather specific.

By the time the men unbarred the door to their lair, we had regained our breath, and the first thing we learned was that Magdalit had been and gone again already.

Oh Magdalit. She was making things so much more difficult for herself—even she, the one who had intended to sound so sensible as she outlined the reasons she could never be Yeshua's wife. Her love for him was young and feverish, for all that. Maybe it was better she learned the truth in her own way. She needed to be in that garden, to be quiet, to mourn Yeshua before she could know that she didn't need to mourn him at all.

I looked round at the talmidim who remained. Every face was a picture of utter bewilderment. They only knew as much as Magdalit knew, after all. They only knew the body of their Lord was missing, and none of them could have stolen it.

"Where's Kefa?" Sh'lomit asked. "He said to tell Kefa especially."

I would have expected a movement—Kefa's shrinking back into his corner, not knowing yet why he was being singled out. But, "Kefa has gone. He went to look at the tomb himself," said Ya'akov. "Yochanan went, too."

"Then she did come here," said Yochanah. "Magdalit," she added when the men continued their baffled expressions. "She took one look at that empty tomb and dashed off, and didn't even get to see what happened next."

"But how did you get in?" one of the men asked. "I heard they posted guards outside the tomb."

"Yes," agreed Shim'on, the anti-Roman rebel who had taken my sons in the night I had decided to become a talmidah. "And at any rate, who moved the stone from the entrance for you? The guards certainly wouldn't have done it. 'Allow us, ladies!'" he mocked, bowing and miming an enormous effort to shift a boulder. Everyone laughed and then immediately became serious again. No one could quite be certain whether the time had come again for jokes or not.

"They were...they appeared to be dead," said Ya'akov's mother. "Because of the earthquake."

The men exchanged glances. They knew how it was to feel the earth rumble beneath their feet. They had felt it the day Yeshua died, and none of them had, it seemed, felt anything of the sort that morning.

"I did say," murmured Yochanah. "I did say the earthquake happened only just in the garden."

"Oh for heaven's sake!" I interrupted. "Will someone just tell them? Yeshua is alive!"

The room went absolutely still for a moment, and then pandemonium broke loose. Mostly it was the men, railing at us for being feeble-minded and allowing our imaginations to run away with us. But they knew us, these men, and they should have known that none of us, women or not, would invent a tale like that. We were the dove Noach had sent out to find dry land after the Flood. We were bringing these men an olive branch of hope. They should have recognized it. A dove had descended on Yeshua once, too . . .

Eventually the essential parts of the story came together —the concern about getting into the tomb, the earthquake, the deathlike guards, the empty place, the angel.

"The angel made the earth shake, I think," said Yochanah. "That's why I thought only we in the garden could feel it."

No one seemed to care about this detail except for Yochanah, but I suppose, especially with men's rampant skepticism, she felt the need to explain why none of them had felt what we described and yet it could still be true. I nodded encouragement.

But, "Kefa," someone grumbled. "Why especially Kefa?" Kefa had obviously not told everyone of his shame a few evenings ago. But either way, I thought such grumbling was absurd, particularly now.

"Does it matter? Didn't you hear what we just told you?" I asked. "Yeshua is alive! An angel said it."

"Anybody," said Shim'on, no longer the joker, "Could see an angel if they were upset enough."

"Particularly a woman," added Natan'el, as if he knew anything about it, unmarried as he was.

Philip, Natan'el's cousin, rose up to defend me, but just then Kefa and Yochanan returned.

"These women say they've seen an angel who tells them Yeshua is alive," said Natan'el, with a rather surly look.

"That's more than can be said for you," Philip murmured, sitting back down. "You of whom Yeshua said you'd see angels ascending and descending upon him. Have you seen that yet?"

Natan'el shot him a venomous glance, but Kefa, out of breath, said, "Well, I didn't see an angel. But the body's gone.

The guards are gone, too. We've got to lay low. They're going to suspect us for certain."

"But he is alive," said Yochanan. "The body's gone, but the grave clothes are still there—folded up as if he changed clothes and had done with that set forever."

I chuckled to myself, still wondering what he was wearing, but no longer fretting about it, mother-like. He had always said our clothing should be one of the least of our worries: "Don't worry about what you're going to eat or drink—or wear. Aren't life and the body about more than food and clothing?...Think about how the wildflowers grow in the fields. They don't spin or sew, but I promise you not even the magnificent Shlomo was clothed as richly. If God dresses the grass like this—which is here today and gone tomorrow—can't you see that he will clothe you even better? Such little trust!"

Such little trust we have. He was always saying that, and it seemed now, more than ever, we needed to trust, but we had spent so much of our time with him not believing. Now that it came time to believe something utterly insane and impossible, some of us couldn't quite do it.

"Such little trust you have," I suddenly heard myself saying aloud.

"What?"

Everyone looked at me. I felt my face redden with the unexpected attention. "Oh," I said. "I just think—didn't he speak of his death to you? Didn't he speak of coming back? And now we're all arguing about whether or not he did." We weren't all of us arguing of course, but I felt the need to try not to be alienating. "Did he ever promise anything he didn't accomplish?" I saw Philip glance at Natan'el, and Natan'el glare back.

"So then, we should just go back to the Galil like the angel said—if, in fact," I added, acknowledging the skeptics, "an angel said it—and find out. If he truly is alive, he will meet us there as he promised. And if he isn't—well, we're probably all still safer there than here."

"He said to go to the Galil?" Yochanan asked. He believed wholeheartedly, I saw. I did not realize until that moment how well I already knew this man I was to call my son. He was ready to do whatever his master asked, and he still believed he had a master.

"Yes," said Shlomit. "He said to tell you all—especially Kefa." She looked at that one hard, and the fisherman looked away and cleared his throat.

"Well, we should go, then," said Ya'akov. "But maybe we shouldn't go all together and all at once. Things could still be ugly with the authorities."

"K'lofah and I are going home tonight," said Miryam. "He says what use to stay in Yerushalayim, when the Messiah has been slaughtered there."

She left quietly then and there. For a little while after that there was discussion regarding who would go and who would stay, and when those remaining would make the journey themselves. I personally thought that if Yeshua really were alive, all of these precautions were rather silly. But I had already said my piece. Besides, I had to acknowledge to myself, I had once believed that Adonai would never let his Messiah die. I had been powerfully mistaken on that count, so I kept silent.

And then there was another knock on the door. It was Magdalit again, and now her face was glowing. Part of the effect came from the tears glistening on her cheeks. Her nose and those great eyes of hers were red, but she looked as if she had never been happier in her life.

37
"HE'S ALIVE!" MAGDALIT SAID

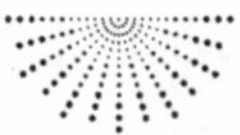

"He's alive!" Magdalit said, and her voice came out like a laugh and a sob at once. "I—I've seen him!"

"You saw him?" a chorus of voices asked all at once.

"Him, not his angel?"

"What did he say?"

"Where?"

"What did he look like?"

Magdalit laughed again, breathlessly, as if her emotions were still running, even though her body had stopped. "I thought he was the gardener." She collapsed on the floor, her laughter having overtaken her, and we were all left waiting for her to regain control of herself before we could learn anything else. Finally she sighed and said, "He said to come back to you and tell you he is going back to his Father and our Father, his God and our God."

"But will we see him?" someone asked. "Won't he come see us first?"

"Don't you understand?" Magdalit asked softly, and almost incredulously. "He is calling his Father our Father now."

"But..." the same voice protested, until someone else hushed it up.

"I don't know," said Magdalit. "He always called us family, but you know how he never gave anyone the benefit of the doubt about belonging to God before. No matter how Jewish we thought we were. And now he's saying we do belong to God after all. I don't know how it happened. I don't know how his death made the world change, but I feel like I belong to him in a way I never did before, and I feel that no one and nothing can take that away, ever again."

Yochanan went to her and lifted her up from the floor to a cushion. Those two believed. They understood each other. "Tell me about it again," he said. Everyone's attention turned to the pair for a moment to see if Magdalit would share any further information, but she just sat quietly for a while, tears streaming happily down her cheeks, Yochanan sitting respectfully nearby waiting for her to be ready to speak.

Conversation in the rest of the room turned back to plans regarding what to do next. There was still so much fear. The door remained shut and bolted. The afternoon wore on and grew quiet. Even if it were true that Yeshua was alive again, no one knew quite what to do about it.

We women crept back into the main part of the house and helped Mark's mother to prepare a meal for everybody: bread and fish and a few fresh vegetables from the tiny garden. It reminded more than one of us of Yeshua.

"Remember the time he fed five thousand men with this?" murmured Magdalit. I had not been there. I had not been a talmidah the time he did that. But still it was what I was thinking, too.

"With less than this," I said.

The afternoon wore on some more. We could just hear the murmur of the men's voices above us. It could not really be such a secret that so many of Yeshua's followers were hiding in this house, could it? And now the authorities surely knew the body was missing. Something was bound to happen before long. We finished preparing the meal and brought it back up to the large room. The air in that room had become very close, and it smelled like people. It was strange, I thought, that Adonai would submit to a life like this—like Yeshua's. A life of smells and hunger and, of course, killing.

The evening got darker, and nothing had been decided. The waiting was almost worse than it had been the day before. Yeshua's death had been unexpected and heart-rending, but also seemed final. Although it would have taken months if not years for most of us to recover, we had all been thinking in the direction that one generally does think, after someone utterly beloved dies. Now there were rumors of something none of us had truly and directly experienced before. We did not even know what we were waiting for.

Some of us began to unroll our sleeping mats. Others sat silently, knees digging into their chests, unable to sleep a wink.

And then there was a knock on the door. It was a quiet, polite knock. In the morning we might have expected such a knock from our own people, but given that so far all of the newcomers had pounded, this quiet tap seemed sinister. No one moved for a moment. Then Yochanan, who seemed to have adopted the role of porter, crept over to the door. He managed to find a chink between it and the wall, and peered through it.

"Oh," he said, sounding almost disappointed, "Miryam and K'lofah are back."

"Weren't you going to the Galil?" asked Andrew, after Yochanan had let them in. "Was there trouble?"

"No trouble," said K'lofah, who, nonetheless looked a little stunned. "We've just seen Yeshua."

"You, too?" asked Kefa. The voice was not the brash,

confronting one of the self-assured fisherman. It reminded me of how he sounded when he came to me and told me Yeshua had called him Satan. For all the "especially Kefa" that had been mentioned this morning, it did seem that those around him were getting to see the Lord before he was. I wanted to remind him that none of those who were closest to Yeshua had seen him yet—not Kefa, but also not Yochanan, not Ya'akov, nor even me, his mother. But I didn't think such an observation would help much. I knew why, in particular, Kefa was upset.

"Tell us," said Yochanan eagerly, having exhausted all the telling that he could from Magdalit some hours before.

"Well," said K'lofah's Miryam, "We set out for the Galil, as you know, although we weren't planning to head very far today. We only wanted to stop at Amma'us. There didn't seem to be any hurry to do anything, did there?"

"But you had just seen angels," said Shlomit.

"Well, I know," admitted Miryam, "but K'lofah hadn't. And I hadn't seen anything else. And I didn't know what it all meant. It was only this morning, but it was already starting to feel like a dream."

"It was really my fault," said K'lofah. "I didn't believe her. We were talking. I was reminding her of all we had seen this festival, and of how we had seen Yeshua really die, and of how people don't just get themselves up from death—particularly not after...not after a death like, er, that one."

"Well, they don't," said Miryam.

"Then a man came up behind us," said K'lofah. "He seemed to be going the same direction, and he asked us what we were talking about. So I said, 'How can you possibly have been in Yerushalayim this festival without knowing what has just happened there?" And he said, which seemed incredible to me, 'What did happen there?'"

"So he told him," Miryam continued. "He also told him that we women had seen angels, but none of us had seen

Yeshua himself, so there was no point in believing that he was really alive."

"Then things got even more surprising," said K'lofah. I leaned forward as the couple talked, trying to catch everything. I already knew what they were going to say. The traveling stranger was Yeshua. That's what they were going to say. Part of me wanted to leap up and demand to know why they were back here if Yeshua was at Amma'us, and why we didn't all just go to Amma'us right away. The other part of me knew he wouldn't be there anymore, and, having finally unleashed my store of words the night before, I just wanted to sit and hear more and more new words about my son. If I couldn't see him for myself, the least I could do was listen to other people who had. I felt as if I were tasting the words—as if they, rather than the bread and fish, were filling me up and nourishing me.

"The traveler," K'lofah continued, "said, 'Silly people! Why do you resist believing the words of the prophets? Didn't the Messiah have to die before he could be glorified?' And then he told us things—things it seems should have been obvious for anyone with the slightest knowledge of Torah—any good Jew. He showed us how, in his life, Yeshua had fulfilled them or made them plain."

"He spoke to us of this all the way to Amma'us," Miryam said. "And we felt...well at any rate, I felt...so much hope. It all made sense, now that this man was telling us these things, and the angels had told us Yeshua was alive again."

"So you invited him to dine with you," suggested Shlomit.

"Yes," agreed Miryam. "We went in and I set to, preparing the food. But when he reclined at the table, there was something familiar, and then he broke the matzoh, and he made the b'rakhah..."

"And then we knew him," concluded K'lofah. "It was Yeshua, of course. It was so completely obvious. Just like the Scriptures were, once we understood them. We stared at each other, and when we looked back, he had disappeared. So we came back here to tell you."

"A ghost," said Andrew. "Yeshua didn't just appear and disappear before. He should never have been killed as he was, and now he has come back to haunt us." Kefa shuffled uncomfortably.

"But he wasn't vengeful," said Miryam. "He was just...alive. I don't know any other way to describe it."

She had scarcely finished speaking when we all heard a small yelp from Magdalit, who had been sitting closest to the door. At first everybody looked at her and then everybody looked at the door, because standing there, in front of the door—the closed door, and on our side of it, too—was Yeshua.

He appeared to be alive. I've never seen a ghost, but he didn't look anything like I would have expected one to look. There was nothing ephemeral about him at all. He seemed more solid and real even than an angel, and the one I had seen had certainly seemed real enough.

I don't know how each person in that room felt in that moment. All I know is that I felt as if I might fall down. And then Yochanan's arms were catching me and I realized that I had. There was my son, my firstborn, given to me directly from God—and he had died. And he wasn't dead anymore. Certainly, he was not dead anymore.

With a rush I thought of all the ways I had imagined he would be my son and my Messiah, all the ways I had worried over him, all the expectations I had had of him. And there he was. He had completely ignored almost everything I had imagined, and he had surpassed my wildest dreams. I thought I knew him, but there he was, having been crucified, and having come back. I didn't even know what the other side of death looked like; how could I know anything about my son—my beloved son? And at the same time, he felt more a part of me than ever. Or perhaps it was that now I felt I was a part of him. I thought I understood why Magdalit had laughed and wept so hard all at once that morning. I wanted to laugh. I wanted to laugh so hard that I couldn't breathe. And I wanted to cry my eyes out. Instead, though, the two things got caught somewhere in the middle of my chest, and then Yeshua was speaking, and I held my breath so I wouldn't miss anything.

"Why are you all upset?" he asked, and as I tore my eyes off of him and looked round, I saw that not all the faces in the room were as rapt with delight as I felt mine might be. Maybe they were afraid he was a ghost. Maybe they were thinking, as I had been, of the ways they had failed him.

For we had all failed him. We had all let him die. Perhaps he really had come to avenge himself on us—but when I looked back at his face, I could see nothing of vengeance. And he himself had begged his Father to forgive his killers.

"Don't let the doubts overwhelm you," he continued. "See my hands and feet? It's me! Here—touch me. See? Ghosts don't have flesh and bones like this." He raised his arms, and there, in the middle of each forearm was an enormous wound. The blood was dry, but there was still evidence of it. Although the wounds somehow did not look like they needed to be tended, they did appear raw, as if they still hurt. I gasped and put my hands over my mouth. Why would he keep those? Surely, if he and Adonai his Father were one, and if he could have risen from that death that had been done him, he would have been able to make those scars disappear without a trace.

He held his arms aloft with something like pride as he waited for us to touch him—to prove him. But no one moved. It was too much. We had spent an entire day speaking of Yeshua's possible resurrection. We could have spent all our lives talking about it. It still was too much terrifying joy to bear when confronted with it in that room, which now seemed absurdly small.

"Is there anything to eat?" Yeshua asked at last. I found myself chuckling. Even chuckling seemed strange, mostly because it in fact felt completely natural to do in the presence of someone who had just defied death by dying—and it didn't seem like it should. Yeshua was talking to us as he always had—we of little trust—coaxing us, prodding us, giving us solid and tangible things to open our minds at last to glimpses of his reality. I got up from my seat on the floor and hurried over to get some of the boiled fish we had leftover from the evening meal.

He took it, eyes meeting mine, holding them, glowing. Then he ate it. The fish seemed to go where it was meant to. It didn't reappear on the floor, or fall out of the folds of his robes. But anyway, I touched his hands when I gave it to him. I knew what he felt like. It was a man standing there, not a shadow.

"This is what I meant when I said everything written about me in the Torah of Moshe, the Prophets and the Writings had to be accomplished," he said. And then, as he had with K'lofah and Miryam, he began to speak to us of these things.

I do not know that any of us were any less dull than we had been all the three years of following him before. But now, at least, we understood that the Messiah had to die. And we had seen him do it. And we had seen him alive again.

38

FOR A LONG TIME THAT NIGHT

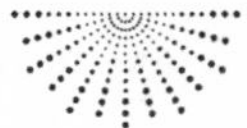

Yeshua spoke to us for a long time that night, and then, as he had always done, when he decided he had said enough for the time being, he stopped. This time, however, he also disappeared. The disappearance was just as sudden as his appearance, and even more unnerving. He had never done this before, and it was hard to imagine how any flesh-and-blood person could. On the other hand, who were we to say what flesh and blood could or could not do, if it had defied death already?

We stared at the spot where he had been, and then we stared at each other, and then we all went to sleep. No one had any better idea of what was to happen next than we had before. But we all had a much more distinct idea that Yeshua would take care of that, somehow, in his own way. All we had to do—all we had ever had to do—was trust him. Everyone slept soundly.

By morning, people began to venture more boldly out of the house. It was already four days after Yeshua's crucifixion, and we had seen neither hide nor hair of the authorities, either religious or Roman. Besides, sooner or later we really were going to have to return to the Galil. Also, someone needed to find T'oma. And I wanted to find my children. I had no idea how they were reacting to the news about their brother's death, though it was impossible they had not heard of it. I could only imagine their skepticism at hearing he was alive again. But I had at least to try to tell them.

Shim'on, the zealot who had seen Yeshua before any of the rest of us besides Magdalit, set out to find T'oma, and I set out to find my sons. I made sure Yochanan knew where I was going. I told him that I would return, but that I might stay with my Ya'akov that night—just that night. Yochanan understood. Yochanan, it seemed, almost always understood.

I walked with Shim'on for part of the way, and then set off on my own up to the house on the Temple Mount where we had celebrated the seder. I hoped my family was still there.

They were, it turned out, but it took me some time to discover this. All the windows were shuttered, the doors were locked, and there was not a sound to be heard, though I knocked at all the apertures I could reach. It appeared as if my sons were taking the same precautions that the talmidim had taken. Their loyalty to Yeshua might have been less easy to prove, but it would have been tricky to disprove as well, as they were his brothers.

"Ya'akov!" I said, as loudly as I dared. "Shim'on! Yosi! Y'hudah! I'm here...it's your mother!" I thought they should have recognized my voice, if they could even hear it. It would be cruel and clever men who would hire a woman to pose as a mother only to ferret out men guilty by association. On the other hand, our authorities had just shown themselves unfathomably cruel, and certainly clever enough to accomplish their desired cruelty. At last I decided simply to sit down and wait. Someone would have to come in or go out eventually. Or I would hear something, and then I could renew my efforts. Surely it would be impossible to keep the grandchildren so quiet indefinitely.

But the sun was warm, and the run of emotions over the past few days had exhausted me more than I knew. I sat on the bench in front of the door, leaned my head back against the wall as my father used to do outside our home in Natzeret, all those years ago, and slept.

"Imma? Imma!" came a hoarse whisper. Someone was also gently jostling my shoulder. "Get inside, Imma." I opened my eyes blearily and saw my second son, my Ya'akov, standing over me. He put his arm around my shoulders and took my hands with his other hand, as if I were an old woman already, instead of just a middling one, and led me into the house.

"He's alive," I said. It was what I had really come to tell them, and I was still too sleep-muddled to remember exactly the way I had thought out. Ya'akov obviously thought I was too muddled even to know what I was talking about. I saw his face seize up with something like pain and he said, "Imma," reproachfully before sitting me down in a chair. His wife brought me something to eat almost immediately, and I'm sure I ate it, but I do not remember doing so, nor what it was.

"No," I said. "You don't understand, and there's no reason you should really, but Yeshua is alive."

I saw my son exchange glances with his wife. They thought I had gone mad with grief. I knew it. "Where are the others?" I asked.

"On the upper level," my daughter-in-law said, warily. "But maybe you should speak to us first. We don't want to upset the children any more than they have been."

"The children are upset?" I wondered, with a slight pang. What did they know about it? Had they any idea how awful it had been? I felt I didn't even know what they knew of their uncle Yeshua. They had seen so little of him in the last three years. The youngest children could scarcely have known him at all. And when their parents had thought so unfavorably of him for so long, what could they make of any of this?

"Their fathers' brother was killed and they wouldn't be upset?" my daughter-in-law, normally calm and sympathetic to me, was glaring.

"Then let me see them," I said. "I have news for everyone, not just for you. This concerns the whole family." I rose and ascended to the upper story. They could have stopped me, but I was their mother, and it would have been unseemly. So they followed, instead.

The upper level of that house was very similar to that of Mark's mother's home, with fewer furnishings because it was rented. I felt as if I were Magdalit the morning before, having seen and experienced something so wonderful I thought I would burst with it, yet cowed by a roomful of beloved skeptics. I looked at the faces of my children and grandchildren. They all gazed back, expecting something, with no idea what.

Yosi brought me a seat, and I sat. "What do you know of the last four days?" I asked them. I decided it was better to start out all together. Maybe, if I started speaking of what they knew, my words would carry them along to what they could never have imagined. And maybe—by some miracle of Adonai, who was time and again a worker of miracles—they would come to believe me.

"Yeshua is dead," said the boy—the beloved little Adam I had held to myself and cried over three years before after the scene in the Temple. He was older now, but his lower lip still jutted forward, and his forehead knit together in an expression of mixed anger and bafflement. "They killed him." That was what they knew.

No one said anything else for some moments. Then Ya'akov said softly, "I was there, Imma. I saw him die. I saw you holding him. I was too afraid to come forward, and it should have been me, not Yochanan, who supported you. I know it should. Imma, I'm sorry."

I saw with a start that there were tears in the eyes of this practical, sensible man. I held out my hand to him. "You needed to be here," I said. "For your family. I am well. Yochanan..." I stopped. I could tell them about the charge Yeshua had given to Yochanan regarding me at some other time. Right now Ya'akov felt sorry enough, and he hadn't the hope I had yet. There was a time for everything, and this was only the time to talk about what had happened with Yeshua.

"Yochanan what?"

"Nothing," I said. "It's nothing." Of course it wasn't nothing. But it wasn't something I could talk about then, either.

Ya'akov let it go at that, and Shim'on said, "Yeshua is dead, Imma. We know it. We failed him. We are staying hidden because of the family, but maybe there is something else we should do. What would you like us to do, Imma? Is there something he wanted us to do?"

I had been, I noticed, staring at my hands holding Ya'akov's hand, but now here was my son Shim'on, asking what to do next.

I looked at all of them again. "He wants you to trust him," I said.

"But he died," protested Shim'on, in spite of his desire to do what his brother would have wanted. "What is there to believe? I was beginning to think he really was the Messiah—my own brother! But now he is dead and everything is just as it ever was."

"No," I said, feeling a smile about to burst onto my lips in spite of myself. "It isn't. Listen to me, my children. This is a difficult story for you, and if, in the end, you think your mother is crazy, well then, so be it. But I promise to you..." I stopped. Yeshua had told us never to swear by anything, and I had been about to swear by the God of our fathers. "It is the truth," I said simply. "Come children," I said then, to the youngest ones. They would believe me, because Yeshua had said truly that the Kingdom of God belonged to people like them. And if their parents doubted, and resented that I had told such an outlandish hope to their little ones, well, it would not be easily undone. Someone in the generations of our family would know that Yeshua was of Adonai, and that he had died, and that he had come to life again.

Adam was the first to come to me. He sat on the floor at my feet, and soon enough his cousins followed, so that I had scarcely begun my tale before all of them gathered around me like chickens. Their parents sat as well, some way back. Everything felt strangely formal, and I wondered if Yeshua knew his mother was speaking to a crowd—albeit a small one—and telling stories, just as he had always done.

"Yeshua was killed," I acknowledged. "He never did anything wrong. I want everyone to understand this. We might not all have understood him, but he never spoke a lie, and he never made a false judgment. They had no right to kill him."

"Of all the people," Ya'akov agreed under his breath, "who ever did not deserve the death curse, it was Yeshua." He was remembering the story of Adam and Havah, the first pair, who had disregarded the warning of Elohim and been cursed with death. Ya'akov's statement startled a smile out of me after all.

"Indeed!" I said. "And so the curse could not stick. It did not stick. Listen to me, children. Yeshua is alive again."

This was the first any in that room except for Ya'akov and his wife had heard of this, so there was a little commotion for a few minutes. Most of the commotion was protest, but so it had been in the other upper room just the morning before. This was a tale impossible to believe without some other sort of sign. But the children...the children, I noticed, believed me already. I was their grandmother. Why would I lie to them?

After some of the noise had died down, mostly because someone remembered that they were hiding and did not want to be heard, I resumed my account. "Believe me or not,"

I said. "I will tell you how I know in good time. But there is something else you need to understand about Yeshua."

I took a deep breath. Never, not even once, had I spoken to any of my children—not even to Yeshua himself—about how I had come by him. I would have to word things carefully, because it was highly likely that none of them would believe me at all. They would think I had been unvirtuous, just as Yosef's family had always thought, and then they would never let me near my grandchildren again. The thought flitted through my mind that perhaps this was why Yeshua had given me to Yochanan's care. He knew his brothers. He knew they would not tolerate me for long.

"Yeshua is your brother," I said. "But your father was not his father."

The room was deathly still for a moment, but I saw jaws and fists clench, and Ya'akov's face turned red. "Why are you telling us this now, Mother?" he asked, slowly, deliberately, his tone daring me to prove myself less worthy of a mother than I already had.

"Because," I sighed, "you have to know this about your brother before you can understand that he is no longer dead."

"Well then," Ya'akov said, in the same cold tone, "proceed."

So I proceeded. Nobody said much, except for me, and I felt sillier and sillier. There were a few choked gasps when I first said that Ha'Elyon himself was Yeshua's Father—really and solely, but there was very little noise from anyone else after that.

It had been one thing to tell the talmidim. They already believed something about Yeshua—he already had their allegiance. I could speak the words I had stored up about Yeshua to them, and even before we knew he was alive—even when those words seemed like a joke in the face of tragedy—they seemed something of a beautiful joke. A beautiful hope, even if nothing came of it. Doggedly I told my children and grandchildren all those same words and names I had learned for

Yeshua throughout his life, but I felt that to them they must sound an absurd mockery. I wasn't even sure they heard anything else I said after the bit where I told them who Yeshua's father was.

But I kept telling. I told them of the angel, the visit to Elisheva and her baby's dance within her womb. I spoke of the shepherds and the magi and of Egypt. I told them of the first visit to the Temple, even though they knew something of that themselves. I told them what I saw and heard when Yeshua was baptized, and what he had told me of the forty days in the wilderness and his testing by the Adversary. I explained, more truly than I had yet been able to, how it was I had become a talmidah, and how it felt, discovering again and again what it meant to be mother to the Messiah.

Then I told how Yeshua had predicted his death, and how we had all tried to imagine that he was telling more parables, because we couldn't bear it. I told how also, he had said he would rise again, and how that made the premonitions of his death seem even less likely, for Yeshua was the only one any of us had seen who could bring someone back to life, and how could he bring his own self back if he ever died?

Finally, I remembered the death itself. I hadn't spoken so much to the talmidim about what that had been like for me. We each had our own memories of that, and it was so new and so raw, even though we knew he was now alive, that the pain was still fresh. I would rather have passed over this part of the story, but it was, really, the main part of the story. I had to make sure my children understood me. I wanted them to know I was as sure as they were that their brother had died—that I had seen the blood and water separate out of his side—that I had held the lifeless body. That I myself had felt the absence of him—of his spirit.

I paused. Still no one had anything to say. Every face was blank. These are my children, I thought to myself in an instant. How can I have so little idea what they are thinking?

And then, lest I lose my nerve, I took a deep breath and finished the story. I told them of the angel we women saw in the morning, and then of Magdalit's encounter with Yeshua himself. I told them of Yochanan and Kefa's failure to find the body in the tomb and of how Yochanan believed. Then I told them how Yeshua appeared to all of us in the room.

"No, Imma," said Yosi, shaking his head sadly. "It was not he. You were all together in the same room for two days. You were overcome with grief. It was some madness—forgive me, Imma, but—some madness begun with the women."

"But," said Y'hudah thoughtfully, and before I could become angry or protest, "surely something did happen to the body. That's worrying. We need to try to find it and get it back. They have already treated him with enough disrespect; did they truly need to disinter him? Is there no respect for the dead?"

This, I thought, ignoring Yosi's slight of a moment before, was somewhat promising, even though nobody seemed willing to believe the truth of what I was telling them. At least one of the brothers was still concerned about the respect due his eldest sibling, even though I had just divulged rather unconventional origins for that same sibling. I was not surprised they didn't believe any other part of my tale yet, save for the detail of the missing body. We talmidim had not believed much more until we saw Yeshua alive with our own eyes, either.

"Tomorrow," Ya'akov sighed wearily. His was the only face I thought I could read, and it said he didn't know what to think. "Tomorrow we will come out of hiding and find what happened. We will try to find some justice at least. And if there's trouble—well, I suppose it's still less trouble than Yeshua went to for us."

I stared at him. He was continually surprising me, my Ya'akov. To change from such coldness and hostility with my revelation of Yosef's non-participation in Yeshua's conception, to a statement of such sibling loyalty was bold, and clearly took some strength.

"For us?" I whispered. I could not believe he had said that, either.

"If he was the Messiah," said Ya'akov, "or if he wasn't—he obviously thought he was. He never did anything for himself. He must have thought somehow that his death would accomplish something for the people—or he must have thought he could escape actual death. At any rate, it was for us, whether it accomplished anything or not."

"Yes," I murmured. "Don't look for the body tomorrow, children. Come with us up to the Galil again. Maybe you will see him, too. At any rate, you won't find his body."

Ya'akov's wife pursed her lips, and Ya'akov sighed. "Let us sleep," he said. "Take your rest, Imma. We will talk some more tomorrow."

But I had had enough of talking. I wanted to see Yeshua again, and I somehow did not think he would appear in the midst of this crowd this evening as he had among the group of his talmidim the evening before. "I am going to stay with Yochanan now," I said. "Yeshua wanted it. He said it before he died," I added. "I'm sorry. But you will always be welcome with us if you choose to come. You can still be his talmidim, you know."

"We're his family," muttered Y'hudah. "Why should we be his talmidim, too? Especially now?"

"Because," I said, "now we know he has all the power in the world, and he loved us enough to come back to us. Because it isn't the same thing." I turned on my heel, not angrily, but decisively, and descended out of the house.

39

UP TO THE GALIL

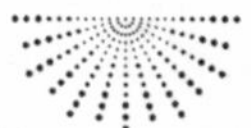

In the end, the group of talmidim, which had grown in size overnight from just the Eleven and the women, traveled up to the Galil in one big cluster, just as we had done when we followed Yeshua about the countryside and listened to his teachings. None of us were much afraid at the moment. Yochanan had, through his connections in the home of the head cohanim, learned that the authorities were, in some respect, absolutely terrified that they could not find the body. We did not think, under the circumstances, that we had much to trouble us from them.

The mood of our caravan was high with expectation. T'oma, who had evidently expressed as much cynicism as my own children, had seen Yeshua only a short time before. On the strength of his and others' assertions, many of Yeshua's original talmidim who did not number among the Eleven, were convinced or at least hopeful. Perhaps we would all see him when we reached the Galil. Perhaps we could follow him and listen to more and deeper truths than we had ever imagined before. Perhaps, even better, he would finally overthrow Rome. It did not seem likely, now that he had died and returned to life, that he would be able to die again. Perhaps this was just what was needed before the great triumph, when the Messiah would rule over the earth and, through him, all peoples would submit to Adonai.

On the other hand, somehow the overthrow of Rome seemed less necessary. It was almost as if, having conquered death itself, overthrowing a human kingdom was too small a hope now. Whatever would happen next, it would be great and glorious, and it would bring Ha'Elyon's Kingdom to earth.

On the second day of our travels, my eldest grandson appeared in the crowd. He was running. "Grandmother," he gasped, well before he had sufficiently caught his breath, "we're coming. Abba sent me ahead to tell you. We're coming!"

My heart lurched, and I embraced him as if he had given me the world, which was impossible, since Yeshua had already done that by coming back. But this was the next best thing. "How soon?" I asked. "How much distance between us?"

"Well," said my grandson as if it should have been obvious, "I'm here. We left, I think, the same day as you, but some hours later. It took Abba forever to decide what to do."

"Does he—" I asked, "Do they believe me?"

"Abba says, 'Well, all we can do is see. And if it isn't true, we won't see anything at all, though we still might not, for all we disbelieved before.'" I smiled. It was how Ya'akov would think—and how I would have thought, too, most likely. But I wasn't sure Yeshua would think that way. He had always taught forgiveness, after all. If he chose not to appear to his brothers, I thought his reasons would be other than those Ya'akov expected. But it was such a great miracle that my children were even considering there to be truth in the tales of their brother, that I couldn't help but hope he would show himself to them, too.

We arrived in the Galil in the early evening and watched

the sky change colors in Lake Kinneret as the sun set. I had always thought the sight very beautiful, the times I had seen it, but that day it seemed so lovely it made my throat ache. It was a glory, I thought, preceding the true great glory when Yeshua would come to us in the morning. He would come then, I felt sure of it.

But he didn't. In fact, for the next little while, very little seemed to happen. No one saw Yeshua at all. Not my sons, not the talmidim, not me. My sons settled back into their old routines without much comment, but Ya'akov, I noticed, was thinner than usual, and did not look as if he had been sleeping. It was with something of a shock that I realized he had wanted to believe me—he still did—only he was not certain that he could. I was less certain myself.

"Sometimes," admitted Yochanan to me once, "I feel as if I dreamed it. Sometimes I have to talk to Magdalit; she seems to be the only one who can't relinquish the idea that she saw him."

"And touched him," I said. "What about T'oma? He touched him, too."

"What about you?" Yochanan countered. I said nothing. Neither Yochanan nor I could find any routine to settle into. I blamed the fact that I was now in K'far Nachum, and most of my home activities had involved my sister, who had returned to Natzeret. But I knew that truly, I had forgotten what it was like to be settled anywhere. Many of us had. Yeshua's words and presence were what we lived for, and we could no longer hear them, or find him at all.

One morning I woke to the sound of quiet discussion in the lower level of Zavdai's house, where Yochanan had grown up and where I had now, a little uncertainly, taken up residence. "I'm going fishing," said a voice that sounded like Kefa's. I thought I could make out Natan'el and T'oma down there, as well as Yochanan and his brother. There was some further murmuring. But they were fishermen first, these men. They had been fishermen before Yeshua had called them, and lacking any other direction, what else were they going to do?

The nets came out—nets that had not been used in months, if not years. "Do you reckon you still know how to do this?" T'oma asked.

"I suppose we'll find out," said Ya'akov, hoisting a netted mass over his shoulder.

"What about breakfast?" I asked. Zavdai's wife, the natural mother of my new son, was stirring, too.

"Not hungry," said Kefa, speaking for all of them as usual. "When we get back."

Hours later, I was outdoors, helping Zavdai's wife wash linens. The noise preceded the men, and we looked up to see them struggling but laughing up the hill, dragging something bulging enormously behind them.

"What on earth...?" I asked, but Zavdai's wife said, "I only saw them once with a load like that before."

It was then that I realized, though it should have been obvious, that the bundle it took five men to drag along was a net full to bursting with fish. Then I realized further that there were no longer five men—there were six. I looked again. The sixth one looked...he looked a little like . . .

"Yeshua!" I cried, and ran forward in spite of myself. I thought probably the men would not want to be interrupted in their progress and their camaraderie, but all the same, I couldn't help it. It was the first I had seen of my son since the day he had come back from death, and I felt I had missed so much.

"Imma," he said, beaming, and holding out his arms to me.

40

THERE WERE FISH TO EAT

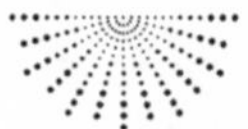

There were fish to eat and fish to sell in plenty in the next few days, and especially that day. Yochanan had come back from that fishing trip more boisterous than I had ever seen him, and Kefa came back quieter. But Kefa also seemed more at peace now. His eyes lost their haunted look, and he smiled more—quiet smiles, as if he had just thought of something that no one would understand to hear him tell it. Zavdai's wife and I prepared a feast for the Eleven and the women that night, and Yeshua stayed with us instead of disappearing like a phantom, and he spoke to us some more.

The horror that had been Pesach that year was now behind us by some weeks, and someone mentioned the festival of Shavu'ot that was coming next. We would go to Yerushalayim again, of course—or would we? We couldn't imagine anything possibly happening at this festival that would be worse—or better—than what had happened at the last one, but maybe, under the circumstances, it would be better for us to stay in the North for a while.

Everyone looked at Yeshua. But he seemed to think it natural that we would go. Obvious, even. And maybe even necessary. "Don't leave Yerushalayim," he told us, "Wait there for what our Father has promised—that I told you about. Cousin Yochanan used to immerse people in the water, but it won't be long now before you are all immersed in the Ruach HaKodesh!"

It sounded to me as if he would not be there with us. This idea left a slightly hollow feeling in the pit of my stomach, but no one else seemed to notice. Or if they did, no one said anything. Perhaps Yeshua wanted us to go to the festival on our own simply because of what had happened at Pesach. Perhaps he would stay here and bide his time until we came back. And then the Ruach HaKodesh would somehow baptize us...I had already been covered with the Ruach HaKodesh, I thought to myself. It had given me a child—this child, who was speaking and always had spoken mysteries to us. But the Ruach HaKodesh itself I had not felt or seen that time. Only the results of its presence. Only the quickening in my womb, the growing of my belly. Only the child who had grown into this man. The only other time I had had any experience of the Ruach HaKodesh was when I had seen it land as a dove on my son's head, and had known it for what it was.

The idea of going to Yerushalayim without the physical protection of Yeshua, and then of being subjected to some other manifestation of Ha'Elyon's own spirit made me nervous. Of all the people eating with Yeshua there that night, I suppose I knew most what to expect. And I did not know what to expect at all. But I knew that, even in spite of everything, too much closeness to Ha'Elyon was frightening. I had no idea what being baptized by the Ruach HaKodesh would feel like or require, but I was sure there must be something.

But maybe this was necessary before Yeshua finally ushered in his kingdom. Perhaps this was why he would wait for us in the Galil. We would receive this baptism, and then we would be prepared to help him bring the kingdom in. Satisfied with this thought, I sighed with relief, wrapped my arms about my knees, and listened to Yeshua talk through the night, until I dozed off.

"No more fishing," said Kefa the next morning, so unlike the one before. "At least, not unless it's for people. Like he told me all that time ago." He chuckled. I asked him what he meant.

"Oh," he said. "Didn't you hear that bit near the end last night? He gave us our purpose, he did. He gave us the next bit of bringing in his kingdom. Last night, he said, 'The authority of all heaven and earth is mine. Considering this, go out to all the people, all over the world, and make them into my talmidim. Immerse them into Abba, and me, and the Ruach HaKodesh. Teach them to obey me—and don't worry, or forget—I'll be with you forever.'"

"But that..." I began. Then I sighed. "It never makes any sense," I said. "His kingdom keeps getting bigger and bigger, but it still seems invisible, to me. Look. Rome is still here, with all its decadence. And our religious rulers haven't changed any either, in spite of losing the satisfaction of doing away with the man they hated most."

"I don't understand either," admitted Kefa. "But I think maybe understanding it all doesn't matter to me as much anymore. I figure, he's going to tell the truth, and whatever he says to do, he'll help us do it. I don't much like the idea of going all over the world. I'd much rather stay right here with my own people, and I don't want to go away from him ever again. But he said he'd always be with us, and I guess I believe he wouldn't say it if he didn't mean it."

"He wouldn't," I agreed. "Whatever else is true, it's that. And he is always able to do what he means, too," I added. "Which is more than some of the rest of us can say."

Kefa gave me a sharp glance and I reddened. "I didn't mean..." I said. "I was talking of myself." He smiled wryly. He knew that I meant what I said, too, and that, like him, I didn't always follow through quite as I had intended.

For a few days, then, life seemed almost like old times, only better because now all of my children were with us, too. My sons, hearing Yeshua had been seen again, ventured down from Natzeret and stayed with various members of the Eleven who had originally lived in K'far Nachum. Their reunion with their eldest brother was a sight to behold—such laughing and kissing and tears and backslapping. I thought maybe it was what the reunion was like between Yosef of the Torah and his brothers when he revealed his identity to them finally—a little bit of shame and sorrow on the part of the brothers, but full forgiveness and delight at reconciliation by the one who had been wronged in the first place. Yeshua even spent some time with his brothers and their families alone. It seemed as if they were all making amends, although surely even they knew Yeshua had nothing to amend at all. When I saw the brothers together—all of the brothers—sometimes I felt as if my heart would leap out of my eyes in a shower of happiness.

But these days were also unlike the old times. Yeshua did not stay in anyone's home anymore, and none of us any longer slept out under the stars because that's where he was, either. He came and went without warning, as he had more or less always done. Only now half the time we didn't see him go—or come. He was just there, or he wasn't. We traveled less. Mostly we stayed in K'far Nachum and waited until someone saw him, and we all came together. Very few people joined us who hadn't followed him with their hearts as well as their feet in the first place. Whether this was because they were afraid of what had happened already, or because they could so little believe in a man who had died and returned to life, that they could scarcely even perceive him, I never knew. Sometimes I saw Yeshua walking down by the boats in K'far Nachum. People glanced up at him, but their faces were expressionless. It was as if they looked at him but could not see him at all.

This mattered little to those of us who did know and love him, however. Sometimes I found myself listening to him speaking and then with a start I would stare at him. This was my son. This was the fruit of my womb. This was a man who had died before my very eyes. Yet he was not dead now. Nothing and no one could be further from death than Yeshua, I thought.

41
YESHUA WENT WITH US AFTER ALL

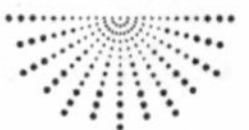

Soon enough it was time to travel south again. Yeshua went with us after all, which buoyed everyone's spirits considerably. We still never saw where he slept, but it was no matter, for he was always sitting, watching over the camp in the morning. There was quite a crowd of us—the Eleven with their families, the women with theirs, all of my sons and their families as well. We made a happy party. Yeshua never said anything ominous, as he had for months before Pesach. The Kingdom of Heaven was near.

We arrived in the vicinity of Yerushalayim just a few days before the festival began, and so, not surprisingly, we went to Beit-Anyah first. Marta and Little Miryam had not seen Yeshua since he had risen, and they both acted as if they were afraid he would break or blow away, until they became accustomed to his presence again. Little Miryam's face streamed with silent tears for quite some time, though she never said anything.

In the morning, Yeshua woke us all himself. Those of us in the house followed him outdoors, and everyone outdoors followed him, too, up the Mount of Olives. Yeshua looked at the city for a long time.

"Lord," asked Shim'on, the one who had once been a zealot—and maybe still was, if it came to that, "Is it finally time for you to restore the kingdom to Isra'el?"

"The Father sets those times," Yeshua replied, cryptic as ever. "It is not for you to know." Once he had told us even he did not know the times. He was not quite saying that this time, but either way, it was clear that once again, the coming of the kingdom was not going to be exactly what any of us expected. "But," he continued, "when the Ruach Ha'Kodesh comes on you, you will receive power to be my witnesses in Yerushalayim, and in all the rest of Y'hudah, and even Shomron, and from here to all the world."

Then he raised his arms and spoke a blessing over us. Over all of us—the Eleven, and the women, and the rest of our families, and Marta, Little Miryam, El'azar, and so many other people who had followed for so many years. There was a crowd on the mountain overlooking Yerushalayim that day. The blessing rolled over and between and through us. I closed my eyes. It felt like a cool refreshing rush of water on a hot day, the blessing did. Or, on the other hand, like warm sun after days of cold, bone-chilling rain. The sound of Yeshua's voice kept its strength, but it began to recede. I wondered if I was falling asleep. I opened my eyes.

Yeshua was not there. I was still facing the exact spot where he had been standing. I hadn't even been very far back from him. But he was gone. This was something new. We had all become accustomed to Yeshua's sudden appearances and disappearances, but he had never been present with just his voice and no body before. Then I noticed everyone staring upward. I craned my head upward, too.

Yeshua was in the sky. I mean, he was actually hovering above our heads. It was almost as if he were wafting on an unseen breeze—except that he was not floating to and fro, but slowly rising straight upward. It was difficult to see his face. He was receding further and further, and I so wanted to see his face. I found myself straining to see. Then, there! He looked down. He smiled. I thought he smiled right at me.

Soon after that, a cloud moved into view, and I never saw him again. I knew, too, even before the angels appeared to tell all of us that he had ascended to heaven, that he had gone to his Father and I would not see his face—his smile—again. At least not until the final resurrection.

They said he would come back and, since the angels had never lied about Yeshua before, I knew he would. But, as Moshe only looked on Eretz-Yisra'el from a distance, and never lived in it though he brought the people through the wilderness, I knew I would not see Yeshua's return. It had been with me as Adonai had said, and so I had brought the Messiah to the world. But I did not think I would see the establishment of the Kingdom.

42

I HAVE NOT SEEN IT

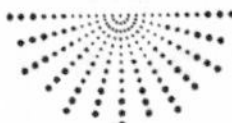

I have not seen it. And, all the same, I have, too.

After the angels disappeared again, everybody—that whole crowd of talmidim from the Galil and Beit-Anyah and Beit-Lechem and Yerushalayim—stood around for quite some time with our hands hanging at our sides and nothing to say. And then Kefa said, "He said to wait in Yerushalayim for the Ruach HaKodesh."

"But what does that mean?" someone asked.

"How should I know?" said Kefa. "And, if it comes to that, why should I know? I expect we'll all know soon enough. In the meantime, here we all are for a festival, which we were going to celebrate in Yerushalayim anyhow. And we do have orders. So I can't see that there's anything for it but to follow them."

This, I thought, was a very sensible plan. With my arm linked in Shlomit's, and with Yochanan not far behind, I began to march back down the hill. I found, marching, however, that my eyes were smarting a bit.

"How can I be sad?" I asked Shlomit. "He's alive, and he has gone to his Father for us—for us all. The horror of Pesach was changed into this great promise...it isn't like he's dead. It isn't like we're grieving that body in the tomb anymore. But I miss him. I miss him already."

Shlomit didn't say anything. I supposed this was because she had the sensible answer as usual but knew me well enough to understand that sensible wasn't what I wanted right then. But then I looked at her and saw that her eyes were moist, too. "I'm not even his mother!" she said, smiling despite her red-rimmed eyes. Her voice caught.

"Imma," said Yochanan behind us, catching up, "Imma, is it wrong to miss him?"

I had, of course, just been wondering the same thing, but something definitive seemed to be called for. And besides, how could missing the son of Ha'Elyon be wrong? It could be startling—for how was it that any of us had been given the privilege even to know the son of Ha'Elyon? To know him well enough to miss him?

"No," I said, looking up at this new son of mine and letting him see the tears drying on my face, "No, I don't think it is."

And so we waited. Everybody stayed in Yerushalayim where they could. There were about one hundred and twenty of us who had seen Yeshua taken up to heaven and who trusted that he would come back, and we couldn't all fit into Mark's mother's upstairs room. But the Eleven and my sons and I stayed up there. Shlomit and Magdalit and the other women stayed nearby, either with their husbands—if they had them and those men were waiting for Yeshua, too—or together in one of the houses set aside for the festivals.

We all met together when and where we could, and we prayed and we prayed. On the one hand, our people pray all the time, day in and day out; as we go about our daily tasks, we speak aloud to Adonai, whether or not he hears us. But this was different. We went about very few daily tasks. We did not even prepare for the coming festival. We just sat together and spoke to Adonai for hours.

Some of us, Magdalit especially, because of her encounter with Yeshua after he had come back to life, even began addressing Ha'Elyon as "Abba." I had some difficulty with this. It was unheard of for anyone to be this familiar with the Master of the Universe, except for Yeshua, of course. He truly was one with that Master, and Ha'Elyon truly was his Father. But also, it felt confusing and wrong to call "Abba" the one who had given me my son. Was I now Yeshua's sister instead of his mother? I supposed Magdalit was right, and certain categories were meaningless where Ha'Elyon was concerned, but it still felt very strange, and it was some time before I could say "Abba" in my prayers.

Nevertheless, we prayed. Once, when the weather was fine, we met all together out of doors. But passers-by noticed, and seemed to find the whole thing either ominous or laughable. Why were we not preparing for the festival? What did we think we were doing? They called out and interrupted and hissed and chortled. Then T'oma reminded us that long ago Yeshua had taught us to pray in secret, so after that we squeezed into the upstairs room during the day and prayed until late at night. It was hot in there, but no one complained. No one wanted to miss the mysterious coming of the Ruach HaKodesh. Besides, we all felt closer to Yeshua this way—meeting all together with others who had known and loved him, praying to his Father who was now somehow our Father. We would have felt adrift otherwise.

We prayed that we might be able to love one another as Yeshua had loved us. We prayed for the city of Yerushalayim and the people who had contributed to Yeshua's death. We prayed for the Ruach HaKodesh to come on us as Yeshua had promised. We prayed for Yeshua to return quickly.

One day Kefa brought up the uncomfortable memory of the K'riot. "Now," said Kefa, "it says in the Psalms, 'Let his estate become desolate, let there be no one to live in it'; and 'Let someone else take his place as a supervisor.' So someone who has been with us since the beginning—since Yochanan immersed Yeshua in the Yarden, should be chosen to take his place."

So we prayed about this, too. Two men's names came up, but lacking a better way to decide between them, we drew lots. "Lord, you know all of our hearts," Yochanan's brother Ya'akov prayed, undoubtedly thinking of the K'riot's black heart as he spoke, "Show us which of these men you want to take the role Y'hudah abdicated." The lot fell to a man named Mattityahu, who had as little to do with tax-collecting as the other Mattityahu had had much to do with it. He bowed his head and we prayed for him, too.

And then the morning of Shavu'ot dawned. We gathered together again early—perhaps earlier even than usual. As he was accustomed to do, Kefa began the prayers, and my son Ya'akov began to pray next, but suddenly the sound of his voice was erased by a much louder sound. Something vast was roaring down out of the sky. It sounded like the wind, but a stronger, much more violent wind than any of us had ever known before. Magdalit, who was sitting near a window, had an instant to glance outside and later told us that to her astonishment, not a blade of grass or leaf of tree moved in that blast, but all of us felt it as it entered the house. It was neither hot nor cold, but each of us felt the shudder of impact, and as soon as the noise ceased and we had recovered enough from the buffeting to look at each other, we saw that we were all on fire. The room seemed engulfed in the blaze, but though I felt a warm tingling, there was no sense of being burnt up.

I cried out in surprise and a little bit of fear. Then I cried out again in the next moment when I remembered Elisheva's Yochanan prophesying that the one coming after him would immerse with fire. As I watched, the flames began to separate, and soon each of us had tongues of fire resting on us, though the room had returned to itself. Yochanan my son began to speak, and I stared at him, for the words coming out of his mouth were not Aramaic. They reminded me a little of a language I had heard before, but only very rarely. It was a sound one could occasionally hear among the more exotic traders in Yerushalayim, and also, if my memory served me, similar in sound to the speech of the magi who had come to worship Yeshua so many years before. The strange thing was that, although I could tell the language was one I had never learnt before, I could also understand it. Yochanan was speaking of Yeshua and of his love, of his life and death and resurrection.

I suddenly had a flash of insight. "Children," I said, because they had all taken to calling me "Imma" by this time. I noticed with less surprise than I might have a moment before that my tongue and lips were not making shapes to which I was accustomed—that I was speaking in another language myself. I only hoped everyone could understand me as I had understood Yochanan. "Children, we are the messengers of Ha'Elyon. He lit up a bush in the desert to speak to Moshe and urge him to bring freedom to his people. Now we are the ones who are burning but not consumed. We are the message of freedom, and we are also the ones to bring freedom to the people. There are people of every nation in Yerushalayim today, here to celebrate Shavu'ot and to worship the God of Isra'el. Listen to us! We need to go outside and tell them!"

People were already standing. Everyone was speaking now, and no one sounded the same. It was as if the curse of the tower of Babel was happening all over again, only this time we could understand, and the languages were uniting us instead of driving us apart.

When we got outside, there was already quite a crowd of people milling curiously about the house. Whether they were there because they had heard the rush of wind, too, or because, in our excitement, we had all been speaking loudly enough to be heard out of doors, I do not know. But it kept growing as we kept speaking. I began telling of the names I had learned for Yeshua since he was born, and a woman in the crowd roughly grabbed my elbow and said, in a language I had never learned, "What did you say? How do you know my speech?"

So I told her of the Ruach HaKodesh coming upon me and giving me a son, and how that son had grown up and been killed and returned to life. I said how he had gone back to his Father, the God of everything, in order to send the Ruach HaKodesh back to me—to us—and that that was why we were speaking as we were. She looked at me as if I had lost my mind, but I don't think she could have faulted my speech at all.

Then I noticed some whispering. It was as if Yeshua were there again, and there were dissenters in the crowd just as there had always been. I thought to myself that if the Ruach HaKodesh were really from Yeshua, because Yeshua really was one with Ha'Elyon, then perhaps he was indeed right there with us, though in a completely unaccustomed form. I thought I should not be surprised at all when I overheard a man say to his awestruck companion, "They've just had too much to drink!"

I laughed a little bit. I thought of the night Yeshua had first shown himself as the Messiah to anyone but me—the night he had given an entire wedding celebration more wine than they could hold. I thought I did, indeed, feel a little bit giddy like that, except that my mind, although overwhelmed, was quite clear. I laughed again. People would think of anything to avoid uncomfortable conclusions.

"We are not drunk," I said. "Drunk people don't miraculously learn other people's languages."

But apparently I was not speaking his language, because he looked at me askance, and then rolled his eyes at his friend. His friend, half-convinced by him, nodded.

But this was wrong! Something about it was funny to be sure, but here we were, speaking life to people so that they could hear about it without translation, and some unhelpful characters were trying to make light of it. I made my way through the crowd back to Kefa, who was the first of the Twelve I could successfully reach. "Kefa!" I said, and found myself speaking Aramaic again, "They're saying we're drunk!"

He looked at me and chuckled, and I thought I saw him remembering the wedding, too. But then he said, "That's crazy. Drunk people don't act like this."

"I know!" I said. "Tell them!"

He nodded then, and grabbed T'oma's arm. "T'oma," he said, "Get the rest of the Eleven—I mean, the Twelve. We need to stand together and show that we're united in all we have to say."

T'oma went one way into the crowd, and I went the other, and soon enough of the men who had lived and laughed and worked and eaten with Yeshua every day for three years were all assembled on the outer steps of the house.

Once they were there, Kefa began to speak. It didn't take the crowd long to quiet down; they were obviously intent on some sort of explanation, whether or not they were equally intent on believing it. "You people of Y'hudah!" Kefa called out. He was definitely the right one to do the speaking. His voice was loud even when he was trying to be quiet. "And all the rest of you staying here in Yerushalayim! Listen and I'll tell you what all this means!"

They were listening.

"None of us are drunk, as some of you are suggesting. Please. It's only nine in the morning!" At this, some of the people nodded, and others chuckled and shrugged.

"No," Kefa went on, "this is what the prophet Yo'el spoke about: 'Adonai says: "At the end of days, I will pour my Spirit out onto everyone. Your sons, and your daughters, too, will become prophets. Young men will have visions, old men will dream dreams. Even on the lowliest among you who serve me, both men and women, I will pour my Spirit out in those days; and they will all prophesy...'""

He went on further with the prophecy of Yo'el. I was impressed. I hadn't known he was so well-versed in the Torah—this fisherman son of a fisherman. But perhaps the Ruach HaKodesh had given him this as he had given foreign speech. Or perhaps Kefa had learned more of such words from Yeshua than I realized.

"'And then,'" he finished his quotation, "'absolutely anyone calls on Adonai's name will be saved.'"

"People of Isra'el!" he was still speaking. "Listen up! Yeshua from Natzeret was a man whose miraculous signs clearly showed you he was from Adonai—Adonai did these works through him before your very eyes. It was God's plan ahead of time that Yeshua be arrested, and with the help of people not tied to the Torah, you nailed him up on a cross and did away with him!"

No one said a word.

"But God has brought him back to life! He has released him from death; it was impossible for death to keep hold of him."

A few people raised their heads with renewed interest as Kefa then showed how our great King, David himself, had prophesied someone resisting the decay of death. He could not, Kefa showed, have been talking about himself, for we all knew where David's tomb was. "Therefore," Kefa explained, "since he was a prophet to whom God had a perpetual descendant on the throne, he was telling in advance the Messiah's resurrection. It was the Messiah, not David, who was spared abandonment in Sh'ol and spared the decay of his flesh. God raised Yeshua from the dead! And we here have all seen it!"

At this, some of us cheered. We could not help it. We were witnesses of it—of this astonishing thing.

"Now Yeshua has been brought up to God's right hand. He has received the promised Ruach HaKodesh and is pouring that gift out on us now—it is him you are seeing and hearing. So then," he concluded, after making reference to David once again, "Let all Jews know that God has made into our Messiah and Lord this one you killed on the cross!"

At this the crowd let out something like a collective moan. I looked at their faces with surprise. Here, in this same city where a mob had sent my son to death some six weeks before, now they were—they genuinely appeared—sorry for it. "Friends," someone called out heavily, "what do we do now?"

Kefa had a ready answer. "Turn away from sin back to God, and then everybody be immersed on Yeshua's authority for forgiveness. That way you will receive the gift of the Ruach HaKodesh, too. This promise is for you and yours and...and everybody Adonai might call to himself!"

The speaking, the questions, the pleading went on for some time, and I remembered what Yeshua had said. About his being with us. About our making more talmidim and baptizing them in his authority. This was exactly what Kefa was trying to do. I found myself praying. I did not know how people could be talmidim of Yeshua when he was no longer physically present. But somehow it must be possible, because here we were, talking about it, and he had commanded it, and he was, I knew, still very much with us. I could feel him as if I were carrying him in my womb.

Everything has come back to the beginning, I thought with wonder. I was being asked to bear the Messiah to the world once more. But now everyone was being asked to do it. I looked at the people around me whom I had grown to love as we had grown to love Yeshua together. I looked at the people who rose up in response to Kefa's words and said they would be immersed, and said they would become talmidim. There must have been thousands of them.

Even with so many, there were still so many who would not respond. There were still those who would say we were crazy, I mused. Or drunk. Like there had been people who thought I had been unfaithful to Yosef when I was asked to bear Yeshua the first time. Things were often, I thought, not as they seemed.

Bearing the Messiah would always be something of a scandal, I knew. He could not be present without making somebody uncomfortable. More often than not, and I smiled to myself, that somebody would be the bearer. But I had known that from the beginning. I would continue to learn wonders about my son that I had never known before, and I would continue to be shocked by him. No doubt I would continue to fail him, too. I found myself seeing him hanging from that crossbeam again. I had not thought I would ever need to remember that. I found myself crying a little bit. Yes. I would continue to fail him.

But, astonishingly, Adonai was still, even knowing me—even knowing that—asking me to bear his son again. I was the favored one. We talmidim were all the favored ones. Let it be to us as You have said.

ACKNOWLEDGMENTS

As this book is the result of some spurts of concerted writing interspersed with a lot of contemplation and mental percolation over a span of nearly twenty years, crafting a thorough page of acknowledgments is a tricky business, because I'm quite sure I will inadvertently leave someone out. However, as *Favored One* really did not come about solely through Jenn-and-a-Bible-in-a-vacuum, I will do my best to acknowledge those individuals and institutions who had a direct impact on the creation of this book, with a sincere request for grace on the part of those who should be named here but who I may, in the moment, have forgotten.

That said, I am grateful to still have enough of my middle aged wits about me to thank the following:

- Matthew, Mark, Luke, and especially John, who, with the help of the Holy Spirit gave us reliable narratives about Jesus without which this book would have been impossible.
- Bill and Marty Sturdivant, who first introduced me to the practice of *lectio divina*—the biblical

interpretation tool I engaged most thoroughly and consistently throughout the writing of this book.

- Dr Craig Blomberg, renowned New Testament scholar and professor, and John Weeks, writer and story theorist, each of whom graciously and expertly provided first read-throughs and critiques before I was ready to engage other beta readers.
- My family, who have been undyingly supportive and appropriately un-pushy regarding my writing endeavors—with special thanks to my Hebrew Bible expert sister-in-law, Dr Emmylou Grosser, and my pastor father, Rev F James Grosser, for input about geography, topography, culture, and theology.
- All of my Bible professors of both the "Old" and "New" Testaments, from each of the institutions of higher learning I ever attended, whether I completed a degree at them or not: Wheaton College (undergrad), Denver Seminary, Gordon-Conwell Theological Seminary, and Bethel Seminary of the East.
- Participants of the Pilgrimage who acted as beta readers and provided endorsement and volunteer editing help.
- Pastor Tom Sparling, for enlightening my understanding of Jesus' last word on the Cross, via the sermon "My God, My God, Why Have You Forsaken Me?" preached 24 September 2017.
- David H. Stern, who doesn't know me but whose translation/paraphrase of the Hebrew and Christian Scriptures together (*The Complete Jewish Bible*) helped give this goy a little bit of Jewish Biblical insight and terminology during a lamentably long era of life during which I didn't personally know any Jewish people myself.

ABOUT THE AUTHOR

Jennifer A. G. Layte is a pastor, spiritual director, and founder of the Pilgrimage, an online spiritual formation community. She provides spiritual mentoring, formation, and direction for any seeking to deepen their relationship with God—or encountering God for the first time—facilitating movement toward wholeness in Christ and participation in local churches.

A writer, teacher, and spiritual caregiver at heart, Jenn loves team building, introducing people to Jesus, and teaching things she is also learning. A lot of that happens via the written word, as in the book you've just read. She has also been published as Jennifer Anne Grosser.

facebook.com/thepilgrimageOSF

twitter.com/PilgrimageOSF

instagram.com/onpilgrimage

CPSIA information can be obtained
at www.ICGtesting.com
Printed in the USA
LVHW111016290719
625691LV00002B/374/P

About the Author

Staci lives in a little lakeside town in Iowa with her husband, elderly Pomeranian, Stella, and a sassy fat cat named Tapanga. Her grown daughters and son-in-law live adventurous lives close by, providing all kinds of stories to add to the fire that keeps her up at night, endlessly writing about the next dark tale. Suspense and thrillers are her genre, as she says, “The best thrill rides in life are the ones keeping you breathless, hanging on by your nails and screaming for more.”